# THE STARGAZER'S EMBASSY

# THE STARGAZER'S EMBASSY

BY ELEANOR LERMAN

MAYAPPLE PRESS 2017

Published by Mayapple Press
362 Chestnut Hill Road
Woodstock, NY 12498
*mayapplepress.com*

ISBN 978-1-936419-73-9

Library of Congress Control Number 2016918834

ACKNOWLEDGEMENTS

Cover design by Judith Kerman; cover art    . Photo of author by
. Book designed and typeset by Amee Schmidt with titles in Lithos
Pro and text in Californian FB.

# CONTENTS

# PART ONE: 1990

I

THAT AUGUST, I had a job cleaning a townhouse in Greenwich Village. It was a movie actor's East Coast place; he'd had a party the night before and left the house a mess. In the afternoon, as I was trying to get red wine and God knows what other kinds of stains out of the carpeting in the living room, I had watched the actor's handlers help him down the winding staircase—a coil of glass and wood that was hard to navigate even stone cold sober—and out the front door to where a limo was waiting to take him to the airport for a flight to L.A. No one said a word to me. Why should they? I was just the cleaning lady. Amid the scrub brushes and spray bottles of cleaning products, I probably looked just like anybody else. Of course I did. That was my goal.

The agency that sent me had told me not to show up until late in the day, so after the actor left, I had to work well into the evening. I labored diligently, as I always did, rarely stopping, paying total attention to every task I had to complete. I kept my headphones plugged into a CD player the whole time, listening to discs that I carried with me whenever I had a job. I didn't much care what the music was; I had a stockpile of used CDs that I bought at flea markets, and just scooped up a random selection whenever I had to go to work What was important—what was always important when I was alone—was to keep my attention focused and my mind occupied.

By the time I finally finished my work and locked up the house, it was just about nine. The streets of the Village were busy, as always on a weekend; straight couples, leather boys, kids from the suburbs were all wandering in and out of the bars and restaurants and window shopping the hand-made jewelry and sandal shops that stayed open late. Usually, there would be a crowd hanging around Sheridan Square where the Christopher Street subway stop let out and gay dance bars faced each other across a small park, but that wasn't so much the case tonight. Instead, I noticed that an unusual number of people seemed to be meandering west, towards the Hudson River piers. I suddenly realized why that was: this was the first night of the Perseid meteor shower. I had read about it in the newspaper last week. The arrival of the Perseids was always predictable but in the sodium glare of city lights, they weren't usually as visible as they were expected to be on this clear, cloudless night.

Normally, the thought of making a detour to watch a meteor shower would never have entered my mind. I generally just tried to get from one place to another—home to work; work to home, mostly—by keeping myself to familiar routes and my mind on automatic pilot, as much as possible. Tonight, my plan had been to walk home from the Village, straight downtown rather than veering even a few blocks west, but it was a hot night and I didn't have air conditioning. There would probably at least be a breeze down by the piers, so I decided to allow myself to follow the crowd of strangers heading towards the river. Even so, I didn't plan to stay very long.

By the time I crossed over West Street, there were dozens of people hanging around the rickety Christopher Street pier, which pointed straight across the Hudson towards the construction sites where new hi-rises were being built on the Jersey side of the river. Some people in the crowd were drinking, some were smoking weed. A few policemen were strolling around, checking things out, but an amnesty for petty crimes seemed to have been declared for the night because even the cops seemed more interested in the coming light show than who was getting high on what. I imagined everyone was hoping that because it was a little darker down here, away from the streetlights, they would get a better view.

I found a spot on a bench facing the river and had been sitting there for about twenty minutes when I saw someone point up to the sky and yell out, "Here they come!" I tilted my face to the night sky but I couldn't see anything much; maybe some thin streaks of light so faint that they seemed to be an apparition, more imagination than reality.

"Why don't you try these?" a voice suddenly said to me. "You'll be able to see much better with binoculars."

I looked up to see a man standing over me. He had dark hair, a striking face—not handsome, exactly, but angular, serious—and was, I thought, considerably older than me. I was twenty-seven; the man offering me a very fancy looking pair of binoculars was, I judged, somewhere in his forties. He was wearing jeans and a green polo shirt; just a casual summer outfit. I always studied the clothes of anyone who approached me—I had to. Sometimes, it was my first clue about just who was coming my way.

But I knew immediately that this man wasn't a concern to me. Still, I was disinclined to accept the offer until he smiled at me and despite myself, I let the smile disarm me a bit. I liked the smile, and actually, now that I was here, waiting for the meteor shower to really get going, I thought, *Why not? What's the harm?* "Thanks," I said. I pointed the binoculars at the sky and what I saw was a revelation; this first wave of nearly-invisible shooting stars became glittering traceries of light, bright trailways through the sky that existed for a few moments and then disappeared.

I watched these bursts of light live and die for a brief time, and then handed the man back his binoculars.

"Beautiful, aren't they?" he said.

"I guess," I said. "Sure."

He looked amused. "You've seen better?"

"I used to live upstate," I told him. "On a clear night, if you went out into the fields where there were no lights, you'd always see shooting stars. A meteor shower could fill the sky."

I had spoken without caution, a mistake I did not often make, and so thought that perhaps I sounded like stargazing might be some particular interest of mine. Immediately, instinctively, a kind of recording began to play in the back of my mind, a denial that I had an interest in anything connected to stars or the far horizons of night and space. *No, no,* I would tell people when I was younger—anyone who assumed I might be interested in things like that—*that's not me, that's my crazy mother. You know how she is.* As a defense, a way of separating myself from her, I had learned to talk about my mother's supposed interest in observing comets and meteors, along with the seasonal progress of the constellations across the night's great, dark vault. That, I would swear, is what took her out of the house at night. *That's why you might see her walking on the road,* I could say, heading across the fields, towards the woods. Hunters, fish, swans, dogs, scales and lions; I had made myself

7

memorize the names and shapes of the constellations in order to claim that she had told me, that she knew them all.

"Where upstate?" the man asked me.

"Freelingburg. It's near Ithaca."

"Ah, the gorgeous gorges. It's beautiful up there, but it does get really cold in the winter."

So thankfully, all we were doing now was making small talk, this stranger and me. Well, that was a better direction for the conversation. Besides, I liked the idea that he had introduced the topic of chilly weather. On such a hot night, just the idea of lower temperatures brought some relief.

"By the way, my name's John Benton," the man said. "And you are?"

"Julia Glazer," I told him.

"Well, Julia, would you like to go have a drink with me? We can wait out the Perseids until they decide to show up in full force. That won't be for an hour or so."

I thought about it and was going to say no until he smiled again. There was something about the way it softened his angular face that I liked even more now that I had seen it again, so I said yes. I even admitted that I was hungry—apparently, half a tray of canapés wasn't enough for dinner—and John Benton said he was, too.

I assumed he had some bar in mind, but instead, we ended up just walking across the street, where an enterprising vendor had set up a hot dog car to cater to the crowd strolling down to the river. John bought a couple of franks and two bottles of beer from a cooler that the vendor had stashed under the cart and then we walked another half block until we found a stoop to sit on. This was all okay with me. It was nice. Just sitting around and having a casual talk with someone was not an experience I'd had much lately. Well, really, not for a very long time.

We talked some more, and I asked John where worked. I didn't expect the answer he gave me, that he was a doctor. And then there was that smile again, though this time, it had an element of Cheshire cat about it. "Actually," he said, "I'm a psychiatrist." He waited a moment and then looked over at me with a raised an eyebrow. "Nothing? No reaction? Usually, when I make that particular confession, people either run away or start telling me their problems."

I held up the half of the hot dog I had left and said, "I'm still working on this, so I'm not going anywhere. And I don't have any problems."

"That makes you the first person I've ever run into who doesn't, but I'll take your word for it." He drank some of the beer and then studied the label for a moment, providing himself with a pause in which to consider what else to tell me. Finally, he added a little bit more to the biography he had just begun to sketch. "I see patients but I also teach. Or did teach. Taught." Then he named a university uptown, so famous that even I had heard of it. "I head the department of psychiatry. Headed," he corrected himself, looking rueful about how he was getting tangled up in his own language. "It's a long story." Maybe just to change the subject, he asked me, "And you?"

"I clean houses, apartments. There's an agency that sends me out on jobs."

"And?"

"And what?"

"What else do you do?"

Now it was my turn to smile. "You mean do I really want to paint or write or want to act and so I clean houses while I pursue my real calling? Well, no. Nothing like that. Really—I just clean houses."

"That's probably not what you went to school for, right?"

"School? Does Freelingburg high school count? They were still teaching home ec when I was there. Cooking and sewing. I can make a pie and mend socks if I ever need to."

I knew what these questions were about. John Benton, the psychiatrist professor—okay, maybe not professor; there was certainly some kind of story behind those past tenses he was getting so tangled up in—was asking himself what he was doing sitting on these steps with me. He had picked up someone (which was exactly what was going on; we both knew that) who was obviously way too young for him and he was trying to figure out why he had done that. I was attractive enough, I suppose, even in my cleaning lady disguise of old jeans and thrift-store shirt, which on the street converted themselves into casual cool. I had straight brown hair, brown eyes—all fine, but not remarkable. So if I wasn't remarkably beautiful or a secret ballerina, what was keeping Dr. Benton here, talking with me?

I decided to give him something, some hint that at least I had some kind of inner life.

"I read a lot," I told him. "And music. I almost always have music on."

I pulled the CD player from my shoulder bag and showed it to him, evidence that I was a person who told the truth—sometimes, anyway. To my surprise, he took the device from me, just as I had taken his—the binoculars—from him. He opened it up to see what I was listening to.

"Mood music?" he said, reading the label. "So what's your mood?"

"Oh, pretty mellow right now, I suppose."

"Then you're lucky," he said. "I've spent the evening with people who definitely are not."

He reached for the bottle of beer again and then busied himself with his food. I read this sudden turning of his attention away from me as a signal that even allowing such a slight hint about his work—the private problems of his patients, I assumed—was not something he usually did.

Like me, he recovered quickly from whatever lapse of judgment he thought he'd exhibited and we went back to chatting. He asked me what books I liked, what movies I'd seen lately, still trying to figure me out. Then he asked where I lived. I explained that I rented an apartment on Canal Street and then John told me about his place, an old, converted carriage house on Paper Lane, a few blocks away. The narrow lane, which was just the length of one city block, was still cobbled and it took its name from the printing businesses that used to be quartered there in the late 19th century. Now, there was still one press left—the Socialist Workers Party was housed in a small warehouse on the west end of the lane. On the east end, there was a recording studio that was famous for letting the bands who used the facility sometimes pay their fees in cocaine instead of cash. Either way, John said, he felt like he was living in the last bastion of an old Village culture: drugs, rock and roll, and outsider politics surrounded him from all directions.

We finished the food and the beer but kept on talking for a while. Finally, John suggested that we walk back to the pier.

There were even more people gathered by the river now, looking up at the sky, or just using the light show as an excuse to hang out at the edge of the Hudson. John and I sat on the bench where he had first found me and passed the binoculars back and forth between us as we tilted our heads back to watch the meteor shower. There were more of them now, dozens and dozens a minute, and probably many more that we couldn't see. With the bright, lively sky overhead, the river lapping at the pilings and the soft buzz of conversation rising from the groups of men and women all around us, the night felt peaceful, pleasant. Even the meteors streaking silently across the sky seemed to be keeping quiet on purpose so they wouldn't disturb anybody.

We sat and watched the sky for about half an hour, which was enough for me. I stood up and told John that I was going to go home. He wanted to get me a cab but I said I would walk, which had been my plan since I'd left the townhouse earlier in the evening. No, he told me, it was too late; he insisted on a taxi and that he was going to take me to my place.

We flagged down cab, but when we got in and I told the driver where to go, he looked puzzled. On the rare occasions that I took a taxi at night, the drivers always seemed confused or asked me if I had the right address because I was directing them to a neighborhood that, in those years, was a commercial area. It had no clubs, no nightlife, and as far as most people knew, no apartments. But I insisted that the driver to just go where I said; I must have sounded sharp, but John either didn't notice or it didn't bother him.

It didn't take long to reach Canal. This wide street, where long ago there had indeed been a canal, was now lined with stores that sold industrial products—glass, plastics, hardware, tools, paint. They were all locked and shuttered at this hour. I lived above a store that sold uniforms and work boots, in a railroad apartment that had housed the original owner and his family when he had opened the business before the second World War. The place probably still looked much the same as it did back then: a living room with a kitchen off one end and the bedroom right in line after that. The living room faced Canal, the bedroom looked out on an alley and the bathroom still had a pull-chain toilet, but I had gone to some small lengths to make it look a little less like I was reliving someone else's tenement days. I had painted the walls white, hung posters, draped Indian-print blankets on the couch (paisley prints in one living room, elephants and temple bells on the bed) and piled my books and tapes on wooden planks separated by thick glass bricks that I had found tossed out as scrap. The place was perfectly presentable, but—for a number of reasons—I wasn't about to invite John Benton up for a viewing, or anything else for that matter. I said goodnight to him in the cab and stepped out, heading towards the door next to the store's front entrance, which led upstairs.

But John called after me. "Hey," he said. "Come back a minute."

I knew what he was going to ask and I could easily have pretended not to hear him. Maybe I should have just gone up to my apartment and these days, in a certain frame of mind, I might be inclined to hold long arguments with myself about what kind of difference, if any, that would have made to everything that happened later. Perhaps a lot. But in any case, that's not what I did. Instead, he asked for my phone number and I gave it to him. Maybe he wanted to see me again for no other reason than to try to solve whatever mystery he thought was involved in his attraction to me, but I had something else on my mind, so it's possible that I gave John my number just because, at the moment, I was too distracted to come up with a reason not to. There were other issues I had to deal with at that moment.

Facing my front door, I was facing the rest of the night, which meant I had to get to the top of the stairs and then down a long hallway to reach my apartment. The apartment itself had never been violated, but the hallway had been, more than a few times. Tonight, all I could do was steel myself for a confrontation but hope, as I always did, that nothing—literally, no *thing*—was waiting for me once I went upstairs.

# 11

JOHN CALLED a few nights later and asked me out to dinner. He suggested a restaurant on Jane Street, not far from his house, and I said I'd meet him there around eight o'clock. I had been on the Upper East Side all day, where I had two apartments to clean in the same building, so after I finished work, I took the subway downtown to my apartment and let myself nap for a while.

I got up at the hour when the stores were closing and the bumper-to-bumper traffic on Canal Street was beginning to ease up. Because it was so warm outside, I had my windows open, and I could hear cars and trucks rumbling along and even the voices of people walking beneath my living room window as they headed home. The sky was streaky, blue on blue on blue, displaying a small moon shaped like a thin white disc, rising as slowly as if it wasn't sure it was really supposed to appear tonight. It was easy for me to feel isolated and a little lonely at such an in-between time, so I turned on the lamps in my apartment and put on the radio to try to lift my mood. And then I tried on clothes, hoping to find something that didn't make me look like a cleaning lady playing dress up. My closet didn't provide many options but I settled on black jeans and a black top. The outfit was a little severe looking, but it was going to have to do.

I got to the restaurant a few minutes late, and found John waiting out-side. He was wearing slacks and sports jacket over an open-necked white shirt—the doctor at ease, I supposed. We looked unmatched, in age, in dress, in everything. And yet, once we sat down, just like the other night, we fell into easy conversation.

John told me a little bit more about himself—he had been born in Chicago, had done his medical training at Harvard, come to New York to do his residency and then never left. He had been married, was long divorced, and had no children. In addition to seeing patients, he told me that recently, he had been writing and publishing a lot—mostly articles in various magazines and journals, though he had also just started a book. When I asked about what, he said, "Oh, I guess you could say I'm considering the mysteries of human experience."

I waited for him to elaborate, but he didn't. I wasn't going to pry, so I turned my attention to the menu. Maybe then John thought he should tell me a little bit more, so he said, "I've written a book about depression and another on the treatment of mental states that manifest hallucinations and behavior predicated on hallucinatory directives, but I guess I've gone off into some unchartered territory now—both in my writing and my research. Which is why I'm not teaching at the moment. The university takes its Ivy League status very seriously—and its fundraising. So, they would rather that I stick to more standard pathways."

"Can they actually tell you what you can do?"

"I certainly don't think so. That's why I have a lawyer who's trying to work things out with the academic review committee that's been set up to evaluate my work, as well as with the president of the university—he's not too thrilled with me, either."

The waiter came to the table and we ordered food and wine. When we were alone again, John said, "So now your turn to tell me about yourself." He took my right hand and turned it over, so that the inside of my bare wrist was exposed. "Let's start with that tattoo," he said.

The tattoo. I'd had it since I was a child: two dark blue circles separated by about half an inch from three smaller circles, all inked with points, like Christmas stars. It had long ago occurred to me that if you connected the three small stars, the result would be an almost perfect isosceles triangle.

"My mother did it," I told John.

He seemed to need a moment to process what I'd just said. It was a measure of how comfortable I was already feeling with him that I'd even mentioned this fact, which I usually kept to myself; I'd told other people before and I was aware that it seemed peculiar. Well, more than aware, really—when I was growing up, the kids around me made sure I knew that. When I was a child, nobody had tattoos except bikers or guys who were in the Navy. Mothers certainly didn't go around tattooing designs on their little girls. But then, my mother was different. Everybody knew that, but especially me.

"Your mother?" John said, sound incredulous. "Why in heaven's name would she do that?"

I shrugged. "She had the same thing on her wrist and she said that it made us both special. She told me that she read about how to do it in a book. The ink is actually some kind of plant dye; it never seems to fade. I've had it since I was about six or seven."

John looked at the tattoo again, seeming to study it. Then he looked back at me. "She must have been an interesting person, your mother. What's her name?"

"Her name was Laura." I said.

"Was?"

"She died when I was thirteen." I rushed on, not giving John a chance to say he was sorry about that and he didn't try to interrupt me. "But yes, she was an interesting person. She always had her own ideas. Her boyfriend, Nicky said she was a hippie before there were hippies."

Now I could tell that John was doing mental calculations in his mind. "She must have been very young when you were born."

"She was seventeen. I was born in 1963, in Rochester, and from what she told me—which was never very much—her parents kicked her out. After that she—we—lived in a couple of different towns upstate until she met Nicky and ended up in Freelingburg. I was about eight years old by then. He owned a bar and she worked there. We had an apartment upstairs."

"So you're still living above the store."

"I hadn't thought of that," I said, picturing, first, my bedroom above the bar and then my rooms on Canal Street and the uniform store downstairs. There really wasn't a similarity, but still, it made me wonder if I wasn't being analyzed. Gently, maybe, but analyzed all the same. I looked over at John and asked, "Are you maybe in psychiatrist mode?"

"I don't think so, but if you do, I promise to stop," John said genially. Then he asked, "Did you ever meet your father?

"Nope. He was some high school infatuation of my mother's. I got the message that she wasn't interested in connecting with him and I wasn't really, either. Nicky was around for most of my life and he was a good guy. I mean, he was always very nice to me. I didn't feel like I was missing anything. We still keep in touch. After I graduated from high school, I might have even stuck around except there really wasn't much for me to do in Freelingburg. He did ask me to stay; he said he'd be happy to pay me a salary to work at the Stargazer's Embassy, but..."

John suddenly interrupted me. "He would pay you to work where?"

"The Stargazer's Embassy. That's the name of the bar."

"I love it," John said. "It's a wonderful name."

"It was Laura's idea," I told him. "When she met Nicky the place was called the Whiskey Wind or something like that. But Nicky changed it for her."

Impulsively, I reached into my shoulder bag, which was hanging over the back of my chair, and pulled out my wallet. Tucked into one of its compartments was a piece of laminated cardboard with my name written on one side under the word "Passport," which was stamped in big, block letters. Printed on the other side was the following information: *Official Document. Issued by the Stargazer's Embassy to the World.* Underneath, in dark blue ink, was a mirror image of my tattoo: the two dark blue stars with the three smaller ones off to the left. I showed it to John and he laughed. "I guess you all had a whole script you were working from up there in Freelingburg. Though it is taking the joke a little far to brand your own child," he added.

As I put the passport back in my wallet, a feeling came over me that I decided was embarrassment, but maybe really wasn't. *Why did I hold onto that thing?* I asked myself, probably for the millionth time. I had such mixed feelings about it and everything it represented. Sometime after he changed the name of the bar, Nicky had begun giving them out to customers, but had presented me with the first one. I remember that even as I took it, I wasn't sure that it was something I wanted. And yet, here it was, with me still.

I led the conversation elsewhere. John told me about a trip he'd taken last summer to New Mexico to interview a Native American tribal leader named Richard Killdeer, who had spent hours talking to him about shamanistic practices and beliefs. "One of the things he told me," John said, "is that we are all capable of traveling though time and space. He said that human beings have always known how; they've just forgotten. He said that if you ask the moon to invite you, it will and your spirit will fly away for a visit, just like that. I was thinking about what he said when we were watching the meteor shower the other night; I wondered if I was watching traveling spirits instead of just interplanetary dust."

As John talked about what Killdeer had told him, the tension in the sharp planes and angles of his face seemed to relax; his whole aura of intensity seemed to lighten. It was obvious that he was talking about something he found fascinating.

"Is that what got you into trouble at the university? Are you doing research into things like that?"

"That's a part of it," John said, and I assumed he was answering both my questions. "But it's a little more complicated."

Again, he didn't seem to want to say any more on the subject, so I didn't push. We talked about other things for another hour or so, through dessert and more wine. Finally, as he was paying the bill, John asked me if I had to work the following morning and I said no; I didn't have a job the next day.

"Then come back to my house," he said. "There's a garden. We can sit outside and have another drink."

We walked the few blocks from Jane Street to Paper Lane, and if he hadn't shown me where the top of the lane was, between two longer streets that ran east-west from the river to Sheridan Square, I wouldn't have realized it was there. Halfway down the cobbled lane was a heavy wooden door set in stone façade; again, it was something I would have missed if it hadn't been pointed out to me. The squat, square stone building, with dark stained glass windows on the second floor, hardly looked like a cozy place to live.

But inside, everything was different. The front door opened into a small vestibule where a straight-back chair sat beneath a framed canvas on which some artist had painted bands of sea green, one on top of another, like layers of a summer ocean. This was a waiting room; beyond it, another door led into John's office, which held a desk and a more comfortable-looking chair than the one outside. There were no more paintings because the walls were all covered by bookshelves that held hundreds of volumes along with an assortment of artifacts that included a woven basket, decorated with a zig-zag pattern, that appeared to be wind-weathered and well-used; a small ceramic vase as deep red as the rug; and a stiff-legged metal horse that looked like some kind of totem object. Yet another door led into the main area of the house, which was smaller than I had expected. There was only one bedroom, and that was at the end of a hallway; just beyond the office was a kind of sitting room that did, indeed, open onto to a small garden with a square of paving surrounded by flowering bushes and potted plants, all enclosed by the brick walls of the surrounding buildings. Inside, showing me around, John led me up a short flight of stairs to the second floor, which, he explained, had been a hayloft at the turn of the century—this was, after all, a carriage house. Here, there was a small kitchen with a trestle table and two wooden benches, a living room with a television on a stand, along with a couch and two armchairs all covered in dark yellow corduroy. The stained glass windows, which went from the floor to the ceiling, were the replacement for the original hayloft doors.

I loved the house from the first minute I entered it. There was something about it that reminded me of Freelingburg, an old north central New York town with a two-block main street where most of the buildings had a history that reached back before the turn of the century. And like John's carriage house, they were all reclaimed from some earlier purpose: one had been the company store for a now long-abandoned mill; another had been a bank that made loans to farmers. But by the time I lived there, as a child, the businesses that had replaced their outmoded ancestors—the "new" hardware store, the produce market, the pharmacy—had themselves become obsolete because a depressed economy and changing times had driven many of the locals out of their small upstate towns. From the Hudson Valley to the Finger Lakes region, people were leaving and businesses were closing up shop.

It was only the Stargazer's Embassy, under a dozen different names, that had survived in its original incarnation. It had always been a bar—after all, everyone drank; the mill hands, the farmers, the mid-century workers who drove to the factories in nearby towns. But just as it seemed to be in its death throes, Freelingburg—and in particular, the Stargazer's Embassy—was born again because of the influx of hippies and back-to-the land types who started moving up to central New York State in the 1960s. Cornell University in nearby Ithaca also provided new customers for the bar. Bikers mixed with the long hairs who mixed with disaffected professors marking anthropology papers in the corner, nursing a Genesee Cream Ale.

I had a complicated relationship with Freelingburg; it was home but it was also a place where I had been deeply unhappy. And angry—viciously so. But from the first time I saw it, the carriage house on Paper Lane seemed to soothe those feelings, which I still nursed. The wood and stone, the iron f ittings on the doors, the beamed ceilings and creaking floors reflected the same long, repurposed history as the houses of Freelingburg, but in its current incarnation as John Benton's home, these elements of the house combined to make me feel at ease. Not safe, exactly—I was never safe; that I knew well—but for the moment, I was willing to settle for standing down from the constant state of alert that was my usual condition. Sometimes, when I was working, or plugged into my headphones, or lost in a book, the needle on the internal meter that measured my level of watchfulness would move down to middling. Tonight, though, when John and I went back downstairs and I settled myself into a chair in his walled garden, with just a small square of late-night summer sky above me, I closed my eyes and felt almost relaxed. The meter was hardly registering any disturbance at all.

John brought out a bottle of wine. We sat for a while and had a drink, then, without either of us saying a word about our intentions we went inside, to bed. I hadn't slept with anyone in a long time and I got the feeling that neither had he, but the attraction between us was strong, and from the beginning, I think we both knew this had already gone far beyond whatever we had—he had—originally thought was happening between us. This felt serious. It seemed so very quickly.

His bedroom, probably the horses' tackle room once, was small, and so was the bed, which meant that when we finally fell asleep, we continued to be entangled. I liked that, I liked feeling his arms around me, I liked feeling the strength of his body, even deeply at rest. I slept for a few hours; whatever dreams I had did not linger with me when I woke around three a.m. John was lying on his side now, facing away from me, but still close enough that when I slid out of bed, I was careful to move as slowly and as quietly as I could so as not to wake him.

I put on his shirt, which was too big for me but comforting, as if we were still enveloped in each other. But why was I awake? I went upstairs, to the kitchen, and drank some water. I opened the refrigerator and ate some grapes out of a bowl. But I was neither hungry nor thirsty, and I knew it. I also knew where I was going next.

Down the stairs, out into the garden. A familiar sense was pulling me: the state of high alert was back. The needle on my internal meter was threatening to push past the edge of the dial. That hadn't happened since the night I had met John, though even though I had felt some inward tremor of concern when he'd left me on the street outside my building, the rest of the night had been uneventful. I had gotten upstairs and locked the door behind me without incident. But that was days ago. That time was past. I knew this time was going to be different.

It was dark outside as I entered the garden, but there is always ambient light in the city. People are up late and their windows blaze; the sodium glow of streetlights is ever-present; cars drive up and down the streets with their headlights pushing through the heaviest hours of the night. So I could see well enough in the small, enclosed garden to make out a figure standing in a corner just at the point where the walls of two of the surrounding buildings met.

It was wearing a long, ill-fitting tan raincoat with prominent epaulets and a pair of what looked like white go-go boots. On its head was a baseball cap pulled low over its face, and it had completed this ridiculous outfit with a pair of oversize sunglasses that might have been worn by some would-be glam rocker a decade ago.

"Is this what you think people look like now?" I snapped at the thing.

The *thing*—my own word, the only one I would use to describe these beings—took one step away from the shadowy corner and made a high-pitched sound that varied in tone. Perhaps, as always, this was some attempt at communication, but I never understood what was being conveyed and I had no idea if they understood me—though that didn't compel me to keep silent.

"I've told you and told you," I said, "You and all the others. I don't care what you want from me. I never have. I never will."

And then I turned away and went back into the house. I would have slammed the garden door, but that would have awakened John, so I just quietly closed it behind me. But before I returned to bed, I found my shoulder bag and removed my CD player so I could fall back to sleep listening to music. In the next moment, though, I changed my mind and put the device away. Instead, I just wanted to fold myself back into John's arms, hoping that would be enough to take my mind off the thing in the garden, which was probably gone by now anyway, since they never seemed to hang around very long. And it was hardly about to come into the house because then it would have to show itself to John and I knew it wouldn't want that. It—they—never did. I was always alone when I saw them; I was the one they always approached, never anyone else I was with though of course, I rarely was with anyone else. Except now, maybe, I was.

As I slipped back under the blankets and closed my eyes, I conjured up a picture of the carriage house and imagined myself moving through its rooms, talking to John, doing everyday tasks, simply living my life. In this scenario, the things not only stayed outside, they grew so tired of my ignoring them that they stopped showing up—though perhaps by the time I invented that possibility I was already asleep and the story I was telling myself was just a dream.

# III

AUGUST PASSED, so did September. October brought cold weather so I put away my tee shirts and got out my long-sleeved sweaters. I didn't try to hide the tattoo on the inside of my wrist but I was always conscious of it, sometimes more than others, so I was a little more comfortable in the cold months when it was less visible because of my clothes.

Clothes became another kind of issue when John asked me to go to a dinner party with him. I was surprised; we had seen a lot of each other since the night we'd met, but it was always just us: we went out to eat, we went to the movies, we took the subway to Central Park and sat on benches, bundled up in our jackets, watching children ride the carousel or ducks floating on the pond near the Boathouse. Pleasant, normal things—for me, especially so. We enjoyed each other's company and the attraction between us only seemed to strengthen. But we also spent a significant amount of time apart because I was working during the day and John was often seeing patients at night.

The dinner party, John explained, was being given by the dean of one of the other departments at the university and most of the guests would be faculty members. "I got the black sheep invitation," he joked, but I got the feeling that it was important to him to see these people, to reconnect with them. Over the past few months, he'd told me a little more about his problems with university administration, saying that the situation was turning into a full-blown argument about academic freedom and people were taking sides, some his, some the university's, and since he had tenure, the problem was even more complicated. "When they hired me," he'd explained, "what they got was a Harvard-trained psychiatrist with twenty years of teaching and treatment experience, along with a portfolio of research grants. But for the past few years, what they ended up with, in their estimation, is some kind of new-age hippie who has some pretty far out ideas about the nature of reality and the role that spirituality may play in our lives—and even beyond that." I assumed he was talking about his work with Richard Killdeer and others like him: Native Americans, shamans, people and beliefs I had zero experience with. I did not connect them to myself and I said nothing to John about the part of my life that, given his interests, might have particularly interested him. I didn't want that kind of attention from him and it would have been useless to both of us, anyway. I knew the things I encountered were not ancient guides or spirits, not ghosts or wandering souls. They were real enough—I understood that without question—but I had been successful, so far, at keeping them at the margins of my life and that was where I wanted them to stay.

John seemed pleased about the invitation to dinner, but for me it posed a number of problems, including one I had confronted on the first night we went out together: finding the right clothes. For a dinner with his friends, I didn't own anything that I thought would be appropriate to wear. Even if I could get away with pants and a nice blouse, I didn't have those things and besides, I was pretty sure that I was supposed to wear a dress. I couldn't even remember the last time I'd even owned a dress; there certainly wasn't one hanging in my closet.

The party was on a Friday night, so the Wednesday before, after I'd spent the day cleaning an apartment on the upper West Side; I took the train to the Village and walked up and down West Eighth Street, looking in the windows of clothing stores. I couldn't imagine myself in a big, midtown department store—I would have been overwhelmed by the choices, let alone the prices—so this seemed more my speed.

It was already dark outside. As I wandered along, the stores with their lighted windows looked to me like shadow boxes posed with mysterious displays. What was I supposed to buy? I understood myself well enough to know why I was having trouble even walking into a store and trying things on: it was because I found myself in a role that was both unfamiliar and disorienting. Not only was I going to step outside the invisible, self-imposed barrier that usually served to separate me from the rest of the world, I was actually supposed to do something with myself that would make me stand out. After all, I was going to this dinner as John's girlfriend—which was who I was now, wasn't I?—and if I were John Benton, I would like the young woman on my arm to look attractive. But attractive in what way? This girlfriend of his who considered a pair of black jeans to be formal wear: what was she was supposed to look like?

I didn't know the answer to that question, but the more I thought about her—*me*—the girlfriend, the more I warmed to her. John Benton found her appealing; he liked her; he wanted to spend time with her. And now, he apparently wanted to introduce her to his friends. So why shouldn't she dress up, if even for just one night? She could at least try it out, see how it felt to be pleased about herself.

I finally made myself go into a small boutique where the air was scented with incense and some kind of Indian music was playing in the background. I looked through the racks of dresses and picked out a few, which I tried on in a curtained stall. I didn't like the first two, but after I pulled on the third and turned to look at myself in the mirror, I almost didn't recognize the person I saw reflected there. The dress was a deep green, and something about the color and cut made me feel transformed. With the smoky incense braided through the air and the unfamiliar music tinkling in my ears, I looked to myself like a person of contrasts, someone perhaps a little bit edgy and interesting. Was that what a girlfriend looked like? Yes or no, that was the person John was going to be presented with.

"Wow," he said on Friday night when he came to pick me up, so it seemed that I had picked out the right dress after all.

"Don't act so surprised," I told him. "I don't always look like I'm getting ready to do manual labor."

"And even when you do, you don't," John said. "Which is one of the interesting things about you." He gave me an odd look, like he wanted to say something else, or something more, but for the moment, thought better of it.

I put on my coat and we went out into the hallway. John waited as I locked my door. He shook his head as he watched me, a small sign of exasperation that I didn't think he was even conscious of, but I knew what it meant: he couldn't understand why I felt comfortable here, in this place. He'd said as much on the occasions when he'd come here before, as he had a few times. He seemed particularly bothered when he arrived at night, a time when the shop downstairs was closed and there was no one else in the building. The other rooms on this floor were used for commercial storage and so the hallway was dark, with only one light fixture illuminating the top of the stairs. I had told him, honestly, that it didn't bother me—I was certainly used to being alone and darkness was not a condition that affected the one real problem I had one way or another; the things were as liable to show up in daylight as well as at night (not that I had any intention of telling him any of this)—but my answer never satisfied him.

We were headed for an address that was in walking distance of my apartment. John put his arm around me as if to guide me through the narrow streets, some, like Paper Lane, still cobbled with pavers from the last century. We were surrounded by buildings with dark, cast-iron facades and grimy loading docks, the survivors of an age of downtown factories that made hats and shirts and coats, furniture, paper goods, carpets, ink, thread, tools. Though some were now being converted into artists' lofts, there was still little foot traffic here and few streetlights, so we seemed to be traveling through a lonely landscape with the stars overhead stretched out like a pathway leading back to civilization.

After we walked another few blocks, up ahead I could see the lights of Washington Square, but John stopped before we got there, leading me towards a doorway covered with a rectangle of riveted sheet metal. He pushed a buzzer and after a brief delay, someone responded. He opened the door for me and we went inside.

Up two flights of stairs, we found the party in a vast duplex loft hung with enormous abstract paintings. On the way over here, John had explained that the dean's wife was a painter so these, clearly, were her works. They both greeted us at the door; the genial husband in jeans and a sweater, the wife in a short, svelte black dress and smoky eye makeup. She looked slender and sharp-edged, and I got the impression that the outfit was meant to signal that no one should mistake her for the academic in the family.

They welcomed John effusively and smiled as he introduced me. The husband looked a little puzzled, though he tried to hide it. The wife widened her smoky eyes. Apparently, they had expected John to come alone and they had no idea who I was.

John led me into the living area of the loft. A hired waiter offering appetizers was circulating among the dozen or so guests, then briefly disappeared into the kitchen and returned with a tray of glasses filled with white wine. John took two glasses from the tray, handed one to me, and then was pulled away by someone. He glanced back at me with a look of concern but I smiled, meaning to assure him that I was fine by myself. I sipped my wine and walked over to one of the large paintings to get a better look at it. I immediately recognized the style—the sea-green abstract in John's waiting room must have been painted by this same woman.

The artist herself was soon standing beside me, her satiny black dress seeming to present itself as a separate presence, a mindful thing that its owner had cunningly persuaded to drape itself around her.

"Do you like it?" the woman asked me, gesturing at the painting with her wine glass. I remembered that her name was Samantha; she had introduced herself when we met at the door.

I looked up at the great, ragged-edged swaths of color—reds and pale oranges intersected by cerulean blue lines of variegated density—and gave her an honest answer. "I do," I said. "But I was just trying to picture it in my apartment. It's almost as big as my whole place."

"Oh?" Something in the tone of that one syllable conveyed the fact that Samantha had gleaned a world of information from that one abbreviated reference to my apartment.

"Where do you live?" she asked.

"Canal Street," I told her.

She nodded, as if agreeing with something I'd said that was deeply profound. "I suppose it's still affordable down there. You wouldn't believe what we're paying in this building, but it's worth it. We searched forever for a place where I had enough space to work."

"I guess the neighborhood is changing," I said.

"The whole city's changing," Samantha replied.

"Well, I'm okay where I am. For now, anyway."

Maybe tonight I was dressed as the girlfriend, but the cleaning lady was still with me and she, in invisible mode—the girl mopping the floor, scrubbing the sink in dozens of pricey Manhattan apartments—had overhead enough casual talk by people who barely remembered she was there to understand that Samantha and I were having two conversations at the same time. In New York, the cost of apartment rentals, the prices for buying a co-op or condo, were always being discussed, but they also conveyed personal information as well: your level of income, the kind of job you might have, even your ambitions, if you were planning to move from a cheap neighborhood to a more expensive one. But I wasn't giving Samantha anything like that and I could tell that it was frustrating for her. She wanted to know who I was—at least, in relationship to John—so finally, she came right out and asked me.

"And how did you meet John? Are you one of his graduate students?"

"No," I said.

"Well, I mean, he's not teaching right now..."

She let the remark trail off but I could have finished it for her: *That would make it alright, even romantic.* The sort-of-disgraced professor, the admiring student. But she had guessed wrong, and now she was even more annoyed.

She took a sip of wine and turned away from me, pretending to study her painting. I imagined that I could hear the wheels turning in her mind; she was trying to decide how much further to pry. Finally, she turned back to me.

"Don't tell me you're one of his experiencers?" she said.

"His what?"

She gave me an appraising look. I got the impression that finally, she had found out something about me that pleased her: she knew something about John that I didn't.

"He hasn't told you?

"Told me what?" I asked. I really had no idea what she was talking about—though of course, she was eager to tell me.

"Well, I suppose you're lucky he hasn't started in about all that with you," she said. "I mean, it all sounds so horrible. I know John doesn't necessarily think so, but I just can't imagine how you could turn that sort of experience—whether it's real or not—into anything good."

She waved at someone across the room and I could see that she was about to walk away from me. Instinctively, I put my hand on her arm to stop her. And, though I was sure she felt that she had just put me in my place—because apparently, I at least looked young enough to be a student, therefore too young for John, which meant I was also too young and probably too stupid to be at this gathering, not to mention the fact that I didn't know something very important about him that she did—I didn't let go until she faced me again.

27

"What are you talking about?" I asked.

She rubbed her arm. I was probably supposed to feel bad about grabbing her, but I didn't. I just stared at her, waiting for an answer.

Finally, she said, "Oh, all that crazy alien stuff that's gotten our eminent psychiatrist friend into so much trouble."

"What alien stuff? I don't understand."

"Really? I would have thought he'd be eager to tell you all about it, since that seems to be the only thing he does nowadays. All he writes about; the only patients he sees: they've all been visited by little green men. Or gray, actually—I think that's what color everyone says they are now. Gray."

Then she did walk away, leaving me alone with the chaotic rags of colors that loomed above me, on the wall. I think my mind went blank for a moment because trying to think about what she had just said was too bizarre. Too much, too wrong for me. When I came back to myself all I could think was, *Of all the things. Out of everything it could have been, it had to be that.* And, I was angry. Very angry; and the object of my anger was John.

He came back to me when Samantha announced it was time to sit down for dinner, but we were placed at opposite ends of the table. John was seated next to our hostess and I saw her say something to him and laugh before turning away. As she did, a look passed across his face that changed his expression to one that I read as unease, especially when he made a point of looking in my direction and trying to catch my eye. I wouldn't return his gaze and as the dinner progressed, I could see him glancing at me once in a while with an increasingly worried look on his face. It wasn't hard to imagine what Samantha had said to him—*I'm so sorry, dear heart, I had no idea you hadn't told her about, well, you know*—and I knew why that would have him concerned about how I would react, but I wasn't about to make things any easier for him. I was too upset. All I could think was that, like Samantha, he must have thought that I was stupid or at least, too naïve to be let in on the big secret about the work he was really doing, which everybody seemed to know about but me. Why else to keep me in in the dark except to think I wouldn't understand what he was doing, or why he was doing it? From the little he'd told me about the research he was involved in—*very* little, I now realized—in my mind, I had characterized it as New Age mysticism, and left it at that, since I wasn't all that interested. The idea that he might be chasing aliens had never crossed my mind. Perhaps I simply hadn't allowed it to—but I wasn't going to blame myself for that. I blamed him.

I deliberately turned to the man sitting at my left, which meant I was facing away from John, and pretended to be deeply interested in a conversation he was having with the person next to him. They were talking about movies, and I managed to join in now and then by making some innocuous comments. I had actually seen one of the movies they were intellectualizing about, an old hippie cult film about a gunman with stigmata that had recently been revived in a local art house. I thought it had been pointless and gory, but I kept that opinion to myself. An hour went by, and then another; food arrived and was taken away only to replaced by different dishes; and all along, the waiter kept filling our glasses with wine. Throughout the whole dinner, I never once looked over at John.

Finally, Samantha said everyone should bring their drinks over to the part of the loft that served as a living room, so we trooped over to an arrangement of couches and chairs decorated in the same blazing reds and pale oranges as the painting that had served as the backdrop to our earlier conversation. Almost immediately, John was at my side. He put his arm around me and I moved away. It was a signal, and he got it.

He shook his head and said "Alright, Jules," using a nickname I had not heard from him before. I knew he meant it as a term of endearment, a way to coax me to pay attention to him—and he said it loud enough for everyone to hear. Then he finished his thought: "Maybe we should be going," He was trying not to look worried, but I knew he was. Whatever was wrong, he wanted to get away from all these people and make me tell him what it was.

But Samantha wasn't pleased that he wanted to leave. "Already?" she said archly. "I was just going to force everyone to climb upstairs, to my studio and coo over my new work."

But John had gone ahead and found our coats and was holding mine out for me; I had no choice but to put it on. I didn't exactly want to go with him but I hardly wanted to stay here, either.

"John, really," Samantha said. "Have we all become so much more boring in comparison to...well. Everything else?"

She was mocking him now; her tone was unmistakable. I didn't know if the object of her derision was me, who I imagined she now viewed as the trophy girlfriend (apparently, the cleaning lady had done well by disguising herself in dress-up clothes) or John's "crazy alien stuff," but either way, he seemed to be in no mood to engage her. He simply said, "It was a lovely evening, Samantha. Thank you. But Julia and I have to go."

Once we were outside, on the dark street, John said, "So. Do you want to tell me what's going on with you? Did I do something or was it them? I hope it was them. My supposed friends. I think they actually mean to be supportive but maybe it's not coming across that way."

"It's not them," I told John. "Your friends were perfectly fine."

"Then maybe just Samantha? I saw you talking to her. I know she can be a little...critical."

"You think I care about that? I'm really not interested in her opinion of you, or me for that matter."

"I see." John said. Then he waited a moment while a car rattled by, bumping along the cobblestones. When it was gone, he said. "You want to tell me what you do care about?"

"Nothing," I replied. "Haven't you figured that out by now?"

"All I've figured out is that you'd like me to believe that, but I don't."

With every word he said, I was growing more furious. "I am not going to have this discussion with you in the street."

"Then name a place where you want to have it because I'm not going to just let you walk away from me."

"Why not?" I spat back at him. "What do you want from me?"

He waited a moment before he answered. "I could ask you the same question."

He looked tense, and I felt like hitting something—a bad, bad reaction, though hardly unfamiliar to me. I was ramping up for a confrontation that had nothing to do with this argument—well, maybe it did, in a way, which was why I was feeling so angry—but I knew I had to get myself under control.

"Alright," I said finally, telling myself I was being generous by giving in. We weren't far from MacDougal Street, where there were a dozen cafes and restaurants. I stalked off in that direction, with John silently following me.

Soon, we were seated in a coffee house, the first one we came to. We arranged ourselves on spindly chairs, at a table with one leg balanced on a matchbook so it wouldn't tip sideways. Long ago, someone had painted griffons and gargoyles on the walls but they were yellowed now by time and cigarette smoke; that didn't matter much anyway, because the lighting was dim so that you could hardly see the creatures glowering at you with their faded, fiery eyes.

"Well," John said, looking around, "this is pretty unpleasant."

He almost sounded amused, which made my anger flare up again. "I like it," I said belligerently.

"Okay, I get the message. Let's order some coffee and then why don't you try to tell me what I've done?"

Eventually, a waitress with kohl-rimmed eyes brought us cups of espresso and a couple of bitter, brittle cookies on a paper plate. After she went away, I looked straight across the table at John and said, "I want to know what you do. What your research is about. Why they suspended you from teaching."

"Not just from teaching," John said evenly. "They won't even let me back into my office."

"Why? Do you have secret photos of an alien army locked up in there? The real, final, one-hundred-percent proof that they exist?"

"I thought so," John sighed. "Samantha told me that she talked to you. She has a way of putting things that can be pretty catty."

"Yes. Samantha's been talking to me. Why haven't you been?"

"Was I obligated to, do you think?"

"Yes," I said. "At this point, yes."

"You mean, at this point in our relationship."

"Yes. That's what I mean."

He paused; took a breath. Apparently, I had said at least something that he wanted to hear me say. I had validated that we had a relationship—no, more than just that. I had told him it was important to me; important enough to jeopardize. If I really didn't care, I would have shrugged off anything about him—about us, together—that bothered me

"OK," he said finally. "That's fair. I'll tell you, but let me start with this: the reason I haven't really opened up to you about my work is because of exactly what's happening now. Most people think it's not only totally crazy but genuinely dangerous. To me, to my patients—probably to the field of psychiatry in general. But I imagine those aren't your concerns so the next thing we're going to have to straighten out is why you feel so betrayed right now. But for the record, Jules, let me clarify one thing for you: I have never seen an alien, or a photo of one that wasn't doctored or didn't turn out to be something else entirely. I have absolutely no proof that such beings exist— except that my patients tell me they do. Most—though not all—describe abduction experiences. I'm sure somewhere along the line you've heard about this. They wake up in bed to find alien creatures surrounding them, or they're driving on a road and see a craft hovering above them and in the next minute, or seemingly so, they find themselves on an examination table in what I guess would generally be described as a UFO. What happens to them next varies, but usually it's extremely traumatic."

I listened to what John said and tried to phrase my reply very carefully— all I wanted to do was repeat what he'd said. "Your patients think they've been abducted by aliens."

"Yes, aliens. The people I work with—my patients—have had experiences that involve aliens. Not always UFOs—often, but not always. Usually, these people are called abductees, but I don't like that term because it implies a one-sided event, which I think is not what we're dealing with. At least, I hope not. So I call my patients experiencers. Just that small change in how they view the things that have happened to them—and I have no doubt that *something* has happened to them—seems to help a little. It integrates them into the event rather than making them simply a victim of it. So that's what I'm doing, or part of it anyway. I'm working with experiencers. There's more to it than that of course but before I go on, I need to know why you find this so particularly upsetting, which you obviously do. Most people just laugh or tell me that I've gone off the deep end. Way off."

"I thought what you were doing involved New Age stuff. Mysticism, spiritual beliefs—that sort of thing."

"It does. What you're calling 'that sort of thing' has been helpful to me in trying to grasp at the potential for something enlightening to come out of what are otherwise horrific experiences. I'm looking for understanding anywhere I can find it. Does that somehow sound better to you?"

I must have looked like nothing was going to make any of this better for me because John raised his hand from the table, tilted up his fingers. Did he even know he was doing that? *Stop*, he was telling me. *Hear me out.* And so I listened while he continued to talk. "Before you tell me that I'm playing shrink by asking why you feel the way you so obviously do—why you find my work so disturbing—let me promise you, I'm not. As a matter of fact, I can't remember a time when I felt less like I had any ability to figure out what was going on with another human being. Namely, you, Jules. So please, explain to me. Help me out here."

*No.* Every instinct in me said *no*, but as much as I was trying to make myself get up and walk out of the café, I found myself rooted to my seat. I simply couldn't leave him. Not now, not yet. I kept thinking about the impression I had formed of him the night of the meteor shower, and afterwards, in the time that we had spent together: he was a thoughtful man. Calm, genial, even gentle. And he had a heart full of light. *And that, I told myself, all of that and more are the qualities you have come to rely on. In particular the last one because it is something that you do not possess.*

"I've been through all this before," I said. "And I have to tell you, I hate it."

He sipped his coffee; he waited for me to explain while I tried to think of how. In my I mind, I saw Laura—my mother—walking down an empty country road and then turning off into a cornfield under a pale winter moon. At the edge of the cornfield was a woods; miles of old-growth trees that stood on protected public land where no one was permitted to hunt and even hiking was difficult because there were no paths. In this image of Laura that I held in my mind, all around her, in the vast clarity of the rural landscape, stars adorned the night sky. The image was a reflection of my memory, which I trusted; which I knew to be true. But if I changed it just slightly, if I put a pair of binoculars in Laura's hand—much like the pair John owned, the ones he had given to me on the night we met—or even had her lugging a telescope through the cold cornfields, then I could present her as an eccentric, a harmless stargazer. I had already laid the groundwork for that story when I had told John that it was my mother who changed the name of Nicky's bar. But that wouldn't be enough to explain how upset I was—what did some harmless stargazing have to do with aliens? I was going to have to add in more details, more reasons for my behavior.

Finally, I said, "It's because of my mother."

"Oh yes, the tattoo artist," he said lightly.

I glared at him. He wasn't going to distract me by remembering the few odd things I had told him about Laura. He wasn't going to diminish the impact of the story I was about to construct.

"That's the least of it," I said coldly.

"Okay," John said, getting the message that I wasn't joking with him. "Then tell me what we're talking about."

"My mother had an obsession. Anything to do with UFOs, aliens, abduction stories—she was totally hooked. Totally fascinated. She read everything she could get her hands on about the subject, she subscribed to magazines about UFOs; she talked about aliens and Roswell and Area 51—things like that—all the time. Everybody in town thought she was a little strange."

*Was that enough?* I asked myself. Instead of the Laura-as-stargazer story, I had substituted this more elaborate explanation, one of the alternates I used when someone asked about her. It had been so long since I had any reason to describe Laura to someone who didn't know her—or worse, who did—that I wasn't sure I had supplied enough details to explain why I didn't particularly want to discuss her or anything about her. Why I didn't have the same sentimental memories of home and mom that most other people did. Most other girls. Of course, nothing I had told John was completely true. Not even partly true, actually. UFOs? Roswell? Area 51? I got that stuff from watching tv, not from Laura. But what I said made sense to John, as I figured it would.

"A lot of people are interested in those things," he told me. "UFOs, aliens—it's become part of popular culture." Then he stopped himself for a moment; maybe he thought he was making light of something that was deadly serious to me. "I'm sorry," he said. "I imagine it wasn't like that when you were a kid."

"No," I snapped. "It wasn't. When I was a kid, mothers were supposed to be home baking cakes or organizing book sales for the PTA or helping you with your homework. Well, that's not what my mother did. Not Laura. She had no interest in anything like that. Besides, half the time she wasn't around. She would just leave whenever she felt like it. Walk off somewhere down the road and disappear until the next morning."

There. That, at least, was closer to what had really gone on: the disappearances, the nights that no one knew where she was except, of course, me. And probably Nicky, though I couldn't be sure how much he was aware of because we rarely talked about how Laura must have spent her missing nights. And certainly, I never had a conversation with Laura about the secret life she was living because I wouldn't allow it. Not from the time I was a small child. I had made that clear enough, I guess, in my own way. And so her secrets—which were now mine—had lived their life in some un-crossable space that yawned between us year after year after year. And it was those secrets that drove us apart.

I never forgave my mother for all this, for being so strange that she made me seem strange, too. Well, maybe I was, but I blamed her for that, as well, and it made me angry. And even after all these years, that anger was still close to the surface. Still there, still boiling away, and since Laura wasn't here for me to be angry at, for the moment, John remained my target.

"Well," John began, "I can see how that would make things...complicated."

"Can you? How kind. How understanding you are, doctor."

He frowned. "You're not giving me an inch, Julia. What can I do here but listen to you? And I am listening."

*Good*, I thought. *Then keep listening. There's lots more to say.* "Freelingburg is a small town," I told John. "Everybody knew that something pretty strange was going on with Laura. It may have been the psychedelic years somewhere else, but not where I lived; people had dairy farms or they worked for the gas company or laid tar on the roads; those kind of people thought my mother was outrageous. Besides the alien stuff, some of them thought she was off at night practicing witchcraft or group sex or cooking meth or who knows what. And what the parents thought, their children thought, so you can imagine all this didn't exactly make me the most popular kid in school. In fact, it made me something of a freak—I was the kid with the crazy mother who lived above the Stargazer's Embassy, which by itself probably would have been a reason to think I was weird, since whatever hippie types did start drifting up there always found the place. It was like someone had put a sign out on the road into town that said, hippies and aliens welcome."

"So this is quite a coincidence," he said. "Of all the gin joints in all the world."

I knew what he meant; he didn't have to quote *Casablanca* to me. And it didn't help. "I don't know what it is," I said, "but you should have told me. You let me think..."

"I didn't let you think anything," John interrupted. "I just didn't tell you everything. That would also make us somewhat similar, wouldn't you say?"

"Oh? Do you want to hear about the mysteries of how to clean a bathroom?"

"Jules. I wasn't talking about the work you do, and you know it."

"I've told you everything there is to know about myself," I insisted. "You want me to sum it up for you? Small town, crazy mother, etc. etc. She died of cancer. I finished school and ran away to the city. That's all there is."

"And that, of course, is *nothing* like all there is about you. Which is probably one of the reasons I'm here."

"I don't know what you mean."

"I'm not sure myself. But what I do know is that I'm not getting up and leaving," John said, "and it seems that neither are you, so let's try to get one step closer to figuring out what's going on here between us. To begin with, let me guess why you're so angry with me right now. What you saw in me—or thought you did—was a steady, normal person. *Normal* being the key. You go to work, I go to work, and then we meet for dinner or we go to the movies or we just talk a lot about nothing in particular. Right? Sound like you and me? Of course there's also the attraction between us, which doesn't need a lot of explanation. But instead of all that, all that normal, everyday life—suddenly, what you realize you may have involved yourself with is exactly what you were trying to get away from: a man who is in the throes of an obsession with some pretty high strangeness, and you want no part of it."

He was right; of course he was right. And because he was, as well as how direct he was being with me, how honest, maybe I began to soften a little. Not completely though: I had my defenses in place for a reason and I wasn't comfortable with the idea of admitting to anyone—even John—how strong they were. How long and how carefully I had worked on erecting them.

"Well, let me tell you something," he went on, "I wouldn't have chosen this work for myself—in a million years, it would never have occurred to me that I would be spending a good part of my life listening to people tell me that they've encountered aliens. Aliens, for God's sake! But it's what happened. And not just to me—what happened to me is hardly important; I'm just the witness. I'm just the one who listens to the stories. What you want, Jules—safety, security, the comfort of having at least some control over what happens to you from day to day—is what all my patients want. But it's not what they get, and I'm trying really, really hard to help them find a way to live with that. " He sighed deeply. "Nobody invites this into their life," he said, "these experiences with...the others, whoever they are. Whatever they are."

I could have told him he was wrong about that—at least I thought he was—but because I didn't really know, I said nothing. What I did know, I still wanted to keep to myself. That was safer for me, that remained the only way I knew to live. Safer, too, to change the subject now; to let John talk about himself rather than keep asking questions about me.

"Your patients—are they all abductees?"

"I use the word experiencers. We're trying to figure this out together, to understand what's going on, what's really happened to them." He fell silent for a moment as if it was now his turn to retreat to his own thoughts, but he kept his connection to me; he reached out, across the table to touch my hand. "I didn't answer your question, did I? Yes, all the people I see now are experiencers. And there are so many of them..."

His voice trailed off as he seemed to be deciding how much more to tell me, or maybe just how to tell me everything he had managed not to say up to now. Finally, he began.

"Until about ten years ago," John said, "I had a conventional career. Well, actually, let me go a little further than that, just for the sake of this conversation. Not just conventional: I was at the top of my field. I told you that I wrote several books; what I didn't mention was that one of them was a biography of Winston Churchill that analyzed how his depression affected his decision making and essentially helped to plot the trajectory of his life. It won a Pulitzer Prize and after that, I had my fifteen minutes of fame. I was interviewed a lot, I gave speeches—that sort of thing. Eventually, after the head of the department of psychiatry at the medical school of my university retired, I was appointed to take his place. So I was writing, teaching, seeing patients; everything was going along just fine and then...then a patient came to me through the student counseling service. Her name was—is—Alice Giddings. Alice was the one who brought all this into my life. She was the first experiencer I ever met, though maybe she wouldn't even have known that was, in fact, what she was if she hadn't ended up in my care. So I'm responsible for everything that happened after that. Me. Nobody else."

He broke off suddenly, perhaps gathering himself for where this story was leading next. Finally, he resumed. He said, "I know how it seems to people, many people, anyway: that I've gone down some crazy path that leads away from rigorous science and accepted medical practice into the realm of New Age malarkey. Alien abduction. I mean, could there be anything more ludicrous for a Harvard-educated psychiatrist with sterling academic credentials and a Pulitzer Prize, no less—which is how I am generally described when someone is about to review something I've written in order to rip it apart—to now devote all his time to? Even *I* realize how bizarre all this seems. And yet, I've never been as fascinated with anything in my life. I don't think I've ever come close to the edge of anything that may be more profound."

Suddenly, he smiled. "I probably sound like an evangelist for some fringe religion. But I'm still who I've always been: organized, stable, dependable—and committed to my work, wherever it happens to take me. Though I have to admit that this work, my patients, the mystery of what they're going through—it can be overwhelming. Fascinating, absorbing, but overwhelming. I get lost in it, Jules, and what I've lost is what I seem to have found with you. Some balance. Some personal life completely apart from everything else."

"And you think *that's* who I am? Some nice, dumb girl you can play house with?"

John regarded me across the table, which now held two cooling cups of coffee and the untouched plate of thin, bitter cookies. When he spoke his voice was steady but intense. "Not dumb," he said. "Far from that. But otherwise, yes, you're right. You made a mistake about me, and I made the same mistake about you because whoever you are—and I'm not going to pretend I really understand all that much about you yet—just some nice, ordinary girl hardly covers it. But together, you and I seem to have worked something out, haven't we? Created some semblance of normal? Maybe we're pretending, but we're doing a good job of it, don't you think?"

"But we're on opposite sides," I said. "You want to know more about things that I want to forget."

"So maybe we can meet in the middle," John said. "It might do us both some good."

I considered what he said and knew in my bones that he was wrong. But my judgment was not always the best—it was too colored by isolation, most of it self-imposed—and because of that, I had made mistakes before. My life had provided me with no reliable guide, no one to talk to. There was Nicky, sometimes, but while he sympathized, he really was no help. So I began to soften even more, I began to give in. Maybe John *was* right—if only just a little. Maybe the world I did not want to live in was the only one in which I could comfortably exist, as long as I remained in control of its boundaries. But all I knew about that world was from my own experiences. I didn't trust anyone else's, not really, but maybe it was time I found out what else—if anything—there was to know.

So I offered my version of an olive branch—at least, maybe the promise of one—by asking him to talk to me some more. "Tell me about Alice Giddings," I said.

"I'm surprised you don't know the story," he replied. "Almost everyone else I run into seems to know her name. She and Jim Barrett give interviews all the time. There was even a television movie about her."

"Jim Barrett," I said. "*That* name does sound familiar."

"I'm sure he'd be happy to hear that," John replied, with a wry smile. Then he asked, "How late do you think this place is open?"

"We're in the Village," I said. "Probably all night."

He called over the waitress with the kohl-rimmed eyes and asked for fresh cups of coffee. Then he began telling me about the girl, the events, and the mystery that had changed his life.

# IV

"SO," JOHN BEGAN. "Alice Giddings. It's a complicated story, but I guess the place it starts is with an owl."

"An owl?" I repeated.

"Just wait," John said. "Listen."

Alice was, he told me, a pretty, fresh-faced blonde from the Midwest, who enrolled in his university about a decade ago because she had won a scholarship. She was thrilled to move to New York and had plans to eventually major in political science.

Everything was fine for the first semester of her freshman year but in the spring, her dorm mates started noticing that Alice was becoming depressed. She started skipping classes, and then missed an entire week of school. She wouldn't get out of bed, barely ate, hardly spoke to anyone. The school sent over a counselor who insisted that Alice go to the student crisis center, which she did, reluctantly. At the university, there was a rotating roster of doctors and psychiatrists on call to respond to cases that the counselors felt merited some kind of emergency intervention; it happened, that night, John was the physician on duty. He went to the counseling center and spoke to Alice and, he told me, ten years later, he remembered exactly what she said to him: "There's an owl watching me. He sits on a bench in the park across from my dorm. I can see him through my window. Sometimes he comes into my room and gets into bed with me. I hate him," she had said, vehemently.

He thought she was hallucinating; perhaps she had been taking drugs or was in the early stages of schizophrenia. But she said—and he believed her—that she had never even experimented with any kind of narcotics and except for the story about the owl, she reported no other experiences that John could classify as being out of touch with reality. If he would just get rid of the owl, she said, if he could protect her from it, she would be fine.

He kept her in the university's infirmary overnight, and since there were nurses on duty, Alice seemed to feel safe. The next morning, John told her he thought that maybe, together, they could figure out what to do about the owl, and she said yes, maybe. So, that was how he took her on as a patient. He put her on medication and asked that the school change her room so that she wasn't facing the park; he thought that maybe if the potential for seeing the owl was reduced, that would also reduce her anxiety but it didn't work. Her fear of encountering the owl continued—in fact, it increased. John told me that he saw Alice twice a week for six months, but the only progress they made was to discover, as they talked about her family and her past, that the park across the street wasn't the first place she had seen the owl; she began to remember it watching her from a field beyond the schoolyard when she was in the elementary grades. Sometimes it even came into bed with her at home, when she was a child and later, as a teenager. Alice even realized that one of the reasons she had been so eager to come to New York—a buried reason, one she had never consciously admitted to herself before—was that she thought by moving across the country, she would escape the owl.

Alice, John continued, completely puzzled him. He had been a practicing psychiatrist for nearly two decades; in addition to his private practice and teaching at the university, he had worked in clinics, hospitals, and prison wards, and had treated people across a spectrum of disorders from what he considered mild neurosis to severe, full-blown psychosis—but Alice didn't fit any pattern he had come across before, or exhibit any symptoms he could categorize. She had one bizarre obsession—the owl—which seemed to have followed her throughout her life, but John could find no reason for it, no organic problem, no particular family dysfunction, no traumatic event, nothing in the medical records he obtained from her home-town physician, and nothing he did seemed to help. Alice grew more withdrawn, more fearful. Eventually, she dropped out of school but because she wanted to continue in treatment with John, she stayed in New York. She rented a room in a house in Brooklyn and got a job working in the windowless stock rooms of a department store, where she felt safe. John continued to see Alice several times a week and grew more and more frustrated with himself and his inability to break through whatever barrier it was keeping them both from understanding what was really wrong with her because surely, there had to be something behind her terrifying fixation on the owl, which continued to plague her.

One day, John said, he decided to try a technique he would have used with a young child—he asked Alice to draw a picture of the owl. Now, pulling a pen from his pocket, he sketched some lines on a napkin and then turned it around so I could see the picture he had drawn. It was recognizable as the flat, oval-shaped face of an owl but with very peculiar eyes—they were lidless and elongated, and John had colored them in so they were completely black.

I glanced at the sketch and then turned away. One quick look had been more than enough for me, but all I said was, "It's kind of strange looking."

"It is," John agreed, briefly studying what he had created. Then he folded it up and put it in his pocket with the pen, as if there would have been something wrong with simply leaving it on the table to be swept away later.

John continued the story. He said that a few days later, as he was walking along a street in the Village, near his house, he happened to glance into the window of a bookstore and then stopped dead in his tracks. There was a book on display in the window, written by a man named Jim Barrett, and the title was *Alien Abduction: Real or Imagined?* On the cover was what has now become an iconic image but was not, back then: a flat, gray face, shaped like an elongated oval and dominated by huge, black, lidless eyes. It was the face of an alien with the eyes of Alice's owl.

John bought the book, read it from cover to cover in one sitting, and then contacted Jim Barrett. What interested him—fascinated him, he said—was Barrett's description of "screen memories." Abductees, Barrett wrote, often did not remember their abduction experience for a long time but many of them reported being bothered by dreams about owls and other large-eyed creatures.

"They always seem to remember the eyes," Barrett told John when they first talked on the phone. John was careful to protect Alice's identity, but he did tell Barrett about his patient and the owl who not only watched her, but often "came into her bed." Barrett suggested that John bring Alice to see him, but John was reluctant, especially when Barrett explained that he had no medical training. He was, in fact, a journalist; his interest in alien abduction stemmed from the experiences that a cousin had confessed to him. Over the years, the cousin said, he had been plagued by frightening memories of shadowy beings coming into his bedroom and flying him up to a kind of craft floating in the clouds above his house. For a story he had written about hypnosis some time ago, Barrett had actually learned how to hypnotize people and he decided to try to use the process on his cousin to see if they could figure out what the memories really meant. He said he had expected some kind of hidden history of mental illness or suppressed family trauma, but nothing like that turned out to be the case. Not even close.

Under hypnosis, Barrett's cousin was able to reveal that the beings were small, gray humanoids with expressionless faces and extraordinary, penetrating eyes. The craft was a spaceship, and the cousin recalled being sexually assaulted by at least one of the beings, who told him they were conducting "experiments."

With his cousin's permission, Barrett had published the account of this abduction experience in his local newspaper and it was picked up by the national news services. As a result—and to his great surprise—Barrett was soon inundated with people who wanted his help. Eventually, that became his main occupation: working with what he termed the alien abduction community. People came to him from all over the country, most desperately in need of someone who would listen to their stories without ridiculing them. Some of them had clear and terrifying memories of their abductions; others were deeply troubled by half-remembered glimpses of bizarre beings, or unexplained hours of lost time. It was those individuals, Barrett had explained, who benefitted from hypnosis; as traumatizing as it was to confront what really happened to them, Barrett strongly believed that it was better for them to understand what they were dealing with than to think, as many of them did, that they were going crazy.

John said that after a long debate with himself, he decided to ask Alice if she wanted to try hypnosis. She agreed, but he did not bring her to Barrett— not at first, anyway—but to a colleague, a psychiatrist who sometimes used the technique in his practice. He did not tell Alice, or the other physician, anything about his conversation with Jim Barrett. All he said was they were trying to discover what—or who—the owls might represent.

"And there it was," John said to me. "Not all of it, not all at once, but under hypnosis, Alice began to remember being abducted by non-human entities. I think—I know—my colleague didn't believe what she was reporting. In fact, after a few sessions he refused to work with Alice anymore more because he felt that he was doing her more harm than good."

"How did Alice react to all this?" I asked.

"While we were still conducting the sessions, under hypnosis she was given the suggestion not to remember anything. I decided that it was best for me to tell her. To help her remember, consciously, little by little. I thought it would be less frightening."

"Was it?"

"Unfortunately, no," John said. "Once I started revealing her own memories to her, they came flooding back in great detail and she became terribly upset. Suicidal, I thought. So, I did what, at the time, I thought was the best thing I could do for her—I called Barrett. He had told me that he helped to facilitate group sessions for abductees so they could talk to each other, help each other. I thought that might be the best thing for Alice; at least if she understood that she wasn't mentally ill, which is what she believed, and that, in fact, others had had similar experiences to those she was describing, it would help."

"And did it?" I asked.

John was quiet for a moment. And then he said, "You don't know how many times I've asked myself that question. The only answer I can come up with is both yes and no. Yes, certainly, it was comforting to her to find that she was part of a community of people who were having this same bizarre experience. But I think it became—has become—almost the whole of her self identity. And she's Jim Barrett's star pupil; his Exhibit A."

"That doesn't sound like you and Barrett have a friendly relationship."

"We did at first," John said. "In fact, he began sending patients to me. For most people, the experience is bad enough, but what it does to them afterwards can be shattering. It destroys their sense of having any control over their own lives and of course, they doubt their own sanity. Many of them can't work; their marriages break up, and they live with constant fear. Over time, my practice became centered on these people. As I told you, almost everyone I treat now is an experiencer."

But returning to Alice, John said that she eventually allowed Barrett to hypnotize her and with each session, the events she remembered became not only more intense but lurid, as well. At least, John thought so. By now, he had talked to a large number of experiencers, some during Barrett's group sessions and others, privately, and he knew that some of them recalled forced sexual encounters but Alice was the first to bring up hybrid babies.

By now, John said, this was a well-known element of alien abduction reports, but a decade ago, it was virtually unknown. Alice was the first person to describe, in detail, how, during one of her repeated abduction experiences, she had undergone what seemed like a gynecological proce-dure, and a year later, when she was abducted again, she had been shown a strange, pale-looking infant with enormous eyes and understood it to be a child that had been created by mixing her genetic material with an alien's.

After Alice divulged this experience in a group setting, other women began to admit that they, too, had been shown alien-seeming babies that they felt, deeply, were theirs. Some men described being forced to ejaculate or to having sperm removed from their bodies through the use of invasive and painful instruments. Barrett, apparently, became convinced that the aliens were not only real and the abduction incidents increasing, but that there was a purpose to them: the extraterrestrials were conducting a breeding program with the intention of creating a shadow race, hybrids, with which they eventually intended to replace the earth's population of human beings.

Barrett published a book espousing this theory, which created quite a sensation and, with Alice's permission, he not only described her experi-ences but used her real name. Alice began appearing on television interview programs with Barrett, reinforcing his warning about the aliens' dangerous intentions.

John, meanwhile, said nothing publicly about what he was doing. In part, he explained to me, that was because as more experiencers began seeking him out—some through Barrett, others through the network of abductees who were in touch with each other—his ideas about the phenomenon began to change. Some of the people who came to him, particularly those who did not need hypnosis to recall their interaction with the humanoids and had been aware of every detail, from the moment the experience began to when it ended; had very different stories to tell. They were no less astounded by their experiences than others John had talked to, and no less confused, even troubled, about why they had been singled out as a target for the phenomenon, but they also had positive feelings about what had happened to them. They often reported their sense that the aliens had been trying to help them in some way, or perhaps to warn them about a coming peril to life on earth such as an environmental catastrophe. Others felt that their abductors where actually trying to lead them toward a spiritual awakening, both on a personal and across the whole spectrum of humanity, as well.

Which brought up a question that none of the experiencers—those who classified their abductions as horrific and those who came away feeling oddly uplifted—could really answer. How did the aliens communicate? Not one abductee could recall any kind of coherent vocalizations (though they did report that the aliens made "peculiar sounds" they could not clearly describe; I listened to this particular piece of information with interest, but said nothing); they remembered being shown images or having "feelings" about what the aliens were trying to tell them. For John, that remained a central mystery: how to interpret the intentions of these beings—which humans who interacted with them seemed to view in wildly different ways—since the beings themselves could not, or would not, declare the purpose of their actions.

Given these divergent experiences and individuals' reactions to them, John began to wonder if he wasn't viewing the phenomenon of alien abduction in too narrow or specific a context. He, Barrett, and others who more and more were exploring this field, were dealing with alien abduction as if it was something that could be understood through logic, analysis, and the collection of evidence, which was admittedly, hard to come by. In other words, to apply the Western world's scientific method to defining a problem and then solving it in a way that complied with all the known laws and principles of what was considered to be indisputable reality.

But what if, John began to think, the abduction phenomenon was something that manifested itself in the realm of our physical reality but was not necessarily *of* that reality? He began to find himself looking far afield for ways to answer his own question, reading widely in literature that ranged from ancient mythology to New Age philosophy and found himself wondering if the clues to understanding that he was searching for might be found somewhere beyond the values and teachings of the post-Industrial-age, Judeo-Christian-thinking Western world he had been raised, schooled, and trained to accept as the only framework for comprehending human existence.

I took in all this information with interest, but continued, mostly, to stay silent. I was just waiting to hear how the story played out. I sipped my coffee, and listened as John explained that over time, Jim and Alice's fixation on the idea that the aliens were conducting a breeding program only grew stronger. John thought that he and Jim, at least, had simply agreed to disagree until they both appeared on a popular tv interview program and the host led them into a debate. By then, John had published a few articles about his theories; nothing that had attracted any great attention, but apparently, the interviewer had read them, and his aim was to pit Barrett against John in an argument about what was already both a controversial and sensational topic.

"It got a little ugly," John said. "Jim was adamant that not only should every single person on earth be alarmed about the aliens' agenda but that there should be some international convening to decide how to respond. It seemed so ridiculous to me that I laughed and Jim took great offense. I said that I wasn't trying to oppose him and that I was still in the early stages of forming my own beliefs but I certainly did agree with Jim's position that abductees were reporting experiences that were 'real,' in whatever terms one understood the concept, and that they had significant and lasting consequences for the abductees' lives. Still, I didn't think anything particularly noteworthy had happened during that interview: I thought people would view us as a stodgy academic and a hyped-up journalist having an argument. But a few days later, I found out that was not how the university saw it. I was called to the provost's office and told that the president of the university was embarrassed because he'd had calls from major donors demanding to know why they had a crackpot on the faculty who was arguing, in public, about alien abduction with another crazy person. I was told that an emergency board meeting had been conducted by telephone and the trustees agreed with the president's decision to suspend me from the faculty pending what they termed a review of my current work. I was pretty shocked; that's a very extreme action to take against a tenured professor."

"When did that happen?" I asked.

"About six months before you and I met. I have a lawyer and we're fighting them. As I've explained before, it's an issue of academic freedom; I should be able to conduct whatever research I want and treat my patients in whatever way I think will help them the most."

Choosing my words carefully, I said, "So you think that if some sort of alien beings are interacting with humans, their purpose is one thing or the other: either to replace us or enlighten us."

"Not necessarily," John said. "I don't think it's anywhere near being so black and white. Their purpose could be anything at all; anywhere between those two opposites or something else entirely. I'm just predisposed to hope, I suppose. And I hope I can find that something...oh, let's say something elevating for the human spirit is involved in all this. I want to believe that, for my patients' sake. And for mine as well, I guess."

For a moment or two I communed with the gargoyles on the wall. I noticed that glass jewels had been pasted to a few of the paintings so that the eyes of two or three of these fantastical creatures glittered through the dim light. They were not at all like the eyes of owls or the secret "others" they might conceal.

Because I was quiet, John prodded me. "So how do you feel about all this?" he asked. "Can you deal with it?"

"That depends," I replied. "How much *do* I have to deal with it?"

"That's up to you. But I'm going to appeal to your sympathy. I'm in disgrace," he said, but he was smiling. "I could use some tender loving care."

"I don't know if that's my strong suit."

"Maybe you're better at it than you know. We could at least test it out, don't you think?"

I didn't react, at first, because I wasn't sure what he meant. Well, that's probably not true—I knew exactly what he meant but maybe I just wasn't ready to hear it. "What are you asking me?" I said.

"I want you to come stay with me. Come live with me, in my house."

"We've known each other three months," I pointed out.

"What difference does that make?" John asked. "You pretty much know everything about me now, while I..." He stopped himself there, and smiled again. "I was going to say that I hardly know you—who you really are. You're a closed book, Julia. But that's okay; I'm not going to pry. See?" he said, crossing his heart. "No shrink in sight; not tonight, anyway."

"There's not all that much to know about me that I haven't told you. As I've said: small town girl, eccentric mother. That's the whole bio in a nutshell."

"The more you say that, the less I'm going to believe it. I already told you I'm not going to pry but that doesn't mean I don't want to know about you. I do. I want to know everything you want to tell me—when you want to tell me. Come on, Jules," he coaxed. "Let's go home."

And I gave in. It was either that, I realized, or give him up, which—with my anger gone now—I could not do. Maybe love compelled me, or something like love, as close to love as someone like me could get. Someone who should have told her secrets that night, but had practiced secrecy too long to deliver them up even to the one person who would have believed them. But I believed that would change everything between us, and I wasn't ready for that to happen. I wasn't even sure that I would ever be.

There was, however, one thing I still had to know. "What happened to Alice?" I asked John.

"She's still my patient," he told me. And then, because I must have looked surprised, he added, "It's complicated."

I had no doubt that it was. As far as I could tell, everything in this life was. And maybe it had just become even more so.

# V

I LIKED LIVING in John's house. It was extraordinary, really, how quiet and isolated it felt, even though it was in the heart of the Village. Coming home from wherever I was working on a given day, I would usually end up taking the subway to Sheridan Square and then walking down to Washington Street where I would turn into Paper Lane. As soon as I did, it was like crossing the threshold from the world of noise and business into place that was protected from the intrusions of the city. And once inside the old carriage house, with its dark wood floors, trestle table, and stained glass hayloft windows, I felt that I was even further away from everyday life. The house was its own country to me, and I was content there. Maybe even happy.

What also added to my sense of calm was that I didn't see many of the things in the first months that I lived in the carriage house. They were never completely gone but even when they did make themselves known, they stayed at the top of the lane, standing on the cobblestones in one or another ridiculous outfit—a caftan paired with neon-hued sneakers; an ice-cream man's ragged summer uniform, topped by a sailor's hat—and never even showed themselves in the garden again. Which meant to me that after I had moved from my apartment to this house we had reestablished our boundaries. There was always a palpable undercurrent of hostility between us, but they never came too near me. They wouldn't dare. I hated them, and they knew it. I always had. I blamed them for everything that had been difficult about my life—which was almost everything. But I may have blamed Laura even more.

Did I love her as well? Though I could only summon up a faint memory of that feeling now, I supposed I must have loved her once, because she was my mother. But we had come to an impasse early, a separation that I imagine often, if not always, happens between mothers and daughters, but much later, as they age and naturally grow apart. Our separation—mine from Laura, Laura from me, the breaking of a bond that would never be repaired—had a date, a time, a place.

I was seven years old. Laura and I were living in a trailer park at the end of a two-lane road, surrounded by cold, wintry fields. Every day was pretty much the same, every night—until one particular night, when Laura woke me up, bundled me into a jacket and said we were going for a walk. A walk. In the middle of the night. I kept asking why but all Laura said was, *Don't be afraid, Julia. Be brave. Everything will be okay.* Still groggy and confused, I followed her down the road, across the hard furrows of a pumpkin field long harvested and plowed under for the winter, and then into a woods.

Laura had a flashlight. Its thin beam helped us pick our way through the fallen logs and leaf litter. Above us, through the branches of the bare trees, I could see the moon and stars, distant, disinterested observers of our midnight trek. I held my mother's hand but already, I was beginning not to trust her, not to believe that whatever mission we were on was one I should be taking part in. Measuring this experience against all I knew, what I knew, even then, was that no other mother was leading her child—at least a child I was acquainted with, a friend, or even any other little girl I could imagine, except maybe some poor doomed child in a dangerous fairytale—through a forest in the dead of an autumn night.

We walked on for maybe ten or fifteen minutes. Laura led me through the woods until we came to a gap in the trees where she pushed aside some branches as if opening a leafy gate and led me into a clearing lit by a circle of light that seemed to have no source. And there, waiting in the clearing were the things: a group of them, maybe five or six. Most were not much taller than me, though one stood out because it towered over the rest. It was nearly seven feet tall and as thin as a gaunt, gray stick. All the things—except for the tall one whose face was hidden because, bizarrely, he was wearing some kind of mirrored motorcycle helmet—shared one feature in common: huge, almond-shaped eyes that were black, depthless, and unblinking.

51

My immediate reaction was terror: their appearance horrified me. Perhaps that was because to me, a child, the small things appeared to have the nakedness of a child—something I knew was private; little children did not show their naked bodies to anyone except a parent. What was worse, these naked, child-sized things looked like their bodies had been turned inside-out in some monstrous way because their grayish skin seemed more like the tissue that internal organs would have been made of than flesh that covered bones. Or perhaps, I remember thinking, they were something else entirely; not children, really, not adults, not even something that was alive. I even wondered, actually, if they were dead. Not that I necessarily even understood what death was at that age, but what I might have meant was simply *not alive*, in the way that I was alive, or Laura was.

I barely had time to form these thoughts when the tall one started to advance towards me. As it did, I registered the fact that in addition to the helmet, the thing was wearing the kind of outfit I associated with tough-guy characters I had seen on tv: a black leather motorcycle jacket, boots, and a pair of jeans. These impressions flew at me and then disappeared as I looked up at my mother and saw that she was smiling—not at me but at them. At the things. She knew them—that much I understood. And they knew her.

What I did then arose from two immediate and intertwined assumptions that must have been rooted in some deep-seated survival instinct: first, that no matter *what* they were, the intention of these things was to hurt me, and second, that Laura wasn't going to stop them. So without thinking in any rational way about what I was going to do, I broke away from Laura and lunged towards the tall thing—not away from it, but towards it, deliberately, with all the speed I could muster—and bit it. I sank my teeth into its arm and bit down with a vengeance that contained rage, hate, pure vitriol. And I remember what that bite tasted like: it was bitter, like tasting poison. Swilling venom. When I finally let go, the thing howled in pain from behind its helmet; it shook its wounded arm and screamed at me, making agonized, wordless sounds that I didn't even try to understand.

And then I ran away. I don't know how I found my way back to the trailer but I did. And I locked the door. Laura didn't come back until dawn, and when she did, she could only persuade me to let her in by promising I would never have to go back to where the things were. It was a promise she kept, but our relationship was never the same. She tried to pretend that it was—maybe she really meant it to be—but I could not. I never trusted her again. I was too shocked by what had happened and the only way forward for me, though I couldn't have put it into words then, was to harden my heart against her. And so I felt, even as a young child, that though I was fed and clothed and tended to in all the basic, necessary ways, I was really on my own.

At first, when she met Nicky and we moved in with him, to the rooms above the Stargazer's Embassy, I remember hoping that the things would disappear from her life. But that didn't happen—in fact, once she had someone to leave me with, she seemed to be gone even more than before. In a way, that was fine with me (or at least, I thought it was); I became close to Nicky, the only person who shared my secrets about Laura, though even as I got older, we rarely discussed them. We both just *knew*, and that seemed to be enough. He was often the one who fed me dinner, helped me with my homework, kissed me goodnight. So, even when Laura was around, I spent as little time with her as possible. Mostly, I would retreat to my bedroom where I was allowed to close the door and have my privacy. My own room, my own books, my own records and even a television, where I watched, with constant devotion, the examples of what I thought were a more normal life that were presented to me by actors who I never quite believed were just mouthing words that had been scripted for them.

Everything changed when Laura died. I had been told that she was sick and there had been multiple stays in the hospital, though if Nicky hadn't gone to visit her every day I wouldn't have believed that the hospital was where she really was. I went to see her once or twice though I always harbored some suspicion that she wasn't really ill, that this was some new form of disappearing that she had figured out. Of course, I was wrong. She had cancer and she died in a hospital in Ithaca one night when I was home watching tv. It was Nicky who told me. I don't even remember crying.

I had never seen the things again after that long-ago night in the clearing—until one of them showed up at her funeral. At the graveyard, it stood under a nearby tree, dressed in a black smock that appeared to be on backwards, and a black velvet hat with a veil, one of the many bizarre outfits that from then on, they always appeared in. A week later, one of them was sitting on a bench outside the Stargazer's Embassy. Sometimes, when I looked out my window, I could see them standing in the fields.

They never actually came into the bar until the year I finished high school and started working there. At first, it was every couple of weeks, and then it happened with more frequency: one or two of them would walk through the front door and take a seat at a table—but they were careful to show up only when the bar was nearly empty and I was the only one working. They always wore sunglasses, but other than that, they were clearly trying to dress like workmen in those days, turning up in stained denim shirts and dungarees—as close as I ever saw them come to donning clothing that at least resembled what people might actually wear. Over time, I had decided that the outfits were some misguided attempt to make themselves seem harmless to me, but I wasn't fooled: never once did I even think of letting my guard down when they were around.

Sometimes, for spite, I would ignore them—I let them sit in some gloomy corner until they seemed to grow tired of watching me and leave. Or if I was in an angry mood—which was often the case—I'd walk over to them and simply hiss, "Get out," though a couple of times I did that carrying a loaded shotgun Nicky kept behind the bar. They'd make the weird noises I had become accustomed to, as if they believed that one day I'd finally understand them, but once I demanded that they leave, they always did.

It was because of them that I finally left Freelingburg the year after I graduated from high school. I told Nicky the reason and at first, he tried to persuade me to stay. He said that he wouldn't let me work alone anymore, that if they showed up when he was around he'd confront them for me, but that never happened. I knew it wouldn't. Nicky couldn't be with me every second of every day, so their visits continued; I didn't see them sitting in the bar anymore but when I was driving, I'd see one of them standing by the side of the road, or on my way to the kitchen, one of them would be lurking in the hallway. After a while, I'd had enough. I thought that by leaving Freelingburg and the Stargazer's Embassy, I would leave them behind.

Except, of course, they found me on Canal Street and then followed me to Paper Lane. And so I became used to them all over again; we were enemies, but I knew that I had the upper hand. They would only come within a certain distance of me and no more. Even all these years later—if years even meant anything to them; how was I to know?—they were still afraid of what I might do, and they had good reason to be. I myself wasn't sure how far I would go if I had to, nor did I have any idea how much physical harm they could actually sustain beyond that bite I had been able to inflict, as a child, on the thing I had come to think of as The Biker, but they seemed to understand that they shouldn't test me. And so far, they had not.

All of this was on my mind one chilly December morning as I waited for John to get up so we could have breakfast together. I didn't usually do this—most days, I was dressed and gone before he was out of bed—but there was something I wanted to ask him.

"Christmas," I said, as he made coffee. "You haven't mentioned any plans."

He got mugs out of the cabinet; brought milk and sugar to the table. I had the feeling that he was considering how to reply, as if he might have been husbanding a series of choices and was sorting through which one to present to me. "I was thinking of a restaurant," he said. "Someplace ridiculously fancy and expensive. Would you like that?"

"Is that what you usually do?" I asked.

"No. Usually, I go to one friend or another. And there have been years that I've hosted Christmas dinner here. I can actually cook," he said genially.

"So can I. Ham, turkey, pudding and pie—you'd be surprised what I can whip up when I want to."

"I wouldn't be surprised at all," John said. "I've already gained five pounds eating the dinners you've been feeding me."

He wasn't protesting; in fact, he sounded pleased, and that pleased me. The night we had sat in the café under the gloomy gargoyles, he had half-joked that he needed some loving care and, to my great surprise, I seemed to have taken that as a mandate. Without specific intent, at least that I was aware of, I had become the keeper of this house; I did the shopping, I cooked most of the meals, I carried sheets and towels to the laundromat and swept the floors. And maybe it was that sense of having a home, of being safe here, with the things as an intrusive but not particularly threatening presence, that made it safe to think of my other home and allow myself to miss it. After all, other than my difficult relationship with Laura—if it could even be called a relationship—I had been safe in the Stargazer's Embassy for many years, too, until I had inherited the part of Laura's life that I despised. The presences that had infected even my relationship with Nicky, who I had come to love. After I left, I had only been back a few times to see him, never even staying overnight. I did call him though, every once in a while, but it had been too long, now, since I had done even that. And I was feeling guilty. He had been as close to a parent as I had ever had and it would be nice, I thought, to show him that my life had gotten a little better. Maybe better than he thought it would have turned out when I left.

"What if we went to Freelingburg for Christmas?" I asked John.

"Really?" he said, sounding cautious. "I'm a little surprised that's where you want to go."

"I'm a little surprised myself, but it is. What do you think?"

"Sure," John said. "If that's what you want, then that's where we'll go. Christmas at the Stargazer's Embassy sounds perfect."

I phoned Nicky later in the morning. He was happy to hear from me, and happy that I wanted to come to Freelingburg for the holiday. Then I explained about John, and Nicky said he was happy to hear that I was bringing someone with me. I said we'd drive up early on Christmas eve and stay over for Christmas day.

So, when I got home that afternoon, I thought everything was set. The door to John's study was closed, which meant he was with a patient, or even a group, so I went upstairs to the living room and turned on the television. It couldn't be heard in John's study when he had the door closed, so I wasn't worried about disturbing anyone.

The weekend before, John and I had bought a Christmas tree at a church fair on Bleecker Street. We had set it up near the hayloft windows, where the winter afternoon light, filtered by the stained glass, gave the bare tree a sort of wistful look, like a lonely character in a child's storybook. There wasn't really anything on the tv that was holding my attention, so I decided to have a start at decorating the tree with the ornaments and tinsel that we'd also bought at the fair. It felt like a hundred years since I'd had the chance to decorate a Christmas tree, so I was enjoying myself, sitting on the floor, unpacking the ornaments and deciding where to hang them, when I suddenly heard footsteps coming up the stairs.

"Hey!" I called out, "there are some little horse ornaments here. They're probably happy to find themselves in a carriage house."

The response was not at all what I expected. "Who are you?" a woman's voice asked.

I should have realized that I hadn't yet heard the front door open and close, and that the person on the stairs might not have been John. But that had never happened before; I did sometimes here people coming and going between John's study and the small bathroom downstairs, but no one had ever come up to the second floor.

I put down the decorations I had been playing with and got to my feet. "Hi," I said. "I'm Julia Glazer."

The woman, a severe looking, wisp-thin blonde, stood completely still on the top step of the stairs as if considering whether or not it was safe to approach me. Though John had never described her appearance to me, I knew immediately who she was: Alice Giddings. She gave off the same sense of being on alert, highly—even brutally—aware of everything around her that I recognized in myself, only I was much better able to mask it.

But I knew something else from that very first moment, as well: this tense individual dressed in a gray skirt and a long-sleeved white blouse clearly didn't like the idea of there being anyone else in John's house. Especially not someone like me, a young woman around the same age as she was but also something of a total opposite in appearance: I was wearing jeans and an old sweater, no shoes, and a pair of green and red striped Christmas socks.

"What are you doing here?" she asked me.

I wasn't sure how to answer her. Of course I could have said, *I live here,* but my instinct about always being cautious led me to hesitate. Besides, I wasn't sure what John would have wanted me to say. What had he told her, what would he want her to know?

"I'm decorating this tree," I told her, as if I was back in cleaning lady mode; just the hired help, doing chores around the house. I must have also sounded pretty stupid—either that, or deliberately evasive. Nevertheless, she seemed to lose interest in even acknowledging my existence and quickly walked past me, to the bathroom. When she left, she didn't even glance in my direction.

About half an hour later, I heard Alice saying good-bye to John in the vestibule outside his office. By the time John finally came upstairs, I had started dinner and was sautéing scallops on the stove. I had the radio on, tuned to a news station. I wasn't actually registering whatever events or evening traffic problems were being reported: as usual, I just wanted the background noise for comfort. John had caught onto this habit of mine and without bothering to ask—which was fine with me—he changed the station to one that played some soft, soothing music, then sat at the table to read the newspaper while I worked. At the end of the kitchen was a glass door leading to a tiny balcony that overlooked the garden; the long rectangle of glass, now, was the color of night and the kitchen was pleasantly dim, with the only light coming from the pendant lamp hanging above the table. All this would have made for the perfect domestic tableau except that I was feeling a little unsettled, like there was something I was supposed to say, only I was pretending I didn't know what it was.

But that was one secret too many; as I took the scallops out of the pan and set them on a serving dish, I said, "So I met Alice this afternoon."

John put down the newspaper and looked over at me. He seemed a little surprised, but not overly concerned. "Really? Did you run into her downstairs?"

"No. She came up here to use the bathroom."

"Did she?" He stood up to help me bring the food to the table. He took the salad out of the refrigerator and opened a bottle of wine. "Oh well," he said, after we both sat down and began to eat, "I guess she's curious about you."

"Why?" I asked.

"She knows I'm living with you. Well, with someone. It's not something I've tried to hide. Your things are downstairs, sometimes—you know, a jacket, shoes, maybe your backpack. And people like Alice, who I've been working with for so long, can probably sense that something is different about me." He smiled. "Maybe my aura has gotten a little stronger."

"But why would she care if you're living with someone?" I asked, though I could guess—thinking about her now, I realized that if Alice had an aura, it would have radiated a level of jealousy that would have set off a Geiger counter—and I'd have been surprised if John didn't know that himself. But as much of an expert as I was at compartmentalizing, perhaps he was better, and occupied with thoughts about so many other things, maybe this was one problem that somewhere inside himself he had decided not to acknowledge. Or, at least ignore. He knew how to help people reveal the things that troubled them so I imagined he was equally good at using that skill on himself for its opposite result when he needed to.

And indeed, Alice, specifically, was not the subject he chose to address when he replied to me. "I guess the only way to answer that is to tell you about how I work with the experiencers," he said. "It's different then what you probably imagine. It's more personal—and interactive than with traditional patients."

"Do you mean they know as much about you as you do about them?"

"Not exactly, no. But I have found that with experiencers, it's important to create a deep sense of trust, even friendship. I can't just be the shrink; I have to be a kind of partner, working through their memories with them, as well as the effects on their everyday life. That means I interact with them in different settings; some of them pretty informal. As a matter of fact," he continued, "I was going to ask you something about that."

"Okay," I said, and waited. I had a feeling that I had better be cautious about whatever was coming next.

"Freelingburg," he said. "The plan was to be there on Christmas eve, right?"

"Right. I thought we could drive up in time for dinner. It takes a couple of hours, but we'll be fine if we get on the road around lunchtime."

"Easy enough," John said, but I heard something else in his voice; some hesitation I couldn't let pass.

"But?"

He smiled. "There's no but. Nothing that would interfere with our plans. It's just that the night before, there's a kind of get-together I should probably go. I'd like you to come with me but you don't have to if you don't want to."

"Why wouldn't I want to? Oh," I said, as the reason suddenly dawned on me. "You're talking about...what? A party with some of your patients?"

"Not a party. Just hanging out for a while. A lot of my patients and others in their network don't have much family support so it helps them to see each other outside of a therapy setting, and it seems to be useful if I'm there, too, once in a while. Like I said, I'm a partner in trying to incorporate their experiences into the way they cope with their lives; I'm not an expert, not a guide. I have my own ideas about what might be involved in their experiences, but they're still developing, so...well, it's important to me that the people I work with know that I see them all as human beings, not just patients."

"Alice asked you to come?"

"She did."

*Of course she did*, I thought. *Right after she saw me here, in your house.*

"So," I said, "everyone there will be alien baby people."

It was a nasty thing to say, but I didn't regret it. John knew, and didn't let it pass. "Jules," he said, "that's not like you."

I wasn't giving in. "How do you know?" I responded. "Maybe it is." Then I pushed some scallops around on my plate while he waited for me to change back into the person he wanted me to be. I gave in soon enough, but turned the conversation around. I didn't want to hear any more about what was or was not like me. There were too many answers, many of which John would probably not have liked very much.

"Alright," I said. "I'm sorry. But it's hard for me to understand how you can try to figure out what might be useful about interacting with aliens when your patients—people like Alice—think it's all horrible."

*Aliens.* Just saying that word made me cringe inside. I never used it, not even to myself. I knew the main narrative of stories that involved aliens—who could avoid it? And of course, John had told me about Alice's experiences. Such stories always centered around a gaggle of unfeeling humanoids who lived in spaceships and invaded people's bedrooms or stopped their car on a lonely road and then floated them up to some examination chamber in the sky. Alice had apparently added the extra detail about hybrid babies, as had others. I could relate to none of this—I had never seen a UFO for example, not even that one time, with Laura had there been anything that could even remotely be described as a spaceship or any other kind of craft hovering around—and I didn't want to. There were *things* in this world, yes—but I didn't have to give them power or purpose or intentions. And I didn't have to give them a name. All I wanted them to do—if they wouldn't simply vanish—was to stay where they were, for me, lurking around corners in their bizarre outfits, making their incomprehensible sounds. I could deal with that; I knew how to and I did it very well, as far as I was concerned. So I listened to John talk to me about "aliens," because then he was talking about something I didn't have to acknowledge. Still, I had to make an effort to listen to what he was saying, to pay attention, because I really didn't want to.

John said, "I can only hope it helps the people I work with to know that maybe there is something to be learned from what happened to them, and in a number of cases, continues to happen. Something that will eventually prove to be beneficial to them. Enlightening. But I don't try to impose that idea; I can't make judgments about what other people experience, especially in a therapeutic relationship." Then he smiled and shook his head; he seemed to be listening to a private joke he was making with himself. Out loud he said, "I don't think the possibility of enlightenment will be a big topic of conversation at Jim Barrett's house. I imagine you'll hear just the opposite."

"Wait a minute. This get-together is at Jim Barrett's? Isn't he the reason you got suspended from teaching?"

"No," John said firmly. "The administrators of the school are the reason. I don't blame Jim for their small mindedness. He and I disagree, but he's been trying to mend fences with me lately and I'm inclined to see if that will work. I do have to respect him, Julia. He was the first person to offer abductees any real help; the first to treat them as if their encounters weren't a manifestation of some kind of mental aberration or disease. He deserves a great deal of credit for that, even though now I think he's gone way off track. I'm just hoping that if I keep the lines of communication open, someday we can find some middle ground that will be helpful to everybody."

*Middle ground:* wasn't that what John had said he and I should be trying to find? Well then, how could I disagree? So I said that whatever he hoped for, I hoped for too, but it still felt like I was mouthing a sentiment I had read about in a manual offering suggestions for how normal people should behave at dinnertime.

We finished our meal and as we were cleaning up, the phone rang; John took the call on the phone in the kitchen so I could hear he was talking to someone about some kind of house repair. When he hung up, he said, "That was the guy I told you was coming to look at the heating system; I really don't think it's working right. We made an appointment for Friday at three. I'm pretty sure I'm free, but I should have checked my calendar."

"I have a job in the morning but I can be back by then," I said. "I can deal with it."

He patted me fondly on the back. "Taking over now, are you? Good." he said. "I like that."

We put away the rest of the dishes and then John took out the trash, which had to be carried to a dumpster at the end of the lane. When he came back, I said, "I'd like to go to the party. If it's important to you, then I should be there."

"Are you sure you'll be comfortable?" he asked.

"I'm always comfortable when I'm with you," I told him. Another response from the manual but this, at least, was almost true.

# VI

JOHN HAD an old Volvo that he kept in a garage on Jane Street, a few blocks away from the house. On the evening of the party at Jim Barrett's we went to retrieve the car, walking along under a darkening sky with night sliding closed above us from horizon to horizon. There was snow on the sidewalks, slippery sheets of ice laid along the curbs. Once the garage attendant brought us the Volvo, we sat for a while, waiting for the car to warm up before we started on our way.

Barrett lived in Brooklyn, which I didn't know very well, so I expected churches and brownstones standing together in tight brick rows. Instead, after a long drive on the Belt Parkway that looped around the marshland near Kennedy Airport and then passed by seemingly endless miles of towering, terraced apartment buildings marching alongside the highway, John took an exit that led us into a quiet neighborhood of elegant old houses. We drove down several avenues occupied by private homes with wrap-around porches and landscaped winter lawns decorated with mangers and electric reindeer, then another turn took us to a more modest street of two-story colonials with bay windows strung with holiday lights. John finally parked in front of one of these houses, which had a huge holly wreath hung on the front door.

He rang the bell and the door was opened by a man whose appearance momentarily startled me: he certainly wasn't like anyone I was expecting to meet tonight. He was in his late thirties, I thought; thin, with dark hair caught in a rubber-banded ponytail, but it was his body piercings that made a statement about him he probably wanted everyone to take note of—*Watch out, I'm a bad boy.* He had several small steel rings clipped through his nose and a narrow bar fastened under his lip; one ear was lined with a mass of silver loops while the other had an oversized black disk inserted in the lobe. These adornments were accompanied by multi-colored tattoos: I could see the head of a snake curling around one side of his neck and what looked like the tail of a dragon rising up from beneath the collar of his black sweater. The backs of his hands were also tattooed: I saw a mandala on one, a yin-yang sign on the other. The tattoos, though way more prominent than my small half-bracelet of stars, made me a little self-conscious; as we walked through the door I jammed my hand in my pocket to hide my own markings.

We went into the vestibule and John introduced us: the heavily deco-rated greeter at the door was named Kel. He told us that everyone else was gathered in the living room, so we left our coats on bench near the door that was piled with winter gear and walked down the hall, heading towards the sound of voices and music.

There were at least a dozen people in the living room, a mixture of men and women of different ages, ranging from about twenty to well over seventy. With the exception of Kel, they all presented a pretty normal appearance; no one in particular stood out to me. The room itself was nondescript but comfortable-looking: a brown-patterned couch and some matching arm-chairs were ranged around a coffee table where cheese, crackers, nuts and potato chips had been laid out. A Christmas tree sporting tinsel and colored balls was standing in a corner and nearby, a radio tuned to a local station was playing pop versions of Christmas carols. It seemed to be a pleasant enough scene, but something struck me as being just a little off: there was some weird kind of tension the air. People were smiling and chatting, but the joviality seemed a little forced. Of course, I told myself, the problem could have been me rather than anybody else: my sense of the environment around me was almost always tinged with wariness.

As soon as we walked into the living room, Jim Barrett came up to John and said hello. He was instantly recognizable to me from his photo on the books he'd written that I'd seen in John's house: slightly overweight, sandy hair, a graying beard. John introduced us and then stated making a circuit of the room, saying hello to everyone. That left me alone with Barrett.

"So you're Julia," he said. He was trying hard not to seem like he was inspecting me, and I tried to pretend that I didn't notice. I was going to try to be accommodating tonight—at least, that was my plan.

"I'm glad you could come," he continued. "Want something to drink? There's beer and wine in the kitchen. Help yourself." Despite the edgy feeling that I couldn't shake, Jim Barrett seemed harmless enough and he was clearly making an effort to play the genial host with me. He stood beside me for a while, asking innocuous questions and responding with pleasantries. I began to relax a little—the plan was working; I was going to be nice. Besides, I decided, sometimes I was too much on guard for my own good. But then I saw Alice.

I hadn't noticed her when we walked in—maybe she had been in another room—but now she was standing in a group of people who had gathered around John. Her straight, ghost-blonde hair framed her face in a way that made her look much younger than she actually was and almost cripplingly vulnerable, like the wrong words would make her shatter. But I didn't think so. I didn't think so at all.

I decided to keep my distance from her: she was welcome to fawn over John if that's what she wanted to do, which was my guess. She was standing close to him and kept touching his arm as he spoke.

I watched this tableau for few brief moments, while Barrett went to answer the doorbell and greet another guest. Seeing that I was now standing by myself, John called to me to join him. After I walked over to where he was standing, he put his arm around me and someone wandered away to get something to eat, so the remaining group of people rearranged themselves. Alice was now positioned opposite me, and, unlike Barrett, she made no attempt to disguise the fact that she was giving me a thorough inspection. Perhaps she was trying to decide if I looked any better than the last time she saw me. I thought I was: I had considered wearing the green dress again, and though I had opted for something a bit more casual, the slacks and blouse I had on were still more upscale than my usual outfits. I even had on a fancy pair of shoes with high heels. More lessons from the manual on good behavior: dress appropriately for all occasions even if you're not exactly sure how to do that. Given time and repetition, you may learn.

The conversation gradually began to shift from general chatter to the issue that they all had in common—though it wasn't their own personal experiences they started talking about but an abduction incident that Jim Barrett had become involved in. Apparently, some months ago, a number of people had reported seeing multiple UFOs in the night sky over Virginia, just a few miles from Washington, D.C. A woman who lived in the area had recently contacted Barrett because she claimed to have been abducted on the same night and returned to her bed sometime around dawn. She had gone through a familiar pattern of experiences that most people in the conversational circle seemed to be familiar with: lost time, strange memories, panicky dreams. She had finally begun to piece together what had happened to her, and having recalled hearing Barrett interviewed on a radio show once, she had gotten in touch with him to ask for help.

Barrett picked up on the thread of the conversation as he joined us. "This could be an important case," he said. "It coincides with UFO sightings that we may be able to document by putting out a call for photos or video. I mean, this happened near Washington, in a heavily populated suburb. It gives me hope that there's some real concrete evidence we can follow up on."

"Did they show her the babies?" Alice asked. "You haven't said if they showed her the babies. In so many of the new cases, even men are beginning to report that they're being shown infants and young children. Even hybrids that are older than that."

"She hasn't volunteered that information yet," Barrett said. "I'm going down to Virginia after the holidays to talk with her in more detail, but I wouldn't be surprised to find out that she's part of the breeding program. They do seem to be stepping up the pace."

"It's so horrible," Alice said. "Beyond words. And we still don't know how to do anything about it."

"That's what we're working towards," Barrett replied. "Every piece of information we can gather will help us figure out what to do. There has to be a way to stop them before they create more hybrids than there are human beings."

Though Barrett was speaking to the whole group that had now assembled around him and John—maybe eight or nine people—he really seemed to be directing his remarks to Alice, as if she was not so much an experiencer as some sort of co-researcher. I guess by the framework John had described for me, she was, since Barrett probably treated the people he worked with in the same way John did—as partners in trying to solve the mystery of alien abduction. Still, there was something conspiratorial about their conversation that put me off, like it was meant to exclude the others, not draw them in. I did notice, however, that as the conversation progressed and John took his arm from around my shoulder, Alice managed to once again insert herself next to him. She put her hand on his arm and kept it there. Maybe this was a signal to me; maybe also to John that even if he disagreed with what she and Barrett were saying (as I assumed she knew he probably did), her regard for him remained unaffected.

As hard as I was trying, I found everything annoying: Alice, the conversation, even John, at the moment—the fact that he was allowing Alice to be so cloying was beginning to get to me—so I told him that I was going to the kitchen to pour myself a glass of wine. As I started to walk away, Alice took a small step backwards so she could turn to watch me; the look on her face was decidedly unfriendly.

There was no one else in the kitchen, so I took my time opening a bottle of Shiraz. Just as I was putting the wine back in the refrigerator, the kitchen door swung open and Kel walked in.

"Hey," he said. "I just wanted to see if Alice's death stare had turned you to dust yet."

Finally, something made me laugh. "You noticed that, did you?"

"Oh, she can be quite the bitch," he said. "I know. She's gone after me a couple of times."

I was surprised by that; I suppose I had expected there to be some kind of unbreakable camaraderie among this particular group of people who probably talked with each other about things they kept secret from most everyone else they knew. Perhaps Kel guessed what I was thinking because he said, "This isn't exactly a lovey-dovey crowd. Straight types mixed with freaks and weirdos. We don't always get along."

"So I guess the aliens don't discriminate. They go after just about anybody."

"You know what?" Kel said. "I think you're being sarcastic, but that's okay. Maybe somebody's got to make a joke or something once in a while, right? Take the edge off. I mean, things can get very serious with this bunch."

"I can imagine."

He gave me a long look. "You know, I bet you can. I bet you've got your own theories, right? I mean, you seem like the type."

"Oh really?" I thought I should have been offended, but I wasn't sure why. "What type is that?"

"What type? A girl with a tat." He raised his right hand, the one heavily inked with a mandala, and pointed his finger at my wrist. It was warm in the kitchen and forgetting my earlier wariness, I had absentmindedly rolled back my sleeve, exposing my own tattoo. "So come on," he said. "Your boyfriend thinks we're getting messages about peace and harmony from our misunderstood friends while Jim and Alice think the end is nigh. Humans being replaced with pod people and all that. So there's two theories. Want to tell me yours?"

I pulled my sleeves back down over my wrists with practiced nonchalance. "Not right now," I said. "No."

"Good choice," he replied. "Why get into it if you don't have to? As for me, in case you're wondering, I've got no theory. I prefer to just drink."

With that, he walked over to the refrigerator and removed two cans of beer. He opened one and put the other on the table. "I'm going to finish this in a minute," he said, jiggling the can he was holding. "Stay here, will you, then we can go back outside. I'm having one of my dark nights of the soul when I don't like being alone in a room by myself."

"I use headphones for that," I told him. "I plug myself into some music and just try to ignore everything else."

He sipped from his beer and seemed to be giving some serious consideration to what I'd said. Finally, he asked. "Why would you have to do that?"

I answered him first with a shrug. Then I said, "I thought everybody did."

"Now I know you're being sarcastic," he told me, "but okay, if that's the way you want it, I won't push it"

As he predicted, he finished his beer pretty quickly and started on the next. I watched him, saying nothing. Outside the window behind him, I could make out a pair of bare trees displayed against the winter night. There was nothing else to see.

"So where are you from?" Kel asked eventually.

"Upstate," I replied. "Tompkins County."

"No kidding? Me too. I'm from Trumansburg."

Again, I was surprised. I could indeed hear the flat, upstate tonality in his voice—a trait I had worked to erase from my own—but I didn't expect him to be from a town in the same county where I had grown up. "So maybe once we were neighbors," I said. "I'm from Freelingburg."

"Is that where you got the tat?" he asked. "It's not bad—better than I would expect from some amateur scratcher." He paused for a moment, and I figured he was waiting to see if I knew that he was referring to an unlicensed tattoo artist. Of course I did; I worked at the bottom of the economy, where a lot of the things people needed or wanted had to be acquired in some off-the-grid fashion. I saw street-made tattoos all the time, though mostly on guys.

I frowned at Kel. He took that as a rebuke, which he seemed to find amusing. "Well," he said, "if you ever want to add anything a little more creative to your ink, come see me. I've got a tattoo shop on St. Mark's, in the East Village."

"That's okay," I replied. "Mine can stay the way it is."

"Sentimental value?"

"No," I said. "Long story."

He nodded. "Fair enough. But if you ever want a real work of art, stop by my place; I keep it open all the time. Maybe that's my version of your headphone trick: there's almost always a customer in the shop because people want tattoos at the craziest hours of the night and day so if I'm there, with somebody, then I'm safe from the creepy crawlies. At least, that's what I think."

I knew what he meant. "Is that what you call them?"

For a fleeting moment, he looked embarrassed, as if he had spoken a child's name for the boogey man. But he quickly erased that expression from his face. "Why not? They look like bugs, with those big eyes."

"Owls. That's what I heard."

"Did you now?" He pointed the second empty beer can at me, just as he had pointed his finger, earlier. "See? We're getting closer to a theory. That's the screen memory business, right? Well, that was never my issue—I remember everything that happened to me. Which is a different kind of problem."

"I'm sure it must be," I offered, though really, I'd had enough of this conversation and didn't want to hear a description of his experience, which I knew was the next thing that was going to happen. What I did want to do was leave, but as I was about to turn and go, Kel started talking again, and it would have been to awkward to just walk out. So I leaned against one of the kitchen counters and listened to him tell me what his creepy crawlies had done to him. It was, as he had already said, very different than what anyone else in the group had reported.

"That's one of the reasons I have trouble relating to them." Kel said. "Alice and all the rest. John keeps telling us how it will help to share each other's experiences—it helps validate them, he says—but sometimes even the other abductees think I'm making things up. When the creepy crawlies came after me, they didn't do anything physical to me—no examination, nothing like that. And they never said anything to me about babies or hybrids. Instead, they showed me a movie. That's all that happened. They showed me a movie about death."

"What?" I said. That sounded alarming to me. Way, way beyond anything I wanted to hear about. I began mentally measuring the distance to the kitchen door, telling myself to just put one foot in front of the other and start moving.

"It's not what you're probably thinking." he said as he walked back to the refrigerator to get yet another beer. "It wasn't threatening. I mean, some of it was scary, but a lot of it wasn't. There was nothing violent and I didn't get the sense they were trying to frighten me. Mostly what the creepy crawlies showed me were pictures of men and women, even children, who seemed to be dead—I mean, they were laid out in coffins and on funeral pyres, but who knows? It all looked sort of staged. Other people were standing nearby, crying over their supposedly dead loved ones. Then they showed me all kinds of funeral processions, and after that, some Egyptian-looking stuff: you know, a guy with the head of a jackal, holding an ankh and raising people from their graves. There was a lot of that, actually; different rituals from different cultures where people died and then some magical person brought them back. To tell you the truth, though," he continued, "a lot of it was very cheesy, like they had tried to make a movie but they were bad at it. Like they thought they knew what they were doing but they didn't, really: they were just trying to imitate things they'd seen somewhere else. And the actors were all creatures like them, little, gray, bug-eyed things dressed up in cheap costumes, trying to look like human beings. If I hadn't been so scared and confused, I probably would have thought it was...well, stupid."

That caught my attention. Maybe he called them by another name, but Kel had just expressed something I also observed about the way that the things I encountered usually outfitted themselves: it was as if they were trying to mimic the way humans dressed, but there was always something off about their choices, something wrong. Some fundamental disconnect that they couldn't seem to make up for, though they must have been trying.

And indeed, as bizarre and horrifying as they were, there was a strangely comic element to their mistakes. That helped me, sometimes, because I could almost convince myself to see them as clueless and dumb.

And, the description gave me a bit more patience to continue the conversation with Kel. "Did you ask them why they were showing you those images?"

"I couldn't communicate with them," Kel said. "Not really. They just make weird sounds—like cats, sort of. Maybe they understood me, but I sure as hell didn't understand them. I'm no pussy." He laughed at his own bad joke and finished off the rest of the beer. He must have been a little drunk by now but he hardly showed it except for his eyes, which were beginning to look glassy. As for me, I was thinking about the distance to the door again.

"I wish I could have understood them," Kel continued, his joking tone all but gone. "It's been years since that happened but not a day passes that I don't go over and over it in my mind. What did they want from me? What did all that mean? Should I have figured it out by now?"

I had no answers for him, so I just kept quiet. He looked over at me, seeming to assess my silence. "Too much information?" he said to me. "I know—who wants to hear about all this, right? Maybe we can try another topic of conversation."

Suddenly, He grabbed my right arm and pushed back my sleeve so that my tattoo was exposed again: my two dark stars and their three smaller companions. He tapped the tattoo with his finger and said. "Or maybe we can just go back to talking about this." He was holding onto me tight now, and I knew he wouldn't have let me go no matter how hard I pulled away. "Somebody marked you, my friend. So what's the short version of the long story? Where'd you really get that tat?"

He wasn't drunk at all; I could see that now. He was dead sober, dead serious, and he thought he knew something about me that he had no right to. It was the tattoo—the fact that he'd seen it when he wandered into the kitchen. Everything after that was a charade he had carried out to get me to talk to him, to get information he wanted and was guessing that I had. But he was wrong; I knew nothing that would help him. I had made it my life's goal to ensure that was true.

"Let me go and I'll tell you," I said. "Maybe."

He gave me an appraising look, trying to gauge the weight of that *maybe*. Finally he released his grip.

"You're a real jerk," I said to him.

"Wait until you get to know me. You might think I'm even worse."

"I think that already," I said. "because you're going to a lot of trouble to hear a very boring story." I told him what I had told John—that my mother had etched that tattoo onto my wrist with homemade dye, and that it matched a similar tat she had. Then, I heard myself add that she had gotten her tattoo when she was with some boyfriend who was having himself inked; while she was waiting with him, she decided to get a tat herself, as a lark. The part about the boyfriend was a spur-of-the-moment invention, though why I bothered to add it, or even to respond to Kel at all, was a question I should have asked myself. But because I didn't—and didn't even try to stick to my own *maybe*—I grew annoyed, though probably even more with myself than with him. "It's just a design she saw hanging on the wall in the tattoo shop," I insisted, "A random thing. It could just as easily have been a rose or something like that."

"Really?" Kel said. "*That's* the card you want to play? *It's a random thing.*" He positioned himself closer to me. "Listen, sister: I've seen these markings before. And it wasn't in any tattoo shop."

He finally let go of me. I moved away from him, but he kept talking. "One of my creepy crawlies also had those same five stars tattooed on his wrist, in that exact same configuration. Though maybe it wasn't exactly a tattoo—it looked more like something embedded under his skin. If they call it skin, if they have wrists...oh fuck," he exclaimed. "Who knows what they call anything."

I just stared at him; he seemed to be working himself up to some kind of rant. But instead, he took some breaths and calmed himself down. "Come on. Help me out here, will you?" he said. "What do they mean, those stars?"

"I told you. Nothing."

"And I think you just told me a lie. You don't believe that at all."

"I believe you've got an overactive imagination," I spat back.

Kel took a step back and shot me a look of disdain. "Oh," he said. "Okey doke then. You're bringing out the big guns: *It's all in your head, Kel. You're imagining crazy things, Kel.* So, I suppose that's as far as we're going to get for now. And if that's the case, you'd better run back to your boyfriend before he wonders if maybe you haven't been snatched away by the creepy crawlies. Stranger things have happened, right?"

"I just can't help you," I told him, and finally left the kitchen.

Back in the living room, there were now about a dozen men and women standing around. The different groups of people who had been chatting to each other when I left had now formed into a kind of impromptu circle: everyone had perched themselves on the couch or on a chair and seemed to be engaged in a back-and-forth discussion. I found a spot next to John, who I had almost forgotten I was upset with earlier; the conversation with Kel had completely taken over my thoughts. If I'd had my CD player with me, or even a book, I would have slipped off to some other room and fixed my attention on something other than the noise in my mind.

Instead, I tried to pay attention to the conversation. Alice was sitting next to Jim Barrett, who was speaking. For the moment, the blonde ghost seemed to have realigned herself with her mentor instead of her therapist.

Barrett was in the middle of explaining something—it took me only a few moments to pick up the thread of the conversation because he was still pontificating about the gradual alien takeover of humanity by hybrids. However, it seemed that as soon as I sat down, he turned the conversation around. It was almost as if he had been waiting for me to return in order to confront John.

"I do have to note that I'm getting out of Dr. Benton's comfort zone again—isn't that right?"

The fact that he'd just called John "Dr. Benton" didn't escape my notice: since all the people here tonight—including Barrett, earlier, had been referring to John by his first name—the formal title sounded like mockery. If it was, however, John did not allow himself to be provoked.

"I think the question is what everyone else is comfortable with, not me. My job is a luxury; all I have to do is listen. I don't have to go through the pain and fear that our friends here have all experienced."

"But you still want us to consider your trans-tribal theory, right?" Barrett asked. "Because I hear through the grapevine that you're going to start publishing again."

I thought he was making it sound like "Dr. Benton" was about to publish some sort of manifesto that would challenge the beliefs of everyone in the room. I knew very little about this. John had told me that he was working on a new book but we had never discussed what it was about, specifically. Of course, in general, I knew what the topic was going to be but that was as far as it went. I had no idea of what "trans-tribal" meant, but apparently, I was the only one in the group who didn't.

"That's true," John said. "And to some extent, I've discussed my ideas with everyone here."

"Except that we don't agree," Barrett replied. Perhaps he was speaking only for himself; perhaps he meant to be understood as representing everyone sitting around the circle. It was unclear to me, but maybe, for the moment, the distinction didn't matter.

"We don't agree, John said, "which is fine, as I think I've always made plain. We're all working toward the same end: trying to understand what's happening to experiencers."

"Except in your construction, we also have to try and...what? Dig deep into our own troubled souls in order to understand the aliens' motivation? That's nonsense. We know what their intentions are, and we don't have to be touchy feely about it. We have to find a way to fight back. How can you not understand that?"

Barrett seemed to be intent on baiting John, trying to get him to enter into an argument, but it didn't seem to be working. In fact, John seemed to deliberately call on his placid Dr. Benton persona in responding: he brought both his hands together in front of him and leaned forward, as if projecting all his energy into the room. "I do understand how you feel. "I've just arrived at a different conclusion. Or non-conclusion," John said wryly. "I don't have an answer, I just have ideas that I'm still in the early stages of developing, but yes, I have been referring to it as trans-tribal contact. What I mean is that there seems to be some kind of highly complex interaction going on between humans and another type of being. It may be recent or it may have been going on since we began scratching pictures on cave walls. I don't know. And I don't know what these 'others' want. Their intentions may indeed be purely malevolent, but I am convinced that there is room to consider other possibilities. And perhaps the first step we could take in that direction would be to try to be less afraid, as difficult—tremendously difficult—as that seems because it's possible that they don't mean to be as threatening to us as we experience them. Maybe it's just a disconnect between cultures—ours and theirs—that neither of us knows how to overcome. It's also possible, of course, that just like human beings, some of them are more well-intentioned than others, some are almost emotionless, and some seem capable of deep feelings, even though we don't understand what it is they are feeling."

"*That's* where you're going with this now?" Barrett said. "Then are we supposed to believe you've abandoned your last theory—that the aliens are in our reality but somehow not of it? And that's where the disconnect stems from?"

"I think it's all the same idea," John replied. "Maybe it's just hard to see each other—understand each other—across the distance that separates us. The unimaginable distance. Time, space, who knows?"

Jim groaned. "Really? Are you really proposing that we're...what? Humans and aliens, all just like the lost tribes of Israel, wandering through time and space? Glimpsing each other through the murk?"

"I don't know," John said, mildly. "Maybe something like that."

I knew him well enough to understand that he knew exactly what he meant and could have delivered an hour-long lecture on the subject but chose to disengage simply to tamp down the growing tension. It seemed to work for a few minutes—different conversations were starting up again around the living room—but then everything suddenly changed.

"Julia doesn't believe any of this," Alice said, speaking out as loudly as if she were onstage. The suddenly not-so-fragile ghost intended to dominate the room.

"Me?" I replied. It seemed that my strategy of avoiding her had backfired—maybe because she just didn't like being ignored. "What difference does it make what I think?"

John put his hand on my arm, a caution to let him handle his patient. "Alice," John said, "Julia isn't involved in this. She just came with me tonight as my guest."

"But she thinks we're ridiculous," Alice said. "It doesn't matter what we say—Jim has his ideas, you have yours—but she thinks they're all stupid. She thinks *I'm* stupid, that I'm making things up, don't you, Julia?"

I could still feel John's hand resting on my arm but I couldn't keep myself from responding. "I actually don't know all that much about what happened to you," I said, which was sort of the truth, since I only knew what John had told me. But she wasn't satisfied with my answer.

"But you think I'm imagining things," she said

"Why would I think that?"

"Because you do."

I shrugged. "Believe what you like," I said. "But if it makes you feel any better, no. I don't necessarily think you're imagining things."

*Necessarily.* I couldn't help myself—I had added that qualifier deliberately, and it set Alice off. "Liar!" Alice cried. "You're lying. I can tell."

"Really?" I said. "How?"

This back-and-forth was quickly becoming some sort of twisted version of the conversation I'd had with Kel in the kitchen, only Alice wasn't as shrewd as he was. In fact, I thought she was on the verge of becoming hysterical. Quickly, John stepped in to try and smooth things out.

"Alice," John said, "maybe we can find another time and place to figure out why you think Julia has some sort of ill feelings towards you. She doesn't."

At that point, Barrett suddenly broke in. "Look, John, if Alice is sensing something from someone in the group, it might be useful to explore exactly what's going on."

"This isn't a therapeutic group," John pointed out. "And having this conversation right now isn't going to do anybody any good."

"Well, I think your...uh, friend...is being a little disrespectful towards Alice and, in fact, *that's* what's not helping."

I knew that I really should have kept my mouth shut at this point and let John deal with all this antagonism, but before he even got a chance to utter another word, someone else inserted himself into the conversation— someone I would have never expected to defend me: Kel.

He addressed himself neither to John nor to Jim Barrett, but to Alice. You know what?" he said to her. "You do this all the time. You always assume that everyone is against you, but Julia didn't do anything to make you feel like that, so why don't you just leave her alone?"

"Why are you standing up for her?" Alice demanded.

75

"I guess I'm just a natural-born nice guy." He smiled; the kind of don't-believe-for-a-minute-that-I-mean-this kind of smile you'd expect from someone whose faced was pierced by steel and had a fanged snake tattooed on his neck. "Besides," he said, turning to me, "Julia never said anything about you imagining things, did you, Julia?"

Since maybe ten minutes ago, that was exactly what I had accused him of doing, there had to be a reason that he was playing the role of my champion. I couldn't imagine why—except it occurred to me that maybe he was banking points, laying the groundwork for some next conversation he wanted, perhaps expected, that we would have. That was exactly the kind of dodgy thing I knew that I was capable of myself—but what was Kel's motive? That part I couldn't quite figure out.

Meanwhile, Kel repeated what he had just said to me. "Did you, Julia? Even imply that Alice was imagining things?"

"No," I said, hoping I sounded less disgusted with this whole evening than I really felt. "It's not my place to have any opinions about what's happened to anyone here. How can I? I don't know anything about any of it."

That finally seemed to defuse the drama, and the conversation turned to more mundane subjects. Some new guests arrived, others departed. John and I finally left a little while later. We got in the car and he turned it on, but before he pulled out of the parking spot he said, "I have to apologize to you for all that. I'm sorry, Jules. It was not a good idea to bring you there. We won't do anything like this again."

He smiled at me but looked worried, like I was going to be angry at him. All I could think was. *I really am not a good person if that's the first thing he thinks.*

"She's jealous," I said. "Maybe you don't realize it." And then I went a step further, hoping to recover some tiny fraction of the poor judgment I had pronounced upon myself a moment ago. "I guess she can't help acting like that."

"You're right about Alice," John agreed. "But maybe not exactly in the way you think. She tries to play Jim and me against each other—it's like a competition to see who's right. If I am, there's hope. If Jim's right, there isn't. It's like she's deciding her fate based on the opinions of two different people, and the likelihood, of course, is that neither one of us knows what we're talking about. So my job is never to buy into the competition, never to try to guide her one way or another. But that's all the more reason I made a mistake tonight, and you got caught in the middle. I'm afraid, though, that I didn't do a very good job of getting you out."

*No, Kel did.* That was what was left unsaid, and I could only guess how much it bothered John. I wasn't even sure how much—or even if—it bothered me.

"I'm fine," I told him. "Really."

He frowned, deeply. "I don't know," he said. "I promised you we'd find some neutral ground in all this. I suppose we have to work on that. Or at least, I do."

"Things will be better tomorrow, when we get to Freelingburg. You'll like Nicky and he'll like you. It'll be nice."

Reminding him that we were off on our road trip in the morning seemed to finally lighten his mood. "Absolutely," he said. ""Let's go home, get some sleep, and head up to the Stargazer's Embassy."

He laughed, because he really did like that name. Or he liked the idea of it. I said nothing, letting him believe that I did, too.

# VII

*MIXED FEELINGS, mixed feelings.* The further north we drove, heading through a landscape carved out by ancient glaciers and scoured by Canadian winds, the more those words reverberated through my thoughts. Why had I done this, set in motion this trip back home? Freelingburg was the place I had fled from, so why return? To see if I could stand it? If I could recover the good memories that were buried under the bad? Peering out the car window at the cold white sky that looked as if it had hardened into an ice dome fixed in place above the bare, wintry fields, I began to feel trapped. I had the urge to get out of the car and start running, but there was no place to go. It was different in the city, where distance didn't exist and isolation was a choice: I could get on a bus or subway and go anywhere; I could be alone but surrounded by people whose presence made the daytime safe, the nighttime endurable. Here though, in these rural counties, each little town was an island surrounded by farms in the valleys and gorges fed by winter rivers; there was no place to go on foot, miles to travel to get anywhere, even by car. John had the radio tuned to a station that was playing cheery Christmas music, but nothing changed my mood; I felt the apprehension of someone peeking around a corner and fearful of what they might find.

We followed I-81 for a long time, passing billboards that advertised holiday specials at motels and diners along the highways from the Finger Lakes to Montreal. But we weren't going that far; as we neared Ithaca, John took an exit that led us west onto Rt-96; another half hour and another turn took us down an inclined road and then up again onto a familiar sight for me: Main Street in Freelingburg.

It was late afternoon now, with a weak sun sitting low in the sky. We drove past the few shops at the south end of the street that served the diverse needs of the locals: a diner, hardware store, a hair salon, and then a place that sold candles and incense, all housed in hundred-year-old brick buildings crouched close together along the narrow sidewalks. John eased the car through the center of town—one crosswalk, where the Presbyterian church faced the tiny post office—and, following my directions, drove a few more blocks until we came to the last street in town before the road stretched out again into the countryside. And then there it was: the Stargazer's Embassy.

I didn't have to tell John that we had arrived because even if you weren't sure what you were searching for, the Stargazer's would be hard to miss. With its dark green façade and iron benches guarding both sides of the entranceway, it looked completely different than any other structure in town. But perhaps the most striking feature of the building was that above the front door hung a huge shield-shaped escutcheon meant to represent the great diplomatic seal of the Stargazer's Embassy to the World, the bar's official name, which was lettered around the edge of the seal in silver paint. Also there for anyone to see was a larger image of my tattoo, set right in the center of the shield, heavily silvered, though somewhat dulled by time. The twin stars and their three smaller companions.

John got out of the car, and smiled as he looked up at the seal. "Well," he said, "I certainly recognize that."

"I guess it does stand out," I replied, instinctively tugging at my sleeve as I opened the door and led John inside.

Probably no one entering the Stargazer's for the first time could be prepared for how dark and cavernous it was. There was also a definite theme to the décor, which announced itself as soon as you looked up at the ceiling, where a machine that Nicky had bought from a demolished discotheque in Ithaca projected a revolving universe of stars and colorful planetoids. Up front, the wall opposite the bar had been painted to look like a map of some distant, starry sector of the universe that included a rendition of the five stars that made up the bar's logo. Nearby were framed posters of kitschy science fiction movies like *Plan 9 from Outer Space* and *The Blob*. Further back, under strings of dim Christmas lights, there were tables and chairs, and at the far end of the space was a stage that could easily accommodate a full band on the nights that some local group was booked to play. But it looked like there wasn't going to be live music tonight; instead, a movie represented by one of the posters on the wall was being shown on a screen that had been set up on the stage. It was a perennial favorite of the Stargazer's customers: *The Day the Earth Stood Still.*

And then, there was Nicky himself, coming towards me. He didn't look very different from when I'd seen him last: lanky, long-haired, grayer than I remembered, his face more lined, but still handsome. How old was he now? Somewhere in his sixties, I thought, though he didn't really look it. More cowboy than old hippie; a guy from rural Missouri who had ended up on a commune outside Ithaca a couple of decades ago and then found a job at the bar, which he later bought with a loan that he was probably still paying off.

"Julia!" Nicky exclaimed. "Finally. There's my girl."

He hugged me and I felt better than I had all day. Now, I could let myself believe that there was a reason to have come home: I very badly needed to see Nicky. I hadn't realized how much until I felt his comforting embrace.

I introduced him to John and they exchanged pleasantries about the drive up and then, about the weather, which was biting cold. As the two men talked, I looked over at the screen and saw that the movie had progressed to the point where Gort, the giant robot, had stepped out of a flying saucer, opened the visor on his helmet, and let loose a death ray that destroyed the weapons trained on him by a battalion of soldiers. I had seen this movie countless times and was enjoying the familiar action when John wandered over to stand beside me.

"So how does it feel to be home?" he asked.

"It's good," I said quickly, the answer I would have given no matter what. "Fine."

On the screen at the back of the bar, Gort now stood motionless on a vast green lawn near the White House while onlookers ran from him. Soon, Klaatu, the humanoid alien who had brought him to earth would begin his own adventures, trying to convince people that he had come in peace. I took one more quick look at the movie and then turned away and walked over to John.

"Come on," I said. "Let's go upstairs. I'll show you my old room."

We left Nicky tending bar for the few customers who had wandered in for a late afternoon beer and went up to the second floor, where my room was at the far end of the hallway, in the back of the building. The rest of the living space—another bedroom, the living room, kitchen and bathroom— were down the hall, near the top of the stairs.

No matter how unusual its façade was, this building, like all the others in town, was an old structure and not much had been done to fix it up. The ceiling in the hallway was stamped tin; the carpet on the floor was thread-bare. Still, the rooms up here were comfortable enough, though Nicky seemed to be using my bedroom partly for storage since it had cases of Genesee 12 Horse Ale stacked along the wall. That didn't change how familiar this place seemed to me, as if I had just stepped away a few minutes ago. My bed near the window, which looked out into a bare pumpkin field, was covered with a wedding ring quilt that had been there since I was a child and my books, records, even a few old stuffed animals were still sitting where I had left them, in a bookcase opposite the foot of the bed.

John put his arm around me. "It's sweet," he said, looking at the room.

"That's what Nicky will tell you: that I was a sweet little girl," I told him. "Not that we have to believe him."

"Well, we'll try to," John said. "He seems like a nice guy."

"He is." I walked over to the window and looked out at the fallow pump-kin field. There were patches of snow on the hard ground; snow edged the narrow road that separated the fields beyond. Out there, somewhere, was where my mother used to go wandering. *She's gone stargazing,* Nicky always told me when I would look for her at night and find her gone. "He certainly loved Laura," I said to John, "though I don't think she made it easy."

"What do you mean?" he asked.

"Oh, free spirit and all that," I said vaguely. "I've told you," though I had and I hadn't, really. Being back here made me feel her presence very strongly, but that didn't necessarily translate into an urge to talk about her. Not now, anyway, and not with John. I turned away from the window and starting taking clothes out of the weekend bag we'd brought and hanging them in the closet.

A few minutes later, Nicky appeared at the door. "Julia," he said, "want to take a run with me to pick up what I ordered for the buffet?"

"Sure," I said.

The tradition at the Embassy was to offer a free buffet on Christmas eve; buy a couple of beers, help yourself to burgers or chicken and fixings and watch the movie or play the jukebox. It wouldn't be all that busy because even the serious drinkers were generally home on Christmas eve, but people would still come in for an hour or two, along with whatever students from Cornell had decided that upstate New York in the dead of winter was still a more congenial place than being home with their family.

I told John we wouldn't be gone long. Downstairs, Nicky said the same to the bartender, who had just come in to start her evening shift. I climbed into Nicky's truck—the same old Ford he'd been driving for what seemed like the last century—and headed about fifteen minutes down the road to the grocery store where the prepared food Nicky had ordered was waiting to be picked up.

On the way over, we chatted about nothing in particular; at least, nothing serious. Local gossip, local business, the comings and goings of people I sort of remembered from the past, but not always. At the grocery, we retrieved foil-covered pans of food and desserts and loaded them into the truck, along with a dozen cans of sterno to keep the hot dishes warm. Then we turned around and started back to Freelingburg.

On the way home, though, Nicky took a different route. We traveled down a stretch of rural road that was hilly and lined by thick stands of pine. He drove on for a mile or two until the road turned away from the woods and headed towards the one place on the outskirts of Freelingburg that could be called a scenic overlook—or so claimed an old road sign, pocked with damage from hard rain and hail. This is where Nicky took us, parking the truck at the edge of a flat plateau that a glacier had long ago sheared away. Once, perhaps, a river had snaked its way through the broken valley below, but some other upheaval had dried up the river's source and pushed its rocky bed back towards the land above so that now, there was only a narrow creek to look down on, maybe twenty feet below us. In the winter, ice dams and the landscape's drifting litter—stones, twigs, dried leaves—kept the creek running shallow and slow.

The truck's heater ticked on, quietly, as we sat for a moment, one of us waiting for the other to speak. I had sort of expected this—a talk. Nicky doing his fatherly duty. Nicky worrying about me, even though I thought I had given him no cause. Of course, I was wrong.

Finally, Nicky said, "I thought we'd just take a few minutes. You know, to check in. It gets so busy around the bar that I figured we might not get much time alone."

"I'm okay," I told him. "Nothing to worry about."

"Nothing?"

"No."

"So I have to ask—what does that mean? Everything's better, or just the same?"

I looked away from him. Because we were sitting in the truck, I couldn't see the trickle of icy water below us, but fixed my gaze on the ragged ridge-line on the other side of the creek bed. Beyond that, there were only hard, flat fields, frozen into ragged rows that had been last plowed in the long-past spring of this fading year.

"The same," I replied.

"So you're still seeing them," he said. "Your...things."

*Not mine*, I thought. *You know that. Hers.* But the distinction hardly mattered. "Yes," I said.

Nicky cracked the window then lit a cigarette, settling in for a longer conversation. "You still don't know what they want from you?" he asked.

"All I know is what *I* want from them: to stay away from me. Most of the time, they do."

"But not always."

"No. They try to disguise themselves but they can't even get that right. I think they're stupid," I said—and realized that I sounded like a child. Like some mother's daughter, complaining to her about her friends.

Nicky smiled. "I have a feeling Laura would have argued with you about that."

"I don't care what she would have said."

I spoke with a vehemence that surprised even me, only because I didn't expect it right now. I thought I had all those feelings under control. Nicky's reaction was different—he reached over and touched my hand. I knew this small gesture, small connection, was the best he could offer. Nicky and I each had our separate experience of what Laura had brought into our lives and while it helped me, at least, to acknowledge those experiences—

which is probably why I'd come home, to Nicky—they couldn't really be shared.

"Does John know that you see them?" Nicky asked.

Lost in my own thoughts, it took me a moment to refocus. "No," I finally replied.

"Why not?" When I didn't answer, Nicky prodded me. "I know who he is, Julia. Just because you're mother's gone doesn't mean I can just pretend nothing ever happened. So I kind of follow the stories. I hear things, I read. And a lot of what I've read in the past few years, John Benton has written."

"So?"

"So it seems odd that you haven't told him anything."

"I told him about Laura. Sort of." I reached back into my memory, trying to recall what I'd said to John about my mother. "I told him she was interested in Roswell and Area 51. Stuff like that."

"Julia. Really?"

"That's what I always told people," I said, and almost added *Didn't you do the same? That was the whole point of the way you decorated the Stargazer's wasn't it? All the stuff I see you've never even changed?* That feeling of wanting to strike out flared up in me, but it was unwarranted in Nicky's company, and I immediately regretted it. Quickly, it drained away. "I didn't tell him anything about me."

"Then why did you pick him, of all people? Honey? Have you asked yourself that?"

The honest answer to that question would have been no, of course not, never: instead, I kept my headphones on, I kept my eyes on the pages of a book. I cleaned houses, rode the subway, cooked dinner. I kept myself going; that had always been my plan, my one and only. Just one foot in front of the other, allowing as few questions as possible from myself or anyone else. Questions about anything.

But there was also another answer, an easier one, and I believed it enough to share it with Nicky. "When I met him, I didn't know who he was, so I guess I just thought he would be a safe person for me. Like you were for Laura."

"But at some point, he must have told you what he's involved in. The kind of work he does."

"Yes," I said. "He did."

I wanted to leave it at that. I didn't think I could even begin to explain how complicated my relationship with John had become—for me, at least—and was hoping Nicky would just drop the subject. I thought he was considering doing just that because he was silent for a few moments, but when he finally spoke again, it was with surprising certainty.

"You should tell John," he said.

"It's too late," I replied. "How could I explain now? Besides, the things he believes...all that spiritual stuff about how even the most bizarre experiences can have some sort of deep meaning—they have nothing to do with me. What happens to me."

"You don't know that."

"I do," I insisted. "I absolutely do."

"Then maybe you could tell him that."

I shook my head. "And then my whole life with him would be about the things. My way is better: as long as I go on treating them like nothing more important than stray animals that show up once in a while..."

Nicky finished my sentence for me. "Then you can pretend that one day they'll disappear."

I looked out the window at the darkening sky, the empty fields. We could have been anywhere, I thought. There were no markers, no signs. "Yes," I said. "Maybe."

I must have sounded unhappy—more than that, probably—because Nicky hardly seemed to think about my answer before he offered me a different one. "Do you want to come home?" he asked. "You could tell John you need a break for a while."

"No," I told him. "He wouldn't believe that."

"You'd be surprised what people will believe," he said. "But then, maybe you wouldn't. Not you."

That seemed to be the end of our conversation. Nicky started up the truck again and we drove back to the Stargazer's Embassy. John had come downstairs and was sitting at the bar, chatting with one of the regulars, a man who liked to call himself a holiday farmer: he had sixty acres about a mile outside town on which he grew Christmas trees and Halloween pumpkins. When the holidays were over, he grew marijuana. One of his Douglas firs stood in a corner of the bar, decorated with popcorn balls and strings of colored lights. There were also a number of ornaments hung on the tree: several of them, I noticed, were little tin flying saucers.

On the stage at the other end of the bar, the movie had reached its conclusion. Gort the robot and Klaatu, his humanoid handler, had issued their warning about the perils of earthly violence and departed in their spaceship for parts unknown. The credits rolled and then the movie began again; it would repeat over and over again all night. Meanwhile, the bartender had turned on the in-house music system, which was playing *Hotel California*. In other words, the Stargazer's Embassy to the World was doing what it did: offering sanctuary, music, rest, intoxication—whatever you thought you were looking for when you walked through the front door.

Nicky and I brought in the foil pans of food and started setting up the buffet. John came over to help and I showed him how to get the sterno going and where to find the paper plates and cutlery that needed to be laid out. Outside, night overspread Main Street, traveled down the roads and over the fields. It laid itself over the hillsides and set out the constellations, cold points of light in the shape of warriors, animals, and creatures of the deep.

People came, people went. Not a lot, but enough to eat most of the free food and keep the bartender busy. John and I sat at a table drinking beer and eating hamburgers from the buffet; Nicky joined us when he wasn't walking around talking to people he knew, which was almost everyone.

Official closing time in the county was one a.m., but on Christmas eve, Nicky had last call at 11:30 so he could shut down at midnight. Afterwards, we helped him pack up what remained of the buffet, which would go to a local food pantry tomorrow. The bartender and the waitress who had come on shift for a few hours did a quick clean-up, and then we all said goodnight and went up to bed.

"So that was Christmas eve at the Stargazer's Embassy," I said to John as we climbed under the quilts I had found in a closet and piled on the bed. There radiator in my room was clanking away, but it was still chilly; wind leaked through the old window frames, rattled the eaves.

"I loved it," John said. "In fact, as much as I want to go back to teaching, if things don't go my way, maybe we could move up here and grow Christmas trees. I could teach math at a community college. I was actually very good at math in school."

I didn't even comment on this fantasy because I couldn't imagine John living anywhere except the carriage house; I couldn't imagine him without the city as a backdrop, the tiny garden in the courtyard to sit in and look up at one small, familiar patch of sky. Sun and clouds and stars; only what you could see right above you, framed by neighboring rooftops and chimneypots.

"How's that going?" I asked, meaning his dispute with the university. I didn't often ask about the case he had brought against the school for trying to stop him from publishing his work with abductees and he rarely mentioned it, though I sometimes heard him on the phone with his attorney.

"We're making progress," John replied. "There's been much more support than I expected; people may think the subject of alien abduction is way out there, but it's begun to dawn on my colleagues that the concept of academic freedom doesn't apply to me and my work, then who's next? Any kind of research could be called into question because some faction doesn't like it. Besides," he said, sounding a little drowsy now, "my lawyer has been telling me that one or two of the donors who have been bending the president's ear are actually in favor or reinstating me. Maybe they've had some kind of experience themselves. Who knows?"

He lifted himself up on his elbow to give me a kiss. "Go to sleep, Jules," he said. "Everything will be alright."

I didn't know if he meant for him, or me, or both of us, but it didn't really matter. I just wanted to believe him.

****

The next morning, Christmas, we all got up late. Nicky made breakfast in the upstairs kitchen and then we exchanged gifts. We had bought books for Nicky, who liked whodunits, and a Yankees cap and sweatshirt, since he was a fan. He gave me CDs and for John, he had also bought music: I'd told him that John liked Elvis, though you'd never expect that, and Nicky had found some old, classic albums at a shop in Ithaca along with an Elvis bobblehead doll, for fun. I got sweaters from both men, and a silver necklace from John.

Late in the morning, Nicky went downstairs to start setting up for the afternoon; the Stargazer's was one of the few bars in the area that was open on Christmas day, so he would be busy. We offered to help but he said no, and suggested I take John out to the nearby state park to walk the trail though the gorge. It was a beautiful place and John had never seen it, so we put on warm clothes and boots and drove off down the road.

The parking lot at the entrance to the gorge was empty and the trail was officially closed, but there was no gate barring the way, so we set out along the rocky path. I knew it well, stuck in their patches of soil and snow looked so absent of spirit, so lifeless that it was hard to since I had walked here many times. The first part of the trail took us through a woods. The bare trees imagine they would ever come into leaf again. Eventually, we emerged into a different landscape: the trail took us along the edge of a rock ledge that seemed to jut out from beneath the earth like a tilted plate. On our right was a high ridge, as sheer as a wall but also damp, running with ice melt. Below us was a stream littered with stones.

Because the way forward was narrow, we walked in single file for about twenty minutes, with John following me as the trail took us down towards the stream and then up again, making a steep climb back towards the woods. But then, as the trail wound around a sharp turn where the cliff face jutted out over the icy stream, we came across a spot I had forgotten about: a bench set into a recess that had been carved into the rock. In the spring, the melting ice up in the hills sluiced down through an old riverbed and created a waterfall here, on the other side of the gorge, and formed a pool where local kids liked to swim. This bench was a perfect place to sit and take in the view. Now, of course, there was no waterfall, but we decided to rest here for a while, anyway.

It was cold enough to turn our breath to mist but we were dressed warmly, so we were comfortable. John and I sat together in silence, listening to the sounds of winter in the path of ancient glaciers: a twig snapped, a bird called out, an animal scurried through the brush.

"There must have been a lot of stories told about this place," John said, finally.

"Sure," I replied. "Who got who pregnant here, who got so drunk that he had to be carried out, who told all his friends to meet him here but forgot to bring the pot."

He laughed. "I wasn't thinking about your high school days. I meant before that. Long ago, people must have walked through here and been amazed. This gorge—it's like a giant crack in the earth. People must have had some kind of explanation for how it happened."

"Like what?"

"Oh, maybe a lightning bolt thrown by the gods. Or a ship sailing through the sky, trailing its anchor."

"I get the lightning bolt. But a ship in the sky?"

John leaned back against the bench and looked up at our particular sky, which resembled a blank ice dome; white, depthless, without features. "People have seen all kinds of things in the sky for tens of thousands of years. Ships, crosses, angels, fire, wheels, galloping horses, flying men; sometimes these visions aligned with religious beliefs or cultural practices. Sometimes what people saw—or what they see now—is inexplicable."

"Like UFOs."

"Maybe. But there's a lot more tied into those visions—or maybe sightings is a better word. Stories about people ascending into the sky and others who descend from above. There are tales like that going back tens of thousands of years ago, from almost every culture we know about."

"So people always tell the same stories about things they don't under-stand. Is that what you're saying?"

"Not the same but similar in interesting ways. Each age, each culture, though, adds its own elements. Or else they are added for us."

"You mean the aliens are adding pieces to the story. The grays."

"Well, whoever's out there. Whoever's stopping by. Maybe they don't even mean to add to the story, but that's the effect, at least on some of us. Me in particular, I think." John glanced over at me and smiled. "You're sur-prised. You would have expected me to say that my patients are the ones most affected. But now I'm telling you my secret," he said. "I'm so sorry that they suffer so much. But the rest of it...the mystery of it—I can't tell you how much it fascinates me."

"That's not so much a secret," I told him, though I don't think he heard me. He just went on speaking.

"I'm a good therapist, I'm responsible to my patients, and dedicated to helping them. But the God's honest truth is, Jules, that the more I study the abduction phenomenon and listen to the stories that the experiencers tell me about it, the more I find its connections to ancient myths and new age mysticism and everything in between, the more I want to know. I want to go back to teaching but if I can't, that's not going to stop me. I'm going to be trying to figure all this out for the rest of my life."

"Do you think you will?" I asked him.

"No," he said. "Probably not. Maybe nobody will, not for a long time—if ever. It could be we're not supposed to."

"Oh? And who would be the one deciding that?"

He shrugged. "It could be the *ones*—plural—but then, I don't know that either." He laughed. "When you come down to it," he said, "I really don't know very much at all."

I was getting cold now, but John seemed unaware of either of the falling temperature or how long we had been sitting on the bench, looking across at the bare rock face, at the absence of a waterfall. He said, "It has occurred to me that maybe our visitors don't know, either. Maybe they're as clueless as we are, just acting on a plan that makes some kind of sense to them but in the long run, who knows?"

He smiled at me again. "Too much malarkey?" he said. "I don't know what's gotten into me. Can I just blame it on the Stargazer's Embassy? Maybe it's having an undue influence on me."

"You can blame anything you want on that place," I said. "I certainly have."

He stood up then and asked if I thought we should walk the rest of the trail or retrace our steps back to the parking lot. I told him that from this point, there was another path that would circle back to where we'd left the car so rather than follow the rest of the trail, which was slippery and steep, we should take the other route. The path of least resistance, John joked, and I said yes, something like that.

In the afternoon, after having an early Christmas dinner together, John, Nicky and I headed back downstairs, to the bar. The same bartender from last night came in and switched on the stereo system. Neil Young's sad voice began singing to us about queens and peasants and burned out basements as Nicky began setting up games on some of the tables. There was no movie tonight but the drinkers could play chess and darts and backgammon, if they liked.

Once the front door was unlocked, I sat at the bar with John for a while, drinking wine and watching the Stargazer's Embassy to the World slowly come alive. This was always my favorite time here, when it was getting dark outside and I could convince myself that the bar, with its great, starry escutcheon facing out into the night was the headquarters of some harmless, secret society that drew its members from the little towns and far valleys of this northern region, the people who didn't quite fit in elsewhere, who needed a place to hang out and think their own thoughts in their own time.

The cook came in just as the bar was getting busy and I followed her out to the little kitchen behind the stage so I could help out the way I used to, plating burgers and French fries and serving up nachos with melted cheese. It was another good way to keep myself occupied, and I enjoyed it for a couple of hours.

Around ten, I told John and Nicky that I was tired and was going to go upstairs, to bed. They were both drinking Scotch at that point and deeply involved in some sort of round-robin chess tournament with a pair of grad students from Cornell, so they said good-night to me and returned to their game.

I went upstairs, but didn't get into bed right away. Instead, I sat in the window as I had many times when I was younger, looking out at the night sky. There was a half moon tonight, wrapped in the cold rags of wintry clouds, but some of the constellations were visible: I could pick out Orion, adorned with his luminous belt and sword and accompanied by his pair of hunting dogs who prowled the southeast horizon.

The conversation I'd had with Nicky yesterday was weighing on me, as was John's confession about his fascination with where the experiencers' stories might lead him (hardly news to me, as I'd told him, but still, not something I needed to hear repeated). I couldn't block out the words, the questions, couldn't stop them from making me ask myself how long, really, I could go on pretending that I was just a bystander, that all I knew about contact with the things was from my mother's stories, or from what John himself had told me. But if I revealed my own experiences to him, then I was going to become a study subject, just like his other patients; I was sure there was no way of preventing that. I'd end up as just another case, another couple of paragraphs in his next research paper—and then I would lose what I had, the safety and security of a relationship, a home, where nights and days went by like anyone else's, where things were normal, where the man and woman shared meals and sex and figured out the grocery list together and decided what movies to see. That was what I had and what I desperately wanted to hold onto.

Finally, I went to bed. I slept and woke and slept again. I felt John lie down beside me sometime after midnight and could tell when he'd fallen asleep because his breathing changed, his body relaxed. I closed my eyes once more and dreamed.

Sometime before dawn, I got up to go to the bathroom. But when I was finished, I found myself walking downstairs to the bar. *Go back to sleep*, I warned myself, but the warning only served to rouse me from drowsiness to being fully awake. A familiar feeling of alertness had taken hold of me and at this point, there was no shaking it.

I got to the bottom of the staircase and unlocked the door that led into the bar. The big, cavernous space was almost completely dark, but the front window let in some dim light from the streetlamps outside, enough so that I could see a small figure standing near one of the tables where a chess set was still set up, waiting for someone to play.

I stayed by the door, waiting as the figure—one of the things; what else would it be?—slowly started to advance in my direction. It was wearing what looked like a pair of ill-fitting overalls with nothing on underneath so that it looked like some bizarre parody of a farmer, maybe one of our neighbors down the road. It kept moving towards me, walking as slowly as they all did, always, as if movement, for them, was like wading through heavy water.

I never had any idea if I was seeing a particular individual multiple times or if each time, my visitor was different—for me, only their varying heights and outfits differentiated one from another. This one had the same features I was used to seeing: a vaguely triangular face with huge, black eyes, a thin, linear mouth—not much more than a slit, really, near the bottom of a long, narrow chin—and no visible nostrils. It was about four feet tall and had hands that resembled a human's in size and number of digits but otherwise appeared weak, almost boneless. As it came towards me, it tried to point one of its thin, gray fingers at me, but seemed to be having trouble doing this. Finally, it managed to make its hand into a fist, with only the second finger held out straight.

This was a new way of approaching me but I wasn't afraid; they knew not to come too close. Or so I thought—this one kept coming forward, seeming to struggle just to push its body through the air. *Go ahead*, I thought, as I watched it. It was so fragile looking that I was sure I could smash it in the face and send it reeling if I wanted to, which wasn't the first time the idea had occurred to me. I had always promised myself that was what I would do if one of them ever tried to touch me, but I didn't do anything, yet, because I couldn't keep myself from staring at that pointing finger.

So, I let it come near. It was just a few inches away when it finally stopped. I was looking at its face, which seemed blank to me, emotionless, as the mask-like faces of these things always were. Perhaps that was why part of me was able to see them as unreal, more like bizarre, animated toys than some sort of living being.

I made myself peer straight into its huge, black eyes, thinking I could stare it down, but its gaze was focused elsewhere. Still seeming to struggle with its movements, it slowly pointed its finger at my wrist, where the tattoo was hidden under the sleeve of the sweatshirt I had been sleeping in, and made a tapping gesture: *tap, tap*. And again: *tap, tap*, slowly and deliberately.

Even though there was that small distance between us—the thing never actually tried to touch me—I could feel the pressure of something that felt both cold and electric pushing against my skin. Without even thinking about what I was doing, I pulled back my sleeve to look at the tattoo, thinking I would see some sort of indentation on my wrist, but I did not. The sensation of pressure faded almost immediately and when I looked up again, this time the thing was staring at me.

And then it opened its mouth and let out a wail. Or, for a moment I thought it was a wail but no—that wasn't really what it sounded like. There was a better description for what I heard come out of the slice of darkness that was the mouth of the thing standing in front of me: it was a cry. A particular cry that contained within it both a hissing sound and a high pitched growl.

It was the sound of a cat. A cat that was angry. Or maybe, I thought—startled by the idea that was beginning to form in my mind—not angry, exactly. Lost, maybe. Or tired. Tired—exhausted—and completely, totally alone.

# VIII

KEL.

His name was the first thing that came to me in the morning, when I woke up. I had listened to the thing cry for a moment or two and then turned my back on it and went upstairs. In the pre-dawn darkness, I had lain down beside John again and almost instantly, fell deeply asleep. That was another way I removed myself from my interactions with the things—if it was even reasonable to call the times I came upon them waiting for me an interaction. I could plunge down into the depths of sleep and stay secreted there, safe and sheltered as if I was resting on the bottom of the sea.

But when I woke and consciousness flooded back to me, I was immediately aware not only that I was thinking of Kel but why he, in particular, had come to mind: it was because the thing had not only mimicked Kel's gesture of tapping his finger on my tattooed wrist, it had made a sound that Kel had referred to as the cry of a cat. I could not remember having ever heard one of the things make any sound since that time, years ago, when I had bitten the arm of the tall being my mother had led me to and it had yowled in pain. Considering all this, I was sure that the thing I had encountered last night had meant not only to reference Kel, but to do so deliberately, in a way that I would understand. And so I had—but what did it want me to glean from that? I wasn't sure, but what it did make clear to me was that the things could invade my life in ways I had never understood before. It was a chilling thought and one that I tried to quickly put out of my mind.

But the awareness of what had happened would not leave me. The things wanted me to think about my conversation with Kel. They wanted me to understand that they knew it had taken place. Was this a threat? A warning? If so, then why had the thing sounded so troubled, disturbed? It didn't make sense, but very little of this did, even after so many years of having them in my life. My thoughts kept going round and round as I dressed and went out to the kitchen in the upstairs apartment, looking for John who had not been in bed when I woke up.

I found him drinking coffee with Nicky. They both teased me about sleeping late, but they probably could tell I wasn't in the mood to be joked with, so they let that go. I poured myself some coffee and devoted myself to reading a copy of the local paper that was lying on the kitchen table while the two men talked about the traffic that John and I might encounter on the drive home, since we planned to leave soon. After a while, John said he would go pack up our things so we could get going.

When I was alone with Nicky in the kitchen, he sat quietly for a while, simply looking at me. I was aware of his gaze, but kept my sight focused on the newspaper. He let this go on for a few minutes, until he suddenly reached across the table and pulled the paper away from me. "Fascinated by the town planning commission's concerns about the sewers? Or is it the school board election slate you're studying?"

"I'm just reading," I said.

"No you're not," Nicky replied.

I tried to take the paper back, but he wouldn't let me. "Julia?" he said, giving me a penetrating look that was meant to get—and hold—my attention, "this is me, remember? I know you. I know when something's bothering you. So do you want to tell me what's going on? Did something happen last night?"

I really didn't feel like I was in the right frame of mind to go anywhere near the subject of *Did something happen last night?*—not even with Nicky—so I went around it. Sort of.

"I need to ask you something," I said. "Did my mother ever tell you what they sounded like? The things? I mean, their voices?"

He seemed surprised by the question. "No," he replied.

Maybe it was just my mood; I was feeling edgy, confused. Something new, something I didn't understand had been added to the way the things approached me. They usually just stood in my line of sight, as if all they wanted was for me to be aware that they were around. Fine, I had incorporated that experience into my life as best I could. It was like accepting that I had hallucinations that would pass without my having to acknowledge them in any active way. But one of the things had broken a barrier last night; it had tried to communicate with me, or so it seemed. I had no idea what it wanted from me and I didn't have any desire to find out. But maybe that wasn't up to me because none of this was. It never had been—and the one person I could blame for involving me was not around to be questioned. But someone else was.

"What was she really doing with them, Nicky? My mother. What was going on?"

"You've asked me that before, Julia, and I still have the same answer, because it's the truth: I don't know."

I looked at Nicky across the table: the denim work shirt, the faded blue eyes, the gray ponytail caught at the nape of his neck with a beaded rubber band. My cowboy hippie sort-of-stepdad who I loved but who, suddenly, I was beginning to wonder about. Just as the things had crossed a barrier with me last night, maybe—without even meaning to and probably, without wanting to—I felt like I had just crossed a barrier with Nicky as well.

"How can you not know?"

"She was your mother, Julia. I could ask you the same thing."

So there she was again—Laura. The person who had brought us together but also kept us apart. Because our lives had revolved around her, even though she had been gone for years, she still exerted her influence. And because neither of us could explain her, no matter how well we got along, this always happened: one of us blamed the other, or we each blamed ourselves, for letting her mystify us, just as we had blamed ourselves for the fear we both carried around when she was still alive that if we didn't leave her alone when she wanted to wander off, she would go away and leave us alone for good. Just as I tried, with relentless determination, to keep the things as far away from my conscious thoughts as possible, I had also done my best to banish this aspect of my relationship with Nicky: there was love and good will, yes, but also unspoken accusations of responsibilities that had gone unrecognized, accountabilities that had been met with nothing but a blind eye. We had carried our different relationships with Laura as separate burdens and the weight had been heavier because we did not share it.

At that moment, John walked into the kitchen, carrying our bags. He glanced at me and then at Nicky. "Everything okay?" he asked.

"Sure," I told him. "We were just saying good-bye."

Later, in the car, when we were miles away from Freelingburg, John lowered the volume on the radio, which I had turned on the minute I climbed into the car. "I won't pry if you don't want me to, but I think, judging by your mood, you might want to talk about whatever I walked into back in the kitchen."

"My mood?"

"Jules. You can disappear inside yourself when you want to—and right now, you seem to want to—but we have a long ride ahead of us and I have to tell you, if you're just going to stare out the window and brood, it's not going to be pleasant for me."

I made myself remember that I cared about how he felt. "I was just asking Nicky about Laura."

"Something in particular you wanted to know?"

"I would like to know anything he could tell me. There's so much about her that I don't understand. It's...difficult for me."

"You're angry at her," John said. "That's normal. Children get angry at their parents when they die. It feels deliberate—like the parent went away on purpose. Even though, when you're older, you can think your way out of that box and realize that of course, your mother or father had no control over their death, that doesn't necessarily make the feelings go away."

John glanced over at the road map that I was holding in my lap. I was supposed to be navigating our way home, but I wasn't exactly doing my job. He didn't say anything about it, just turned the map to check something and then smoothly changed lanes.

"And in your case," he continued, after he had completed his maneuver with the car, "you also probably have a lot of guilt about her. Not only about blaming her for dying but I'm going to guess that the two of you had some tough times in your relationship. It's inevitable, particularly because children are very good at defying their parents. And when children become teenagers, they get even better at that. But something they rarely know how to do is ask their parents questions that provide any useful answers about who their mother or father is, as a person. That's probably because it's hard to think of your parents are real people until you're closer to being an adult yourself. Your mother died before you had a chance to experience her as a person, a human being."

While John was going on and on, I had barely been able to sit through what sounded to me like some sort of psychiatric infomercial. Finally, I couldn't stand another moment of it. "Are you finished?" I asked him.

He sighed. "Am I never supposed to offer an opinion on this subject, even when you're clearly upset? Anytime we get even close to discussing your mother..."

"I cut you off," I said. "I know."

"Why?" John asked.

*Why?* Because guilt, defiance—the unknown mother, waiting to be discovered by her dear daughter when she reached maturity—had nothing to do with me, or Laura. He was talking about the kinds of women he probably used to treat before he wandered off into alien land (that was a nasty thought but it expressed, perfectly, how nasty I was feeling): whiners, I thought, all of them, condemning these unknown patients with their neurotic mommy-daughter issues. I immediately hated them all. Let them—let him—have lived one day of my life with Laura. With the things she left behind and then see what they'd have to say.

"Can we just get off the subject for now?" I groused. "I'm tired. I didn't get much sleep last night and I'd like to take a nap." And then, because I didn't want him to ask me why I hadn't slept—I didn't actually want him to ask me any questions at all—I said, "Didn't you hear the cat last night? All that noise kept me up."

"I didn't hear anything," he replied. I could tell that he was reluctant to let himself be distracted from the conversation we were having—or not having—but was resigned to losing this battle once again. "A cat got into the house?"

"Into the bar, downstairs. It happens. Probably because Laura used to feed them."

I had made that part up, just adding to my story. Maybe John believed me, but he still had one last question.

"And you think they remember that after all these years?"

"Yes," I said. "I know they do." And then, finally, I closed my eyes.

*****

Back in the city, we mostly stayed around the house through New Year's, which we celebrated by ourselves, drinking a glass of champagne in front of the tv as we watched the glittering ball above Times Square drop down to signal the change to a new year. Then we picked up our routine: I went out to my cleaning jobs; John saw his patients and worked on the book he'd begun writing about the experiencers. He'd also started going to a meditation class at a yoga center nearby. He had asked me to go with him and I had tried once, to please him, but I couldn't do it. I couldn't clear my mind as I was instructed to, I couldn't concentrate on my breathing or become one with the universe or whatever else it was that I was supposed to be doing.

Why? Maybe because I couldn't relax. Not that I ever did, really—not completely—but since we'd returned from Freelingburg, I had felt even more than usual that I was on the alert. John could tell that something was bothering me and in his own way, his most practiced non-intrusive-but I-can't-help-being-a-therapist way, kept gently pushing me to talk to him. He had not been dissuaded by the argument we'd had in the car driving home from Freelingburg, and despite my continuing refusal to open up to him, he kept trying. More often now, he filled the silences by talking about himself and about his work, if only in a general sort of way. I would listen, interested despite myself—which sometimes only served to make me more irritable. He must have thought that I was drawing away from him, and he was probably right. The visit to Freelingburg had put me on edge and being me, my sense of worry about something I couldn't define just made me turn further inward. I knew I was not good company these days but felt powerless to remedy my behavior.

And so our lives went on like that for a while until one night in mid-January when we were both in the upstairs living room, reading. We sat on either end of the yellow couch, surrounded by soft lamplight that seemed to keep the night-darkness framed by the windows safely contained beyond the glass. I was engrossed in some police procedural, which was a good thing for me to concentrate on since I had to keep track of characters and clues, which kept my mind from wandering off into unhelpful thoughts. John was reading something quite different: a heavy, hardbound volume that I thought was a textbook of some kind. At one point, he got up to go to go to the kitchen to get something to eat and came back with some crackers and cheese on a plate. I put down my book to reach for some of the crackers and as I did, I saw that the book, which was now lying on the couch beside him, was open to a section of photo reproductions. Even upside down, I recognized what I was looking at: a photograph of Michelangelo's Pietà. It seemed like an unusual subject for him and that spurred me to ask him about the book.

"Are you reading about art?" I asked.

"Not exactly," John replied. "This is a study about archetypes. The kinds of ideas and images that seem to arise from our collective unconscious and help form our notions about religion, mythology, legends—but also about how we approach daily life. What we value, what we don't..."

I closed my book and looked over at him. "You mean, what's real and what's imagined, in someone's opinion."

"I guess you could say that." Then John smiled. "You think that's what's on my mind, don't you? Well, you're probably right: in one way or another, I suppose I'm always thinking about how to reconcile those concepts. Or maybe they don't have to be reconciled, exactly. The real and the imagined could both exist at the same time: it might depend on who's doing the imagining—just as you said."

I pointed to the photo of Mary and her dead son. "So the mother and child are archetypes?"

"Ancient ones. But so are other concepts, like saviors and demons." Again he smiled. "Love and death. Dark and light. People have probably been telling themselves stories about these things from the beginning of time. As a matter of fact, the ability—the drive—to tell stories is one of the main characteristics that distinguishes human beings from any other species—at least that we know of."

"You had to add that in."

He laughed. "I did. But it's true. Humans are great storytellers. Although of course, one has to allow for the possibility that even some of our most outlandish stories are true. Or partly true. Or should be true. The good ones, anyway—the ones in which things work out in the end. The hero wins, the lovers are reunited, the gods forgive whoever angered them and provide a bountiful harvest."

"And then everyone lives a long and happy life."

"Exactly." He smiled, and his whole expression lit up with that gentle joy that always pleased me so. "Maybe something like that actually happens sometimes. It would be nice, don't you think?"

"Yes, I guess it would be."

"So why don't we agree to take it on faith that it does? Maybe sometimes, things just work out the way they should and everyone ends up where they want to be." He closed his book and leaned back against the couch. He seemed relaxed, comfortable. "You have to believe in something to get through this life," he said to me. "It doesn't have to be the right thing—if there is anything like that. Just *something*."

This was the first time in what felt like forever that we'd had a conversation that didn't have some kind of undertone of tension in it, which I knew was mostly my fault. Realizing this reminded me of what I was doing here, why I was living in this house with this man—because I liked him. Because he was smart and funny and even though what I thought I had wanted was to hide in the shadow of his strength, it was his vulnerability, his uplifting sense that there was something good to look for in the world, that comforted me even more.

I moved over on the couch and put my head on his shoulder. He actually seemed a little surprised, which made me feel awful: I really had been unpleasant to him lately and he didn't deserve that. I promised myself I would do better; I would be a better person, a kinder, more loving companion.

So, even though I was still feeling that I should be putting all my energy into being watchful, I dialed back my anxiety a little, or tried to, and threw myself into caretaker mode. For the next few weeks I cooked fabulous meals. I cleaned the house. I seduced John in the middle of the day and generally acted like a normal, happy person—or at least, I acted out my idea of how a normal, happy person in a loving relationship would behave. And actually, all this domesticity did help me a little: I felt like I was somehow shoring up my fortress, fortifying my nest. If I could have added bricks to the walls

I would have done that, too. I would have constructed battlements. I would have dug a moat.

All for nothing, as it turns out. All for nothing at all.

# IX

ON A FRIDAY in February when I was still carrying out my campaign of being the nicest girl in the world, I had a cleaning job that only kept me busy until around one, and then I was free. I was working uptown, so I caught the subway back to the Village and went shopping, since I was planning on cooking a steak for dinner, the best I could find. My first destination was a butcher shop on Bleecker Street, where I had a long conversation with the owner about the quality of his New York strip but was eventually persuaded to buy rib eye. Then I went to the liquor store and bought a fancy bottle of merlot. The meal was going to cost more than I'd made for five hours work, but I didn't care: I was on a mission to make John happy. I had made up some formula in my mind about how his being happy equated with my being safe. It didn't matter that the idea made no sense: it soothed me, and so I let it be true.

It was bitterly cold outside and the streets were icy, so I was careful as I walked down the lane to the carriage house because the uneven rows of cobblestones were slick and treacherous. Once I unlocked the door and closed it behind me, I turned on the radio, loud, and went up to the kitchen. I wanted to marinate the steaks and then take a shower. John wouldn't be home until later: he had arranged a rare day for himself when he wasn't seeing patients, so he'd had the morning free but was scheduled to see his lawyer in the afternoon and then he was going to take a meditation class. He'd told me that he thought he'd be back around five.

I was out of the shower and dressed but hadn't yet finished drying my hair when the doorbell rang around four-thirty. I thought it was probably UPS or a late mail delivery: John was always ordering books, so it wasn't unusual for packages to arrive almost every day. But when I peered through the peephole, the person I saw standing on the doorstep was someone I would never have expected: Jim Barrett.

I unlocked the door and said hello. Barrett asked if John was home and I said no.

"I left a message on the answering machine," Barrett said. "Do you know if he got it?"

"I don't," I said, and realized I hadn't even looked at the answering machine, which was on the desk in John's office, by the extension phone. I almost never checked it because the only messages that might be left there for me were from the cleaning service I worked for and I usually called them every morning to confirm my schedule.

"I was supposed to come over earlier this morning, but I couldn't make it," Barrett explained. "I did try to reach him."

John hadn't said anything to me about expecting Jim Barrett today, but he had barely mentioned the man's name to me in weeks. Both Barrett and Alice seemed to be topics we just didn't discuss anymore, though John had made one or two offhanded remarks that had led me to believe they had reached some sort of truce again, at least when it came to their work. And, occasionally, when I was home in the afternoon, I did still hear Alice coming and going. Even if she didn't say anything when John opened the front door, I knew when she was around; maybe it was the sound of her particular footsteps or some subtle charge in the air that I was attuned to, but I was always aware of her presence when she was in the house.

Barrett stood on the doorstep, clearly waiting to be invited in. I couldn't just keep him standing there, so I pulled the door open wider and let him into the vestibule. "Thanks," he said, stamping his feet on the mat inside the door. "Is John going to be back soon? He did mention he had appointments this afternoon, but I'll hang out, if you don't mind."

"Of course not," I said, though of course, I did. "I can make some coffee."

He took off his coat and draped it over the chair in the vestibule and then followed me upstairs to the living room. He was carrying a manila envelope with him, which his placed beside him on the couch when he sat down.

Gesturing at the envelope he said, "This is what I wanted to give John, but I would have just put it through the mail slot if no one was home."

It was probably because I didn't like him that I thought he was imply-ing it was my own fault I had to play hostess for him, but I smiled and went into the kitchen to put on the coffee. I told him that it was brewing, and then excused myself to finish drying my hair.

A few minutes later, I was back in the kitchen, pouring coffee into mugs and checking the clock to see how long I had to spend alone with Jim Barrett until John got home. Fifteen minutes? Twenty? It could be longer. John walked home from the yoga center where he took meditation classes and sometimes stopped in a store along the way to buy something: fruit, magazines, or if he was in the mood—or thought I was—some fancy dessert from the bakery a few blocks away.

I brought the coffee to Barrett, who took a few sips and then put the cup on a table beside the couch. Now that I had no more tasks to complete and he had no props, we were going to have to have some kind of conversation. I was trying to think of some innocuous topic to bring up—the weather seemed appropriate; we could spend a good few minutes on the subject of what a cold winter it was turning out to be—when Barrett plunged right into something entirely different.

"Actually," he said, "I'm glad we have a few minutes alone. I've been wanting to talk to you ever since the night of the party."

"Oh?" I said. I could think of few things I wanted less. Besides, I knew I didn't like this man; now that feeling grew stronger. I looked over at him with narrowed eyes and waited for whatever was coming next.

"I was wondering if you had any thoughts on why Alice took such a dis-like to you—out of nowhere, it must have seemed to you."

I took note of that *must have seemed.* "Why don't you ask her?" I replied.

"I have," he said. He paused for a moment; the wait he imposed on us both until he spoke again was deliberate. He was trying to gauge what my reaction might be to whatever else he was going to say, but I knew enough to make my face into a mask. He was going to get nothing from me—unless I decided otherwise.

Barrett picked up his cup of coffee again and took another sip. "It may just be that she thinks you're distracting the great Dr. Benton from his work."

Offering a jab at John was bait I wasn't going to take. Besides, I wasn't sure, yet, what he was after, though it was obvious to me that he had some kind of agenda. "I don't believe that's possible," I replied.

"Well, that's good, because I've got something important for him to review for me." Again, he gestured at the manila envelope beside him on the couch. "The Virginia case—you probably heard me talking about it at the party. I've been down there a couple of times, interviewing the woman who was abducted. She seems to remember everything very clearly and I taped our conversations. I told John I wanted him to listen to them."

"If he's not back by the time you have to leave, I'll make sure he knows you brought him the tapes."

"I have some time," Barrett said, leaning back against the couch. "I can wait a while. If I'm keeping you from anything, please, don't feel you have to keep me company."

"I need to get dinner started," I said, though I didn't move from my chair.

Barrett took note of the fact that I remained seated. "Well, if you have a few minutes, maybe you'd like to hear about the case. Some of the details that the Virginia abductee reported might be particularly interesting to you."

I said nothing. Watching me closely, Barrett said, "This woman—the one in I went to interview—said that she was taken from her bed a few months ago by three grays and carried up to some sort of craft hovering in the sky. It isn't the first time this has happened to her; they've taken her twice before. Each time she undergoes something she calls a medical examination, but no matter how much she pleads with them to explain to her what they're doing, and why, they don't answer. Perhaps they can't communicate, or have given up trying. It's all beyond terrifying, as you can imagine. The woman—let's call her Mary—usually has trouble recovering her memories of these events without hypnosis but this time, she made an effort to register and remember as much as she could, and it seems to have worked. One thing Mary remembers very clearly—a new detail she's never mentioned before—is that when one of the aliens was holding her down on what she thinks is an examination table, she saw something on his wrist. A picture or maybe a tattoo—what would call a tattoo, I suppose. Do you want to see a drawing of it?"

"No," I said.

But Barrett was already opening the manila envelope and pulling out a sheaf of papers. They seemed to be covered with sketches—I caught a glimpse of what must have been Mary's drawing of the aliens: small, with gray bodies, thin appendages—and the big, dark eyes, of course. Depthless, unblinking, cold.

"Maybe you'll reconsider," Barrett replied. He leafed through the papers and pulled out a single sheet, which he then held out to me. "Here," he said. "I'm sure this looks familiar."

I did not take the piece of paper so, after a moment, he put it down on top of the envelope, face up, so I could see the drawing he wanted me to look at: two large dots, in close juxtaposition to one another, and then three smaller ones, off to the left, in an arrangement that looked like a triangle with one straight side.

"So?" I said.

Barrett pointed to my wrist, where the tattoo was clearly visible, since I hadn't thought to make any effort to hide it. "Quite a similarity," he said. "It's interesting, isn't it?"

So Kel wasn't the only one at the party who had noticed my tattoo—Barret had, as well. *Never mind,* I told myself. I knew how to deal with that. I was about to give Barrett one of my several stock answers about the tattoo—probably, I was going to use the one about it being a meaningless design my mother had glimpsed in a tattoo parlor—when all of a sudden, something very disturbing happened to me.

Whenever I consciously thought about the tattoo, it was almost always coupled with a mental snapshot of its origin, so what I saw in my mind was Laura's hand holding a pointed stick dipped in plant dye. But at that moment, in the living room of the carriage house, with Jim Barrett sitting across from me on the yellow corduroy couch, that image faded away and was exchanged for another. I tried to blink away the picture that was developing because I didn't want it to be there, but it was too late: I had seen what I had seen—not my mother's hand holding the stick but a thin, gray arm with a small gray hand and fingers that looked almost boneless but were still able to grip some sort of device, something that looked like a needle, and the needle was drawing stars on my wrist.

I felt panicky, almost on the edge of losing control of myself, but I wasn't going to let that happen in front of Jim Barrett. I took one breath and then another, and then bought some time by finally taking the piece of paper from Barrett and pretending to study it. Then I handed it back. I was still feeling shaky, but I knew that I could get through this moment. I could slam shut the box of memory that had just begun to open itself—if that *was* a memory I had just glimpsed rather than some bizarre manifestation of my own hidden fears.

"That's just a bunch of dots," I said. Deliberately, I held out my wrist and displayed the tattoo with its carefully inked, stylized stars; each an unmistakable jagged point of light. "Mine are much more elegant, don't you think?"

I was beginning to calm down now, to regain my footing. I was good at this, at faking my way through difficult moments until the persona I wanted to be present in a particular moment actually became who I was. And who I wanted to be, right now, was someone who was more than a match for Jim Barrett, who could be as combative as he was, but maybe even better—trickier, more sly. It was going to take a lot of effort, though, because the image I had just shoved away was not going to stay locked up forever. I knew that; it was too vivid, too troubling. Soon enough, I was going to have not only my own memories to deal with—images sliding over each other like alternative theories of a crime that brought up the question of who, really, was the tattoo artist, my mother or one of the things?—but I was also going to have to content with the testimony of some random woman I had never met. Once I was alone again, once my own thoughts started slipping through the barriers I built out of music and books and tv, what I had been told this afternoon was going to be hard to dismiss, since I had heard it before, at Barrett's party. When we were talking in the kitchen, Kel had told me the same thing: that one of the creepy crawlies he had encountered was tattooed with the twin stars and their three smaller companions.

And that was exactly what Barrett was insisting on, even though he didn't know about Kel. "The pattern is the same," Barrett told me. "There's no mistaking it, particularly the triangle stars."

I still had another useful tool that I could use to swat away this accusation. If denial didn't work, perhaps sarcasm would be better. "Well," I said, "maybe there are tattoo parlors all over the universe—even on space ships. And maybe they all use the same stock art. But the skill level—I have to say, your aliens need to take a few classes or something."

"Maybe so," Barrett said evenly. "But while Mary just drew dots on this piece of paper to show me the pattern she remembered, she described the alien's tattoo as looking like stars."

I shrugged. The message was, *I don't care, I'm not interested.* But Barrett was not to be deterred. He touched one of the bigger dots on the piece of paper he was now holding and slid his finger over to its twin. "I'm pretty sure that those represent the double stars of Zeta Reticuli," he told me. "Mean anything to you?"

*Zeta Reticuli.* I silently repeated the words to myself. They sounded science fiction-y, like Gort, the giant robot from outer space, last seen by me on a movie screen at the Stargazer's Embassy. So I said, "To me, all that means is the Stargazer's Embassy. That's my stepfather's bar. Those stars are the logo. They don't have any other meaning."

"Except that Mary says she saw this same tattoo on the body of an alien being. On the exact same part of the body as yours." He slipped the sheet of paper back into the envelope, a signal that by itself, the drawing wasn't important anymore—what it might imply *was* important, though I guessed that he didn't have anything concrete to confront me with. But perhaps someone else had an idea, as quickly became clear when Barrett said, "It was actually Alice who pointed out the similarity to me when I showed her the drawings."

So she had noticed the tattoo as well. I realized that she might have seen it back in December, when I first met her—the afternoon she had come up the stairs and I was decorating the Christmas tree. I wondered if it had triggered something in her memory even then, something she had been holding onto all this time. And while I was asking myself questions, another one occurred to me: was it possible that Barrett was not here by accident? That he had deliberately come to the house at a time when he knew John would be out but likely, I would be home? The cleaning lady, who probably didn't work a regular eight-hour day, who, in her other role as helpmeet and adoring girlfriend, might be home at this time in the afternoon, preparing dinner.

Now, my inner weather was changing over to anger, which also helped with deflecting my earlier panic about the image of the gray hand drawing stars on my skin. But I was wielding a doubled-edged sword against myself: my anger also made me a little careless. While I was good at setting up rules for myself, I was often bad at following them, especially when provoked, as

I was now. Or felt that I was. So while I knew I should move on to some other topic—the miserable winter weather was still a subject waiting to be explored—I couldn't keep myself from challenging Barrett to say whatever it was he really wanted to. I was tired of waiting to hear exactly what it was.

"Listen," I said, "is there something specific you want to ask me?"

Barrett kept his eyes trained on me and I met his stare. In the back of my mind, that boneless hand was still poised above my wrist, but I kept it at bay. *Later*, I told myself. *We'll get to that later.*

Finally, Barrett lowered his eyes. He slipped the papers he was holding back into the manila envelope, as if he was finished interrogating me. But apparently, that was just a ruse because he suddenly caught my gaze again and said, "Yes, actually, there is. Do the names Betty and Barney Hill mean anything to you?"

Just then, I heard the front door creaking on its hinges. Immediately afterwards, John's voice came wafting up the stairs. "Jules? Are you home?"

I waited just a beat before I answered. "In the living room," I called back. "We have company." I had kept my gaze on Jim Barrett all this time and as I listened to the sound of John opening the downstairs closet to hang up his coat, I finally answered Barrett's question. "No," I said. "Should I know who they are?"

He turned away to pick up his coffee cup, and when he turned to face me once more it was with a bland smile indicating that our near-confrontation had come to end. Once again, he was nothing more than a guest being entertained by the householder's companion. "Never mind," he said. "Maybe we can pick this up another time."

John came upstairs and greeted Barrett. They talked for a few minutes, remarking on the confusion about the time they had agreed to meet, and then moving on to the reason for the meeting: the tapes and drawings in the manila envelope. John took the envelope from Barrett and told him he'd try to get a start on reviewing the material later that night.

Barrett left after that, and I finished the preparations for dinner, which I served around six o'clock. John and I sat at the trestle table in the kitchen, with just a few lamps on in the living room and tea lights in a saucer on the table between us. John was in a good mood; he'd had what he called a productive meditation session but more than that, his appointment with his attorney had brought hopeful news. The lawyer said they had made significant progress in their negotiations with the university. Continued pressure from John's colleagues both within and outside the university—including letters of outrage to the university president and chair of the board signed by dozens of academics and educators lamenting the repercussions for academic freedom if John's suspension was allowed to stand—had finally convinced the administration they had to do something to rectify what they now called "a hasty decision" by a review committee that probably didn't have the authority to censure a tenured professor. Therefore, they were willing to discuss terms for reinstating him. They would consent not to throw up any roadblocks to the research he was doing for the book he had started to write about the experiencers if he would agree not to publicly discuss or write about his battle with the administration. For now, that was a sticking point: once John published the book, it was likely to garner significant interest and he didn't think he could talk about the process of writing it if he didn't include the kind of prejudice about abduction studies that he had encountered from his own university.

I listened to everything he said and made the right responses, but my attention was continually distracted by the manila envelope sitting on the couch. Several times, I almost told John what I already knew it contained—at least one drawing that, despite my own protests, bore a marked resemblance to the tattoo on my left wrist (which now had a new story attached to it that I was still refusing to let myself think about) along with a taped interview with a woman who said she had seen the same markings on the wrist of a bug-eyed alien. But I just couldn't bring myself to speak. I wanted this quiet, congenial time to go on and on. I thought that when it ended, and John went into his study with the envelope, it might be the last untroubled hour I had for a long while.

But the clock moved on relentlessly. By seven-thirty we had finished our meal. John retrieved the envelope from the couch and went downstairs. I cleaned up, washed the dishes, and turned on the tv. For two hours I watched one of the home shopping programs, fixing my attention first on the features of a food processor they were selling and then on various items of jewelry and clothing that were being offered. I neither wanted nor needed any of these things, though I did manage to spend some time thinking about whether I could use a new watch, and if I did, would I want one that came with changeable cloth bands in a selection of patterns that included daisies, peace signs, and paisley? No, I decided. Probably not.

John came upstairs just as the program hosts were introducing a new product line they were about to start selling and he laughed when he saw what I was watching. I had been paying such close attention to the program—playing my usual trick on myself of keeping my thoughts so occupied with some kind of visual and auditory input that I didn't have to think, consciously, about anything else—that I was actually startled to see him standing in front of me.

"Oh yes," he said, pointing at the tv, where a pretty woman with a wide smile was holding up a triple strand of faux pearls, "that's just your style."

"It might be," I said, hitting the off button on the remote. "Someday. You never know."

"Okay," he said, "when you're old and gray, I'll buy you pearls. Real ones. For the time being, though, how about we just watch the news and then go to bed?"

He sat down beside me on the couch and turned the tv back on. Then he pulled me close and kissed the top of my head.

"Listen," he said, "do you know I'd be lost without you?" He patted his stomach, "Thinner, maybe, but lost all the same."

*Why?* I wanted to ask him. *And why are you telling me this all of a sudden?* For the past few hours, I had been distracting myself from an imagined scenario in which John marched up the stairs and said *Julia, I think there's something we need to talk about,* but instead—this. As close to a declaration of love that he had ever made to me; certainly, I had never said anything like that to him.

I wondered if he was still just blissed out from the meditation and the promising news from the lawyer. But surely he'd spent the evening doing what he said he was going to: listening to the taped interviews with the Virginia abductee and studying her drawings. If both Jim Barrett and Alice had something to say to me about them—not to mention Kel, who didn't even need anything but his own intuition to start asking me questions—why wasn't John doing the same?

At the moment, I had no answer. I just mumbled something dumb but appropriate, like, "No, you'd be just fine on your own—just like you were before you met me." John didn't even respond to that; he just hugged me tighter and kissed me again.

We watched the first half hour of the news, then went to bed. John fell asleep almost immediately, but I couldn't get anywhere near even feeling drowsy because my mind was racing. I was thinking bad thoughts, scary thoughts, and I knew I had to find yet another way to distract myself, so I plugged a pair of headphones into my CD player, tuned in an FM station and turned up the volume.

Eventually, I fell asleep. When I awoke around dawn, I still had the headphones on and some pop song I didn't recognize was pounding in my ears. I turned off the CD player and found myself looking at the thin bands of light coming through the bedroom window. Silvery light, but dull and chilly. It was cold in the bedroom; instinctively, I moved towards John's side of the bed to curl up against him, but he wasn't there.

I thought that maybe he'd gotten up to go to the bathroom but then, through the half-fog of waking, I heard voices. For a moment, I thought I'd make a mistake about turning off the CD player and somehow, it was still on—maybe what I was hearing was a commercial, or the hourly news. But it only took a few moments for me to realize that the voices were actually coming from the sitting room down the hall from the bedroom.

I got out of bed and walked down the hallway to the sitting room that led out to the garden. Here, there was a couch, an armchair and a wall of shelves filled with books. On a side table in the corner, an old country cottage-type lamp with a yellow shade decorated by the silhouettes of black bears had been turned on.

And on the couch, two people were sitting, John and Alice. He was facing Alice, with his back turned towards me, but she was looking in my direction. She was shoeless, and all she was wearing was a pair of faded pajamas. Her blonde hair was wild and disheveled, and her whole body seemed to be shaking.

As soon as she saw me, a crazed, fearful look came over her face. Then she raised her hand and pointed at me. And began to scream.

"JULIA, WOULD YOU go make us all some coffee, please?"

John spoke in a strong, deliberate tone that I recognized less as an instruction to me than a signal to Alice that she should focus on his voice, his presence, in order to try to calm down. Nevertheless, without a word, I did exactly as he asked, hurrying up the stairs to the kitchen and putting on a pot of coffee—the same thing I had done yesterday, for Jim Barrett, except that now, I saw my hand shaking as I poured water into the coffee maker. Downstairs, Alice finally stopped screaming, though I could hear her gulping air like someone who had survived a near drowning.

When the coffee machine beeped to announce that it was finished with its chore, I poured the brew into cups, tipped some milk into a cow-shaped creamer, and placed sugar and sweetener packets on a small plate. I put all these things on a tray and started back down the stairs realizing, as I went, that what I had produced—the cups, the ceramic cow, the cheery yellow and white packets—looked like the ingredients of weekend brunch. I had a bad feeling that the Julia I was being right now, the kind and helpful sweetheart of a girl, might be living her last hour, but she was still roaming the kitchen, doing her best to make things seem normal and nice.

That ended as soon as I walked back into the room where Alice was sitting with John. As soon as she saw me, she started screaming again. The screams quickly morphed into a wail. John put his arm around her shoulders, trying to comfort her, to get her to quiet down. I placed the tray on a side table near where John was sitting and silently turned to leave the room.

I had gotten only a few steps when Alice was on me. She had broken away from John and rushed across the room to attack me. She grabbed my hair, yanking me backwards, and then had her arm around my throat, putting so much pressure on my windpipe that I immediately began to choke.

Later, I wasn't sure if I had fought her off or if John pulled her away from me; everything happened very fast and my memory of who did what was a little blurry. But what remained sharp and clear were the words she screaming at me when we were finally separated and I turned around to face her.

"You're one of them!" she yelled. "You're a hybrid. That tattoo on your wrist—they put it on all the babies!"

I took a deep breath; I imagined silence as a response but spoke to Alice anyway. "You're crazy," I said to her.

"The babies!" she cried. "That's how they mark the babies! Don't pretend you don't know."

John was standing between me and Alice now, with his arms wrapped around her to keep her from coming after me again. But she managed to turn herself towards me, anyway, and kept on yelling.

"You're one of them! I knew it from the first time I saw you!" And then, again, she spat out the worst thing she could accuse me of. "Hybrid! Hybrid! *Hybrid!*"

"Julia," John said, before I could get out another word, "would you go back upstairs please? Right now?"

I didn't move. I felt paralyzed. Something was happening inside me; some feeling was weaponizing itself, readying a trigger.

"Tell him!" Alice cried as she struggled to break free from John. "Tell him you're one of them! You're not human. *You're not human!*"

I turned away from her for a moment because I needed all my attention to look inside myself. And when I did, I found a name for what I was feeling: murderous rage. Pure, unadulterated wrath: such a black, depthless hatred that I feared I could not control myself. Most of my life had been an exercise in exerting control over my perceptions, my reactions, even my thoughts, so to be gripped by a wave of emotion I felt I might not be able to control was frightening. Disorienting.

"*Julia.*" John repeated, so sharply that my name now sounded like a reprimand. "Please. Go upstairs."

I listened to him only because I didn't trust myself to be in the same room with Alice; there was no telling what I might do to her. Standing in the upstairs living room, as the gloomy daylight pushed through the tall windows, I realized that I was still wearing the tee shirt and sweat pants I had been sleeping in. I couldn't go back down to the bedroom where my clothes were because Alice would see me and whatever had just happened would likely start all over again. So, I went into the bathroom and pulled a pair of jeans, a shirt and a sweater out of the hamper where I had dumped them last night. Then I went out to the living room and without even thinking about what I was doing, I began to pace. Like my clothes, my CD player was in the bedroom downstairs, so I couldn't distract myself with music. And I knew that turning on the television wouldn't work. I was too angry to sit still, too agitated to come up with a strategy for calming myself, so I walked in circles. I counted my steps and talked to myself about how violent I felt. And how strangely familiar the feeling was, considering the last time it had come over me.

I knew exactly when that was: in real time it was decades ago, but for me, that time was always just yesterday: the moment I had run across a clearing in the woods and sunk my teeth into the arm of a dough-gray thing nearly seven feet tall and wearing a biker outfit. The moment that helped to create me, that separated me from my mother and made me believe that the only way to survive this life was to be stronger than anything that might come at me from anywhere, at any time, in any form. Maintaining that strength required an enormous amount of control, and the fuel for the energy it took to exert that control was anger.

But now, suddenly, something new occurred to me—a new constellation of thoughts or maybe they were, in fact, old ones I just refused until this moment to acknowledge: why had I run across that field? Why was I already so angry that I hated the things on sight? Why did I think they were going to hurt me? What evidence did I have? And perhaps most important of all, why was I so sure that whatever they did to me, my mother would not prevent it? That she would, indeed, be complicit. Why did I so distrust her? Why? *Why?*

What had just happened with Alice was barely on the horizon of my mind now. Instead, I was far away, back in the clearing where my rage had propelled me forward. And as I ran towards the thing once more, the box of memory I had tried to slam shut yesterday afternoon, when Jim Barrett was here, broke itself wide open. It disintegrated. It had taken less than a day for me to find myself confronting the day of reckoning I had known would come.

So here was the truth: that midnight in the clearing, I was already angry because it wasn't the first time I had met the things, it was the second. The first time was when the tall one had given me the tattoo. He—*it*—had used some thin, glowing machine with a stinging needle-like tip and inscribed five blue-black stars—two large ones and three smaller companions, arranged like a triangle with one straight side—onto my wrist. The procedure was not painful but I hated it, I hated what was being done to me. Somewhere, on some television show or in a movie, I had seen cattle being branded and I thought that was what was happening. I screamed for Laura to make them stop, but she didn't. She barely even tried to comfort me, at least as I remember the scene. She just kept saying, *Don't be afraid, Julia. Be brave.*

And so perhaps I was—except, by the second time Laura led me to that clearing, my courage took the form of defiance. Or at least, defiance presented itself to me as an option, a possibility. It might not have been what she intended, but I probably got that idea from my mother as surely as I was branded with a tattoo she already bore: Laura was different than everybody else. She listened to no one but herself. Why then, did I have to listen to her?

I didn't. But even defiance can be worn away by time. I could cling to my anger at Laura, and at the things, but it was harder to wrestle with myself, with my own memory. There was no avoiding it now: I had to accept the truth. I had no choice.

*So not Laura. Them. One of the things gave me the tattoo.* I said those words to myself as I faced the idea that they were no longer deniable. And once I did, the image of the tall alien and his glowing needle affixed itself to whatever gallery of the mind it is that displays pictures of the past that cannot be altered or repudiated. But there was a caption to that picture—another truth that I didn't like. Yet there it was: the fact that I had something in common with Alice and with many of the abductees: I had invented a screen memory. I had allowed myself to live on one side of that memory for many years, seeing Laura as the tattoo artist instead of the tall thing. But I was on the other side of the screen now—way over. *Not Laura. Them.*

"Julia."

I heard my name and turned to see John coming up the stairs. By the look on his face when he saw me, I must have had the appearance of a wild animal, pacing in circles, making sounds in my throat, sounds of fury and outrage.

John walked over the couch and sat down. He held out his hand. "Come over here," he said. "Come sit with me."

"No," I told him.

Slowly, he lowered the hand he had held out to me. I realized that he looked upset and exhausted and at any other time, I would have run to embrace him—but that was what the good girl would have done. The homemaker, the girlfriend, the selfless companion. But as I had guessed, she was nowhere to be found The sweetheart of a girl I had invented was gone, lost somewhere in the distance I had crossed again as I took myself back to that clearing and raced towards the thing I had to be strong enough to kill. Or at least, strong enough to make it believe that was my goal. How could a good girl live with such intentions etched on her heart just as surely as a tattoo of five stars was etched on her wrist? She could not. And so she was no longer in this house. Banished. Probably to be seen no more.

"I want to tell you what happened," John said.

"Don't," I told him. "I'm not interested."

"I'm going to tell you anyway so you might as well listen."

I shrugged and seated myself on a chair opposite the couch. *Let him talk,* I thought. *It won't change anything.* I kept my gaze fixed towards the window as John spoke, though all I could see was the solid brick wall that was the back of the building on the other side of Paper Lane.

"Alice says she was abducted again last night, from her apartment, and when they returned her, they left her here, in the lane. I woke up when I heard her banging on the door. You had your headphones on, so I guess you didn't hear the noise."

I turned back to face John. "Really? You believe that story? Why would they dump her here?"

He rubbed his hands across his eyes, and shook his head. "I don't know," he said. "I honestly don't know. If there's a message here, I'm not getting it. I'm sure Jim will come up with something, though. It will undoubtedly be a chapter in his next book."

"Jim Barrett?"

"Alice wanted me to call him, so I did, and he drove over. He's downstairs in the office with her now."

Had I been pacing that long? Lost in my own thoughts that long? But I was out of my mental coma now, and I could hear well enough how defeated John sounded, even sarcastic in speaking about Barrett, which was not like him at all. The nice girl would have tried to comfort him, but all he had now was me. Vicious, vengeful me. My heart was empty. It was ice.

I said, "I want to know why you let her say those terrible things to me."

John leaned back against the yellow couch cushions, which appeared to be leached of color in the cold morning light. The stained glass of the old hayloft windows seemed able to admit only the thinnest illumination into the room.

"I guess I'm trying to do the right thing by everybody," John said. "It doesn't always work."

"I'm not everybody!"

He sat forward. He looked over at me, focused on me, wanting me to understand that now, his attention was here, in this room. "I know that, Julia."

It was too late: what he said didn't matter. No words were going to be good enough. I was wounded, aching from wrongs done to me new and old, which meant by Laura, yes, but now even by John—or so I felt. And I would not be dissuaded. I wanted to lash out even if I was the one who ended up the most badly injured. "Then why didn't you shut her up? It's because you think she's right, isn't it?"

"Why would I think that?"

I pulled back the sleeve of my sweater and held up my wrist. The tattoo looked like it had been inked with black blood. "Because of this, just like she said. Barrett did, too."

"Jim? When did he talk to you?"

"Yesterday. When he brought you the tapes And the drawings."

"You should have told me that Jules."

I didn't even acknowledge what he said. I just kept piling on my evidence. I didn't care if it hurt him. I wanted it to, even though it was likely to hurt me much more. "Kel said that he also recognized the tattoo.

Now John looked startled. "Kel? He told you he's seen these markings?"

"Yes," I spat back. "How come you don't know that? You're his shrink, aren't you?"

"My patients don't tell me everything, Julia. They don't remember everything. Or they remember but they don't understand what's behind their own memories."

"Well, everyone seems to remember this," I said, thrusting out my wrist again. "Even that woman in Virginia. I was sure you were going to say something to me about that last night."

"And you're upset that I didn't?"

"Upset?" I cried. "I'm way beyond upset." I glared at him. "So, doctor," I said, "why don't you tell me your theory about why I have this mark? You must have one."

After listening to me rant, John closed his eyes and sat silently for a moment. When he opened them again, he stood up and walked over to one of the bookcases near the hayloft windows that looked down on the long dining table we never used. He must have known what he was searching for because he quickly located a volume on a high shelf and carried it back to where I was sitting. Standing beside me, he quickly paged through the book until he came to a photo he said he wanted to show me.

But before he handed me he book he asked me a question. "Do you know who Betty and Barney Hill were?"

"Barrett asked me that same question."

"Did he?" John said. What he tell you about them?"

"Nothing. And I wouldn't have listened if he tried. Those are stupid names, like cartoon characters." I was behaving horribly now, even to the point of saying the first thing that came to my mind, no matter how ridiculous. I knew all this but I didn't care. I would have found any excuse to resist being soothed. Any excuse to be petulant. Mean.

But John paid me no mind. He apparently wanted to tell me about the Hills and he just went on talking, hoping, I suppose, that despite myself, I would listen.

"Betty and Barney Hill were a husband and wife who were involved in one of the most well-known abduction cases on record," John began. "This was in 1961: they were abducted, together, when they were driving along a road in New Hampshire. They said they were taken aboard a spacecraft and put through painful physical examinations by alien beings who told them that they were analyzing the differences between our two species. Sometime after the incident, under hypnosis, Betty Hill reported that one of the aliens had shown her a star map. She said she thought he was trying to explain where he and the others were from. That's the map," John said, as he finally handed me the book and pointed to a photograph of a crude, hand-drawn image that showed a number of small, dense black dots set off to the left of two larger, almost identical black circles.

"There's been a lot of work done in relation to this map," John continued. "If you read through the literature..."

That was too much for me. *The literature*? I suddenly felt like I was being lectured by Professor Doctor Benton, and I hated it. "What literature?" I snapped at him.

"Abduction literature. There's a tremendous amount of it. Some of it is nonsense but I have to admit that the analysis that has gone into figuring out this map has been very thorough. It's generally accepted now that these two larger circles represent the twin stars of the Zeta Reticuli system. And these three small dots," he said, sliding his finger to the left, touching first one, then two, then a third of the group of black markings set off to the side of the circles, "are called the triangle stars."

John took the book from me then and returned it to the shelf. When he came back, I could hardly bring myself to look at him. "How long have you known?" I asked.

"That what's tattooed on your wrist matches the pattern of the Betty Hill map? What difference does that make? It doesn't necessarily mean anything. You said your mother was interested in all kinds of things connected to aliens. Certainly, then, she must have seen this map somewhere."

"Don't talk about my mother," I said angrily. "You don't know anything about her."

"No," John replied quietly. "Not much. Just what you've told me."

"And how much did you believe?" I asked

"Everything you wanted me to," John said.

Perhaps he meant that kindly, but it didn't sound that way to me. "You knew," I repeated. "You knew something was wrong and you never said anything to me."

"All I knew was that I recognized a pattern I had seen before. And even that didn't occur to me for a long time. Once it did...really, what good would it have done to bring it up with you, Julia? You made it clear that these were things you didn't want to discuss with me."

"You're right. Maybe it wouldn't have done any good at all. But at least I would have known what you really thought about me and so I wouldn't have let you keep me as a pet. A patient."

"I don't know where you're getting these ideas. Besides, I would never do anything like that," John said. "Never." He sighed deeply. "Still. We always seem to find ourselves back here," he said. "There are things I don't tell you, things you don't tell me. Maybe it's time to stop that, don't you think?"

"I don't think anything," I said. "Nothing. Maybe you should just leave me alone."

"I don't want that. I don't believe you want that, either."

When I didn't reply, he spoke again. "Jules," he said, "I don't understand. I really don't. What's really so terrible? What am I missing here? If your mother was so interested in the idea that human beings have experienced alien contact, it's very likely she knew the Betty and Barney Hill story. In fact, it would have been hard *not* to know it and to have seen picture, some-where, of the star map. So when she talked Nicky into changing the name of the bar, she came up with the idea of using the stars as the logo and then she not only had them painted on the wall in the bar, she inked them on her wrist, and on yours. Granted—and I've said this to you before—it's a little strange to give a young child a tattoo, but you said she was kind of a hippie. She probably just thought she was doing something that included you as part of the tribe."

"Tribe?" I cried. "*Tribe?*"

"It's just an expression."

Maybe he thought he was explaining everything away, but of course, he was wrong. And because I was no longer his good girl, I had to tell him that. More: I had to take something away from him, just as I felt that I was losing everything. And what I was going to take away was the last piece of any illusion that the life we had been living was something that could continue, because I knew it couldn't. Not now. Not when he found out who I was—whatever that meant. Because maybe it meant something I didn't understand myself.

"It wasn't Laura who put the tattoo on my wrist," I said. "I made myself think it was, but that's not true."

John paused. Perhaps he thought he shouldn't ask me the next logical question but like me, couldn't prevent himself from saying things—asking questions—that led into dangerous territory. "So who did?"

"Alice already told you. It was the grays."

That was Jim Barrett, breaking into our conversation. John and I had been so absorbed in what we were saying that we had been aware of nothing else, which meant that Barrett had come up the stairs without our hearing him. Now, he was standing in the living room, with Alice cowering behind him as if she had to be protected from me—and maybe she still did. "I believe her, John," Barrett continued. "I believe everything Alice just told me—which means there are some things Julia needs to explain to us. We need to know how she's involved in the abductions."

"For God's sake," John said. "She's not involved. Accusing her is just making all this worse."

*Whatever he really thinks, he's defending you.* I tried to register that thought, to store it up in case I needed it later. In case some of the ice melted and I was able to feel something for him again. Something loving, kind.

Barrett continued, seeming to relish his confrontation with John. "All what?" he asked. "What are we really talking about here, John?" The look on his face was that of a man who knew that he had uncovered some sinister secret and was about to prove its existence.

But John wasn't going to be baited. "Jim please, just go," he said. "Take Alice home and I'll talk to you both later. I'll phone or I'll come to your house but we can't go any further with this. Not here and not right now."

"Why not?" Barrett said. "*Why not?* Because you can't accept the fact that your girlfriend has been lying to you?" He moved away from Alice and came forward to stand in front of John, who rose from the couch to face him. But I couldn't bear to be near him—I didn't even want to look at him.

I jumped up and brushed past him, heading for the kitchen just so I could be in another room. I walked past Alice as well, who was standing to the side of the stairs. When I went by her, she moaned as if my very nearness might cause her to faint.

I walked over to the door at the far end of the kitchen, the door that overlooked the garden, and pressed my face against the glass. The cold seeping in from the chilly morning made me feel that I was between worlds, as much outside as I was in this house with these people who were talking about me. I looked down into the garden, then peered up at the winter sky where a ragged wind was rearranging the gray clouds far above me. For a few moments, I focused on those things—sky, wind, clouds, empty garden—as I listened to John and Jim Barrett arguing. Their voices were like the wind to me; they reached me, flowed around me, but then faded away. I wasn't really listening to whatever they were saying to each other. I didn't want to know.

Suddenly, I had a familiar feeling—a bad one; not unexpected but unwelcome. Always unwelcome. Slowly, with my fingertips, I pushed myself back, away from the door, the sky, the knife-edged wind, and turned around. I walked one step, then two, then three, so I could look down the stairwell into the hallways below that separated the ground floor room the faced the garden from the waiting room outside John's office.

And in that hallway, I saw one of the things standing at the foot of the stairs. It was dressed in one of the bizarre costumes they appeared in—this time, a parka trimmed in ratty fake fur that was a gelatinous green color and a matching pair of slippers. The clothes seemed blurry, as if the thing was in my world but its clothing was still partly in some other place.

As I stared at it, the thing came closer to the foot of the stairs. Then it appeared to pull something from—where? Some void beside it that was invisible to me? From some wormhole between wherever *here* was for me and *there* for the thing? I had no idea, but I watched as its hands and arms seemed to disappear and then became visible to me again, clutching a small, lozenge-shaped object wrapped in a blanket.

Then, in an instant, it ripped the blanket away from the object so I could see it was an infant, or something that looked, to me like an infant but misshapen, large-headed, limp.

Dead.

And then the thing held the dead baby out to me and threw back its head, opened its mouth. No sound emerged but I knew what it would have been if I could have heard it: I knew immediately, viscerally. It would have been a wail of grief.

What I saw, Alice saw too. From where she was standing, the bottom of the stairs was visible to her as well. When she saw the thing hold out the dead baby, I thought she would start screaming again but instead, she turned to me and said—sounding almost as dead as what the thing held in its arms—"It's you. This is all about you. Tell them," she said. "Tell them!"

*Tell who? Say what?* Tell John and Jim Barrett that there was a thing downstairs, clutching a dead baby? Tell the thing to go away, to leave Alice alone? Trade myself for her? *What was I supposed to do?*

I did what my instinct told me to—what had always saved me in the past, or so I believed. I rushed down the stairs, past the thing, which stepped back as I pushed by and vanished into shadows that seemed to stretch themselves out from the corners of the room to enfold it and then shrank back again, molding themselves to the walls. In the hallway, I grabbed my coat and backpack from a chair and pulled open the front door.

I went out into the lane, into the winter, the cold. And then I ran.

# XI

*GET AWAY, get away, get away.*

That was my only thought as I ran through the streets. It was mid-morning now; a grim, winter day that displayed a small, weak sun above the rooftops of the Village below Seventh Avenue. I kept on running until I got to Fourteenth Street, which was crowded with workday traffic. I finally stopped there, on a corner, to catch my breath. My face felt blistered by the wind; my hands were stiff from the cold.

Enough sense returned to me so that I thought to move into the shelter of a doorway. There, I reached into my backpack for my wallet and counted how much cash I had. Not much, but I did have a credit card and that gave me an option; maybe many—how far could I go with what I had? Where *should* I go?

The answer came to me immediately. There was only one place, and one person I had to talk to. Someone who maybe had lied to me—had been lying to me for a very long time. There was no question now: I had to go back to the Stargazer's Embassy.

I walked another twenty blocks to the Port Authority bus depot and waited for two hours for the next bus to Ithaca. From there I could take a local bus to Freelingburg; there was always a bus that traveled the rural roads out to the towns at the edge of the county. I might not get there until nighttime, but that didn't matter. Nothing mattered but that I make it home.

In the Port Authority, I went into a drug store that also sold anything else you might want to have with you on a long bus trip and bought a cheap transistor radio and a pair of headphones, since I had left my CD player back at the house. I plugged myself in and tuned to an all-news station; it wasn't that I cared anything about what was happening in the world but the carefully modulated voices of the announcers and the repetition of the sports, traffic and weather calmed me a little because they gave me something to focus on. I was trying hard not to think about the scene I had left behind me. I didn't believe that John and Jim Barrett had seen the thing and its horrifying burden—only Alice and I had. The men had been standing on the other side of the room, oblivious to anything but the argument they were having. Alice, however, would have told them by now, about how the thing had held the dead baby out to me. Would John believe her? I wasn't sure anymore. But certainly, Jim Barrett would.

Whatever he thought, John would be worried about me—more and more, probably, with every hour I didn't return. But I couldn't begin to even think about that; I didn't want to think about anything until I got to Freelingburg. So, once I boarded the bus, I found a seat in the back, buried myself under my coat and closed my eyes. Sometimes I dozed, sometimes I listened to the news; the stations drifted as we traveled north, so local New York reports of traffic problems and apartment fires faded away and were replaced by deep album cuts being played by a student-run radio station at a university in Connecticut, and then, as those songs broke up into static, the signal was once again taken over by a news station—this one broadcasting from the Hudson Valley. I heard about a bridge collapse over an icy river, a town holding a cider festival, an overturned truck at a crossroads. I felt like the voices speaking in my ear were all that kept me tethered to world; without them, my own thoughts would take over and they were so confused that I might disappear inside them and never be able to escape.

It was twilight when I got to Ithaca; fully dark when I boarded the local bus that headed out into the countryside. It was just after eight o'clock when I stepped off the bus in Freelingburg and started walking towards the Stargazer's Embassy to the World.

There was no moon in the sky, no people on the street because all the shops were shuttered at this hour. It was on winter nights like these, when I was a child, that I had once seen a lone deer walk down the center of Main

Street, right under the hanging traffic light that no one paid much attention to even during the day.

When I entered the Stargazer's, there were a few customers sitting at the bar, a few more at the tables in the back listening to music playing on a tape deck. Led Zeppelin was climbing the stairway to heaven. In some bar, somewhere in rural upstate New York, they always were.

I didn't see Nicky around so I asked the bartender where he was. She remembered me from Christmas but was clearly surprised to see me suddenly standing in front of her. Instead of answering, she blurted out, "Did you just drive up here tonight?"

"I took the bus," I told her, and then asked again, "Where's Nicky?"

"He's upstairs."

"By himself?"

"Yes. He's doing some paperwork."

I didn't even know why I'd asked that question—who would Nicky be with? A girlfriend? Even though he seemed to be alone at Christmas, that didn't mean he wasn't seeing someone. But the fact that I was even thinking about this was a measure of the fact that part of me was feeling like we were strangers. Still, I had to talk to him and it couldn't be in front of anyone else.

I practically ran up the stairs. I found Nicky in the living room, sitting on the couch with a calculator and some papers spread out before him on the coffee table. It was a familiar scene to me: he always preferred to work up here instead of in the cramped office behind the stage at the back of the bar.

He looked up when I walked in and took off his reading glasses as if he couldn't believe that it was me he was seeing and needed a better look "Honey," he said. "What are you doing here? Is something wrong? Where's John?"

I heard him, but I was past answering. I had questions of my own. "I need to know something," I said to him. "And I need you to tell me the truth."

He had started to stand up, to come towards me, but now he sat down again. "You came all the way up here tonight to talk to me?"

"Yes," I said. "That's exactly what I did."

He gave me a long, steady look. He opened his mouth and then closed it without asking the dozen questions he probably had in mind. "Alright," he said. He gestured at a chair opposite the couch. "Sit down," he told me. "What is it you want to know?"

I did not sit down. I stood by the door and said, "Am I a hybrid?"

"A what?"

"You heard me. A hybrid."

"Honestly, Julia. I don't know what you're talking about."

"Yes you do. I know you do."

Now, as he kept his eyes trained on me, he seemed to be searching my face in a way that he had never done before. What was he looking for? Traces of Laura, I thought; traces of the one person he could never have told even the smallest lie to.

I was studying him, too, but it was impossible for me to get any sense of what he was thinking or feeling because he suddenly seemed drained of emotion, as if he had sent the lighthearted part of himself away. As if he—like me—was capable of being one person inside but plastering the outside with a different mask most of the time. What I was seeing now was who he was when he wasn't trying to be someone else. "Alright, Julia," he said, gesturing at the chair again. "Sit."

I walked across the floor, feeling the vibrations of the music playing downstairs. "Okay," I said, as I lowered myself into the chair. "Here I am." I took a breath. "Nicky. Am I a hybrid?"

"No," he said. "Of course not."

At least he knew what the word meant—but that only made me more suspicious. "How do you know?"

"Because your mother was your mother—we both know that—and she told me who your father was."

"Yeah, right. High school boyfriend. What if that's not true?"

"Maybe it's not. But it can't be what you're thinking, either. Do you remember when you were ten and you had to spend the night in the hospital in Ithaca because you had an intestinal infection and were running a high fever? It turned out that the real reason you were so sick was that you had a bad reaction to the first antibiotic the doctor gave you, but because he didn't figure that out for a while, the hospital ran all kinds of tests: blood tests, a bone scan, an MRI. Don't you think that if there was anything...odd about you, it would have shown up? Nothing did."

"Who told you that? Laura or the doctor?"

"I don't even remember," Nicky said. "But so what? There is no reason on God's green earth to think that you are anything but a perfectly ordinary girl."

"If I'm so ordinary why do I have this?" I thrust out my wrist so he could see my tattoo. My mark.

"Your mother..."

I immediately interrupted him. "No," I said. "Laura didn't do it."

He paused for a moment, touched one of the sheets of paper on the table in front of him and then withdrew his hand. He was simply letting a piece of time pass so he could consider what I'd said.

Finally he spoke—but there was a wariness in his voice, a distance that surprised me.

"That's what you both told me. Always."

"But it turns out that wasn't true."

"OK," he said, and took a breath. "Then who did?" he asked.

"What do you mean, *who*? It was them. The things."

"Really?" he said.

I waited for him to say something else, something more, but he didn't. He moved some papers around again and sat back against the couch. I felt like suddenly, he was a million miles away from me—and retreating even further.

It was that distance opening, widening, that made me rush on. I wanted to tell Nicky more now; I wanted him to hear me, to come back from wherever he was disappearing to. "There's this woman—a patient of John's. She says she's been abducted multiple times. And she said they show her babies; one of the babies was hers. The last time—last night?" I shook my head as if that would clear the clouded sense of time I suddenly seemed to have. *Was* it last night that Alice would have been abducted? This morning she showed up at the house? Today—all day—that I had been traveling to get here, get home, get to the truth, the lies, the beginning and maybe the end. "Yes," I finally assured myself. "Last night. They showed her that the infants they've created all have this mark, in the same place. And this morning, one of the things showed me a baby that had died."

"That sounds horrific."

"I don't know if it was real."

All I meant was what I had seen that morning, nothing else. The things had exhibited so many new behaviors recently that I was no longer certain what else they might be capable of. Maybe showing me the supposedly dead baby had been some kind of new trick to get my attention, to shake me up in some way. But Nicky must have heard something different. An opening. A chance to say what he must have wanted to say for years and years.

"I suppose there's always that question, isn't there?"

It took a moment for me to understand what he meant—and maybe what he meant could have been taken a dozen different ways—but not for me. The message I heard was unambiguous: it sounded plain-spoken, absolutely flat-out and clear. What he was telling me was that he had never known for sure whether what Laura and I had both told him—about everything—was fact or fiction. I didn't want to believe that but after all, he had never seen anything out of the ordinary; all the evidence he had that anything strange had happened to either one of us was the stories that my mother and I had shared with him. And yet, all these years, I had held fast to the idea that Nicky was the one person I could talk to about the things because even if he had never seen them, they were still a part of his life, just as they were of mine. But apparently, it wasn't so. He was saying that to me: it wasn't exactly so.

"I'm sorry, Julia," he continued, "Maybe I shouldn't have said that, but I don't know what else to tell you. Dead babies...even your mother never went that far. She never said anything like that."

Meaning what? That I had gone even further over the edge than she ever had? Even if that was what he really thought, he owed me something. Information, explanations...*something*. Anything. "Then what did she say? What did she tell you about them? She must have said something."

Now we were back to the same conversation I had tried to have with him at Christmas, but this time, we were having it in some new territory—some terrible place where I lived all alone and Nicky did nothing to help me sustain myself there. Nothing that would make it easier.

"At first," he admitted, "yes, she did try to tell me about the visitors. That's what she called them. She said she was helping them."

"*Helping them?* Jesus," I said. "Helping them do what?"

"I honestly don't know—I've told you that over and over again, and it's true. All she ever said was that when you were younger, she had tried to get you involved, but you wouldn't cooperate. She said you had attacked one of the visitors and she could never get you to go back to them."

"That's what she called them? Visitors?"

"Yes," Nicky said. "That was the word she used."

*Visitors, creepy crawlies, grays, things.* And, oh yes, one more word: *Aliens.* These were now my collection of names for the slim gray creatures in their array of bizarre outfits whose presence was my mother's legacy to me. That is, if I accepted that they were all the same, that despite the very different ways they acted with different people, these phenomena—these presences—were all members of the same...well, what? Race? Species? Group? *Tribe?* More words. And maybe none of them really mattered, at least not to me. Not much. Because while John and Kel and Jim Barrett and Alice used different terms for them, they were all meaningless to me—except maybe *alien,* though not in the way everybody else meant it. Whatever the things really were, wherever they were from, how could something that I always knew existed seem alien to me? In many ways, my own mother was more mysterious to me than they were. My mother, who had made me motherless twice: first by caring more for her visitors than for me and then by dying. She had left me, both body and soul.

"You should have helped *me,* Nicky," I said, to the one person I thought I deserved to say that to. "You should have tried."

"How?" Nicky said. "What was I supposed to do for you? I didn't even know anything was wrong until your mother died. And before then..." His voice trailed off for a moment; maybe he was sorting through his own memories, reasons, rationales for how he had lived his life. That must have somehow summoned back the feelings he had tried to banish earlier because he suddenly sounded anguished.

"For God's sake, Julia," he said. "There are things you just don't understand. I changed everything for your mother. I changed my life, I accepted conditions I knew were practically untenable for any normal human being. But it all happened so gradually that I guess I just...went along with her. For her. That's what you do. You figure out what you can't live with and what you can, and if the pile on one side is bigger than the other, you pick up that pile and carry it around for the rest of your days." He went on, sounding even more like he was speaking from a place of great pain. "But do you know what I did do? I changed this place, I set it up so that it would be the kind of hangout where a strange, eccentric woman wouldn't stand out so much. That was the whole point of The Stargazer's Embassy—to give your mother a story to tell. 'Oh, I live with that weird, long-haired guy who runs the sci-fi hippie bar.' Not that she thought she needed a story, but I thought so. I thought...oh God, I don't know what I thought—except that the way people talked about her, I thought someone would try to have her committed. Or maybe I would. Should have. Sent her to a shrink or something."

"Then why didn't you?"

"Because I loved her. And because that was the deal I made with her, eventually: that I wouldn't ask too many questions. In the beginning, I was so crazy about her I would have agreed to anything. Besides, in those days, we were all high all the time. We took a lot of psychedelics and everybody saw all kinds of things. Believed all kinds of things. And even later—well, I wanted her to stay with me and that was the only way: to just leave her alone, when that was what she wanted. Let her disappear whenever she said she had to. We just let it be. She'd come and go, and I wouldn't ask where she'd been or what she'd been doing, and that's how we lived."

*There are things I don't tell you, things you don't tell me.* I didn't need to hear that complaint again, even if it was true, so I brushed it away.

"And what about me, when I started telling you about the things? What did you think about me?"

"You didn't really say all that much either, Julia. At least not at first. And when you did, I thought that maybe it was just your way of keeping your mother alive. I didn't want to feed into it, though, so I never told you any of the crazier things she said. Like that business about helping them."

That was a startling idea; infuriating, even—especially from Nicky. "Really? You thought I was hallucinating...well, what should we call them? How about visitors from outer space? That sounds sufficiently crazy, doesn't it? You thought I was conjuring up spacemen *because I missed my mother?* Then you should have had *me* committed."

"I didn't say..."

I wouldn't let him speak. "Never mind," I said. "Never mind. Let's just stop talking, okay? Let's just stop."

I couldn't bear another word. Our conversation had led us through a dark tunnel that I thought neither of us might ever emerge from. Certainly, we weren't going to do each other any good by going on with this—at least not here, not tonight. Whatever compact had existed between us was broken, maybe—probably—irreparably. But I just couldn't think about it anymore, I couldn't speak and I couldn't argue for one more minute. I felt as if I had finally stepped into some realm that was beyond even anger and was falling deep into what felt like a black depression.

I told Nicky that I was going to bed and went down the hall to my room. I stripped off my clothes, pulled the blankets over my head, and went away. That's what it felt like, that night—instead of going to sleep, I felt like I let go of myself and disappeared.

Sometime in the night, I was awakened by the sound of my bedroom door opening. I wasn't afraid—I hardly felt like I was still alive, so what could happen to me? Besides, I knew it wasn't the things because they wouldn't dare come into my room. After a moment, I sat up, looked toward the door, and in the dim light from the hallway, I was able to see that it was John standing in the doorway.

"I thought of everywhere you could have gone," he said, "and I knew this was the only place."

"I could have been carried off in a flying saucer," I answered.

"Stop," he told me. "Not that. Not now."

He pulled off his clothes and slid into bed beside me. I faced away from him but he wrapped himself around me and waited for me to speak to him. I was so tired, so empty, that it seemed hard to even begin. But I had to, and so I did.

"I am not what Alice thinks," I said, though in the back of my mind I was thinking, *Well, maybe not. Probably not. But that's what I am going to believe.*

John, at least, believed it, too. He said as much, and he meant it. "I know that, Jules."

"Still. There's a lot I haven't told you."

John sighed. I felt his intake of breath, the slow exhale. Pain was in that sound, great sadness. "I think I knew that too," he said. "Which is why what you said to me this morning may be true, if just a little—that at times, I've treated you like a patient. Though I always tried not to, and maybe that's the problem. I tried too hard, I succeeded too well. So instead of helping you, I think I've made your situation worse. Whatever you're...confronting, you had coping mechanisms. I've managed to involve you with people who stripped those away."

"So now it's time to tell you, right? What I'm confronting." Because I had used his word—not something I would normally have said—John seemed to think I meant to respond with bitterness. Perhaps I did. Perhaps I still had that left in me; I wouldn't have been surprised.

"Yes, you need to tell me," he said. "But not because I can fix it. Not because I'm curious or it will fit some theory I have. Not because of anything it will do for me or Alice or Jim, or anyone else. It's because I love you, Jules. There's no other reason but that."

I thought that might well kill me—to hear John say almost the same words Nicky had said about my mother. John had never told me before that he loved me, not in those words, and this was a terrible way to hear them. In my wrecked and weary state, it turned out that bitterness wasn't what was left inside me but something like grief. The love that now wanted to speak of itself seemed not to belong to me but to Laura. It appeared in my life too late and with the same encumbrances that she must have recognized: this love was helpless, misdirected from the beginning. It knew too little, waited too long to find its voice. But still, it had its effect, now: it made me tell the truth.

"Those *things*," I began, "they're around me all the time," I said. Not every day but enough; enough so that I can never pretend they aren't real. It all started when Laura died. They used to just show up, standing somewhere, by the side of the road or in a corner, somewhere—outside my school, in a store. They'd just look at me, like they wanted me to know they were there, but they never came close. Lately, though—lately, it's like they want to tell me something. Maybe they want me to do something. I don't know. But I won't let them near me. Never."

John waited a moment before he spoke. He was being careful, trying not to say anything that might make me push him away. "What do you think they want?" he asked.

"I don't know. I don't care. I don't want *them*," I said, with whatever vehemence I could still muster. "I just want to be normal."

"I'm sorry I couldn't give you that," he said quietly.

I didn't respond to him directly; I just pressed on, needing, now, to get it all out. "One of them was in the house this morning, when you and Jim were arguing. It showed me a dead baby. I think Alice saw it, too."

He was silent for what felt to me like a long time. Finally, he said, "Maybe Jim is right. Maybe whatever is happening—whatever they're really doing—is dreadful. Horrible. Nothing else but that."

"Is that what you're going to believe now? Because of me?"

"No, not because of you. And right now, I'm not sure what I believe."

Again John was silent. I thought he might actually be falling asleep but suddenly, he spoke again. "All they do is show themselves to you?"

"Yes."

"They've never tried to even touch you?"

"Well, they've tried. But they don't anymore."

"Do you know why?"

"Probably because when I was a child, I bit one of them."

John sat up. I finally turned so I was facing him. "You're joking," he said.

"I am not. My mother had to pull me off."

"Your mother was there?" He sounded incredulous.

"Oh yes. She was there. She must have been involved with them before I was even born," I told John. "She brought me to them. Jim Barrett guessed right: it was one of them who gave me the tattoo. But the next time I saw it...well, maybe it wasn't the same one—I can never really tell. But it didn't matter: as soon as I was near enough, I sank my teeth into its arm. It howled like it was dying."

"Did it say anything to you?"

"I have never heard them speak. At least, in any way that I can understand. Sometimes they make different sounds. When we were here at Christmas, I went downstairs to the bar after you were asleep and one of them was there. It made a sound like a cat."

"They make sounds like cats and when you were a little girl, you took it upon yourself to bite one of them." He nodded, seeming to give himself a few moments to absorb everything I had just told him. "Well, Jules," he said finally, "that's quite a story."

"It's not a story."

"I know it's not," he said. "I know."

I was already exhausted and this conversation was just making me feel worse. So, maybe despite myself, I let myself relax into John's arms, I let him kiss me again, try to soothe me to sleep. But I couldn't rest yet. My mind had started racing again.

I whispered to John, "Do you think it's because of them—the things—that we met?"

"We met because of a meteor shower," he replied.

"Do you really believe that?"

"I'll tell you what I don't believe. They don't control fate. They don't control the universe."

"How do you know?"

"I just do," he said. "There's just too much."

"Of?"

"Everything. Whatever they know—and maybe they do know more than us—it still can't be everything. And the more I think about that, about them and us, what can possibly be going on between us, the only answer I can come up with is that the mystery deepens."

"I don't know what that means," I told him.

"Nobody does," John replied. "Least of all, me." He sighed deeply, on the edge of sleep. "Close your eyes, Julia." he said. "There's nothing to be afraid of."

I had heard almost those same words before of course, in another room, in another small upstate town. *Don't be afraid, Julia.* But that time, in a late hour, in the long ago, it was Laura speaking. And she was waking me up to go out into the night.

# XII

WE LEFT VERY early the next morning. I told John that I didn't want to see or talk to Nicky, and he didn't ask why. Still, after I went downstairs and got into the car, he walked back into the Stargazer's Embassy and was gone for about ten minutes. I assumed he had awakened Nicky and had some kind of conversation with him. That was John, that was his nature: not to interfere but to leave doors open, just in case. When he returned to the car, he said nothing to me, just smiled, turned on the radio, and headed down Main Street.

I think it was in my mind that I was never going to come back to Freelingburg again, but I didn't have any dramatic feelings about that one way or the other. I was dead inside, numb. The town itself was still asleep; curtains drawn, doors locked. Even the Stargazer's Embassy seemed lifeless: one more old bar in an old town far away from anything that anyone might care about.

As the wintry rural roads gave way to cold highways, I sat silently in the passenger seat, watching cars and trucks streaming by. The colors of the vehicles were dulled by the poor daylight, which refused to brighten. A reluctant sun allowed only one gray hue to replace another across the heavy blanket of the sky. John drove straight through, hour after hour, navigating the highway miles and then the clogged chokepoints of the approaches to Manhattan without a word. Sometimes, he reached over and stroked my hair. Sometimes, he twined his fingers with mine for a moment, or laid a hand on my leg. He was just making contact, just keeping the distance between us something that I guess he felt he could measure by an internal reckoning of his own. But he still didn't try to talk to me. I don't think I could have responded if he did. All I wanted, at that point, was to go home to the carriage house, to get into bed in the small, chilly downstairs bedroom and pull the comforter over my head. I wanted to go back to sleep and maybe never wake up. At least, not for a very long time.

By late morning, we were back in the city. John eased the old Volvo down Paper Lane and parked near the front door of the carriage house. We couldn't leave it in the narrow lane for too long, but John said that since we hadn't even had breakfast that morning, he wanted us both to go inside and have something to eat before he took the car to the garage. He also told me that he'd cancelled his patients for today so we could both rest. I tried to remember whose apartment I was supposed to clean today—who would be furious that their granite countertops might remain covered with crumbs, whose floors wouldn't shine, sinks wouldn't gleam—but I couldn't bring up the calendar I carried in my mind and didn't have the energy, or the interest, to root around in my backpack and find my pocket datebook. Me, the world's most responsible cleaning lady: today I didn't care about anyone or anything, least of all who didn't get the services they expected. Later, I'd make up some excuse for not showing up and both the client and the cleaning agency would have to accept it. If not, I didn't care about that, either.

I let John steer me upstairs to the kitchen, feed me scrambled eggs and tea, and then lead me back downstairs to the bedroom. I wrapped myself in the comforter, put my head down on the pillow, and then heard John leave the house, locking the door behind him. I heard the car's engine start up and fade away, like a voice trailing off to a whisper.

I closed my eyes, expecting to sleep, but that didn't happen. I lay in bed for what felt like a long time, but as tired as I was, I could not drift off. Instead, a familiar feeling came over me: the alert went on. My attention level went up and then shot off the charts.

I threw off the comforter and got out of bed. Cautiously, I went out into the sitting room that led to the garden but it was empty, quiet. I opened the garden door but that patch of paving and bare soil looked as lonely as it had all winter, with its wrought iron chairs and planters pushed away, into a corner. There was nothing out here.

Still, I knew one of the things was around. At least one. I doubted that it was the thing with the dead baby because I had finally decided that particular horror scene had indeed been presented to me only because Alice was there; the shock value, if that was the point, required both of us to have the experience at the same time. But I knew that didn't mean I was going to be left alone today, so where were they? And what kind of new game was this, if it was a game? They never left until they at least had a chance to show themselves to me, whether I actually acknowledged them or not. And they never made me come looking for them, so I considered simply taking a seat in the room off the barren garden and waiting, but I was feeling too edgy for that. Some new component of my interaction with the things had been added this morning, some level of anxiety that I hadn't quite experienced before. I began searching through the house, looking in every room but found nothing.

I was standing in the vestibule outside John's office, deciding whether or not I should go in, when I heard a footfall on the doorstep outside. Then, I heard the scraping sound of a key being inserted into the front door lock. I knew that was John, coming home from parking the car in the garage. I watched the doorknob turn, asking myself if I was going to tell him how I was feeling, if I was somehow obligated, now, to report every aspect of what I saw or perceived that might relate to the things. The twenty-four hour patient: was that how I was going to live now? Was that who I was going to be?

Selfish, stupid thoughts—later, that was how I would remember these few moments. Because as they flashed through my mind, the door opened and I saw that John wasn't alone: Alice was standing behind him, in the lane.

I never quite untangled the sequence of events that followed, but Alice must have arrived sometime after John left to return the car to the garage. She had hidden in a doorway, waiting for him—but no, that's not right: she was waiting for me, actually. Having no idea of what had transpired after I left the house the previous day, she just assumed that I had eventually come home and patched things up with John—why not? That was how she lived, lurching from one disturbing experience to another and just marking time in between, so she expected me to be home all day. That was how she thought of me, how bad and useless a person she believed I was—well, half a person, anyway—living not only in John's house but also on his money, since she had no idea that I worked. Not wanting to announce herself, since that might have given me, at least, the chance to slam the door in her face, once she arrived at the lane she waited until the moment that someone opened the door to let her slip into the house.

She didn't have to wait long—and it was John who let her in. But he didn't really intend to: he pushed open the door, saw me standing in the hallway and smiled at me. I read that smile almost as a reply to my own racing thoughts: *I'm home, I'm home. Everything will be alright.* But then he heard Alice behind him and turned to look at her.

"Alice," he said. That was all, just her name. But that one word, spoken as two syllables, seemed to emerge into the air on the stream of John's breath. I almost thought I could see it, spelling itself out as he spoke. *Alice.* The name began constructing itself out of a sense of surprise but it soon filled up with the other elements of the connection that existed between these two, which stretched back into a time when I was no one to either of them, nothing. I heard concern, fondness, even friendship, but also another note, the one that ended everything he breathed into her name, a new factor that I knew was attributable to me. In John's voice I also heard apprehension.

Standing behind John, I saw Alice's face contort into a mixture of grief and rage. "Why did you send me away yesterday?" she demanded of John. "Why did you tell Jim to take me home?"

"Come inside," John said to her. "We have a lot to talk about."

"I don't want to talk," Alice cried. "I am through talking. I've talked and talked and talked for year after year and nothing helps," she said. "Nothing! And then you let that...thing into your house! You let yourself fall in love with one of them."

*Thing.* The bizarre idea flashed into my head that Alice was reading my mind, that she had picked out my word from the collection of descriptions we all used for the beings who troubled our lives. Maybe the idea *was* crazy, but if it were true, I don't think I would have been in the least bit astounded. Indeed, in that moment, I thought that nothing could startle me anymore, nothing that I could conceive of happening might not suddenly present itself to me, traveling over the human horizon with a smirk on whatever face it was wearing and mouthing a greeting that went something like, *Oh, you thought this was impossible? Really? Whose life have you been living, anyway?*

But my attention quickly shifted back to the scene being played out in front of me. Standing on the doorstep, John didn't even try to address Alice's accusations. Once again, he tried to persuade her to come into the house. "Please," he said. "Let's figure all this out together. I know that I can still help you."

"I don't want your help," she said. "I don't want anything from you anymore."

She suddenly lunged past him. John turned, still thinking, I guess, that despite her protests she would push past me as well and go into this office. I thought the same thing so stepped back, away from the office door, but she just kept coming at me, striding into the vestibule until we stood face to face.

"You're not human," she said. "You're a monster. You don't deserve to live. Not anywhere on this earth, but most of all, not in this house. Not with John."

I didn't even try to answer her—I just wanted to get away. I turned and quickly walked out of the narrow vestibule, escaping into the sitting room. There was a sliding pocket door here that we rarely used; I tried to pull it out of its slot to shut off the sitting room from the vestibule but it was stuck. Alice continued to advance in my direction. She was past the stairs now, so I couldn't go up to the second floor and my only other way of getting away from her was to go out into the chilly garden and slam that door in her face.

John was right behind her. He had his hand on her arm but she kept pulling away and I suppose he didn't want to be rough with her. Still, he delayed her enough for me to open the heavy wooden door that led to the garden. And there I stood, half turned toward the door, half turned towards Alice, when she repeated, "You don't deserve to live." And as she sent that last word out of her mouth she also raised her hand. Her thin hand, veins taut, fingers gripping an enormous knife.

I couldn't believe what I was seeing. Me, who had seen creepy crawlies dressed in mismatched tag sale remnants, *things* wearing baseball caps and ragged boys' pajamas patterned with rocket ships—to me, a young woman with a murderous expression on her face and a carving knife in her hand was still an image I could not process. But she was coming towards me at what seemed like a mile a minute, and my brain quickly started telling my feet to move. Message received, but nothing happened. I was frozen to the spot.

Then, suddenly, John was between us. It was almost as if he had moved the air aside and slid into the hair's breadth of space that still separated me from Alice and that knife, which was meant for me. And so, not meaning to—I was her target, I know that, there is no disputing that—she stabbed him instead.

Almost immediately, John slid to his knees and fell sideways, with his head twisted towards the floor. I knew from the way his body lost all its strength in an instant, as if all the power lines had been cut and darkness descended around him, that he was dead. Blood began pumping out of his chest, a stream of it, a red river, soaking into the rug on the floor. The part of me that wanted to pretend none of this was happening sent out a cleaning-lady report—*You'll never be able to mop that up*—before every system in my body and brain that was not marshalling itself to face Alice and the knife she was still holding, completely shut down.

I was now in some sort of automaton-like state: I opened my mouth: I may have screamed—who knows? I was so deep inside myself that I couldn't have heard anything that came out of my own soul, if I had one. I do know that I took a step forward to lunge at Alice, meaning to knock her down or grab the knife or do *something*, when another report was sent from my sentinel self, the guard I had no control over, who never went off duty. The message was, *They're here.*

My impression was that they came in from the garden, but that's just a way of trying to use a description that means something in the context of the world I understood. *They came in from the garden* means the feeling I had all morning that a thing—though now it seemed not just one but several—was, were, somewhere around me. *They came in from the garden* means that a stream of things, maybe three, maybe four, maybe ten—or maybe it really was just one, moving in some way, at some speed that made me think I saw a number of them at once, all dressed in boots and capes and wearing necklaces that appeared to be made out of steel teeth, since I can think of no other way to describe the decorations it, they, were adorned with—entered the sitting room and occupied that same space where John had stood. Their backs were towards me, with their blank-eyed, black-eyed, creepy-crawly, pale gray and unreadable faces pointed towards Alice. They formed a wall between us. And though I didn't want to believe it, I knew what they were doing. They were protecting me from her.

And then the world—or *our* world, anyway, mine and Alice's, though it is a terrible idea, that she and I at that moment occupied the same time and space—asserted itself again. Sound came back, my thoughts, feelings, *self* came back, and I heard Alice scream. I heard her scream over and over again, and saw her drop the knife and begin to back away from the gray things.

Then they turned towards me. I say *they* turned towards me but when I looked into those depthless, unblinking black eyes, I saw only one face, one creepy-crawly thing. It was thin, spindly, almost, but there was also something aggressive about it, a posture of strength and surprising steeliness (which perhaps explained the bizarre necklace of metal teeth, though that would be a only a guess). As it faced me, the thing raised its arm and pointed a jointless finger at me—or I thought it was pointing at me until it moved the finger, slightly, away from my face so that it was gesturing towards the garden door. It wanted me to go outside, to get away from Alice.

The instinct that had earlier sent me in that direction however, did not respond. Instead, some explosive brew of emotions that had been churning around inside me all morning—no, for longer, even: I could say, *since everything that had happened last night, yesterday,* but that would only be a tiny portion of what I was feeling, only a sliver of a slice of a fraction of the emotions that had gathered together, met and marshaled themselves under a meteor shower, perhaps, but really, it was even longer ago, farther back than that—let itself loose without allowing for any possibility of control. All bets were off, all boundaries crossed, all hope hopelessly lost.

"Me?" I cried to the thing. "You want to save me? What about John? You couldn't have come a minute sooner? You couldn't have stopped her before she killed him?"

The thing barely acknowledged me. It just kept its finger pointed towards the door. As always, I could read nothing in its face, but my sense of experiencing a stubborn willfulness emanating from the core of the being standing before me grew stronger—and so did mine.

"No!" I spat at it. "Don't tell me what to do!"

*Oh,* I heard myself think. *I'm talking to Laura.* In my crazed, confused, half-dead state, here she was again, in this room with me, and I was fighting her along with her visitors. *My* visitors. Mine.

That was it: that was my last fully formed thought for a while. In the next instant, so many memories, cries of defiance, fear, and rage slammed together that they seemed to take over, animating every muscle, cell, sinew in my body. There was a small side table standing in a corner just a few feet away from me. I turned, lifted it up, and swung it towards the thing, smashing it in the head. The unblinking eyes never changed but the slit that served as its mouth opened an inch or two and a sound came out—that high-pitched, cat-like mewling I had heard before.

I swung the chair again, then again, and again until my arms began to ache. I heard Alice screaming, saw John's body still bleeding on the floor.

And I saw a field I was being led across, a woods in front of me, a clearing I was being taken to and did not want to reach ever again. I kept on hitting the thing until it finally backed away from me, moved past Alice and seemed to vanish into the shadows of the room. Then, when it was gone, I finally turned to leave and, driven by my own free will, went out into the cold, bare garden and slammed the door.

# PART TWO: 2000

# I

*DEATH IS NOT real to me.*

That was the thought that came to me in a child's bedroom in Tarrytown, New York, as I stopped where I stood, my hand raised to spray glass cleaner on the window. Looking out through the heavy curtains of sunlight that fell across the yard towards the swimming pool filled with bright, blue water and the fence that separated the residential properties on this street from the edge of a suburban woodland beyond, I thought I saw some movement ripple through the lower branches of the leafy elms. It was just out of my direct line of sight, something I saw with the corner of my eye. Outside, out there, it was a hot, thick day; there was no breeze, no one around, nothing that should have caused any kind of disturbance in the foliage.

So what? A few branches swayed, leaves rustled; not everything a person sees, or thinks they do, needs to be explained. But I was not just *a person*, not just anyone, and my thoughts went their own way. Now, they leapt back through the years and returned to me with a familiar conclusion seemingly unconnected to the rustling in the trees, real or imagined, but for me, the connection was made before I even formed the words to think about it.

The connection was Laura, my walker in the woods. In rain and snow, sun and shadow, I had watched her from my window, setting off across the fields, until she was lost to my vision as she entered the deep woods. And because I thought of Laura, I also thought of John. And because of them both, death. The connection was her death, his death, the events and forces that had brought me here, to this ordinary hour of an ordinary summer day, my vision beginning to swim with the starbursts of light that come from staring out into a great brightness, and thinking that I myself could disappear at any moment, dissolve into the sun and shadow and become someone who *is*, and then *is not*. You are and then you are not. Laura was, John was. And now they were not. Had not been for years and years. So where were they? Anyplace, anywhere? Certainly, they were not with me, as I stood at the window, knowing that they were dead but unable to feel anything else about that fact except that it kept recurring to me. And when it did, it was their death—deaths—that quickly dissolved and disappeared. They were gone.

I kept staring out the window, looking, looking. And then, in a moment, a deer appeared at the edge of the woods. Standing in a narrow clearing between the fence and the tree line, it dipped its head to pull some grass from the loamy ground. It raised its head, seeming to stiffen, for a moment, as it sniffed the invisible ribbons of air and then turned to walk quickly back into its world, its life in the realm of elms and pines. I was relieved: there was a plausible reason, cause and effect (deer in its habitat, grass growing in the summer sun) for the disturbance in the heat, the air, the edge of my vision. But I could forgive myself for feeling anxious, if only for a moment, even though nothing troubling had appeared there, off in the margins, for close to a decade. Not that I looked into the margins anymore—not so much, anyway. Blinders on, as tight as could be: that was how I thought of myself. Looking straight ahead, walking a straight line. Still, one thing I did not do, though, not ever, was to let my guard down. Even in this new version of my old life, which is what I had constructed, or reconstructed—all I seemed to know how to do—I never completely relaxed. In terms of time, the kind that existed on clocks and calendars, I knew the difference between the past, the present and the future, but for me, the difference was minimal. My life without John was much like my life before him, just as I could say the same for Laura, and even Nicky, who in a way, was now dead to me, too, since I hadn't spoken to him after the last night I'd spent at the Stargazer's Embassy. These people were ghosts; I made an effort to let myself believe that they always had been. Yes, they had scarred me. Yes, they had added and subtracted from who I was, but as living beings, I had let them go. If they still lived at all for me, it was in the ghost realm, the margins, with the things. That was where I had consigned them; that was where I needed them to stay.

It was for those reasons, all of them, that I didn't take a lot of time to peer out into the summer morning. I finished cleaning the window and pulled down the shade. Then I walked around the pretty, pink-themed room with stuffed animals on the bed, picking up a discarded tee-shirt from the floor, a ruffled swimsuit from a chair beside a child-sized desk. I dropped these things into a plastic basket with other laundry to be done and carried them down to the basement in the empty, quiet, sun-filled house.

Here, it was darker, a little cooler. I took the clothes and sheets I had collected from the rest of the house, put them in the washing machine and turned it on. Then I sat down on the concrete floor, rested my head on my knees and closed my eyes. I had more work to do in this house but I needed a break for a few minutes. For just a few minutes, I wanted to rest.

*****

*Death is not real to me.*

In the long reeling out of weeks and months and even years that passed through me, by me, that began and never ended after the final morning I spent in the carriage house on Paper Lane—the last hour, sitting in the wintry garden, surrounded by blank brick walls and a stack of empty planting pots—there were, of course, many other thoughts I had about what had happened in that place. There were feelings, too, and nightmare-inducing sense memories that were terrible, overwhelming, bathed in grief. But over time, that one idea—*death is not real to me*—forged itself from the lingering features of all the others as they finally began to fade away. And as it took shape, it began to appear unbidden on the message board that, as I pictured it, sat at the front of my mind, waiting to be written upon whether I (me, the Julia up here, out here, in the everyday world of work and sleep and traveling back and forth from here to there) wished it, or willed it, or not. The message board that I nevertheless tried my hardest to keep blank in order to shield me from whatever went on in the deeper, darker reaches of whoever I was then, the me of the aftermath, the after-days. But without my knowing why, or when, more and more often as time went by, a message appeared there, a note from the underground, that seemed constantly to want my attention. *Death is not real to me.* Each time the message demanded that I receive it, I replied, *So what? Shut up.* Who was I talking to? Myself, perhaps. Perhaps the dead. Or others—but I wasn't ready to consider anything like that.

Instead, what I considered was that in my life, I had experienced two very different deaths: Laura's and John's. Laura had died in a hospital—quickly, as far as I knew, though I probably knew very little. She went into the hospital one week and died the next. I saw her once, and that was a reluctant visit; I had no idea how sick she really was and I was in one of my pulling-as-far-away-from-her-as-I-could states, so Nicky had to drag me to the hospital in Ithaca where I sat in a chair and glowered at my mother, who looked, to me, like she always did. Pretty, young, witchy, in a way, with her long black hair and dark, shadowy eyes. I was shocked when Nicky came home from the hospital a few days later and told me she had died. She had cancer; stomach, liver, something like that—I should have always remembered what it was, because he told me, but I didn't. The cause didn't matter to me because it didn't change how I felt, and all I felt was angry at her—fury. How dare she leave me when I wasn't finished fighting with her, punishing her for not being the mother I wanted, the kind of nice, regular person that all the other kids I knew had for a mom? And then, of course, when her visitors began plaguing me, I grew angrier at her, still. How can a person be really dead if you go on living a life so connected to theirs that you cannot release yourself from those ties? If you cannot resolve your feelings about them because your days and nights continue to reference them in almost everything you do, whether you consciously think about it or not. They continue to exert their influence but you continue to deny it by pretending it does not exist.

Now I had John's memory to contend with as well. I missed him, but selfishly, even more I mourned the life we had together for the moments it gave me when I was almost at peace. And I came to believe that, brief as it was, that might have been the only life, the only time, I would ever really be able to share with another human being because, for all the secrets we kept from each other, there was something between us that we accepted equally: the idea that having a normal, regular life, whatever one understood that to be, also had to be understood as—for some of us, at least—a longed-for condition that only existed sometimes. Sometimes other things happened, sometimes other conditions—strange, inexplicable, but manageable, maybe; meaningful, even, if John could have ever found a way to prove that to be so—also applied.

But he never got the chance to prove anything, not even to me. And I blamed him for that, for the fact that as much as I protested that I wasn't listening to him, of course I was, or else, I might have. *Don't be afraid, Julia. Don't be afraid.* As much as I told myself that I never was, as much as that was or wasn't true, I still needed to hear it, wanted to hear him say that over and over and over again. But now, there was no one to tell me that anymore. No one at all.

Was that what I was thinking, that last hour in the bare garden, scoured by the winter wind? Now, I couldn't remember, really—all I was able to conjure up from that first day were images, freeze-frames from a movie that I watched because for the longest time I could not feel like I was actually a participant in my own life, or what my life had become after I slammed the garden door. I do recall the door being opened again by uniformed policemen, about being gently gripped by the arm and guided back through the house, past John's body, which I did not look at, and the absence of Alice, which I wondered about, and then out the front door. I was taken to the police station a few blocks away and answered a lot of questions. I told them what had happened except, of course, that I never mentioned the things. No matter what mental or emotional state I was in, I still knew how to protect myself—that much never changed. I was hardly going to tell a bunch of boys from Brooklyn—the policemen I talked to, guys with outer-borough attitudes and Bay Ridge accents, trying to be at least civil to me, the bereaved, the girlfriend, the victim in the narrative they were creating—that I was alive because beings from beyond here, beyond someplace, had protected me and I, in turn, had tried to murder them, it—whatever. But apparently, that's what Alice told them because the Bay Ridge boys repeated her story to me. I told them she was crazy. She was jealous. She was weaving together her many fantastic stories about alien abduction (*Oh, she's that woman from the talk shows,* one of my boys in blue said to the others; *my wife likes that stuff*) with her rage at me for sleeping with John. I was her target, I explained. I was the one she was after and John had stepped between us. I felt nothing about telling the story this way because it wasn't a lie. It was the truth stripped of the parts they wouldn't believe. And in the end, it didn't change the outcome for Alice, though she changed everything for me.

Here's more about the end—of this part of my life, anyway. The police and the prosecutors I had to talk to found their own way to create a pragmatic frame around a series of events that seemed like the script of a made-for-tv-movie. They did that by treating me, of all people, like I was the only survivor of a kind of cult; the sane one, the girl who resisted the madness. John was the kindly doctor who had suffered exile and defamation by trying to help a bunch of delusional followers of Jim Barrett, the amateur alien hunter who had become famous by feeding on the fear and anxiety of misguided and probably mentally ill people like Alice Giddings. In the weeks that followed John's death, I had many conversations with the Bay Ridge boys and other men and women with neighborhood accents that spanned the boroughs and traveled down the turnpike across the Hudson River (I heard Jersey, Queens, Staten Island), and in their flat, urban tones they told me how they had come to my rescue, as they saw it (*You were just sitting out there, in that garden, in the cold; you would have gotten frostbite or that crazy Alice Giddings would have found another knife in the kitchen and come after you again*), and followed up by telling me, probably, more than they should have about what they believed they knew about all of us. They were serious and thoughtful about compiling evidence, taking statements, but bemused (as much as they tried to hide it) by the characters (as I overheard them describing Jim and Alice) they had to deal with as they constructed their case.

That was how I found out it was Jim Barrett who had called the police that morning. I heard this from one of the prosecutors, a young, no-nonsense beauty who wore either black or blood-colored high heels every day and suits so sharp and tight that I thought of them as steel-cut armor. Apparently, Alice had actually phoned Barrett from the carriage house and told him what she had done. Then she sat down by John's body and waited for the next event to take place, whatever it was going to be. She sat on one side of the door and I sat on the other. I thought about that once in a while. We were waiting for different things to end, and to begin.

Later, I heard that Alice's parents hired a lawyer for her who managed to separate her from Jim Barrett. He had acted as her representative, even her agent for many years, but the lawyer put a stop to that. He convinced Alice to accept a deal from the prosecutors that had her plead guilty by reason of mental defect and she was sentenced, not to prison, but to long-term care in a psychiatric institution. Barrett—the leader of the supposed yes-there-are-aliens-snatching-us-from-our-beds cult that Ms. Steel Suits and the law-and-order boys had talked up so much that, for a while, every newspaper had a story about it, every cable channel had a nightly panel of experts discussing, dissecting, mouthing off about the group—was sued by her parents in civil court and forbidden to write anything more about her, or to discuss the case in any public forum. He was, Steel Suits told me, furious about all this but in particular, he was furious at me.

I already knew that, because sometime during those first hours that I was in the police station, Barrett had been put into the same room as me. It was an interrogation room in the Sixth Precinct on Christopher Street, and it looked exactly like these places look on tv cop shows, which just added to my sense of being estranged from anything that was happening to me, or around me. A catalogue of complaints against bad fortune could be read just by glancing at the battered file cabinets, peeling walls, the chairs that appeared to have been repeatedly punched by bleeding fists. I sat in one of these chairs, at a table that smelled like old coffee and cigarettes, watching the last, bleak edges of the morning scrape against the filthy window opposite me. Then it was afternoon; the light swam by, thick and whale colored. Then it was evening, presenting itself with dark, grim bars of starless, moonless nothing.

I had answered lots of questions, and believed that I had been believed. I had been brought food that I did not eat, coffee that I did not drink. These had been taken away and I had been given a blanket, because someone thought I was cold. I was. I wrapped the blanket around me, and waited while one set of cops left and told me another would be in soon. *Fine,* I told them in my compliant cleaning lady voice. *Anything you want.*

But when the door opened next, the person sent into the room was Jim Barrett. I knew I was supposed to think this was an accident, that some dumb clerk had made a mistake but these people didn't make mistakes; tired and removed as I was, my alert system was still highly functional and went from stand-by to full-on protect mode. The Bay Ridge boys were checking my story. They wanted to hear what the cult leader—as I'm sure they had already dubbed him—might say to me. What I might reply.

Barrett saw me, took a deep breath, and immediately started in. "Did you tell them what happened?" he asked me.

"Yes," I said, still using the cleaning lady's voice. "Alice stabbed John. She killed him."

"That's not what I mean," Barrett said angrily. He lowered himself into one of the abused chairs. "When she called me, Alice told me what she saw."

"What did she see?" I asked. Now the cleaning lady's voice had become weary, subdued.

"Don't fuck around with me," Barrett said. He leaned forward and pointed his finger at me. "I want you to tell the cops what really happened."

"Okay," I said. "What really happened?"

Barrett changed his posture, he changed his attitude. He pushed his body back into the chair, as if it was important to put some distance between us. He scowled at me, because I was only worth scowling at. "This is how you're going to play it? You think this is what John would want?"

"I don't know what John would want," I said. "He's dead."

"My God," Barrett said. "You are a piece of work."

I shrugged. That was my answer, but he wasn't having it, so he tried again. "Julia," he said, and it was hearing my name that finally made me flinch (though only inside; Barrett never saw it) because that was too personal; it did bring John back to me for a moment, a second (*Julia*, I heard him calling me from another room, in what was already another time; *Jules*), "this is too important. You can't go on pretending that you haven't seen them. That they weren't there."

"Alice was there," I said. "And me. And John. That's it."

He couldn't control himself—the pointing finger was back in my face. "You're lying. The grays were there. Alice told me they were—she told me what they did. And now you finally have to admit it. The grays were there!" he cried.

I just looked at him. Never mind who or what had been in the carriage house: what mattered was who was here now. I knew who that was, and so did Jim Barrett: there was a mirror on the wall behind me and on the other side were representatives of law and order. I had already signed my statement, which was bare, believable and straightforward. I had declared Alice crazy and jealous. I had not added, *Oh, and by the way: I was saved by little green (gray) men wearing metal teeth as necklaces.*

"Right," I said. "Of course. The grays were there." The cleaning lady took the edge of her blanket and wiped a spot on the table in front of her. Professional instinct; I hoped everyone took notice. "Is that what you want me to say?"

"I want you to tell the truth. It's important—you know how important. You can change everything. You can literally change the world."

"Me? I don't think so."

"But you know! You know! The grays are here. They're real and they're dangerous. We can work together on this—we can make a difference."

"Oh," I said. "I see."

He glared at me. "You see what?"

"Together?" I said. "What you mean is, you're going to need a new Alice."

"That's what you think? That's *all* you think, after everything that's happened?"

I didn't respond to him; instead I finished my own thought. "That's not me," I said. "I'm not like that. I'm not even Alice-ish."

"You think it helps to mock her?" Barrett demanded. "To mock me?"

"Nothing helps," the cleaning lady told him. Or maybe it was me. "That's the point."

Barrett sat across from me, fuming, trying to think of the next thing to say, the next way to approach me. All he managed to construct was a threat.

"This isn't over," he said, but anything that might have followed was quickly upstaged by the sound of the door opening. A new cop came into the room, a young woman in plainclothes, wearing serious glasses and a gold detective's badge on a chain around her neck.

The detective looked at me, then at Barrett. "You shouldn't be in here," she said to him. He turned his anger on her. "Hey," he said, "ten minutes ago, you people practically shoved me in here.

"It's not a good idea to say 'you people' to anybody anymore. Don't you know that?" the detective said. She grabbed Barrett's arm and tugged him out of his chair. As she led him out of the room, he turned back to me.

"You heard me, right?"

I said nothing. I looked towards the window, which continued to show me nothing at all.

Sometime later—an hour, a day; I had no idea because I had been sitting in that miserable room long enough to totally lose track of time—Steel Suits came in and introduced herself. Actually, this far removed from that time, I don't remember her real name. But I do remember what she said.

"I'm sorry for your loss."

I almost had to think about what she was saying, why she was saying that to me. The first thought I had was that the phrase sounded familiar and then I realized, of course. Television, again; that's what everyone said on cop shows, on tv.

"Thank you," I replied, hoping that I sounded the way I should have sounded, like a person who was shocked by what had happened to her; devastated by what she had witnessed. Which I was—but already I knew that also, I wasn't. Part of me wasn't, anyway, and that was where the message was forming, tentatively at first, but then, with greater and greater insistence.

*Death is not real to me.*

Was that day—those days—really the first time that idea began to transform itself into actual words in my mind? Maybe, but now I have come to doubt it. Given everything that happened afterwards, I think I may have known it all along.

# 11

THE MORNING AFTER I did the laundry and finished thoroughly cleaning the house in Tarrytown, I agreed to do something I had rarely done in recent years: I spent a day working in Manhattan. Or rather, Laura Glazer did, because that was what my name was according to the driver's license and other identification I had gotten with a copy of my mother's birth certificate and some basic ingenuity. No one at the cleaning agency that I now worked for ever questioned the age discrepancy because I labored in a business of illegal hires; it was a plus, I suppose, that I had any legitimate-looking i.d. at all. Ms. Glazer, whoever she was, had an apartment in the Bronx now, and the cleaning agency that sent her out on jobs was based in Scarsdale. When I went to work, I always went north; I rode buses to the bedroom communities ranged around the city, walked suburban streets to houses surrounded by lawns and trees and leafy views. I had an unlisted phone number and a post office box in Laura's name, and did nothing to attract attention to myself—or to me-as-Laura. In and out of my disguise, I lived a quiet life.

And I almost never went into the city, which helped to complete the break with the previous life that I had imposed on myself. Not that I didn't have help in making the decision to disappear, as much as possible, from the life I had led with John; in that respect, I had plenty of reasons, because while the police and prosecutors had treated me with great consideration—and why not? Had there been a trial, I would have been their main witness—the press showed no such empathy. Jim Barrett had it worse than me, which

159

I took some satisfaction from. He had undergone a public battering after John's murder—*Cult Leader Influenced Abduction Blonde* was one particularly creative newspaper headline I could recall now—but the media had not exactly left me alone, either. I wouldn't talk to them but I couldn't prevent them from describing me any way they chose, and often, what they chose was *Slain Prof's Mystery Gal Pal* and various similar and equally colorful names. When the narrative proved juicy enough to be featured on the national news, I became the survivor of the alien-addled killer's jealous rage. And then the story morphed again: it took on new life when it could be portrayed as some sort of lascivious love triangle with an alien cult angle. I would turn on my tv and see a photo of me leaving the police station (boots, long hair, blood on my shirt; a set designer couldn't have dressed me better for the role of mystery galpal) juxtaposed next to some official university snapshot of John, looking serious and ten times my age, along with Alice's Midwest blonde sweetie face—and of course, the now-famous, always repeated rendering of a blank-eyed alien with gray stick arms, its visage void of affect, its soul-less demeanor completely horrifying. Reporters stood outside the door of the house on Paper Lane and made me sound like the Greenwich Village version of a post-hippie-era gold-digger girlfriend, who had moved into the prof's posh townhouse. There was more of that kind of thing every day for weeks. I had to escape it, and part of the way out was to leave at least my part of the city—the mystery galpal's streets, her places, her haunts—behind me.

But today was an exception. I was going to venture back into my personal exclusion zone because of a client who was particularly valuable to the agency since they had a huge house in Larchmont that they paid regularly and promptly to have cleaned, by me, top to bottom every week. The family's only daughter was starting college in the fall and her parents had rented an apartment for her in the East Village, not far from the school, and they wanted it thoroughly cleaned before they moved in any furniture. They liked the work of humble, efficient Laura, and so had insisted that I do the job. The agency told me to go and I couldn't come up with a reason not to, so I said yes, of course: Ms. Glazer would take her skills and cleaning products to East Seventh Street and do her job.

It was Wednesday; mid-week, mid-summer. I took the number 4 train from the Woodlawn Station in the northwest Bronx and rode for an hour, changed for the number 6 local at 14th Street, rode one stop more and got out at Astor Place, a wide thoroughfare with a huge, black sculpture of a cube standing on one corner at its epicenter. The cube, installed in such a way that it could be rotated by passersby who had the impulse to try to spin it, marked the divide between the East and West Village. I walked past the cube without touching it and headed east.

This was an old, immigrant neighborhood of narrow streets with narrow buildings, many were turn-of-the-century tenement structures with dark hallways and railroad flats where one tiny room opened into another. But in the later part of this century, the refugees from Europe's rural backwaters had moved on and the counterculture had moved in. What I remembered from years ago when I used to take an occasional walk down here, was a mixture of the old and new: Ukrainian bakeries and Russian tailors sewing behind the dusty windows of their storefronts along with headshops and tarot card readers and second-hand clothing stores selling flowered skirts and toe rings. The air smelled like marijuana; people sat on stoops playing guitars.

But now, it seemed the area had changed again. Some of the buildings had been torn down and replaced with terraced co-op units; men and women in expensive clothes were hurrying towards Astor Place to ride the subway uptown, to their offices. Health food stores abounded as did bars with ironic names and all kinds of places to work out, from big-name gyms to boutique yoga studios. Against this background, the busboys taking a break for a smoke outside the restaurants where they worked, the dog walkers, the nannies, and the cleaning ladies, like me, all looked exactly like what we were: the hired help. Here for a few hours only, and then gone.

I wasn't as surprised by all these changes as I might have been if I were someone else: I had been through enough unexpected cycles already to just take in the new landscape and walk on. I found the address I was looking for—a hundred-year-old building that had been completely renovated. I had been given the keys so I let myself in, walking through history. A marbled lobby floor was laid over whatever workers' footsteps had trod here in the past; a mirrored elevator took me to the top floor, where what must have been a warren of small rooms had been chopped up and put back together as a trio of spacious units. The apartment I let myself into had a bedroom with a walk-in closet, a brand-new kitchen gleaming with stainless steel appliances, and a bright, airy living room that had tall windows looking out at Tompkins Square Park. The first thing I did was pull the shades; I didn't need to see any parkland today; no trees, not even the semblance of a woods, whether bathed in sun or shadow.

There wasn't all that much to clean in this luminous, empty apartment, but I did my job anyway. As I worked, I listened to my new music player, a brand-new gadget I had bought from a guy who hung around my bus stop in the early morning selling bootleg electronics. A rectangular black box with a grayish LED screen and a round pad with directional control buttons, it was about the size of a deck of cards and easily fit in the pocket of my jeans. It was called a Diamond Rio and played digital MP3 files which, the bootlegger explained to me, could be downloaded from the Internet. I didn't have a computer, let alone a modem or online connection, but there was a place on the main shopping avenue near where I lived that purported to be an Internet café (no coffee, no pastries—no nothing, really except a few refurbished terminals, some clanky printers, and powerful, hot-wired connections to every questionable web site you might want to do a little business with). It was situated in a tiny storefront squeezed between a transmission repair shop and a check-cashing service. I was the only woman who ever seemed to enter the place, but I learned a lot from my fellow low-wage workers who spent their off-hours here, carrying out all kinds of transactions I didn't need to know anything about and then relaxing by searching for porn. They showed me how to access file-sharing web sites and fill my little Diamond Rio with classic album tracks and unreleased demo tunes that people all over the world were uploading for their geek friends, which now included me. I could spend ten dollars for an hour of online time and get hundreds of free songs. So, now, on the top floor of the ex-tenement in the East Village, I kept myself plugged in as I cleaned the already shining surfaces, scrubbed the brand-new tiles, polished the hardwood floors.

By early afternoon, I couldn't find anything else to do, so I loaded my cleaning supplies into my backpack, and headed out the door. Downstairs, lulled into something like laziness by the sunshine and the ease of the day's work, I decided to treat myself to lunch so I went looking for some non-upscale restaurant where I could sit in a cool corner and watch the street life wander by outside, in the light. I thought I would try St. Mark's Place, the more-or-less main street of the neighborhood, where I hoped a falafel place I remembered was still around.

It wasn't, but as I turned onto St. Mark's from Second Avenue, I spotted a pizzeria up the block, so started in that direction, which would also lead me back to Astor Place and the subway. This was a busy area; lots of shops and foot traffic so I walked slowly, looking in windows and taking in the mixed-signal scenery: a boutique selling sky-high priced dresses next to a junk store offering Tibetan trinkets and hash pipes, with a frozen yogurt shop and Karaoke bar across the street.

"Julia!"

I thought I heard someone call my name but that seemed unlikely. I didn't know anyone anywhere around here and no one knew me.

"Julia! Hey, stop for a sec."

I just kept walking. *Forget lunch*, I told myself. *Head to the subway.*

But then a man came striding up from behind me and a familiar face—yes, still familiar, I had to admit—placed itself in front of mine.

"I thought it was you. I saw you from the window of my shop."

The silver hoops in one ear, the black disc in the other, along with the bar piercing under his lip and the snake tattoo curling around his neck— they were familiar, too. His hair was longer, though; even tied back in a ponytail with a piece of leather twine, I could see that it was streaked with gray. His outfit was bad-guy summer gear: a black tee shirt printed with a gap-toothed, grinning skull and a pair of ripped black jeans.

"Hi, Kel," I said. I suppose I could have added, *nice to see you*, but I didn't think it was.

He looked at me with an intensity I remembered from our long-ago meeting in Jim Barrett's kitchen. Bad guy on the outside, maybe, but definitely somebody else inside.

"It's weird, seeing you wandering down St. Mark's like this," he said. "Just out of the blue." That was what he said, but not what he meant; he sounded more like he was asking himself a question—was this just a random event, running into me after so long? Maybe he was deciding that he didn't think so, but I told him otherwise.

"I had a job down here," I said.

"So you're still doing the same thing? Cleaning houses."

I shrugged. "It's work."

"Yeah, we all need to work. Pay those bills, right?"

Again, I shrugged. I was hoping to end this conversation and be on my way—at least, that was what I believed was my wish—but I wasn't exactly pulling away from Kel. I was standing in the street, looking at him, listening.

"My shop's right over there," he said, gesturing to a sign bolted to an iron railing in front of one of the old buildings on the block: it depicted a black snake curling around spiky red letters that spelled out "St. Mark's Tattoos." The tail of the snake ended in an arrow that pointed to the shop entrance, which was below street level. "Why don't you come in for a while and we can talk?" Kel said. He looked back at the sign again, then at me. "It's not as gloomy as it looks. We can sit out back."

"Okay," I said, but before I followed him, I looked at my watch. My deciding to talk to him came with conditions: I wasn't sure, myself, what they were, but there had to be some. Maybe I could begin with putting a limit on the time I was going to spare.

He led me down to the shop where an already heavily tattooed man was in the middle of having a bleeding rose inked on his back. The guy doing the tattoo gave Kel a brief nod but other than that, neither he nor his customer paid any attention to us as we walked through the two small rooms of the shop. The space towards the front was where the work was being done; behind it, an even smaller room, containing a dented file cabinet and metal desk, seemingly served as an office. The walls of both rooms were papered with drawings and designs for tattoos. Music that sounded like it was being broadcast from a death star—what else would have made sense here?—was banging out of a boom box that sat amid the scattered papers on the desk.

But when we walked out the back door the scenery was quite different. We were in an alley that was still below street level, but just above us, separated by only a rusty chain-link fence, was a green, dandelion-dotted yard that belonged to a church on the next street—I could see its spire pointing up at the summer sky.

Kel unfolded a pair of metal chairs that had been leaning against a wall then went back inside. He returned quickly, with two dark brown bottles of beer. I must have looked like I wasn't sure if I wanted the one he handed me because he said, "Come on, let's have a drink. We're old friends."

"Is that what we are?"

"I don't know," he said. "We're certainly something."

I sipped the beer, which tasted sharply of bitter hops and alcohol. Definitely tattoo shop stuff; it went with the heavy metal music.

"So," Kel said. "How've you been?"

Despite myself, I laughed. "Really? You want a summary? We haven't seen each other in what—ten years?"

"I'm making polite conversation," Kel said. "You don't want to do that, fine. I can go back to work and you can just toddle off to wherever you were headed."

"I'm sorry," I said. "I could be nicer."

"As I recall," Kel said, "that's not exactly your style."

I laughed again, and this time, he smiled back. "Okay," he said. "Let's start again. Let's go back to that maybe we're friends, maybe not thing. I did try to get in touch with you...afterwards. After what happened. But I guess you weren't receiving visitors, wherever you were."

"I went back to the house once, just to get my things," I told him, surprising myself with how easy it was to not even think about telling him anything but the truth—at least, not yet. "And then I went to a hotel because I had given up my old apartment. Actually, the place I went was really a divey motel in Queens. One of the cops told me about it; he said it was less horrible than the other kinds of places he thought I could afford."

"Was it?"

"I don't know. It didn't matter one way or the other—I didn't stay very long."

"I figured something like that. But I thought you'd come to John's funeral—I looked for you there, too."

"You went?"

"I did. But not you."

"No. I didn't want to. I couldn't." *Of course not. Death is not real to me.*

Kel had no idea what I was thinking, so he made a guess that must have seemed obvious to him, even though it was wrong. "Maybe because you thought there would be people there you didn't need to see?"

I knew who he meant: Jim Barrett. I certainly had reason enough to avoid him, particularly after the scene at the police station, but at the time, I hadn't even thought about him. And I also hadn't even thought about John's funeral or who would plan it. As it turned out, I didn't have to—he had a sister who lived in Chicago, and she made all the arrangements. I knew her, sort of; at least I knew that while she and John weren't very close, they had stayed in touch. In the past, I had even spoken to her on the phone once or twice. She apparently tried to call me at the carriage house sometime during the day following John's death, but just like Kel, she couldn't reach me. She had done her best, though: she told one of the Bay Ridge Boys about the services and where John would be buried, and he passed on the information to me. But by then, I was already going, disappearing from the life in which she was connected to a person I had lived with. (*Julia; Jules.* That was hardly even a whisper in my ear anymore.)

"It wasn't that," I finally answered. "I just didn't want to go."

"Neither did I, really. I just thought I was supposed to." He glanced over at me, maybe to check on my reaction. "Not a criticism," he said.

"I didn't take it that way."

Kel drank some of his beer, squinted at the sun. "So where are you living now?" he asked. "You don't have to tell me if you don't want to."

"That's okay," I said, because it seemed to be. "I have a place in the Bronx."

"Far away. Well, sort of."

"It is," I said. "Far enough, anyway." And then I added, "For now."

Whatever that meant—I wasn't sure myself; it was just something to say—it seemed to make sense to Kel. We sat quietly together for a little while after that, drinking cold beer in the alley behind the churchyard. We were in a shady spot, in the shadows, really, while the afternoon sunshine stabbed at the grassy world on the other side of the fence.

Suddenly, Kel said, "Have you seen any of them since...well, since that day?"

He wasn't looking at me—he was staring off into the churchyard, so I couldn't read any particular expression on his face. But I didn't have to. I knew what he meant.

"You believed what Alice told everybody? I mean, what she said happened?"

"Yes," he said. "I did."

He was still staring off at the churchyard. This was my chance to say, *Well, if you believe that, fuck you,* and walk away, but I knew I wasn't going anywhere. The truth continued to decide to tell itself. "That wasn't the first time they showed up," I told Kel. "They've been with me all my life."

I never would have expected it, but suddenly, everything I hadn't said to anyone in years came rushing out of me—not since I'd told John the truth about my life. It felt like an enormous relief, like a confession. Like I had been waiting for someone to unburden myself to, and here he was: someone who had once defended me, who had banked on having another conversation that had now waited a decade. So maybe he was someone I should allow to cash in those chips because it was also likely he was someone who would understand everything I had to say.

And so I said everything, told it all. Kel listened without comment, sitting tipped back in his chair and nodding from time to time. When he finished his beer—and I finished mine, hardly noticing that I'd drained the bottle—he brought more, reclaimed his seat and went on listening as I started at the beginning and went through to the end.

I told him about Laura and Nicky, and about the Stargazer's Embassy. And I told him more: all about my life before John and then with him, at the carriage house. And about how that life was terminated; not only with Alice's violent act, but with mine. The coda to my story was also the admission I had started it with: that through all my life, through everything that had happened to me, the defining context of my existence was the bizarre and ultimately mystifying presence of the things.

"But not now," I said. "I haven't seen any of them since that last time, at the house, when Alice saw them, too."

Was that really true? It was—except for yesterday, when I looked out the window into that clearing at the edge of the woods. *But that was a deer,* I reminded myself. And told myself to believe it. "And you?" I asked Kel.

He shook his head. "No," he told me. "Just that one time I told you about, when I was a teenager. Which probably makes me the only experiencer in the world who wants to see them again. I'm not afraid of them," Kel said. "I just want some answers." He squinted up at the sun, then looked back at me. "You're not afraid either."

"After what happened, I think it's the other way around."

"Let's hope so," he said, he said, with a wide smile. "They probably need a little more ass kicking from our team. But most experiencers...well. I guess they're not like us." Maybe it was the use of the term John had taken as his own—*experiencer*—that turned the conversation back to him. "Did you hear that the university posthumously reinstated John?" Kel asked. "They issued an apology for what they put him through and the president made a big speech about academic freedom. Now that John's dead, he can do any research he wants."

I heard the scorn in Kel's voice and let it pass without comment. It was just one more fact that belonged in storage someplace; it didn't require any reaction from me. "I read about that," I told Kel. Sometimes, when I went online to download music, I let myself wander around the news sites and I had seen an article about the university's apology to "the prominent professor and noted psychiatrist murdered by one of his troubled patients." I had read something else, as well. "I saw that they published his book. I didn't think he had finished it."

"I heard that his sister let them have the manuscript, so I guess they published as much as he'd managed to complete. Did you read it?

"No," I said. I didn't necessarily want to hear about it either, but apparently, this afternoon, I was in some sort of free-fire zone. I would answer any question I was asked and listen to anything I was told.

"It drove Jim crazy. Or maybe crazier, I should say. Not a word about the aliens' plans to take over civilization with hybrids. It was all about how to help experiencers interpret their interactions with the creepy crawlies in a positive light—or at least, as positive as possible. Faith, hope and light—all that stuff." Finally, Kel looked in my direction. "I get the feeling that's not what you believe."

"I try not to believe anything, really," I said.

"I can understand that," Kel said. "Not my position, but hey, you're entitled."

"Great," I said. "Thanks."

"In a minute you're going to thank me for nothing," Kel said, "because now I'm going to tell you what Jim Barrett believes. He believes you helped to destroy him. All his work, all those years—he doesn't blame Alice; he blames you for the way the story played out in the papers, on tv, everything.

He came across seeming like a nut job. Like he drove Alice to think the things she did, act the way she did. He's still looking for you, you know? He still thinks that if you would tell the truth, he'd be vindicated. People would take him seriously again."

"People would take him seriously? That's hardly up to me."

"Maybe yes, maybe no," Kel said. "Like whether you and I are friends or not friends. It's a gray area." Suddenly, he let out a kind of sardonic guffaw. "I guess I just made a joke," he said.

Maybe, but I didn't think it was funny. "I'm not going near that man," I said. "I can't help him. I won't."

"I understand how you feel. He made terrible mistakes, especially with Alice. But that's what happens with true believers," Kel said. "They make mistakes. Big ones."

I was beginning to suspect that maybe I'd made a mistake myself. Maybe the thing with the deer yesterday had spooked me more than I thought and I had let my guard down too easily. Maybe I shouldn't have told Kel anything—but letting him know I felt that way wasn't going to help me, either. So I kept the focus on John. "I'm sure John would be so pleased to hear that he was murdered because of a terrible mistake."

"Who knows what he thinks now, wherever he is?" Kel said. "John was a true believer, too—in his own way."

"Wherever he is now? Give me a break," I said.

I decided that it was finally time to end this conversation. Kel must have guessed that, because he raised his hand in a gesture that could have been interpreted in any number of ways: *Wait, have patience, I'm sorry, what do I know, give me a break, too.* However, what it turned out to mean, at least after we both had a moment to reconsider why we were having this conversation, was, *Listen, there's more to say.*

"I guess you figured out that I do still talk to Jim occasionally," Kel said. "But don't worry; I won't tell him anything you said. I won't even let him know that I saw you. Promise. Double promise."

"He wouldn't be able to find me anyway, if he's looking for Julia Glazer. She is currently nonexistent. In theory, anyway."

"Ah," Kel said. "You've created a fake identity. That's always a good move."

Now we were back on better terms again; the bad boy and the cleaning lady with illegal documents had returned to common ground.

"Can I ask you a question?" Kel said.

"As long as it doesn't have the names Jim or Alice in it," I told him, and meant it.

"They're near the edges. But let me get away with that. Okay?"

"We'll see."

"Why you?" Kel asked. "Why do the creepy crawlies act so differently with you? They don't hurt you—they even let you hurt them and still, they protect you. Why?"

"I don't know."

Kel let a moment pass, and then another. A small breeze seemed to move the sunlight around, creating shadows in the grass of the churchyard. The afternoon was passing through its waning hours.

Finally, Kel said, "Are you sure?"

His question took time; my reply did not. "What difference does it make? They're gone."

He gave me a look that I thought meant he was revving up to be philo-sophical, but no: he was suddenly interested in joking with me. "Well, here's my thought" he said, "If they do come back, I certainly hope you're around, because you can hold them down while I beat the shit out of them."

"I thought what you wanted were answers."

"In lieu of that," he said, "I'll take violence, like I said. Want to be my partner in crime?"

"I'll tell you what," I said, "you'll be the first person I call if they get in touch again."

I really did want to go now: my reservoir of good will, wherever it had bubbled up from, was finally running low. I stood up, handed Kel my empty bottle of beer, and lifted my backpack from the ground. But before I left, Kel had one more thing to tell me.

"Did you hear that the carriage house burned down?"

Maybe it was just an afterthought, one more piece of information to add to the afternoon's data dump, but it had its effect on me: of all the things I'd heard and said in the past hour or so, somehow, this was the saddest. Maybe because it was the only thing I would have never expected.

"No," I said. "I didn't know that."

"There was an electrical fire. I think the shell is still standing—the walls—but the inside is gutted. Someone techie millionaire bought it and plans to tear it down to build a mini-mansion. Glass walls, security cameras and priceless art—that sort of thing, I imagine."

"But not yet?"

"No, like I said—I don't think so."

Suddenly, my plans changed. Suddenly, I wasn't exactly ready to get on the subway and go home. Kel—as he had been doing all afternoon—seemed to be tuning in to what I was thinking.

"Are you getting the idea that you might like to go for a walk?" he asked. "Because I'll walk with you, if you wouldn't mind. I'd like to see the place one last time, too."

Another surprise. "I didn't realize you'd ever been there,"

"Oh yeah," Kel answered. "I was a patient of John's for a while." His sardonic laugh reappeared. "I even turned up as a footnote in his book. All that cheesy death and resurrection stuff the creepy crawlies showed me: John couldn't make heads or tails of it, but he thought it was an interesting anomaly."

I thought my preference would have been to take the crosstown walk by myself, but Kel turned out to be good company. For the time being, we moved away from the troubled subjects we had been discussing and instead, I told him about my feeling that, as we walked, we were passing through a kind of landscape where many of the places I remembered—the shop that should have been on this corner, the bookstore that used to be in the middle of that little side street—were not just gone, but seemingly erased. The busy avenues, crowded with young, pretty people, held little evidence and less memory of what had been before. We made our way from St. Mark's to Eighth Street, which took us from the East Village to the West; crossed Sixth Avenue and headed down past Seventh Avenue to Christopher Street. As we continued walking west, in the direction of the Hudson River, I could see glass high-rises cutting into the skyline along West Street, which ran parallel to the riverfront.

I pointed towards one of the towering buildings. "Wow," I said.

"Wait until we get there," he said. "You won't believe it."

On Washington Street, we reached the beginning of Paper Lane—and Kel was right; the narrow street and its surrounds were almost unrecognizable. All the quirky little buildings that had shared the lane with the carriage house, including the recording studio and the Socialists' print shop, had been torn down and replaced with sky-high modernist residences of glass and steel. The towering hi-rises were at the far end of the lane; from where we stood, they laid out their long shadows on the lane's cobblestones, which seemed to be all that was left from the life I had fled a decade ago. But not quite.

"Come on," Kel said, starting down the lane. And then he smiled. "Have some faith."

So I followed him home. That was how I felt as I walked down the lane, keeping my eyes on the familiar cobblestones underfoot. Then, because my feet knew just where to stop, I looked up and a familiar door was just a hand's breadth away.

Kel stepped back and let me approach the house myself. The stone walls, the heavy, wooden door with its iron fittings looked just as I remembered them, but as I moved closer, I could smell the acrid tang of smoke lingering just behind the entrance. So yet again, I stood on the edge of two landscapes at one time: in my mind, the yellow couch, the trestle table and the lamp with its silhouettes of black bears all stood safely in their rightful place. John was reading in his office, or maybe not—maybe he was out somewhere but certainly, on his way home; checking his pocket for his key. But of course, had I been able to open the door (which now I could see was warped from the heat of the fire; even the iron fittings looked like they had begun to melt) there would have been no one there and inside, nothing but ruin. Blackened shards of time.

I put my cheek to the door and closed my eyes. No matter how hard I tried to banish it, the smell of smoke persisted.

Finally, Kel gently pulled me away. "Come on," he said. "Maybe this wasn't the best idea I had today."

"I'm fine, I'm fine," I said, though without even realizing it, I had started, quietly, to cry. Quickly, I made myself stop. *Enough*, I told myself and started to walk away.

I turned towards the head of the lane, meaning to go back the way we came, which would have let us out on Washington Street, but the first thing I saw as I dried my eyes with the back of my hand was a huge truck blocking our way. I hadn't heard it drive up and, judging by the puzzled look on Kel's face as he stood beside me now, neither had he. That seemed impossible—it was a huge eighteen-wheeler with an enormous tractor cab pulling a closed cargo container behind it. The unmarked cab—no trucking company name, no registration tags—was black, as was the container, which stretched all the way back to the head of the lane, and both were so wide that it was going to be impossible to squeeze past them. I couldn't imagine how the driver had managed to navigate this monster down the lane and how we could have been oblivious to its approach—never mind what business it could possibly have for being here.

The truck's engine was off and if there was a driver sitting behind its tinted windows, we couldn't see him, so it didn't look like it was going to move any time soon. Clearly, there was no point in trying to retrace our steps back to Washington Street, so we turned and walked down to West Street. From there, it was just a few steps to the corner where we could turn back towards Seventh Avenue and I could catch the subway. Kel could board a crosstown bus, if he wanted to, or walk back the way we came.

But as we made our way along West Street, Kel stopped me and pointed out towards the river. Another block or so away was the same pier where, years ago, I had gone to watch the Perseid meteor shower and as a result, had first met John. That night, I had followed the crowd streaming down to the pier to get a better look at the sky show; now, as the afternoon mellowed into early evening with soft streaks of blue and gold lacing themselves along the horizon, there was no such urgency to the movement of the men and women crossing back and forth across the street. It was getting on to dinner time; some people were heading home while others were still lounging around, talking, playing Frisbee, or just enjoying the sight of the setting sun. What was notable about the scene, however, was that at the end of the pier, a large movie screen had been set up, as if a film was going to be presented, but no one seemed to be paying any attention to it. And no chairs had been arranged in front of it or blankets laid out for viewers to sit on. No signs indicated what was going to be displayed on the blank white screen.

"Want to go check that out?" Kel asked me.

"No," I told him. Something about the tableau on the pier didn't seem right to me, something was off. But Kel was already standing at the curb, watching for cars as he prepared to cross the street.

"Come on," he said to me. An anxious tone had crept into his voice; a nervousness that projected unease, but there was something else there, too. Some kind of compulsion.

I went reluctantly, but I did follow as he crossed the street Maybe I had been infected by his sense of being driven to see what was going on, or maybe the directive to be his shadow came from somewhere inside myself.

We walked down to the end of the pier to where the movie screen had been set up. The river flowed by, its currents, salted by backwash from the open water of the Atlantic, swirling with golden light. On the far shore, we could see huge construction cranes that were helping to erect the new hi-rises marching along the Jersey waterfront. These giant machines, frozen in place at the end of the workday, looked like monster-sized claws readying themselves to scrape away the sky.

No one on the pier paid any attention to us, or showed any sign of interest in joining us as we stood in front of the screen. "Maybe we missed the show," I said, but that, as it turned out, was wishful thinking.

Just a few moments after I spoke, the late afternoon light seemed to darken all at once, as if we were in a theater where the spotlights had just been dimmed, and images suddenly appeared on the screen. The first scene that was presented was instantly familiar to me: a young woman with long, dark hair walked across a field, approaching the edge of a woods. It was nighttime, and the sky arched above her, ribbed with darkness, nailed with stars. The young woman walked rapidly, deliberately. Soon, the angle of presentation changed as she crossed from the field into the woods so that we had a closer look at her for a moment or two. Though we only saw her back, it was possible to get a sense of what she looked like: thin, dark-haired, dressed in a fringed jacket and worn jeans.

"What is this?" Kel whispered to me, but I thought he had already figured that out. I certainly had. At least, I knew how it was beginning: the young woman we were looking at was Laura.

Then the screen went blank for a moment; long enough for Kel to look around and see that still, no one else on the pier was paying any attention to us or the images being projected in front of us. Of course not: they weren't meant for anyone else to see.

Soon, the screen lit up again and the presentation resumed, though the subject matter had changed. Also, the quality of the film we were now being shown—if it was a film—was notably poor; crackly and burned at the edges, as if it was very old and had been shown many times before. Or perhaps it was purposely intended to look that way. What I did understand, almost immediately, was that the images we were seeing had a familiar quality—for Kel, because surely, he had seen them before, and for me, because I remembered how he had described them to me, years ago, when John and I had gone to that holiday gathering at Jim Barrett's house. In fact, I could recall much of what Kel had said: that the things had shown him a movie depicting death and resurrection. He had mentioned people laid out in coffins, weeping relatives, along with Egyptian-looking stuff, like some human figure with the head of a jackal holding aloft an ankh to beckon people back from the land of the dead. I also remembered him talking about seeing different kinds of rituals from different cultures where people had died and some magical person brought them back. And I recalled him saying that the production was cheesy, like his creepy crawlies had tried to make a movie but they were bad at it. Like they thought they knew what they were doing but they didn't, really: they were just trying to imitate things they'd seen somewhere else. And the actors were all creatures like them, little gray, bug-eyed things dressed up in cheap costumes, trying to look like human beings.

This bizarre production seemed to contain all the features Kel had told me about, and more: in fact, it seemed to go on and on. Finally—abruptly— the screen once again went black and I thought the show we were watching was over. But then, for what turned out to be the final time, the screen lit up and an image appeared before us. It seemed to be the same scene that had first been displayed: a woods, a field, the night sky filled with cold stars.

Then, suddenly, the same young woman we had seen before came walking out of the woods. It was hard to see her face but the impression of her appearance—the long, straight hair, fringed jacket, jeans and boots—conveyed a time, an era: this had to be the old hippie days. The 60s or early 70s: Laura's time.

The woman—my mother—crossed the field and stepped onto a two-lane road; one of those rural byways that are unlit at night and wind through a lonely landscape of gnarled trees and abandoned farm houses collapsing into the earth beneath them. As Kel and I watched silently, the young woman—with only her back visible to us now—kept on walking for a few moments longer until she approached a distinct bend in the road that would have taken her out of sight. But, before she reached the bend, the screen went black.

I kept watching for a while longer, but it was obvious that there was going to be no more to see. The screen looked not only empty, but dead, somehow, as if it had been forever disconnected from whatever source had been generating the images we had been shown.

Finally, I turned away from the blank screen and looked over at Kel. He looked at me. I wondered which one of us was going to speak first.

It was me. It had to be—I thought I had the most to lose. Ten years of peace—or at least, of being left alone; all that was on the line now. The movie had been both a reminder and a challenge—all I wanted was to walk away from both.

"I'm leaving," I said to Kel. "Right now."

He grabbed my arm. "No," he said.

"I have to. This is a bad place for me. I can't let anything else start here. Not again."

"I think it's already too late," Kel said. "They want us to know they're still around."

Again, I thought about the deer I'd seen at the edge of the woods the other morning—if it was a deer. If it wasn't just a better costume. If it wasn't just my own mind creating an image of something I'd rather see than what was really there. That's what people did, wasn't it—create screen memories? I hadn't forgotten about all that. But maybe it wasn't just memories that could be masked—maybe you could make yourself not see something that stood right before your eyes, if you didn't want to. If you didn't want to badly enough.

But I told myself I didn't have to accept that idea. "It's because we're together," I said to Kel. "They're afraid of me, but not you. They're using you to get to me."

"You think you're that important?" he said. He still hadn't let go of my arm and now, I pulled away from him. I meant to walk—to run away—but I didn't. Not yet. "Was that you on the road?" he asked. "That woman—she looked like you."

I could have said nothing. I could have lied. I could have said that I had no idea what he was talking about, but it seemed to be too late for that, as well. "It was Laura. My mother."

He nodded. "I don't know if that's better or worse," he said.

"And I don't know what you're talking about."

"I'm not sure myself but...I think I'd better tell you something."

"No," I said. "Whatever it is, I don't want to hear it."

"Who says I really want to tell you?" he replied. "But I think you'd bet-ter listen."

"Fuck," I spat out.

"I guess that was you saying okay," Kel replied.

And then he was the one who started to walk away. I followed him, walking as quickly as possible because, at the moment, getting away from the pier was the only thing I wanted to do.

# 11

"ALRIGHT," I SAID. "What is it?"

"We might have something in common," Kel said.

"Really?" I replied, with as much derision as I could inject into my voice. "You think?"

Kel frowned at me. "I'm not an idiot, Julia. I don't mean that—them. Not just the creepy crawlies. Something else."

"Are you going to make me play twenty questions?"

"No," Kel said. "Just ask me one. Where was I on the night of my eighteenth birthday?"

"Fine," I said impatiently. "Where?

Kel waited a moment before he answered me. It was as if he was holding onto something important he wasn't quite ready yet to give me. But then he did.

"On the night of my eighteenth birthday," he said, "I was at the Stargazer's Embassy."

We were sitting on a bench near the basketball courts on West 4th street, about halfway between the pier where we had seen what I was now thinking of as the death movie, and Kel's shop in the East Village. Neutral territory; at any minute, I could get up and walk to the train, station a block or so away or Kel could head east, towards his shop. But it was night now; a big moon had hung itself among the stars pooled around its edges like bright little fish. I looked up at this glowing display while I did some math in my head. Kel, I thought, was maybe eight or nine years older than me, which meant that when he was downstairs in the Stargazer's Embassy, I was likely upstairs, in my room, not doing my homework. A middle school misfit already plotting how to get out of town.

"That's not all," Kel continued, before I even had a chance to say anything. "I had an invitation."

He pulled his billfold from his pocket, reached into a compartment behind a few credit cards and pulled out a folded cardboard rectangle. Immediately, I knew what it was: a passport from the Stargazer's Embassy to the World.

"Nicky gave that to you?" I asked. I was surprised; unless Kel was going to tell me that he was a regular at the bar, I couldn't imagine that he would have been given a passport. And I was right.

"Nicky didn't give it to me," Kel said. "The creepy crawlies did."

I couldn't think of anything to say to that except, "Why?"

"I guess they wanted me to go there," Kel said. "And I did." He paused for a moment, seeming to examine the passport, which looked so tattered that I imagined he had done this many times before. "You know how people always tell you that when they were abducted, the creepy crawlies came into their bedroom, or stopped their car on a lonely road somewhere?" He suddenly looked over at me and laughed. "Well, maybe people never told you that because you never went to any abductee meetings, right? Not your thing. But it was mine—for a while, anyway—so trust me, that's what you hear. But that's not what happened to me. I told people it was—and by people, I mean abductees, people in the meetings I went to, like at Jim Barrett's house—because it was easier to explain things that way. The real story sounds even crazier than anything those people had to say."

"Great," I said.

Kel looked over at me. "You just can't let go of that little edge of sarcasm, can you?"

I shrugged. "Sorry," I said in such an exaggerated way that he had to know I really wasn't. But he chose to ignore that.

"You should be," he replied. "In fact, you should maybe just shut up for a while because some of this is going to sound familiar to you." He went on.

"The abduction part—I always lied about that. I heard what people said at meetings and I just added that to my story. I would tell people I had been abducted but it never happened."

That was a startling admission—until I reminded myself that Kel had never actually told me he was abducted. I had met him at a house full of people who identified as abductees, so I just assumed that was what had happened to him. Apparently, I was wrong, but this new realization just made me wonder if Kel wasn't some kind of crazy person who wanted so badly to have extraterrestrial contact that he had fabricated an entire history for himself—Munchausen by alien, or something like that. My expression must have given him some hint of what I was thinking, so he quickly offered an explanation. "That's the only part of what happened that isn't true," he said. "The rest...well, just listen, then you can judge for yourself. Okay?"

"You never even told John?"

"John knew. He was the only one. Except now, I'm going to tell you."

The fact that whatever Kel had to say was something he had once shared with John made me suggest to myself that maybe being scornful wasn't the most appropriate option for me right now. I sat back, finally willing to listen.

Kel said, "What happened to me started when I was standing at my father's grave. It was a dark and stormy night," he added. Then he laughed quietly, and said, ""Actually, it really was."

He continued to tell me the story. "My dad died when I was sixteen," Kel said. "He pretty much raised me by himself—my mother had taken off with some guy when I was a little kid. After he passed, I took off, myself: got on a bus and went to the big city, where I sold pot, couch surfed, stuff like that. It was that kind of time," he said. "Anyway, I survived. At one point—I think I was around seventeen—a friend of a friend of a friend let me work at his tattoo shop. At first, I was just cleaning up and stuff like that, but then I got interested in what he was doing, and he began to teach me. I was just sort of getting straightened out when whammo, my eighteenth birthday came around and that night, I got really ripped with some friends; on top of drinking, we were popping uppers so I was pretty nuts. Anyway, I got it in my head that I should visit my father's grave. He's buried in a cemetery near Trumansburg."

"Which is what?" I said. "Maybe twenty miles or so from Freelingburg? From the Embassy?"

"Maybe that," Kel said. "But I didn't know the place even existed. Believe me, when I was a kid, we did our drinking out in the cornfields. You could drink, legally, when you were eighteen back then but it wasn't even on my radar screen to be thinking about going to a bar. Not then, not on my big birthday, either. I borrowed someone's Harley and went on up I95, in a rainstorm. High as motherfucker. I'm lucky I didn't kill myself, or anyone else for that matter. But I made it to Trumansburg. By that time, my head had pretty much straightened out. I want you to understand that: I was sober as a judge when I parked the bike outside the cemetery. It was prob-ably around eleven o'clock; the entrance was locked up tight but I climbed over the gate and got in. Then I found the plot where my dad was buried and I saw that the grave had a headstone now. That was new to me: my aunts had paid for it but it hadn't been there when my dad was buried. I remember reading what it said—my dad's name, his dates, then something like, *beloved father and brother*—and then I walked around to the back of the stone, sat down and leaned against it. The rain had finally stopped, but it was still thundering in the distance. I was soaked to the skin, tired, but I mean it, Julia: I had all my wits about me. Still, I suddenly felt so, so sad. My dad was a son-of-a-bitch—it really wasn't easy to be his son—but, he was my father. He was all I had. So I remember sitting there, all by myself in the dark, in this godforsaken cemetery out in the country, in the middle of nowhere, and suddenly, I just started crying. Weeping, like I couldn't stop. I think I was wrung out from the drugs and the traveling and I just felt like I didn't know what I was doing with myself, my life; like I had no purpose, and to top it off, I was all alone in the world. Only, all of a sudden, I wasn't."

Kel was still holding the tattered passport in his hands. Glancing down at it, he said, "So here comes the fun part. Like I told you, I was never ab-ducted. I was...well, visited."

*Like me?* I thought. Well no, it turned out. Not exactly.

"I was leaning against the gravestone, crying like an idiot," Kel said, "when I suddenly felt like there was someone else nearby. And there was. A guy came walking through the grass between the graves. For a moment, I thought it was a caretaker and he was going to make me leave, but there was something weird about him, you know? Well," he said with a smile, "yes, of course you know. He was a little guy, wearing sunglasses and a coat that was much too big for him. Sunglasses at night—there's a song about that, right? So I guess my brain switched over to thinking about that because, I mean, how much can you process about a midget-sized guy wearing sunglasses and a big coat, walking towards you in a cemetery late at night? In that kind of scene, you're either dreaming or you're about to get murdered by some crazed clown. So I just sat there, watching, as this guy—only now we know he wasn't really a guy, right?—came right up to me and just stood there, in front of me, looking at me with those damn sunglasses perched on his face and his coat dragging on the ground. His skin was sort of grayish and his head was shaped like a kind of dome-shaped triangle, but hey, it was that dark and stormy night, so I wasn't asking myself a lot of questions. Anyway, Mr. Sunglasses just kept peering at me from behind those shades until suddenly, he reached into one of the pockets of that big coat, pulled out this and handed it to me."

Again, he looked down at the cardboard rectangle in his hand: we both did. Kel turned it over so that we were looking at the side with the logo that matched my tattoo. "A passport from the Stargazer's Embassy to the World. I was reading what it said because I had no idea what the hell it was. I did see that it had an address on it—22 Main Street, Freelingburg, New York. I was thinking well, wow, whatever this place is, it's just down the road. Then I looked up, and Mr. Sunglasses was gone."

Finally, Kel folded up the passport and slipped it back into his billfold. "So tell me," he said, "what would you have done?"

"Me? I'm not offering an opinion about that. You told me to shut up before, remember?"

"I lift the ban."

"Then here's what I would have done—I'd have planted myself back on the bike, pointed it in the opposite direction, and gotten out of there as fast as I could."

"That's because you already knew too much. I knew nothing. And maybe I wasn't as sober as I claim. Maybe the alcohol and the drugs were still filtering through my brain. Who knows? Anyway, I did get back on the bike. But I went to Freelingburg. To the Stargazer's Embassy. I mean, a guy in a cemetery handed me an invitation."

"And unless it was Halloween, most people would think that was a little crazy. A lot."

"Maybe I did think that," Kel said, "which is probably why I went. But I also kind of felt like I didn't have a choice. Like I was on some sort of journey and I had to keep going..." He suddenly turned to look straight at me. "How stupid does that sound?"

"A little stupid," I answered. "But then, I don't really know you. Maybe for you, that's normal."

He suddenly tapped me on the head. "Yeah? What about you? Do you have a setting in there that points to normal?"

Because the only answer I gave him was a shrug, he said, "Do you want to hear the rest of this story or not? Because right now, it's heading straight for you."

*That* deserved a comment. "Really? Do you remember seeing me at the Embassy that night?"

"I don't remember seeing any kids. But I did see your mother—at least I think so. I mean, now, I think so."

"You saw Laura?" High alert—there it was again, that feeling that I had to focus, to pay attention. Listening to Kel was suddenly like hearing witness testimony: someone was going to tell me something about my mother. Someone who knew something I might want to know. Need to. "Why do you think it was her?" I asked.

"Because after watching that movie...look, let me just finish, and you tell me if it was her. Okay?"

"I'm back to shutting up," I said. "Talk."

He nodded. "I got to Freelingburg, found the Embassy on Main Street, parked the bike and went inside. I sat down at the bar and a guy came up to serve me: thin, long hair—that must have been Nicky, right? You told me about him." I nodded, and Kel went on. "I asked for whatever he had on tap and he asked for my i.d. I got out my driver's license, but at the same time, I showed him the passport. He looked at it and then he told me I was in luck: it was movie night at the Stargazer's Embassy, and on movie night, if you had a passport, you got a free beer. I asked what they were showing and he pointed at a screen they had set up on a stage at the end of the bar. He told me it was 'The Day the Earth Stood Still,' so when I got my beer, I turned my stool around and started to watch."

I was beginning to get it now, the point of this story, so I broke my silence again. "Only that's not what you saw, right?"

"Well, I thought it was. I had never seen the damn movie before. I didn't know I was supposed to be seeing a giant robot or a flying saucer or anything like that. So I just watched what was playing...the same thing, over and over again."

"The movie we saw tonight."

"The same one. As far as I remember, exactly the same one, only without the beginning and ending."

"Without Laura."

"Didn't need her in the movie, I guess," Kel said. "Because she was in the bar. I mean, you tell me: pretty, witchy looking, dark hair..."

"Yes," I said. I didn't even need the description. I knew it was Laura.

"I noticed her at one point when I happened to look away from the movie. She was sitting at a table with a tall man. Very tall—way over six feet—and thin. Skinny, like he had nothing inside him. He was wearing a blue sharkskin suit with thin lapels and a skinny tie—a really stylized lady-killer outfit like some guy might have worn when he was going out to a nightclub back in the 1950s, only it didn't fit right: the suit was too tight and the sleeves were too short. I thought about how that was like the characters in the movie, since they were all wearing outfits that looked like they came from some amateur costume shop or something. And he was wearing sunglasses—big wraparound shades—which really gave me the creeps. It was like I was being stalked by some cult that wore sunglasses. I guess it was when I saw him that I got up from the stool and started to leave...everything was suddenly beginning to seem very creepy. But the woman got up, too, and she stopped me."

"The woman was Laura," I said. "That's who you mean, right? You can use her name."

"Okay," Kel said. "Laura stopped me. She walked over to me and asked me to come sit at her table for a few minutes. I didn't want to but it was like all of a sudden, I was frozen. The same way abductees describe that they feel when the aliens come for them. You want to move, but you can't. The next thing I knew, I was sitting at the table, across from the tall guy with the shades. I felt really weird, like I was half in a coma or something. Underwater, looking up through, like, wavy layers of dark and light. The woman... Laura...sat down next to me and she said that her friend—and I knew that she meant the guy in the shades—wanted to know what I thought of the movie. She said they had shown it just for me, and I said thanks—can you imagine? *Thanks?*—but I said that I didn't understand it. Then she asked me if I thought my father was in the movie. I thought that was a crazy question but hey, the whole situation was crazy, right? I wanted to get up and run away but I still couldn't move. So I said no, I hadn't seen my father in the movie. Was he in the cemetery, she asked me? Did I believe that? Or did I think he was somewhere else? I remember my answer to that: I said, are you asking me if I think he's in heaven? That's what a five-year-old would say, I guess, but I was really addle-brained at that point and it was the only thing I could think of. And your mother...Laura...patted me on the hand, like I *was* five. *No*, she said, *not heaven*. Then she sighed; I mean, she let out this really, deep sigh and said, *That's probably not very likely*. After that, she didn't say another word to me. She just waved to the guy behind the bar... Nicky, I guess...and he sent somebody over with a drink. A boilermaker. I remember that because a beer and a shot of Jack is not something you usually see women drink. And actually, she didn't; she pushed it towards the guy in the sharkskin suit and he downed it: one, two, three, gone. He was a drinker; I could tell."

Even to me, Kel's story was beginning to sound a little preposterous. "Are you sure you're remembering this right?"

"Wait until I'm finished," he said, "and you won't ask me that."

Okay, I could wait, but one thing was bothering me now, and I had to ask. "Are you sure Nicky didn't bring over the drink himself?" What I wanted to know was whether Nicky knew who—what—my mother was sitting with. The last time we had spoken, he had denied even believing that her visitors were real. I wanted to try to figure out if that was a lie, but even as I asked who had brought the drink to the table, I realized the answer wouldn't help me, one way or another. From what Kel was describing, however odd Laura's companion looked to him, no one else in the bar had seemed to notice. Maybe that meant that however strange these things seemed to people who saw them—who were meant to see them—when they wanted to pass through this world unnoticed, that's what they were able to do.

In any case, Kel hardly seemed to even register my question about Nicky because he didn't bother to answer me. "Just hold on," he said. "Here comes the end of the story...at least this part. The guy downed the boilermaker, and then your mother went behind the bar, poured another, and brought it to him herself. He gulped that down, too. After the guy had the second drink—or maybe it was his third, or his fifth; like I said, he could have been drinking all night—he stood up, like he was getting ready to go. He was pretty drunk by then; I could tell that because he was really unsteady on his feet. He held onto the chair for a moment and seemed to kind of compose himself. Then, all of a sudden, he stood up straight, looked over at me, and started to pull off his shades. That's when I saw the tattoo on the inside of his wrist—I told you his suit didn't fit. The sleeves hardly reached down to his wrist so when he lifted his hand, there it was." Kel pointed at my wrist. "Those same stars, little sister. The same ones that are on the passport—and on the sign outside the bar."

I had already figured that out; he didn't have to tell me. But it seemed necessary to him—and I guess to me as well, now—that he finish the rest of this story. So I asked the next inevitable question. "What did you see when the guy got the shades off?"

"He seemed to be struggling with them, like they were stuck on his face somehow. But when he finally pulled them away from his face...well, three guesses, none of which I think you'll need."

"No," I said. "I get it."

"That face," Kel said. "The huge black eyes, smooth gray skin. I've seen it a hundred times since. Book covers, magazine articles, drawings by abductees...I mean, experiencers. I see that face in my dreams, still. But that was the first time, at the Stargazer's Embassy. I was so shocked that when the guy finally walked out of the bar, I ran after him. I don't know what I was going to do, or say, but once I was out the front door...well, whatever I had meant to do, I was stopped dead in my tracks because out there, on the street, he wasn't alone."

I could picture the scene: I knew it well. A late, lonely hour in Freelingburg with all the stores locked up, the streets empty, and the cold night clamped down on the town like a black tent zipped tight. This image formed the backdrop for the rest of Kel's story. "There were maybe half a dozen of the short ones waiting for him on the street, like they were there to help him get back to wherever he had to go. As soon as I closed the Embassy door behind me, they all turned to look at me. A whole crowd of creepy-crawlies, staring straight at me. I freaked. I mean, I just totally freaked. I jumped on my bike and got the hell out of there. I drove straight back to the city and spent the next week...alright, that's not even close to the truth. I spent most of the next year, at least, stoned out of my skull. And then it took me a good long while after that before I went back to the tattoo shop and started learning the trade again. All I wanted to do was forget everything I'd seen."

"But," I said.

Kel nodded. "Yeah, *but*. But who can forget seeing something like that? Those faces. Right out of nightmare. And then that," he said, reaching over to trace the tattoo on my wrist with the tip of his finger. "That damn thing. A tattoo. It was like a message to me. I'd seen every kind of design in the tattoo shop where I was working, but not that, and then all of a sudden, it turns up...well, where it did. One night, everywhere I looked—on the passport, on the sign over the front door of the Embassy, inked on the creepy crawly's wrist—there it was. So I couldn't stop asking myself what it meant."

"John told me that the five stars are part of the Betty Hill map," I replied. "I didn't know that when I was a kid. All I knew was that using the stars as the Embassy logo was Laura's idea."

"Oh yeah, Betty Hill. Zeta Reticuli and all that," Kel scoffed. "If that's all it is—a map that leads home—why don't they just go home, already? Why hang around here showing us fucking movies? Following you around in weird disguises?"

"And drinking in bars," I added.

"Right. And drinking in bars in some godforsaken town in upstate New York. I mean, can you explain that to me?"

"No," I said, "I can't." And then I laughed. Probably for the first time in my life, the things seemed funny to me—well, almost. Amateur filmmakers—*bad* amateur filmmakers. Bad dressers. And drunks. It all seemed so stupid that it *was* laughable. And once I started laughing, I couldn't seem to stop. I finally gulped some air, coughed, and got some control of myself. But I was still giggling.

Kel watched me, smiling. "It is ridiculous, isn't it?" he said. "I mean when you string everything together. It's like we're talking about something so stupid it can't be real. And yet it is. So there can only be one explanation: it's the drinking. Maybe everybody all over the universe just likes to get hammered. Little gray creepy crawlies, tall skinny ones, boys and girls from the galaxy next door, and a million more just over the next event horizon: they all enjoy bellying up to the bar. And Jack Daniels seems to be their drink of choice."

I started laughing again, and so did Kel. But we stopped when we were startled by the sound of loud shouts from the basketball court behind us, followed by applause from a crowd gathered around the fencing that surrounded the court. More shouting followed, as what was obviously a frantic competition began to reach its conclusion. Another group of players standing impatiently on the sidelines were waiting to take the court. These games, mostly intense, informal pickup tournaments, could go on all night.

We both turned to watch the action for a few minutes, until a timeout was called. By then, we had settled down—at least, we had stopped laughing. Kel then tried to pick up our conversation where we had left off.

"Maybe that's what we should do tonight," he said. "Go on a bender."

"Not that I don't feel tempted," I replied, "but I can't. I've got to work tomorrow."

"And that stops you?" he sighed. "What a good girl you are."

We both got up from the bench and took one last look at floodlit basketball court, where play was starting up again. I was hungry and tired and ready to go home. I was scoping out a hamburger place across the street, thinking about grabbing something to take with me on the subway when Kel pulled a cell phone from his pocket and said, "You should let me have your number." I must have given him a look of surprise because he said, "Don't start thinking all sorts of cutesy things. I want to be able to get in touch with you in case something happens."

"Because you think something will?"

"Don't you?"

My question, his answer: both were unnecessary. Maybe more years would go by, maybe just an hour, a day, but we weren't going to be left alone. I was certain of that, just as the same instinct told me that my long period of freedom from contact with the things might have gone on indefinitely, perhaps for the rest of my life, if I hadn't run into Kel today. I had to admit that there had been times after John's death when I'd had similar thoughts about him. Had my living with John somehow increased the things' interest in me, or their desire for me to see them, recognize that they were still around me? If I let my mind wander down that path, then the direction it inevitably led was to the idea that the things themselves had somehow engineered these meetings. Was that possible? The idea that they could meddle in the course of my life should have been frightening but it wasn't, maybe simply because my exposure to them had gone on too long for me to feel any kind of fear. Instead, like the release of being able to laugh at them, the thought that they were meddlers, manipulators, just made them seem weaker to me, like bullies who had to go to a lot of trouble to get what they wanted—and in the end, couldn't even control the outcome of their interference. But what was it that they wanted? I still couldn't answer that question, except that craziness seemed to be the result of their desire, whatever it was: bad craziness, accompanied by misery and tragedy and death. Given all that, the message I had for them—whether I ever got a chance to deliver it again or not—was the same one I had been sending them since I was a child: *I am not afraid of you. And I am dangerous, too.* Maybe that was the reason their presence in my life ratcheted up when they could approach me through someone else; John, Kel, even Alice—they were like conduits, direction finders, pointing straight at me, even when I was determined to look away.

These were my private thoughts; I had no wish, at the moment, to share them with Kel. I did give him my phone number, though, and watched with interest as he tapped it into the phone, a fat little black bar with a tiny screen and a small, rigid antenna sticking out of the top. Then we parted and I crossed the street to get my burger. After that, I plugged myself into my CD player and went to catch the subway.

What I needed was the number four train to the last stop in the Bronx, which meant I had to change from one line to another at Grand Central. It was a long ride, rocketing underground, station by station, from the west side to the east, then all through Manhattan and finally, up into the Bronx, where the train emerged from one kind of darkness into another: from the tunnels into the night. The tracks here were elevated above ground; we passed by Yankee Stadium, where the lights were on but no game was being played because the team was off on the road somewhere, then on through old neighborhoods, stopping at old stations with wooden platforms and rusted benches: the Grand Concourse, Mt. Eden Avenue, Burnside, Kingsbridge. Finally, we reached Woodlawn, the end of the line, and I disembarked with the rest of the passengers, just a small group of workers and late-night stragglers heading home to this distant neighborhood, still part of the city, but barely.

There was a long flight of stairs the led down from the station to the street. The elevated tracks ran above a wide roadway; on one side was the edge of Van Cortland Park, with its vast, grassy acreage. On the other, where I descended from the stairs, was the stop where most mornings I caught the bus north to the suburbs beyond the reach of the New York City transit system. Late as it was, there were people lined up here, waiting for a bus to take them to the overnight shift at some commercial bakery or machine shop or, like me—some night-time version of me—to clean stores and offices while the bosses and secretaries slept.

As usual, there were also street peddlers working the line at the bus stop, trying to hawk all kinds of knock-offs: some nights it was watches, some nights, depending on the season, purses and sunglasses or gloves and scarves. People without money were always trying to sell each other cheap versions of nicer things that people with money coveted. Tonight, however, as I stepped off the staircase and started down the street, my attention was drawn to a table set up in the doorway of a shuttered bodega. There was something for sale there that was different than the usual counterfeit junk laid out on display.

Another train, its brakes screeching, pulled into the station overhead as I looked over the items on the table. The guy standing behind the table was a regular. He usually sold portable electronics, like boom boxes and CD players, but tonight, what caught my eye was a small selection of cell phones. They looked similar to the one Kel had, just a little thinner and flatter, but with the same small screen, fat antenna, and narrow buttons on the keypad.

"Do they really work?" I asked the vendor. He was a stocky man with thick fingers: when he picked up one of the little phones, it was almost lost in his hand.

"Sure," he said. "It's a Jap phone."

Well, it did say Nokia above the screen, but I had read about these phones in a magazine and I knew that Nokia was a Finnish company, not Japanese. There didn't seem much point, though, in having a discussion about the phone's pedigree with the vendor, since wherever this phone had actually been manufactured—or put together from various "found" parts—was anyone's guess.

"Doesn't work now, of course," the stocky man said. "You gotta get it hooked up. You know how to do that, right? You go to Besso's."

Yes, I knew how to do that. Besso's was an electronics store on the avenue near the dicey Internet café I frequented. It was one of those stores that always had a "Going Out of Business—Everything Marked Down!" sign in the window, but never actually closed its doors. They sold items similar to the ones on the table before me, as well as cameras, calculators, computer equipment—and cell phone plans. Maybe Besso's minions had secretly installed their own cell phone towers around the city; maybe they were bootlegging signals from legit carriers. I had no idea and I didn't really care; I just knew that they could hook up a cell phone and the service was cheap.

"Okay," I said. "How much?"

"Forty bucks."

That was way less than the couple of hundred dollars these things usually sold for. Forty dollars was just about all the cash I had on me, but what the hell. Maybe I'd find it useful for work to have one—the woman at the cleaning agency who arranged my jobs kept telling me it would be easier to get in touch with me if I had a cell phone.

I forked over the cash and got my phone. The vendor just handed it to me without a box or even an instruction sheet, but I didn't expect anything like that. I slipped the phone into my back pocket and thought about when I could get over to Besso's. Saturday, probably, two days from now, when I didn't have to work. For the time being, the phone could sit in a drawer at home and wait for me to bring it to life.

# III

ON SATURDAY MORNING, on my way back from Besso's, the first call I made on my new cell phone was to myself: I dialed my home phone number and listened to my answering machine tell me that I wasn't around. Well, at least the thing worked: whatever cell towers the signal was surreptitiously bouncing off were blindly forwarding my call through the atmosphere. Or maybe I was unknowingly pirating someone else's cell frequency; I wasn't sure because I hadn't exactly carried out an in-depth interrogation of the kid behind the counter who had sold me a calling plan and set up the phone for me—I was too distracted, and too busy buying other things, as well. The store had been crowded and the customers were haggling with the sales-people in a cacophony of languages. Almost the minute I walked in, I had been assailed by a slick-looking kid standing behind the counter. He was maybe nineteen years old, with a buzz-cut Mohawk and a thick gold chain around his neck. He must have spotted my old CD player since I had my headphones on, and asked me what I was listening to. I knew that he didn't actually care about the music, he was interested in my old Sony because he had a newer model he wanted to sell me. It was a Diskman, also, supposedly, a Sony, except that I realized the name was spelled wrong: I had seen enough of them in store windows: the *k* should have been a *c*. But that didn't stop me from buying it after I signed up for the cell service—I had some kind of bootleg phone now, so why not an equally questionable music player, as well?—along with a pair of earbuds to replace my old headphones. I was happy enough to have all this stuff; the electronics felt like an improved version of the high-voltage fence I liked to keep around myself.

Now, after listening to my own voice on the answering machine, I slipped the phone back into my pocket and continued on my way home, carrying a plastic bag with my other purchases. I was mostly thinking about my work schedule for the following week when, from the corner of my eye, I saw a kid on a bicycle pedal by me in the street on the other side of a line of parked cars. I don't know why I noticed him, but almost as soon as I saw him, I forgot about him—until I reached the corner, and there he was again, stopped, straddling the bike, looking straight at me.

He was a skinny kid, maybe twelve; wearing a tee shirt, basketball shorts and high-top sneakers. As soon as I saw him waiting for me on the corner—because that seemed to be exactly what he was doing—the air around me seemed to become thick, concentrated; the sunlight was like an arrow heading in his direction. And my inner alarm dialed itself over to high alert. I could almost hear it screaming.

My immediate reaction was that the basketball shorts and sneakers were supposed to be a reference to the day that Kel and I had seen the death movie and then sat by the basketball court while he told me his secrets. But this wasn't a thing in costume: it was a kid who I thought I might even recognize from around the neighborhood. It was summer; there were dozens of kids running around, riding bikes, playing punch ball in the street and basketball wherever someone had stuck up a hoop. Maybe because of all that, I couldn't prevent myself from letting a hopeful thought bloom: could I be mistaken about the idea that the things had now come up with some new way to accost me?

Nope. Not at all. I strode up to the boy on the bike, and—still testing—tried to walk around him. As I did, he moved the bike forward to block my way.

I stopped. "Okay," I said to him. "What's up?"

"I'm supposed to give you a message," the boy said. "Some guy wants to see you."

"Some guy?"

"Yeah, some weirdo. A little guy wearing sunglasses and a ball cap. And rain boots. Does it look like it's gonna rain today? Like I said, weird."

"Where did he come from?" I asked.

The boy shrugged. "I don't know. He just showed up. Me and my friends were hanging around the Internet place near Besso's and when you came out the door, the guy was just there, standing in the middle of us, pointing at you."

"What did he say?" I asked, and then caught myself. I had never heard the things talk. They seemed to be good at acting out show and tell with people—presenting star maps to them, for instance, and both living and dead babies—but even Kel had said they couldn't speak. How could they have given the boy a message for me?

Easily, as it turned out. In a way that would never have occurred to me.

"He didn't say anything," the boy said. "He showed me pictures on his phone."

"He had a cell phone?"

The boy looked at me like now I was the weird character he had to deal with. "Of course he had a phone. *Everybody* has a phone."

"Alright," I said. "Of course. Everybody has a phone. So what did he show you?"

"Just the bike path in the park. You go up the clubhouse road to where you see a sign, then turn off. That's where the path is. There's a gate at the end of the path, all locked up. Used to be a picnic area there but they got it blocked off now because it got swallowed up by a sinkhole last spring. Too much rain."

The boy and I looked at each other, experiencing a momentary alliance as we realized that we were sharing a similar thought centered on a pair of rain boots. "That was months ago," the boy said, shaking his head. "What a jerk."

The moment passed, the boy's faced turned stony. He was just delivering information: maybe the task had intrigued him for a while but now he was bored. He spoke rapidly, like he was just trying to get rid of the words. "Look, miss, the guy wants you to ride down the path and meet him at the gate. He left you a bike outside your building. If it hasn't been stolen already," the boy said, removing himself from any further responsibility for the message by ending it with a note of futility. Then he climbed back on his own bike and quickly rode away.

I crossed the street and stared down the next block, towards my building. And there it was, a sleek black three-speed bike, leaning against a brick wall, under someone's window. It wasn't chained up or secured in any way, but I knew it wasn't going to be stolen. If I ignored it, that bike would just sit there day after day, waiting for me.

At first, I did ignore it. I wanted to go to my apartment to put away all the stuff I was still carrying in the plastic bag. First, I had to climb a long flight of badly worn stone steps divided into three sections by landings where cement lions with chipped cement manes and blank cement eyes crouched on broken pedestals. Lions, stone angels and brick arches: every building on my block had at least one of these features, referencing a time when the apartment buildings in this part of the Bronx had been designed with the idea of grandeur in mind. Imitation grandeur, certainly, scaled-down and built on the cheap, but the intention had been for people to feel like they had escaped from the city proper into some suburb-like enclave. Across the street from where I lived was a development called Lafayette Gardens, named for the revolutionary war hero, where the buildings had been set around a plaza with a marble fountain at its center. But it was generations down the line now and what had once looked imposing had settled into weariness and disrepair: the flights of cracked stone stairs were dangerous to navigate, the fountain inoperative, the buildings barely heated in winter and so badly wired that in the summer, turning on a fan and a lamp in the same room was liable to blow every circuit on an entire floor. Women who went up on the roof of my own building to hang their washing out to dry sometimes took a step across the tarred surface and suddenly found their foot dangling through the ceiling of a top-floor tenant's living room.

I lived on the ground floor, safe, at least, from that kind of intrusion. I walked through the quiet lobby, crossing a floor made of some kind of fake black marble. Moving from the bright sunshine outside to the dim shadows here, where—as usual—most of the lighting wasn't working, left me nearly blind. It was easier to see by pretending to see, so I closed my eyes as I slipped my key into the lock on my front door and went inside.

It was a small apartment, just two rooms and a tiny kitchen. I had a tv and a couch in the living room, along with a stereo set standing on a metal file cabinet I had rescued from the street; nothing much more than that. In the other room, I had a bed, a dresser, and a night table holding an alarm clock with a glow-in-the-dark face. The window in my bedroom faced the elevated subway tracks which, from here, were about a block away. I had positioned the bed so that I could lie there at night and watch the trains coming around the curve that led to the Woodlawn terminus.

Now, I dropped my plastic bag on the bed and sat for a few minutes, looking out at the empty tracks. I was just killing time, just delaying what I was going to do next. Pretending that I hadn't already made my choice. But of course, I had: like Kel, I had received an invitation and while in the past, this would have just made me furious—*Idiots*, I would have thought; *Why would I do anything they want?*—the idea of seeing the things again after so long an absence didn't set me off the way I would have expected. Maybe it was because, with Kel, I had been able to laugh at them. Maybe because of the idea that they might be a bunch of loopy drunks—or at least one of them was, at least sometimes. It gave them a dimension of something like humanness—well, maybe not quite that, but *something*: vulnerability, perhaps, or just plain stupidity, that had tamped down my anger, my defenses. My desire to lash out at them.

But at this late date, this point in my life, lash out for what? For not protecting John? For frightening me when I was a small child and then haunting me through all the years after Laura died until I had, literally, driven them out of my life—if indeed, that was what I had done? Oh yes, all I had to do was raise those questions with myself to feel that the anger wasn't really gone, it was just taking a breather. Waiting. Expecting, at any minute, to be let out of the corner where I was keeping it and be set free to rage again through all my days and nights. Except that I didn't want to do that right now. I could tell myself that it was because, in joking about them with Kel, I had discovered a new way of looking at the things and that was true, that was part of the reason that I was feeling remarkably calm right now; even resolute. But there was something else, too, and I knew what it was. I had known all along, from the moment on the pier when what I thought of as Kel's movie had concluded with an image of my mother walking down the road. What drew me on now was Laura, that lonely image of her, the loneliness she had left inside me. I understood full well that I could refuse the invitation I had been given. It was my choice: if I wanted, I could never see the things again. But they had held out a kind of calling card to me and on it was that image of Laura. Where was she going? What was I supposed to think about that? In my mind, all I could see, now, when I thought of her was her back turned, walking away from me. I couldn't let that image linger. I couldn't just let it go. Let *her* go. I could try to fight it all I wanted, but I knew it was impossible.

So. I put my purchases away and went back downstairs. The bike, of course, was still waiting. A black bike, angled against a brick wall, waiting in dusty summer sunshine. The similarities to the story that Kel had told me kept piling up: the movie, the invitation, the bike—though my ride was not a motorcycle, but a girl's bicycle, for a girl's version of the trip, perhaps. Still, as I pulled the bike away from the wall and began to pedal off, I did find myself thinking that here was another characteristic of the things that I had never recognized before. Another possible weakness I reminded myself to make note of: they seemed to have little capacity for imagination, or even trickery. Maybe, whatever they were doing, they did over and over again, using the same elements, the same tools and tricks that, to someone like me, who had been exposed to them for so long, hardly seemed like tricks at all. Even the fact that the boy who had been their intermediary said that they had a cell phone, or more likely, something that to him had resembled a cell phone, didn't seem at all odd to me the more I thought about it. As the boy had said, *everybody has a phone.* Even I had acquired one, so why shouldn't they have, as well? Why not make use of an object that they now saw almost all of us use? That seemed to fit a pattern: they showed us movies on what looked like regular movie screens; they wore human-looking clothes (though granted, with no idea of how ridiculous their outfits were); they left me a bicycle to go find them, not a time machine or a ticket for a ride on a UFO. Maybe this was something else for me to understand about them, too: that they were better mimics than monsters. At least, that seemed to be the case with the things I had encountered all my life, and with Kel's creepy crawlies. It didn't explain the other, more prevalent version of the stories about the things—Jim Barrett's version, Alice's version, even what Betty and Barney Hill reported—that involved abductions, repulsive physical intrusions, and of course, the hybrids, the babies. But that wasn't my concern right now: I couldn't reconcile every contradiction that came to mind as I rode through the sunny afternoon. I had to focus on what I was doing, though I already had a good idea of where I was headed: deep into Van Cortlandt Park, down a bike path that led into an old forest of elms, oak and pine.

Plugged into my music, I had sometimes gone for a walk along the perimeter of the park, keeping to the paved sidewalk lined with benches across the street from the stop where I waited for the bus under the elevated train tracks. The park beyond the benches stretched for over a thousand wooded acres. A map encased in a Plexiglas case near one of the benches showed the location of various bike paths and ball fields; even a small lake where ice skating was allowed when it froze over in the winter. I didn't need to consult the map, though: I had seen the cinder path that led to an old, boarded-up clubhouse that used to serve golfers when the public course here was open. But this was not exactly a golfer's neighborhood anymore, if it ever was, so the fences around the course had been taken down and the rolling fields had been allowed to turn back into weedy grassland.

I rode in the street for two blocks then turned a corner; one more block brought me to the road under the elevated train tracks. I walked the bike across, watching for cars because there was no streetlight here. Then I got back on again, pedaled past the benches and headed up the cinder path.

As I approached the clubhouse, I saw the sign for the bike path with an arrow, pointing off into the woods. I stopped there for a moment, just looking, listening. It was high summer, the middle of the day: I had expected to see other bikers coming along the path, but there was no one. I was alone. Curtains of sunlight surrounded me but the bike path led off into shadow. So, into the shadows I went.

I was surprised to find that the path was paved. It went up and over the gradual incline of a hill so that I soon found myself coasting along under the canopy of overhanging trees. Slender shafts of sunlight filtered through the leafy branches, the trill of birdsong broke the silence. These elements of the everyday made the ride into another experience of being in two places at once: the real world—the one I lived in, moved through—was certainly around me, but I also had the unmistakable sense of being somewhere else, somewhere that looked like a bike path in the park but maybe was not. I felt like I had that day with Kel, when we'd walked through the Village and it had seemed to me like a landscape where layers of time were pulling themselves apart as I passed through them—only here, it wasn't the divisions of time that were separating but of *place*, as if what I saw in front of my eyes was only one facet of what was there. But I had to remain focused on what was—or seemed—inarguably visible because straight ahead, the end of the path was coming into sight and with it, the gate that I had been told to look for.

The boy had said that it was locked, but that wasn't so: it was wide open, beckoning.

*Fine,* I thought. *At least you're making it easy for me.* I got off the bike, laid it down on the grass verge beside the paved path, and walked through the gate. Careful of my footing, I looked for the edge of the sinkhole that was supposed to have swallowed up this part of the park but all I saw was an expanse of bare, stony earth that narrowed into a dirt track leading into a stand of trees. The sense of being in two worlds at once just grew stronger as I crossed the rough ground and followed the track through the trees that soon broke through into a meadow—a bright clearing of grass and wildflowers ringed by a pinewoods so dense that the way forward seemed impassable.

Entering the clearing, my feeling of straddling different realities was strengthened by a strong tide of déjà vu: I knew this place, or some version of it. Memory brought it back from the Hudson Valley town where Laura and I had lived when she first took me to see the things. The only difference was that she had brought me there at night and now, I was standing in a circle of daylight so sharp-edged that it felt unreal, like a stage set that had been designed especially for me—something both familiar and a little ominous. But I wasn't afraid. I thought all this repetition of things that had gone before—the movie, the bikes, this clearing—only showed the same lack of imagination I had guessed at earlier.

I walked across the grass towards a picnic table nearby. There were wooden benches on either side, both empty—or so it seemed at first. But suddenly, the air seemed to shiver, as if it was made of slats that were being opened and shut; the sunlight was momentarily closed off behind a curtain of shadow and then the light returned. When it did, one of the things was sitting at the picnic table.

Without hesitation, I walked over to the table and sat down across from the thing, which was wearing a sunhat and a short, floaty summer dress imprinted with daisies. It looked straight at me with its elongated, depthless eyes.

"Am I supposed to believe you're a girl?" I said to it. "Did you think that would make me feel better?"

Its mouth, a tiny slit almost invisible in its narrow face, did not move. There was no indication that it was even trying to reply.

"Listen to me," I said. "Don't play games with me. Don't show me movies. Don't stand on street corners again and think you can make me pay attention to you. If you're going to start all this up with me again, I want to know why."

Again, it simply stared at me. If it understood what I was saying, which I assumed it did, apparently I had not yet said whatever it was waiting to hear. *If* it was waiting to hear something from me. I took a guess at what that might be.

"Do you want me to tell you I'm grateful that you—one of you—saved me? Did you think that if you waited long enough, that's what I would feel? Well, I don't. It was John you should have saved. Or not driven Alice crazy in the first place, if that's what you did. Is it?" I demanded. I had thought that my newfound feeling of having some power over the things—these stupid, cross-dressing, drunken, blank-eyed creepy crawlies—would keep me from becoming agitated, but that didn't seem to be working. My anger was creepy-crawling itself back towards the surface. "*Is* that what you do?" I said. "Haul people out of their beds at night, stick probes into them and show them mon-ster babies? Do you enjoy that? Making them afraid of you? Ruining their lives? Still not the slightest reaction from Daisy Dress. It simply went on staring at me.

"Fine," I said. "Don't speak. Not that you can. Not that I want to hear your wounded cat voice ever again." I stood up and leaned over the table, pushing my face closer to the thing. Then, without even thinking about what I said next, these were the words that came out of my mouth: "I don't care about you. I never will. Do you understand? I am not my mother. Don't make the mistake of thinking that I am."

The anger that I had talked myself into believing I could deactivate of course, was beyond my control as was the loneliness that never left me because I was a child without a mother, and those were the voices that had spoken from inside me. If it was some vestige of a child's indestructible longing for her mother that had brought me here, then it was the thought of the damage I held her responsible for that also made me deny it. But my outburst, finally, seemed to provoke a reaction from Daisy Dress: it opened its slit of a mouth, though it made no sound. Maybe that was simply a gesture of surprise. Maybe some kind of heightened interest in what I was saying. I didn't have a chance to figure that out, though, because in the next instant, I felt something touch me from behind: there was a slight pressure along my back and down to my thighs, a dull tingle, as if a wire with a tremor of electricity in it had brushed against me.

I blinked, and then there were two things in my view: Daisy Dress was still sitting on the bench opposite me but now another thing, dressed in a similar outfit, was standing beside it. The pair glanced at each other and I thought I saw the one who was standing nod its head slightly. That must have been some kind of communication because, in the next instant, the thing that was seated at the table stood up, positioning itself shoulder to shoulder with its companion. Then, as if in lockstep, they turned and walked rapidly away from me. In just a few moments, they had stepped across the boundary of the clearing, into the trees, and were gone.

I stared at the spot where they had disappeared, but there was nothing to see, nothing to hear. I was surrounded by utter silence.

But then, almost immediately, I felt the ground beneath the picnic table begin to shudder. It was what I imagined an earthquake would feel like if it began slowly, if it had some kind of consciousness and wanted to give you a head start to get away. I jumped up from the bench I was sitting on and walked rapidly across the clearing in the direction of the gate that had led me here. The trembling beneath my feet grew stronger, quickly becoming so violent that I feared I might trip and fall. I began to run.

When I reached the stand of trees that ringed the clearing, I turned around to look behind me. What I saw was a cloud of dirt and dust that had been thrown up by the shaking ground. Some of this thick mixture drifted towards me and I began to cough. Dirt got into my eyes and made them sting. The world before me looked dark. Invisible.

I shook my head, wiped my tearing eyes with the edge of my shirt. When I was able to see again—when the dust cloud dissipated and my eyes blinked themselves clear—what lay before me was a changed landscape, a place that could not have been, and yet was the same clearing where I had just been sitting at a picnic table, only now the table, the benches, and the impossibly bright meadow where they stood were gone. In their place was a huge sinkhole surrounded by brown, scraped earth and broken rocks. The edges of the sinkhole were not stable: I could see puffs of dust rising from the ground as dirt and rocks continued to slowly slide into the abyss.

The columns of air around me seemed to brighten and where before there had been silence, now there was sound. The trill of birdsong gradually returned; I thought I could even hear car traffic somewhere off in the distance. Sunlight poured down again from a great blue sky; it even seemed to soften the contours of the broken landscape before me.

I felt as if I had just experienced a switch being made right in front of me, one scene substituted for another. Now, the scarred ground with its gaping hole was an undeniable reality: they were what really existed, what was supposed to be here. Where I had been a few moments ago—the clearing, the picnic table—where was that? I couldn't answer my own question except to think that it was somewhere else.

Well. There was no point in just standing there, watching sunlight and shadows move each other around. Watching earth slowly collapse into a giant hole. Nothing else was going to happen now. The things, certainly, weren't going to come back.

*The things weren't going to come back.* For the first time in my life, I found myself bristling at the idea that they had walked away from me. They had deliberately brought me here, then said nothing, done nothing except touch me, which I never would have allowed if I had realized that was what was happening. The memory of that brief contact lingered as the impression of an electric shiver that had run down my back. All of this was different than the way they used to behave. In the past, I had always felt that they were trying to cajole me into acknowledging them and I didn't have to if I didn't want to: one way or another, I could keep them at bay. When those rules—my rules—were violated, I lashed out. They knew that, didn't they? Maybe. But now it felt like something had changed, some kind of careful balance that had been established between us had fundamentally shifted.

None of the things had ever really found a way to make me pay so much direct attention to them before without some kind of violence on my part. And not one of them had been able to turn its back on me. Now all that had happened and I didn't like it. Not at all.

I also didn't like the fact that—of course—when I got back to the gate, the bike was gone. It belonged to that other scenario: the one with a clearing, a picnic table and two slim gray things wearing sundresses. I wasn't in the mood for a long walk on a hot summer day, especially since I hadn't brought my headphones with me. As I began to trudge up the bike path it occurred to me that I would have liked to complain to them about that. As if we had a relationship. As if we could talk.

# IV

"IT STOPPED WORKING. I can turn it on, but that's it. It just stays on that home screen, like it's frozen. I can't make a call."

I was back at Besso's, standing at the counter and grumbling at the nineteen-year-old about my phone. Today, he was wearing a muscle tee-shirt and had parked a cigarette behind his ear. We both stared down at the candy-bar shaped slab that was my cell phone, which was displaying the usual image on its start-up screen: two god-like hands reaching out for each other, backlit by a dull, greenish glow.

"You tried restarting it?" Nineteen asked, as he fiddled with the little roller bar underneath the screen that was supposed to allow you to toggle back and forth between the phone's functions.

"A bunch of times," I told him. "Nothing happens."

It was another sweltering summer Saturday morning. I hadn't planned on being here; what I'd wanted to do when I got up that morning was go to the movies—a normal, human movie. I had intended to catch a bus to Fordham Road—the Bronx version of the shopping center crossroads of the world—where an old movie palace had been converted into a multiplex and then figure out what I wanted to see. Given the neighborhood, I knew that my choices were likely to be either superheros or car-chase escapades but I didn't care much either way, since my main goal was simply to spend a few hours in air conditioning. Of course, that was a lie, and I knew it: what I really wanted was to double down on a new campaign I'd embarked on to keep myself occupied. I had spent much too much time this past week allowing my thoughts to drift—no, not *drift*: head like a straight line, like a bullet aimed straight and true, whether I liked it or not—back to the things and my surprising reaction to their walking away. I had come to no useful conclusions about how that had made me feel and all I had managed to do was upset myself. I had walked through the gate in the park believing I had some control over my life but here I was again, letting them take center stage in my life. *Not good, Julia,* I kept telling myself. *Not good at all.*

I had been at the bus stop before noon, but as I waited there, I felt my phone vibrate in the back pocket of my jeans. I thought that meant the cleaning agency was calling me about something like a change in my schedule, since they were the only people I had given my number to. It was when I tried to answer and was unable to that I realized the phone wasn't working. So, cancel the movie, at least for the time being. I had headed back to Besso's.

"When did it stop working?" Nineteen asked me.

"I don't know," I said. "I haven't really used it much since I got it."

The kid gave me a sort of pitying look: what kind of life must I have if I didn't need a phone to keep me connected to my vast network of friends and hookups? I almost wanted to explain that I hadn't even bothered to carry the phone with me all week since I knew where I was supposed to be and at what time, so there was no reason I needed to call anybody. That was when a little *click* went off in my brain: *think about it, Julia. Where has the phone been all week?* The answer to that question was, *in the pocket of these jeans, which I haven't had on since last Saturday—the day I had gone on that bike ride. The day I found the things waiting for me in the clearing.*

Suddenly, I had a bad feeling. And that feeling had had a cold, electric tingle to it—a memory of what I'd felt as I sat at the picnic table when I'd become aware that Daisy Dress number two was standing behind me. Had the second thing somehow managed to do something to the phone?

"Hello? You still with me?" Nineteen was frowning at me now, waving the phone in front of my face.

"What?" I said, since I had stopped listening to him while I thought about what might have happened to the phone last Saturday afternoon.

"Look, I'm trying to help you here," the kid said. "You want to hear what I got to tell you or not?"

"Okay," I said. "I'm sorry. Sure. What do you think is going on?" I now had my own suspicion, but since I wanted to be wrong, I thought I could invest a little more time in hearing an alternate theory of the crime. One I wouldn't have to deal with in a way I was already guessing that I would.

"As far as I can tell, someone sent you some kind of huge image file that's jamming up the phone. It looks like it's attached to a text message. That's kind of cool and all, but I didn't even know you could do that—I mean, beyond something really simple. "

Nineteen now gave me an accusing look; he seemed annoyed that I had brought him a problem that he wasn't even aware a cell phone could have. The phone was still clamped in his hand like a little hostage that wasn't going to be released until I gave up some kind of secret information. But I could hardly do that.

"I don't know what you're talking about," I said.

"Look," Nineteen said, "all you can do with a text message is type words. And with your service plan, the only people you can even do that kind of texting with is other peeps on your same plan. I heard that soon, on the big carriers—you know, like the regular phone companies and those guys—you'll be able to text people outside your network but even then I don't know if you'll be able to send big image files, which is what you definitely got on this phone. So what's going on? You can tell me, cookie. I mean, I don't care. If you're some kind of phone phreak..."

"What?" I said. "Freak?"

"Pha-reak. *Phreak.* With a *p.* Someone who screws around with phones. Come on. You know what I'm talking about." He leaned across the counter and presented me with a smarmy smile. "Maybe you got a boyfriend at home who's into phreaking and he rigged this phone for you? I thought phreaks mostly figured out ways to make free calls on landlines but maybe your guy is the King of the Phreaks and he jazzed this sucker up into some kind of hyperdrive. Is that it, cookie? You figured out how to send each other dirty pictures or something like that?"

"I think you're the freak," I told him, grabbing the phone back from him. "And I mean that with a great big *f.*"

"Listen," Nineteen said, "here's my '*f*—just calm the fuck down. All I'm telling you is that if you know a phreak who can rig a phone like yours, then we can work something out—provided, of course, that he can fix whatever he did, which I'll bet he can. Maybe you just don't get it, cookie, but what I'm saying is that phreaks get paid. So do the people who set up the deal, if you know what I mean. Come on," the kid said, enlarging his smile and pursing his lips, thinking he was cute. "This phreak. Introduce me."

I almost laughed. "You wouldn't like him," I said. "Or her. Them."

"Them?" Nineteen said. "There's a whole ring of them?"

"Yeah, maybe," I said. "A whole ring. A gaggle. Enough for a great, big playdate."

"Hey, no need to get snippy," Nineteen protested. "I'm just saying."

"I know what you're saying," I told him. "Thanks for your help."

I stuffed the phone back into my pocket and marched myself out of the store. Emerging into the street, I was assaulted by sunlight and let my growing anger boil along with the heat of the day because suddenly, I was feeling really upset. Gone was whatever equilibrium I thought I'd earned back this past week by trying to put the things out of my mind again. But now, not only were they front and center, I even had a new word for them: *phreaks*. Because certainly, they were responsible for the broken phone. If there was some sort of image file jamming it up, they had no doubt put it there—I was certain of it now because there was no other explanation. That cold electrical tingle I'd felt had not been just a movement of charged air passing behind me as Daisy Dress number two had made itself known; it had signaled the transference of some kind of message to the phone I'd forgotten to take out of my pocket when I'd gone back to my apartment after visiting Besso's last Saturday and put everything else away.

*Phreaks.* Great. Well, who did I have to blame for the fact that once again, the things had found a way to draw my attention to them? That would be me. It was me who had not only let myself be enticed into actually going to them, going to find them, but had also given them a new conduit for making contact by buying the damn phone.

Or was it just me, just my own fault? I was certainly in a mood to spread the blame around. Some dumb kid clerk in a dicey electronics store wasn't much of a candidate, but I had another one: Kel. Why not? Talk about opening a channel that I thought I had closed: I had lived my life for nearly ten years without even a glimpse of the things and then whammo, all I had to do was spend a few hours with him and not only were they back, they seem emboldened. And they seemed, once again, to have gotten the upper hand.

Oh yes. Time for me to have a little chat with Kel. I wanted to scream at someone, rip someone apart, and he was the first in line. The only one—unless I came upon one of the things on the way home, which didn't seem likely. They had laid down some sort of gauntlet and whether or not I wanted to, I had no choice but to pick it up. In fact, I had already picked it up—it was in my back pocket, inside my phone.

I went home and called Kel on the unhaunted, light-up-dial telephone beside my bed. When he answered, I spewed out the whole story—the cell phone I had bought in the street, the kid I had met on the way home last week, my bike trip to the double landscape beyond the gate in Van Cortlandt Park, and now, the picture jamming up the phone that I was apparently meant to see but could not. When I got to that part of the story, I even repeated the name that Nineteen had used to describe the things, though of course, he had no idea that was what he was doing. *Phone phreaks*, I said to Kel. *Can you believe it?*

When I was finally finished—and realized that I had probably been talking a mile a minute—there was a brief silence at the other end of the line.

"Are you there?" I said.

"That depends," Kel replied. "Do you want me to be? I mean, you could have told me all this right after it happened. You should have. I thought we had a pact."

"A pact? Really? Did we spit on our palms and shake hands? I kind of don't remember that."

"You know, you sound a little hostile. I remember when we first met, that was my impression of you. But then, after all these years, I thought you'd mellowed a little."

"When it comes to them," I said, "have you?"

"Point taken. So of course not. No."

"Then what do we do?"

Silence again. I heard some sounds in the background: pounding head-banger music, people talking. It was a Saturday afternoon; the tattoo shop was busy.

Finally, Kel said, "Actually, I have an idea, but it means we have to go out to Queens. There's a guy I know there...John knew him too."

"John knew him?" I paused. "You mean this guy...he's an experiencer?" The word was almost hard for me to say. I hadn't used it in what felt like forever.

"Well, he's had experiences but not like ours. You'll get it when you meet him."

"Sounds just fabulous," I said.

Kel heard the sour note in my voice. "You're being sarcastic."

"You think?"

"Look, I don't want any of this, either. We can just leave it alone. Leave it the way it was."

"It's too late for that. Something's changed."

"I know," Kel said. "I tried to tell you, remember? I've just been waiting..."

He didn't finish the sentence. Again, I heard the headbanger music hammering against the walls of the tattoo shop. "Waiting for what?"

"For this, I guess. For this."

We agreed to meet that night. Then, like normal people, we fell into a conversation about logistics: in order to get to Queens, where was the best place for us to meet, since I was coming from the Bronx and he was in the East Village? With the way that subway lines crisscrossed the city, we decided that the central point where would could most easily find each other was on the train stop where the downtown and uptown lines met at the last station in Manhattan before plunging through the tunnel under the East River.

"One last thing," Kel said before we hung up. "Do you still have your passport?"

"My Stargazer's passport?" I guessed that was what he meant, but the question surprised me. "Why?"

"Ted Devere. That's the name of the guy we're going to visit and those passports—they're kind of a thing with him."

That was even more surprising. "*Stargazer's* passports?" I said. "How does he even know about them?

"Long story," Kel said. "I'll make it shorter when I see you tonight, okay? Right now, I'm in the middle of inking some barbed wire around a guy's bicep."

That was the end of our conversation. After I hung up the phone, I sat on my bed for a while, in my half-bare room, not ready, yet, to go looking for what I apparently had to find. After a while, I curled up on the bed and closed my eyes. The windows were open but the air was still. I let myself rest in the quiet, under the blanket of immovable light. I think, for a while, that I even fell asleep.

But when I woke, the first thing I did was go to my closet and root around in the back until I found a particular shoebox that held nothing but one item. One little square of laminated cardboard that I had almost thrown away. Almost. I wasn't even sure why I had saved it. When I had moved—fled Manhattan and come here to the Bronx—I was deep in some cold-hearted darkness that laid itself across me like an iron shield. In that state, I was done with Nicky, even more done with Laura, and fighting every impulse to spend my days and nights doing nothing but mourning John. And when I fled with my cold heart and iron resolve, I thought that everything I owned except my talismans of protection—my music player, my headphones, my books and tapes and CDs—deserved to be consigned to the trash. And yet, that's not what I did with this one thing: instead, I had entombed it. Buried it in a box that once held a pair of sneakers. Good ones—running shoes, in fact. If there was any kind of symbolism in that, I didn't see it then and I wasn't about to spend any time thinking about it now. I just opened the box and retrieved my passport from the Stargazer's Embassy to the World. Apparently, according to Kel, it had some purpose to serve. Other than entitling me to a free drink in a certain bar in Freelingburg, I couldn't imagine what that might be.

# V

IT WAS ON the subway to Queens that I found out what was so important about the Stargazer's passport.

"Ted has one too," Kel told me.

That seemed impossible to me. "How did he get it?" I asked.

"He was there once," Kel said, "At the Stargazer's Embassy. He was making an appearance at Cornell and some students took him to the bar."

That information sounded even more baffling. "An appearance? Is he an actor or something like that? I mean, what does he do?"

"He takes pictures," Kel said. "With his mind."

We were on the N train, which had passed through the East River tunnel and was now rattling its way underground, station by local station, towards the north end of Queens. It was about eight at night, and most of the people on the train looked like they were coming home from the kind of job where you never get let out on time but nobody pays you for your extra hours. Occasionally, someone stole a glance at Kel; his ponytailed hair, along with the nasty tattoos and piercings, did not fit in with the working class vibe of the other passengers, but he paid no attention. He had explained that we had to ride the train to the last stop, so he wasn't even watching the stations. He seemed totally absorbed in what he was telling me—or trying to, anyway. It was a noisy ride and we had to lean close together to talk. I thought I was hearing him well enough, but I was still having trouble understanding what he was actually saying. A guy who took pictures with his mind?

"Is it some kind of trick?" I asked

"I don't think so," Kel said. "You really never heard of him?"

"No."

"Well, I guess you were just a kid when he was famous. He used to be on tv all the time—on those late-night talk shows they used to have before they were all hosted by comedians. And I remember a bunch of magazine articles about him—*Life* magazine did a whole spread. He also did appearances, like at colleges. He'd be on stage, and someone would hold a Polaroid camera in front of him. He'd kind of stare at it really hard and then it would produce a picture."

"Of what?"

"Oh, different things, but usually something nearby. A particular building. A dog that belonged to someone in the audience. A random person walking down the street. But sometimes, there was nothing much at all—just blurry images. Ted said he had no control over what the pictures showed."

The train's brakes suddenly screeched; the sound of steel grinding on steel was so loud that it seemed to fill up every inch of space around us. Then the train came to a halt. We were in a tunnel, between stations. The car lights dimmed as they lost voltage. After the noise of the brakes faded away, everyone in the car was silent because even a whisper would have been overheard. Kel, too, said nothing more.

We were in this suspended state for only a few minutes. When the lights came on again and the train began moving, I was the one who spoke first. In the silence before the train had jerked back into motion, a question had occurred to me. An important one.

"Do you know when Ted was at Cornell?" I asked.

"What you really mean is, when did Ted go to the Stargazer's, right? I was getting to that part," Kel replied.

"Because it was when I was there?"

Kel nodded. "It was the early nineteen-seventies, so yes, you were there."

"And my mother. He might have met my mother"

"Yes, I think that's likely."

211

There was something about the way he said that—some deeper story embedded in the bits and pieces of conversation we were having between the train's stops and starts. "Okay," I said. "Just tell me the rest."

"I only know what Ted told me once. Cornell was one of his last public appearances because something happened to him that night. He was on stage, there was an auditorium full of people, and a bunch of Polaroid instant cameras lined up for him on a table. That's all he used, Polaroids. The kind where you snap a picture, then the photo comes out of the camera and develops in a few minutes. Well, Ted picked up the first camera, did his Ted thing—he held the camera right in front of his face and stared at it. Then, all of a sudden, the camera ejected a picture. There was some sort of projection system set up on stage so that when Ted put the photo on the table and it started to develop, the image was displayed on a big screen that everyone could see. So, Julia, what do you think showed up on the photo that night?"

The way this story was going, I knew there was only one answer. "Really?" I said.

"Yes, really," Kel said. "Yes indeed. The very first image was your friends, the phone phreaks. The creepy crawlies. Big, blank black eyes, long gray faces, no nose, mouth like a slit. Sound familiar? Well, for over an hour, Ted made pictures come out of one camera after another, and the only picture that developed was that same one. An alien. Remember, this was more than twenty-five years ago. That long gray face wasn't plastered on book covers and tee shirts yet, so it kind of blew everyone's mind. But afterwards, a couple of students thought it was be a fine old joke to take him to the Stargazer's Embassy and get him a Martian cocktail or something like that."

"Nicky never served anything called a Martian cocktail."

"Julia," Kel said. "I'm kidding."

I shrugged. "What do I know? Maybe he did."

"Anyway," Kel continued, "I guess that night, at the bar, someone gave him a passport. Nicky, your mother—who knows? Someone did."

"And then?"

"And then, I guess he got drunk. Remember..."

"Right. Everybody all over the universe likes to get bombed."

"Ted in particular, I gather."

"And afterwards?"

"Afterwards? I don't know if anything else in particular happened that night, but it did pretty much mark the end for Ted. He gave a few more performances, but from that night on, the only images he could produce were the same. Aliens. Pretty soon, some jerk who called himself a professional skeptic—a guy who actually made his living as a magician, if you can believe that—decided to go after Ted. He wrote articles debunking what Ted did, he went on talk shows, supposedly proving that the cameras were rigged, that he had accomplices who put the film in the camera that was already imprinted with images—you know, like that. Not that Ted was a hard guy to malign: he was always difficult. Alcoholic, paranoid, violent—he got into a lot of fights." Kel smiled at me. "You'll like him."

"Thanks for the vote of confidence."

"Hey, I've never smashed a creepy crawly in the face. You get points for that."

I scowled at him; this wasn't what I wanted to talk about. "You said John knew him."

"He did. Somewhere along the line, when John started researching the abductions and treating experiencers, he must have come across Ted's story because from what I gather, he sought him out, to talk to him. He probably took the same trip we're taking now—Ted's lived in the same place forever. He works as the night janitor at the school near his apartment. Other than that, I heard he's pretty much become a recluse."

"Another downtrodden member of the universal cleaning crew." I sighed. "I probably will like him."

Again, the train braked to a screeching halt between stations, interrupting our conversation. There was no announcement, no explanation from the train crew about why we kept stopping in the dim tunnels.

When the train finally started up again, Kel continued the story. "John actually mentions Ted in his book."

"I didn't realize you read it."

"Of course I read it. I'm in it. At least, I think so. All his patients are referred to by pseudonyms. But Ted wasn't a patient, and there'd been enough written about him, I guess—at least back then, when he had some notoriety—for there to be no real reason for John to protect his identity."

"Did John think he was a fake?"

213

"No. He seemed to believe that Ted had some sort of unusual ability—but that was John, right? Always willing to believe something amazing was possible. In the book, he does refer to documented experiments with something similar called remote viewing. You know about that? The army spent a lot of time and effort trying to develop remote viewing as an intelligence tool they could use: they'd put someone in a room and ask him to draw a picture of some target on the other side of the world that he'd never seen, like a military base or a submarine. They eventually abandoned the idea but before they did, once in a while, it actually worked."

I wasn't much interested in that and was impatient to get Kel back to talking about John, about what he thought of Ted Devere. "So why did he think that Ted suddenly started producing pictures of the things?"

"His theory seemed to be that at Cornell, there was someone in the audience who was an experiencer and that somehow, Ted had picked up on the image of the aliens that person had in his or her mind."

"And how did you end up meeting this guy?" I asked.

"Back when John and Jim Barrett were working together, John sent Ted to see Jim. I guess he felt that Ted might have something useful to contribute to Jim's investigations, but I don't think that went anywhere. Ted did go to some of Jim's group meetings for a while—that's where we met. For a short time, we were sort of friends—you know, two misfits, with one thing in common: we both had Stargazer's passports. Ted used to love to show his to people; I think, in some way, he thought it was real, whatever that meant to him. Which is why I wanted you to bring yours. Like I told you, he can be pretty crazy, so just in case he flips out at the idea of my bringing a stranger around, the passport may help calm him down."

"How long has it been since you've seen Ted?" I asked

"Years," Kel confessed. "I tried to call him a couple of times but all I ever got was an answering machine with one of those robot voice messages. I'm really just assuming he's still at the same address."

The train stopped again—this time at a station. Except for us, all the other passengers got off and no one else got on. Kel turned his head to look out at the platform, finally checking on where we were. "Next stop," he told me. "End of the line."

About five minutes later, we disembarked at an underground station that looked like an arched tube made of white tile. There were metal benches painted orange at each end of the otherwise empty platform, which was so harshly lit it made me blink. As we walked, the sound of our footsteps echoed off the tile walls.

We climbed a long staircase and finally emerged onto the street. I felt a little disoriented: the underground station had been almost painfully bright; out in the summer night, the buildings all around us were dark and the moonless sky had wrapped its stars in dark, drifting clouds.

We were in a commercial neighborhood. A used car lot took up one side of the street; on the other was some sort of ironworks housed in a building that looked like it had been constructed from slabs of black slate. Broken sections of iron fencing were stacked outside in a yard.

Kel led me down this block and then another until we came to a more residential neighborhood where grim, cramped-looking houses clad in aluminum siding squatted one after another behind narrow porches. Sometimes, I could see the light of a television set through the curtains, or hear a dog bark as it picked up the sound of our footsteps as we passed by.

We kept walking. At some point, as I adjusted my backpack I was carrying, I thought about my phone, which I had carefully stowed inside before I left my apartment—the phone that was the reason for our long train ride and now, this seemingly endless walk.

"You know," I said to Kel, breaking the silence we had kept since we'd gotten off the train, "I'm still not really sure why we're doing this. How do you expect this guy to fix the phone?"

"I don't expect him to fix it," Kel said. "Wherever you got that piece of junk, you're probably just going to have to go back and get another. What I am hoping Ted can do is take a picture of what image is inside it and show that to us. Do you have a better idea?"

"Nope," I said. "But how much farther do we have to go?"

"One more block," Kel told me. "See there? Just past the school."

We turned a corner and he pointed to a huge, hulking building that seemed to obscure the horizon. It looked more like a prison than a school; every blank window was hidden behind bars, every entrance to the concrete yard that surrounded the building was chained shut.

We walked past the school, picking our way along the cracked sidewalk under the stale sodium glare of the streetlights. Finally, we came to a building that looked like a brick rectangle pushed up against the night sky. It was an apartment building just a few stories high, rundown and weary looking.

"*That's* where we're going?" I asked.

"Yup." Kel said. "Ted lives in the basement."

We went around to the back of the building where there was a line of garbage cans stacked against a high wall. Beyond the wall was more of the same landscape we had just passed through: dark streets, narrow houses, locked up shops and factory buildings. The far reaches of the borough of Queens, beyond the subway lines.

Kel walked down a ramp that led to a metal door. It had no bell, no nameplate. Kel waited a moment, as if he were listening for any kind of sound inside, and then knocked several times, hard.

"Ted," he called. "It's Kel. Kel," he repeated. "Remember me? I'm a friend of Jim Barrett's."

I noted who he mentioned—Jim Barrett, not John, but said nothing about that as we waited for a response from behind the metal door. There was none.

"Ted," Kel called again. "Look under your door. I'm going to show you my passport."

He reached into his back pocket and pulled out his Stargazer's passport, which he slipped under the door, leaving an edge of the document visible on our side of the entrance. After that, we waited. A few long minutes seemed to pass.

And then, all of a sudden, the document vanished. Someone on the other side of the door had pulled it in.

Finally, the heavy metal door swung open. A man stood in the entrance: thin, almost ravaged-looking, with an unruly shock of dark hair. He stared at us with wild-looking eyes.

"Is it really you?" Ted Devere asked Kel. He sounded not just suspicious, but convinced that someone was trying to play a trick on him. A bad one.

"I promise, it's me, Kel. And this is my friend Julia. Show him your passport, Julia."

I had it ready and handed it over to Ted. As he examined it, studying it as intently as if it really was some sort of official document, I studied him. He was dressed in outdated, ill-fitting clothes—pants held up by a frayed brown belt and a white, short-sleeve shirt that all looked like they had been rescued from a Good Will bin. And how old was he? That was hard to tell, but my guess was that while he was probably in his seventies, he actually looked even older. Maybe that was partly because he was so pasty-looking; his skin gave the appearance of being paper thin, never nourished by the light of day.

Suddenly, Ted looked up and spoke directly to me. His whole demeanor had changed: my first impression had been that he seemed like the kind of person you'd cross the street to avoid if he was walking in your direction, a crazy guy who would be muttering curses and talking to himself. But now, he seemed almost imp-like: his smile was mischievous, his attitude radiated playfulness.

"I have a passport, too," he said, as he handed mine back to me. "I'll show it to you."

I looked at Kel and he looked back at me, shaking his head. Obviously, this nice Ted was not exactly the person he had expected to encounter.

Ted turned and walked into his apartment; Kel and I followed after him, entering a room that, while nearly bare, I could hardly think poorly of, since my place wasn't much better. He had a couch, a standing lamp, a table and a mis-matched pair of folding chairs, along with a portable television set sitting on a low bookcase with empty shelves.

Ted reached under the couch and pulled out an old shoebox that had been painted black and covered with the kind of stick-on silver stars you could buy in a stationery store. He opened the box and pulled out his passport from the Stargazer's Embassy to the World. It did kind of give me the chills that he was keeping his passport in a shoebox, just as I had—though there was more weird stuff to come. He handed the passport to me and as I took it from him he looked at me and smiled. "Your mother gave me that."

Though Kel had already suggested that something like this was true, it was still pretty shocking to hear it so directly from Ted. Besides, how could he know who I was? I looked over at Kel, but he shrugged and shook his head. One surprise was following another.

"That's very nice," I said, realizing, too late, that I probably sounded like I was addressing someone who was mentally challenged. I took a breath and pulled myself past that moment. "But how do you know the person who gave you this..."

"Laura," Ted said, tapping a finger to his forehead. "I remember her name."

"Yes, Laura. How do you know she was my mother?"

"You look just like her," he said. "But that's not all."

"Oh?" I said. "What else? I mean, how else..."

I wasn't sure how to finish the question. Ted went on smiling at me. "You've got their pictures in your mind, just like she did," he said. "I don't always need a camera anymore to see them."

"Them?" I said.

"Oh, you know," he replied, leaning forward, as if trying to peer straight into my head. "Yup," he said, sounding satisfied. "They're in there alright." Now, his mischievous smile grew even wider. "Do you want to see her pictures?"

"*Her* pictures?" Suddenly, I felt my heart start pounding in my chest. "What do you mean?"

"I guess that didn't come out right," Ted replied. "The first picture was hers. All the others are mine, I suppose." Then, as if addressing himself, he added, "Well, of course they are."

He reached out and took my hand, pulling me forward toward a door that led to another room. I looked back at Kel, who simply shook his head again—if he had thought he was going to have any control over this visit to Ted Devere, he knew he had already lost it. He followed us as Ted opened the door and we all walked into the room beyond.

Ted turned on the light and I heard myself gasp. I don't know what I thought might be behind that closed door, but it wasn't anything I might have expected.

On one side of the room were tall metal shelves that held dozens of Polaroid cameras. The only other objects in the room—and there were hundreds and hundreds of them—were more painted shoeboxes covered with silver star stickers. There were towering stacks of these boxes, piled one on top of another. Many of the boxes were open, and out of them spilled what had to be thousands of Polaroid photos. Every surface of the wall space other than where the shelves of cameras stood was also covered with Polaroids, some affixed with pushpins, some with yellowing tape. And each and every photo was of the same hauntingly, maddeningly familiar subject: the things.

"My God," I heard myself say as I looked around. When I glanced over at Kel, he looked as shocked as me.

Ted, meanwhile, was moving around the room, going from box to box, clearly looking for something. Finally, as if a memory came back to him like one of his photo images lighting up his brain, he pushed aside a stack of boxes to get to the far wall. There, he found what he wanted, a photo he carefully pulled from its place in the corner, the only one of the photographs I could see that had been put into a frame.

He handed it to me. The frame was black, one of those inexpensive pieces fronted by a thin sheet of glass that can be bought in any dollar store, but I knew it signified the fact that Ted had made a special effort to preserve the photograph inside. I looked at the picture while Kel looked over my shoulder.

What we saw staring out at us was one of the alien figures—a phreak, a creepy crawly, a thing—with its black, almond-shaped eyes and expressionless, triangular face. I wasn't surprised to see that this one was dressed in a costume—a familiar one, actually, since Kel had already described it to me: a blue, sharkskin suit with thin lapels and sharply creased slacks. When I looked closer, I also noticed that the thin, gray fingers of its hand were wrapped around the handle of what appeared to be some sort of old-fashioned canvas satchel, the kind of item someone going on a trip might have carried in some previous century.

"That's the thing you saw at the Stargazer's sitting with my mother," I said to Kel.

He nodded in agreement and then pointed at the photo. "Look at the background." he said.

I looked, though it was hard to see because the photo had been produced in a nighttime setting, so the figure seemed to be standing against nothing other than a black background. But as I kept looking, the darkness began to assemble itself into objects, as if they wanted me to identify them. There was a doorway, there were iron benches standing on either side of that doorway, and there, surely, was a huge, shield-shaped escutcheon above the door, depicting two large stars and three smaller companions, just like the tattoo on my wrist.

"It's standing right outside the bar," I said to Kel—but it was Ted who replied to me.

"Oh yes, that's the place," he said, sounding actually joyful. "And that's the picture your mother showed me, in her mind. The first time I saw her visitors."

He took the framed picture back and went to return it to its particular spot among the other photos. As he did, Kel whispered, "I guess that's the real story. He didn't pick up an image from a person in the audience—somehow, he connected with your mother."

"Like you did," I said. "At the Stargazer's Embassy."

"Jesus," Kel said. "This is beginning to remind me of some supernatural version *Everybody Comes to Rick's.*" In case I didn't get the reference, he added, "*Casablanca.*"

"I know what you meant," I said. And remembered that John had said something similar to me, years ago, also in connection with my mother. Laura, so long gone from my life, still seemed to be, somehow, the nexus of it.

"Listen, Ted," Kel said, moving away from me. He walked over to Ted, who was still busy arranging the stacks of photos that had been disturbed when he removed the framed image he'd wanted to show us. "Do you still see these, uh, visitors?"

"Oh yes," he said. "I mean, not directly. Not in person, so to speak. But I take pictures of them all the time. Whenever they're around," he said vaguely. "Mostly when they're thinking about traveling. Going from station to station. They think about that a lot, but I don't think they've gone anywhere in a long time."

*Going from station to station?* What did *that* mean? I had no idea, so the best I could do was focus on one fact, one image that stood out from what Ted had just said to me. "Was that why the visitor in the picture you showed me was carrying a suitcase?" I asked. "Because he—they—are traveling somewhere?"

"Yes!" he said. "Exactly." Then, as if sharing a confidence with me, he lowered his voice. "I don't think they really know what suitcases are, though. And I'm sure they don't really need them. It's just that they don't actually know how to dress, do they? Well, why would they?" he said, seeming to be asking himself a question, not me. And then he answered it. "They're not really here—and we're not really there, where they are—so I think all they get is a glimpse of us. We see them better than they see us—that's my theory, anyway. And that's why I think they're so hit and miss with the clothes. What do you think?"

I had no clue of course, but at this point, I was just trying to follow what he was saying—most of which was completely confusing to me, so I simply agreed with him. "Sure," I said.

Kel, though, was much more impatient; it seemed the more Ted babbled on, the more tense Kel became. I could feel it.

"Listen, Ted," he said, "What do you mean by we're here and they're there? I don't understand."

Ted glanced at Kel with what seemed almost like a pitying expression on his face. "Well, here is *here*, obviously. Where we are. The visitors are nearby. Really close. It's not as easy for them to get back and forth as everybody thinks. That's what your mother told me" he said, turning back to look my way. "I only met her that one time, but she was so nice. I could see why they liked to be around her. And around the Embassy. It's a fun place to have a drink. The good ones like to drink," he continued. "They're partial to Jack, I think. Did you know that?"

"I told you," Kel said to me, though his voice sounded a little strangled, like it was coming from a dry throat. He didn't seem totally comfortable with the idea that the joke he had made to me was, maybe, not a joke at all. "Jack Daniels. Tennessee sipping whiskey. Famous all over the universe."

I didn't respond to him because I wasn't all that interested in cosmic drinking habits right now. I kept my attention centered on Ted. "You thought my mother was nice?"

"She sure was to me. Your mother was real sweet, real patient. I showed her the photo and she tried to explain to me who they were. I can't help them, though, poor guys. I'm not very nurturing. I'd be no good at all with babies. I do like cats, however. I like them a lot."

All I wanted to do, right then, was keep quiet and go on listening to him. *Cats, babies*: I knew I should force some deeper conversation about all this but my mind was still laser-focused on the fact that he had met my mother, that he thought she was a nice woman. Sweet. *Sweet?* And patient, as well? Not with me—at least, not that I could remember. I found myself wishing that he would tell me more about her. I was so consumed with that desire I didn't even notice that a cat had, in fact, slipped into the room.

The cat was dark gray, almost smoke colored. It walked up to Ted, moved slowly around him in a circle, then jumped onto one of the stacks of boxes and seemed to turn itself into a statue. It sat and watched us.

"That's Wendy," Ted announced.

The name seemed so unlikely for such a spectral looking animal that I was momentarily distracted. I felt like the cat had disturbed the air in the room, which was only now settling back into place, like thin sheets fluttering down one on top of the other.

"Wasn't your mother nice to you?"

"What?" I said. I thought, somehow, that the cat had become the object of his attention, but apparently he still wanted to talk about Laura. Or about me and Laura. "We had a difficult relationship," I told him. "And then she died..."

He asked when, and I told him. "I guess that's why the pictures stopped."

"Did they?" I said, looking around the room at the seemingly endless boxes and stacks of photographs. It didn't seem possible that he had ever stopped adding to this stockpile.

But Ted said, "Yes. For a long time." He suddenly darted over to a corner of a room and quickly returned, holding a shoebox full of photos. He hadn't had to hunt for this bunch; apparently, he knew exactly where he'd put them. "For years, all I could get were these," he said, handing me the box. I pulled some out and saw dim, blurry photos of someone's lawn, a river winding through a landscape of weeds and cattails, a city block crowded with faceless people. "Boring, right?" Ted said disdainfully. "I couldn't stand it. So you know what I did?" He smiled. It was a wide, almost mischievous grin. "I went back to the Embassy. I had to take two buses. It's a very long trip."

"I know," I said guardedly. *Where was this story going now?*

"Your mother wasn't there anymore. I didn't know that then, when I started my trip. But I know it now. I mean, I know why: because she died. Thank you for telling me."

What was I supposed to say? Using the cleaning lady's good manners, I tried to sound formal, serious. "You're welcome."

Ted nodded. He had put a serious expression on his face, as well, and let it stay there for a few moments. But he quickly reverted to being playful.

"I did get a free drink, though, because I had my passport," he said brightly. "And I watched a movie with a giant robot."

My turn to nod. "I've seen it a few times."

"It was a good movie," Ted told me. "But what was even better was that I knew they were around...the visitors. And as long as I knew where they were, I could take pictures of them again."

"What?" I said. Could I possibly have heard him right? "The visitors live in Tompkins County? In *Freelingburg*?"

"Of course not," Ted said, and now the expression on his thin, bony face changed again. He was regarding me with what almost looked like pity— apparently, I was beginning to strike him as a little dim. "I told you, they live where they live, which is not exactly here. But they know where the Embassy is, that's for sure. I told you, it's a nice place to have a drink. Who doesn't like that?" He put down the shoebox and smiled at me. "Your mother made that place what it was. She welcomed everybody who wandered in."

There she was again: the Laura that Ted Devere had apparently known. Kind, welcoming, friendly. I hadn't known that woman, not at all. I could only wonder, *Who was she?* As if answering me, Ted spoke again. "Julia," Ted said, "do you want to see?"

"See what?" I asked.

The answer came with a mechanical sound, a kind of a click and a *whoosh*, amplified over and over again as the several dozen cameras stacked on the rack of metal shelving suddenly came to life. I looked in that direction and saw nothing—but I could hear them. There was some kind of internal hum coming from every one of the cameras, as if they were talking to themselves.

And then, suddenly, one by one, they began to disgorge their photos. One, two, three—and then ten, twenty, thirty, even more. Maybe there were fifty or sixty cameras on the shelves and now, each one of them was spitting out a photo.

I looked back at Ted, who was once again smiling broadly. "Go on," he said. "Take a look."

I walked over to the rack of cameras and pulled out one of the developed pictures. It was about three inches by four inches, with a white border. The photo itself was dark; its surface was damp. At first, I couldn't make out any shapes or forms, but little by little, moment by moment, the image began to develop, seeming to slowly swim up to the surface from somewhere beneath—inside?—the thin piece of photo paper, as if there was a dimension to the photograph that I couldn't see.

But suddenly, what I could see, and see clearly, was the picture that Ted, apparently, had just caused to appear. I looked at it, looked again, and then pulled another one out of a different camera, and then another and another, until I was holding ten or twelve in my hands. Kel started doing the same thing, pulling photos from the cameras. Each of us was now holding a sheaf of photos we had taken from the cameras stacked one next to the other on the metal shelves. They all showed the same picture: seen from the back, a young woman with long, dark hair, a fringed jacket, jeans and boots was walking on a rural road that ran towards the edge of the photo and disappeared into the white border.

Kel came over to me, his hands full of photos. He said, "It's like a still from the movie we saw. The last scene."

"No," I replied. "It's different. In the movie she was walking towards this part of the road, where it makes a bend." I put down all the photos I was holding, except one. Then, with one finger, I traced the path that the figure—Laura—was walking. "Now, she's passed it. The bend in the road is behind her."

I looked over at Ted. "Where did this come from?" I asked him. "The picture. Where...how did you get it?

He laughed. "You brought it," he said. "It's in your phone."

I had actually forgotten about the phone, which was the reason we had come here in the first place. It was still in my backpack, which I had left in the other room.

Suddenly, Kel seemed to come back to life. Except for the few words he'd said about the photo, he had kept silent for the past ten minutes or so while Ted talked to me. But something had come over him now: impatience, anxiety—something. He threw the photos of Laura into the nearest shoebox and then strode over to Ted.

"Listen to me, Ted. I get that your...friends are interested in Julia's mother. That's all just great. But I want to ask you about something else, something you said before." Kel started speaking very slowly, as if he was concerned that he wouldn't be understood—or perhaps, not paid attention to. "You said something about babies. I mean, I heard you say that, right? Babies? What were you talking about?"

"Oh, they're all making babies. Hybrids, I guess they are," Ted replied cheerily. Kel, however, seemed shocked by this. He opened his mouth to say something, but before he could form the words—perhaps before he could even figure out what to say—Ted had an additional piece of information to share. "All of them. The good ones and the bad ones. You should stay away from the bad ones. That's what I think, anyway." He turned away from us then, bending down to pick up the pictures Kel had let slip from this hands and moving them to another shoebox. Apparently, there was some system to the way he stored the photos, despite the chaotic look of the room.

"What do you mean?" I asked, since I thought his warning was meant for me. *Good ones and bad ones?*

But Kel was on a mission now; he wanted an answer to his question. He grabbed Ted's arm, made him stop his tidying up. "Do you have pictures of the, uh, babies?"

"Oh no," Ted said. "Too sad. Much too sad." He shook himself free of Kel's grip and addressed me again. "That's what your mother said, too. Very sad. She felt bad for them. And I think she felt bad for me, in a different way. But that's how I felt about her, too. She was lonely, you know. She really didn't have anyone to talk to. She told me that," he concluded.

My first thought was to defend myself. *Hey,* I wanted to say to Ted Devere, *she* had no one to talk to? Which meant that *she* was lonely? Want to hear how I felt? But then I reminded myself that Ted couldn't have meant to chastise me about my mother's loneliness, because no matter how psychic he was—if that was what was going on, part of the mystery involved in how he manifested these pictures—how much could he really intuit about my relationship with Laura? He seemed to think that everything between us was fine—and also that I knew more about her and her drinking companions (*and there,* I thought, *another name for them*) than I really did.

"Look Ted," Kel broke in again. "These babies..."

But Ted wouldn't let him finish. His demeanor changed again; suddenly, he was all business. Still pleasant, but clearly done with us. With Kel, at least. He waved his arms, as if swatting away a swarm of intruders.

"I have to go to work now," he said.

Maybe he did, maybe he didn't. But I was done now, too. I had received much more information than I expected—and more, probably, than I wanted. I was ready to leave.

I turned to go but Kel, stubbornly, was still standing in front of Ted as if he meant to block his way. Ted quickly zipped around him, though, disappearing behind a stack of shoeboxes. I thought the boxes were stacked against the wall, but apparently not: there must have been enough room behind them for Ted to slip into some small space that had been left open. He was back in a few moments, holding something in his hand.

"Here," he said, dropping some small object into my hand. "You're going to need this. Your phone is never going to work again."

I looked down. What now lay across the flat of my hand was something smaller than the Polaroid prints. It had weight to it, but looked as thin as a wafer, as sleek as a piece of polished steel.

"What is it?" I asked.

"It's a phone," Ted said. "I have dozens of them. A friend sends them to me because they have great cameras in them. You can't buy them in a store yet, but they're coming." Then he added, "Maybe not this model, exactly, but somebody's working on it. Somebody's always working on something, you can bet on that."

I barely paid attention to his philosophizing, if that's what it was. I was too captivated by the actuality of the object that now lay in my hand. A phone that could also take pictures? Even Nineteen hadn't mentioned anything like that. Staring at the phone, I couldn't imagine how you would use it like a camera because I couldn't even figure out how to turn it on. Ted must have registered how confused I was because, like a magician finishing his act with a flourish, he pointed his index finger at me, waved it around a few times, and then touched the side of the phone. The whole surface suddenly lit up. Instead of the dim little screen on the top of my fake Nokia—now, apparently, deceased—the entire front of this phone *was* the screen. Further, it seemed to glow, like a slender sheet of backlit glass. And it had little icons on it that seemed to float against a deep blue background. I could identify what some of them were: the tiny pictures of a telephone, camera, and keyboard were obvious, but there was one that—though instantly recognizable—conveyed no meaning I could think of.

"Hello Kitty?" I said to Ted, pointing to the round, white face of cat with eyes like blank, black pins and no visible mouth.

"It's an app," he told me. "They're installed on all the phones I got from my friend." I must have looked puzzled, because he said, "Apps," he repeated. "*Applications.* They're coming, too. Just wait."

"What's it for?" I asked, meaning the little cat picture.

"I like cats," Ted told me. "I like to know what they're thinking. That Wendy, for example," he said, turning to point his magician's finger at the gray cat, which I had completely forgotten about. The cat was still sitting silently atop one of the stacks of shoeboxes covered with stars. "She's always got something on her mind."

Suddenly, Wendy made a sound; something between a growl and a sing-songy screech. It startled me, but it made Ted laugh. "Try it," he said, gesturing at the phone again. "Just touch the picture."

I did. I touched the picture of Hello Kitty on the screen of the phone I was holding in the palm of my hand. Its blank, almost featureless face was sort of mesmerizing. Then, suddenly, the black eyes—eyes without pupils—started to blink. And then the phone spoke. Out of a tiny speaker somewhere on the side of the phone came a mechanical voice, robotic and emotionless. "I'm hungry," it said.

"That's it?" Ted said, addressing his cat. "That's all that's on your mind? Oh well. First things first, I guess."

He now made a big show of looking at his watch, tapping it impatiently, and frowning, though he directed the frown at Kel, not me. "I really do have to get to work," he said. "Lots of floors to clean in that school. Summer school classes are the worst. Takes me all night."

He practically pushed us out of the apartment then, shooing us along with the cat following right behind him. Kel was already halfway out the front door when I stopped, for a moment, to pick up my backpack. As I did, Ted came close to me and whispered, "You didn't need the passport, you know." Gently, he touched the tattoo on my wrist; I had the feeling that it was the same way he would touch his little cat app. "I would have known you anywhere," he told me. And then he closed the door behind me. Our visit with Ted Devere was over.

I followed Kel up the stairs to the street. Still processing everything that had just taken place, I said, "That Ted. He's nothing like I expected. I thought he'd be some kind of miserable loser. But he's, like, the happiest guy on the planet."

Kel ignored what I said. He had an agitated, almost angry look on his face. "We have to talk to Jim," he said.

"What?" I said. I couldn't imagine any reason that Jim Barrett was suddenly on his mind. "Why?"

"Why? Because this is all too much for us. For me, at least. Travelers with suitcases? Good ones and bad ones? And they're all making babies? *Babies?* That's what Alice said all along. And Jim. Ted never mentioned anything like that before. At least, not to me."

All I heard was Alice's name, and it irritated me. "Alice?" I said. "You're going to quote *Alice* to me?"

Kel didn't reply. He strode off down the street, as if he didn't care whether I came with him or not. I watched him as he walked through the sickly pink pool of light cast by the sodium glare of the streetlight on the corner, disappearing, almost, into the darkness beyond. I ran to catch up with him.

"Listen," I said, grabbing his arm, "all that back there—that was about my mother. *My mother.* About Laura."

I had to convince Kel of that. I couldn't have explained why, but the strongest feeling had come over me that what I was saying was true. That nothing else Ted said could matter or even be understood unless we both recognized that somewhere in the middle of all the seemingly crazy information Ted had dumped on us was something really important that I had to figure out about my mother. It was ironic—I knew that, I knew it as deeply as I had when I'd gotten on the mystery bike and ridden into the woods to meet the things. I had spent my life running away from Laura, but somehow, now—at least in this moment—she seemed closer to me than she had ever been. And I, closer to her. Whether that was good or bad, I wasn't sure, but I also wasn't going to let anyone else decide the answer for me.

"I'm sorry, Julia," Kel said, "but I can't work out what all this means."

"Then just stay out of it," I said, vehemently. "I can handle it myself."

"*Handle* it? This can't be handled. It has to be confronted in some way; it has to be dealt with. And the only person I know who can do that—who wants to do that—is Jim Barrett."

"Well, aren't you the big, brave guy? You're the one who told me that you wanted to see them again—the things. The creepy crawlies. The Jack Daniels fans. You wanted your questions answered."

"I did. I do. But right now, I'm pretty sure I won't like what I might find out. I never wanted to believe that they're conducting some sort of...well, what? A breeding program? But if they're creating babies, that means they're trying to create hybrids, which means, yes, Alice was right and Jim is right. They're doing something very scary. Dangerous."

"You're afraid of them," I said.

"If I wasn't before—or afraid enough—then I was stupid," Kel said. "But yes, right now, right here, I'm scared shitless of them. You should be, too."

With that, he started walking away from me again and this time, I let him go. I'd had enough of him. More than enough, so I just watched as he walked off into the summer night.

Once he was gone, and I was standing on the street alone, I realized that I might—just might—be a little lost. It was late, it was dark out, I was somewhere deep in the ass-end of Queens by myself, and I wasn't really sure how to find my walk back to the subway station. There was no one around to ask, and on the way over here, I hadn't paid much attention to any particular landmarks I could recall: one rundown house looked just like another, so did the shuttered stores and industrial lots full of junked cars and scrap metal. Well, what was I going to do? I was just going to have to start walking and hope that somehow, I was heading in the right direction.

# VI

FOR THE REST of the summer, August through the warm days of September, I was on a mission to keep myself occupied—or better, to lose myself in work. Exhausting, endless hours of work. I told the agency that I would take on any extra jobs, extra hours they could give me, and they had plenty, so—like Ted, ironically, and the irony wasn't lost on me—I found myself cleaning school buildings at night, along with office suites and stores in strip malls. On Labor Day weekend, from midnight until dawn, I even found myself in the back rooms of a suburban ice skating rink, cleaning the concession stands and locker rooms. As always, I had my CD player, my earbuds and my music with me and on that job, I listened to heavy metal stuff all night; it kept me going. Even better, the pounding music made it impossible to think, which was fine with me because all my thoughts only led me down blind alleys.

Sure, I had stood up to Kel; sure, I had said that I could handle anything that came my way—but the problem was, I had no idea what that might actually be, so I had no clue how to prepare. All I knew to be true was what I had said to Kel: that whatever the things were after, it involved Laura: something about her, connected to her, was at the center of this new, heightened phase of my involvement with the things. But that was as far as I could get in figuring all this out, so there was nothing to do but wait. And since I hated the waiting, I just kept working. I worked myself to exhaustion and then worked some more.

On almost all my extra jobs, the people I worked with—mostly women, some men—spoke no English, or very little. Spanish, Russian, Chinese, Korean, and other languages that I couldn't possibly understand. I got by with nods and hand signals. *Pass me the bleach, I'll do the mopping, you wipe down the desks*—there's a lot of information that can be exchanged with pantomime. Without words. I got very good at it.

So I didn't talk to the people I worked with, but they talked all night. I recognized, now, that everyone in the world—my world, at least, the post-midnight cleanup squad—had a cell phone, and as they worked, they often talked on their phones in their incomprehensible languages (well, incomprehensible to me) to unseen people in some unseen place. Home, perhaps, or laboring away at late-night work of their own, or maybe even in some far away country, living in an hour, a time of day that was the reverse of ours. I had no idea, no way of knowing.

I almost never used my own phone, the new one that Ted Devere had given me. No one but the cleaning agency had my number, and they mostly left messages for me on my home phone, which had an answering machine. But once in a while, I'd feel a buzz in my pocket, where I kept the phone, and pull it out to find that the agency had another last-minute job for me—sometimes, that meant I went from all-night work to all-day, without stopping, but I was getting very good at that, too.

One night, on a high floor of an office tower in White Plains, I was working with a fairly large cleaning crew when my phone rang. I had my earbuds in and AC/DC was hammering away in my head, so I didn't hear it. Maybe, this night, I had bumped it or something and accidentally changed the setting from vibrate to sound. In any case, I had no idea that phone was making any kind of noise until one of the cleaning crew, a woman, tapped me on the arm and pointed to the pocket of my jeans.

I pulled out my earbuds and heard the fake, old-timey ringer of the kind of rotary phone that you used to make calls from in a booth, in the corner candy store. It was something pre-programmed into the phone—somebody's idea of retro Western culture cool—and I had never bothered to change it.

I pulled the phone out of my back pocket and listened to the night-shift supervisor at the cleaning agency ask me if in addition to my scheduled afternoon job in Scarsdale, I could sub a half day for someone who was sick; she cleaned and did laundry in a house not far from my regular client in that town. I had planned to go home for a while and catch a few hours of sleep before going back to work around noon, and if I said yes to this extra shift, I would end up going something like eighteen hours without even a nap. I said yes.

I guess I had been staring down at the floor while I was talking to the supervisor, because when I finally clicked off the call and started to put the phone back into my pocket, I looked up and saw the rest of the crew standing around me in a kind of semi-circle, watching me with wide eyes. At first, I couldn't imagine what they found so fascinating, but I quickly realized that what they were really staring at was my phone.

After I'd first gotten the phone from Ted Devere, I hadn't spent a lot of time thinking about how different it was than anything else I had ever seen before—or anyone else had seen, for that matter. When I had brought it into Besso's to have my calling plan switched over, Mr. Nineteen, who, by now, must have considered me one of his best customers, nearly flipped out as soon as he saw it. Then he offered to buy it from me, or trade me a ton of other electronic equipment if I'd hand it over. After all, who couldn't use a multi-speaker boom box or a remote-controlled helicopter? Well, not me, so I said no and related what I remembered of what Ted had told me about the phone: they'll be available eventually, just wait, this is an advance model someone gave me, blah, blah, blah. What I didn't say was that the phone had become a kind of talisman for me, a touchstone. Every time I switched it from one pocket to another, or stashed it in my pocket or backpack, I thought about Ted Devere. I thought about how happy a guy he seemed to be in the middle of what should have been a life in decline. About his strange pictures, his memories and his warnings. *Your mother was real sweet, real patient. The good ones and the bad ones.* I may have used the phone only occasionally, but I was hardly about to let it go.

Now, as I held it in my hand, its rectangular screen black and blank and smooth as polished glass, I watched the eyes of the others on the cleaning crew watching me. They were all relatives from someplace in Peru, some old village with Mayan roots. I knew that because I'd been on night assignments with them before; the agency called them "the cousins," and often kept them together on jobs because they seemed to work most efficiently that way.

But it was a little weird to have them all staring at me. They all had their own cell phones of course—some version of my fake Nokia, no doubt, bought from the same kind of sketchy street vendor—but none of them had seen anything like my gift from Ted Devere. Wanting the moment to pass, I put the phone away and went back to my part of the job, which was cleaning the desks of absent, unseen workers, wiping up their coffee spills and disposing of their candy wrappers and soda cans.

Finally, the cousins dispersed and went back to their work. They barely even acknowledged me for the rest of the night though once in a while, I'd catch one of them stealing a glance over at me. I was the foreigner here, the odd one, the stranger who had possession of a strange device.

I detached myself from the cousins' crew just after dawn. They all piled into an ancient van driven by some other relative who had come to pick them up, while I walked a half mile to a bus stop and waited for the bus to arrive. At this hour of the morning, the air felt stratified, as if the seasons were laid one on top of the other, like invisible planks. It was still warm outside, but the lower temperatures of fall were twined through the upper elevations of the atmosphere. It was an hour between worlds, an hour of changing light and moving skies.

I worked my extra job, went on to my regular client, and then finally headed home, arriving at another hour that was busy changing its scenery: the red dusk was heated with sunset but chilled by a rising moon, huge and bright. I was exhausted. I made myself a sandwich, wolfed it down, and then, on my way to take a shower, detoured to the bedroom and fell instantly, deeply asleep.

But not deeply enough, perhaps, because I was troubled by troubling dreams. Or at least, one particularly disquieting dream. It was a kind of recreation of the past night's incident with my cell phone, where I stood in the middle of a circle of small people with huge bug eyes, watching me as I clutched the phone. Some of them were carrying suitcases, some were wearing dresses covered with daisies. Some, I knew, had seen a woman in a fringed jacket walking past the bend in a road. They wanted something from me, these people, but I didn't know what. In the dream, I thought I could make a phone call to find out, though I wasn't sure who I should dial. Still considering what to do, I looked down at the phone, at the little icons on its screen, and saw that the black pin eyes of Hello Kitty were blinking.

I woke up, went back to sleep, and had the dream again. And again I woke, now with thoughts in my head that were like the backwash of a time long past, John's time—my time with John—and his belief that you could emerge from the worst experiences with a renewed spirit, a deeper understanding of yourself. But why had this particular idea decided to swim up to the surface? Was this just another random connection? Yes, I told myself, because it seemed far overreaching for me to try to connect the idea of some kind of enlightenment with what was just a jumbled dream, stitched together from disconnected images floating around in the back of my mind—even more so, because when I woke up, twice, I felt as far away from enlightenment as I thought anyone could be. Mostly what I felt was anxious and sad. Restless and sad. Mournful, almost. Almost grieving again. And I didn't know why.

After the second time I woke up, I couldn't go back to sleep. It was nine p.m. Then it got to be ten. Ten thirty. My inner clock was way out of synch with the clock on my wall, and I knew that at this rate, I was going to be up all night. Since I had yet another regular client's house to clean in the morning, my sudden bout of insomnia wasn't doing me any good.

Nor were my thoughts, which continued to be as jumbled as the dream. *The good ones like to drink.* Considering that bit of admittedly fantastical information, I even wondered if I had anything in the house I could drink myself to sleep with: wine or beer or something stronger? Probably not. There was a package of cupcakes in the kitchen cabinet, a couple of frozen meals in the freezer, but I couldn't remember the last time I'd stocked up on alcohol. If I ever actually had.

I was sitting on the edge of my bed, well aware that I was deliberately trying to distract myself by making a mental inventory of the meager offerings in my kitchen, when I suddenly heard my cell phone ring. Or maybe I was imagining it. I was so deep inside myself that the old-timey ring could have been a phantom sound left over from my dreams. But no; I was sure the phone actually was ringing. So, I picked up my jeans from where I tossed them on a chair and dug the phone out of my back pocket. If I'd missed a call, the screen would have indicated that, but when I turned the phone on, it showed me nothing. Well, no—that wasn't true. After a moment, I realized that something on the screen *was* activated: the black pin eyes of the Hello Kitty icon were slowly, steadily blinking. What I had seen in my dream had just replicated itself in my waking world.

And then it occurred to me that on this side of the barrier between sleep and wakefulness, what I had heard wasn't exactly the sound of the phone ringing. Maybe it was something else, some other sound. Something like a wail, a scratching moan. Something that, when filtered through free-form anxiety and maybe ten—maybe a hundred—levels of restlessness, sounded like a cat.

*A cat?* The first thing I thought of was Ted Devere and his pet with the name straight out of Peter Pan. But this wasn't Wendy calling me. This was someone else. Some*thing.* I had heard this kind of hissing wail before. Kel had described it to me, as well. It was the voice, the sound, of things that didn't know how to speak. Or couldn't.

But maybe now, in their own way, they were speaking to me. Maybe my time of waiting was over, or about to be. Maybe it was time to go. And if so, I knew exactly where.

In under five minutes, I had my jeans back on, pulled on a shirt and sweater and grabbed my jacket. A few minutes more and I was out of my apartment, down the stairs and pushing through the front door.

What I expected when I got downstairs was that the bike would be back. The black bike that I had ridden into the woods. But it wasn't there, under the window of one of the first-floor apartments. Not there, not anywhere. The street, in fact, was deserted. Just the squat, brick apartment buildings, old and gritty, facing each other across the empty street. Just parked cars, streetlights, a cold black sky.

It didn't matter, I didn't care. No bike? So what—I could walk. Of course, it might well be a stupid and dangerous thing to do. Something a haunted woman would do in a fairytale—go walking into the woods late at night. (Or a woman in boots and a fringed jacket whose daughter watched her from a bedroom window, seething with anger.) But at the moment, I *was* haunted; that was exactly how I felt. And I knew that I had heard some sound from that phone; well, at least I believed I had. Believed it completely. And the cat's eyes were still blinking; I had checked the phone as I went down the front steps of my building. All I was doing, I told myself, was answering a call.

So I walked down the empty street, turned towards the elevated train tracks, towards my bus stop by the station stairs. A few passengers were waiting there, but not many because this was an off-hour, a time between the night workers' shifts. Only one vendor had set up a table tonight, and all he had on offer were bootleg DVD's that no one seemed interested in.

I crossed the street under the elevated train tracks and walked up the cinder path that led to the shuttered clubhouse. Once there, I didn't hesitate: I turned onto the paved bike path that went up an incline and then down, deep into the woods. I had brought a flashlight with me and switched it on before I started down the path. It produced a few feet of light ahead, which was enough for me to find my way.

I went down the bike path between the bare trees, all looking like tall, flat shadows joined together in the dark, like paper cut-outs. Following the thin beam of the flashlight, I walked all the way to end of the path, to the gate that barred access to the scarred landscape beyond. A lock and chain had been added to the gate since the last time I was here—or maybe it was more accurate to say that this lock and chain were not here to block my way in the summer, when I was able to pass through the gate with ease. This time, I had to climb over the gate to get to the abandoned picnic area. Once on the other side, I didn't move forward just yet. I stopped, and swept the area with the flashlight, wondering which place I would see, which world.

It was the broken world, the world swallowed by a sinkhole. Which was not what I expected.

I kept my back against the gate as I stared at the vast sinkhole. I could make out enough of the scene before me to recognize that there was still a rim of what looked like fairly stable earth and rock surrounding the sinkhole edge nearest to me but I couldn't tell how far across it extended because the beam of my flashlight couldn't reach that far. What I did see, though, as I swung the light around from side to side, was the picnic table—*a* picnic table, anyway—pushed up against a length of chain-link fence that stretched out from the gate into the dark woods off to my right. The table looked like a movie prop left over from a story that had been scripted, acted out, and was now long done. Long forgotten. What remained was just the void and the trees beyond that presumably still stood their ground, though I could not see them on the other side of the abyss.

Walking carefully, I made my way over to the picnic table and was able to slide myself onto the bench that was squeezed between the table and the fence. I laid the flashlight on the table, switched it off, and then pulled my phone from the pocket of my jeans. Looking down at the screen, the blank-faced Hello Kitty icon stared out at me, useless and still. Its eyes, now, were no longer blinking. They looked empty, like tiny, meaningless voids.

I put the phone back in my pocket and sat in the darkness, in the depths of the deserted parkland. The moon slid out from behind some tangled scraps of clouds but it was a poor source of light; the darkness grew a little thinner but it was not illuminated in any useful way. I still couldn't see very far in any direction.

*So,* I thought, *maybe I was wrong about the phone ringing. About the cat's eyes blinking. Maybe those were things I believed had happened but really hadn't. Maybe I really had been dreaming when I thought I was awake.*

Yes, maybe so—but I was wide awake now. No question about it. In fact, I was on full alert. And I was waiting again. In fact, I was sure that was what I was doing: waiting. For someone to come into the clearing in the woods that did not exist, but somewhere, somehow, really did. I was waiting for a break in the darkness, a parting of the curtains. I was waiting for time to stop and start again. Or reverse itself and give me another chance to change my behavior, to change the choices I had made. Which would mean, of course, that I was waiting for my mother, for one moment in the past to reconvene on this spot so that I could say—or she could say—I'm sorry about the way everything turned out. But that was an impossibility that I recognized even as I kept my vigil on the bench, in the dark. My mother was dead, gone. *But death is not real to me. Death is a barrier that I can't make myself recognize. An ending I want to fight against—and since I can't, I want to pretend it doesn't exist. I don't understand it and so I don't believe in it. And it doesn't matter that none of that makes sense.*

Or maybe it did matter. Why else was I sitting here, in the dark, at the edge of a ruined landscape, trying to make myself erase my growing doubt that the cell phone in my pocket *had* rung? Or cried out like a cat? Why else was I wishing that the eyes of the little cat icon were blinking? Why? Because I had come to a point in my life where, if no one was going to get to say, *I'm sorry,* then I needed to hear something else. To know something else. Something important, something to keep me going. Oh sure, I could just go on cleaning houses and stores and offices; I could work twenty-four hours a days and plug myself into one song after another, each one more vicious and violent than the next, and it wasn't going to help. Nothing was going to help from here on in. Maybe death wasn't real to me but my life was—or it was time that it became real. It was time to give up on trying to attack whatever frightened me and then run away. Or worse, ignore it. I had gone far enough for long enough. It was time to stop. But I couldn't without some kind of help. I couldn't because I didn't know how.

So I kept looking into the darkness and waiting. And I knew who I was waiting for, of course. Not my mother—not really. She was the dream I had been having for years and years. Wide awake, all I could be waiting for were the things.

I would have settled for Daisy Dress or one of its companions, wearing a rain coat or a baseball cap or a pair of go-go boots. Or naked as they day they were born—if they were born. I would have settled for anyone, anything to come and sit with me. Because otherwise, I was all alone.

Maybe half an hour passed. Maybe longer. The moon played its game with the clouds, a broken slice of cold white rock scudding in and out of sight. Nothing stirred in the woods, nothing approached me. No good ones or bad ones, no versions of friends or foes. Nothing—no one was coming. There was no one, nothing to see.

Finally, I allowed myself to realize that there was no reason to stay any longer, no reason to go on waiting for something that was not going to happen—at least not now. Before I eased myself out of the spot between the table and the fence, I picked up my flashlight and switched it back on so I could see where I was going. But it slipped out of my hand and dropped onto the picnic table, where its bright beam slid across the surface of the table's wooden planks. What I saw in the stream of light were names and initials people had carved into the wood over the years—friends and lovers, families, kids hanging out on a summer afternoon. There were also symbols I could easily recognize—hearts and crosses—and some I could not, that had probably been left by frat brothers or, on the other end of the spectrum, gang members: there were Greek letters next to a dagger dripping tiny drops of carved blood, and a few inches away, some sort of sword-and-sorcery symbols that probably originated in a video game. The picnic table was like a record of human passage; how many hundreds, perhaps thousands of people had sat here at one time or another, and decided to leave some small evidence of their visit? Of course, the random collection of scratches and scrapes were hardly permanent—once the sinkhole decided to expand again, the table was going to be sucked into the abyss, never to be heard from again, except as mulch for the next generation of grasses and trees. But for now, here it was, displaying its artwork as clearly as an ancient cave wall decorated with handprints and paintings of mammoths.

I suppose it was the thought of the cave walls that made me stay a few moments more. Using the flashlight, I searched the ground around the table until I found a broken rock with a sharp, pointed edge, which I used to make my own carving. Right in the center of the table, where there was a small blank spot. It took me longer than I thought it would, but I was being careful, and I was trying to be exact. It helped that I had an original to copy.

When I was finished, I looked at my handiwork and thought I'd done a pretty good job. Now, on the picnic table, visible for as long as the ground beneath it held, were a set of two twin stars and three smaller ones off to the side, arranged in a way that made them look like an isosceles triangle.

*There*, I thought, *I've left my mark, too.* And that seemed to give the night's walk into the woods some meaning for me. Nothing nearly as important as what I had hoped for, but it helped a little. It helped me feel a little less like an idiot for running off into the night, a little less angry for giving in to the idea that what I was waiting for in this life—if anything; maybe there was no *next*, no big reveal, no answers to questions that should have been forgotten long ago—could be shown to me by the things. The lurkers in the shadows. The weaklings that had to play games with me in order to get my attention.

Well, the next time they wanted my attention they were going to have to ask for it more directly. And maybe I would respond, maybe not. Maybe I would just lash out again the next time they came near.

Being me, even I couldn't predict how I would react to them. Or to anything else, for that matter. Anything at all.

# VII

WHEN MY CELL phone did ring again—when there was no mistake about it, no ambiguity, as well as the time after that, and many more times that followed—it was always the cleaning agency. I had finally figured out how to change the ringtone to something less jarring than what sounded like the squawk of the first telephone ever invented, so when I heard the first few notes of the pop melody I had selected, I answered quickly. It was October now and the weather had changed; summer was gone for good and a windy autumn had taken its place. On a chilly morning, I was back on the bus to the suburbs, headed for one of the private houses I cleaned every week. My cleaning supplies were in my backpack. I was listening to music and reading a book. Over a month had passed since I'd hiked off into the park and I was still sticking to my usual strategy: keep busy, keep occupied. I knew that wasn't going to work forever—too many of the barriers I had spent a lifetime shoring up were beginning to show signs of an absent custodian—but for the moment, I didn't know what else to do. Which remained true, up until the moment that any decision was taken out of my hands.

"Julia? It's Kel."

Hearing his voice coming through the phone was completely unexpected, so I didn't respond. Not immediately.

"Are you there? Julia? This is important."

He sounded agitated. Clearly, this was not going to be just a nice, friendly, social call.

"How did you get this number?" I asked.

"Please," he said impatiently, "the lives we live, how hard do you think it really is to screw around with stuff like that?" He didn't wait for an answer. "Can you talk?" he asked.

"I'm on my way to work. I have five minutes." I actually had longer than that to travel, but I wanted Kel to say whatever he had to and then just get off the phone.

"Okay," he said, and then wasted half the next minute I had given him by saying nothing.

"I'm looking at my watch," I told him.

"I'm having trouble getting started because you're not going to like what I have to tell you and I don't want you to hang up."

"Time," I said, "is ticking away."

He sighed. "You're not an easy person. You know that about yourself?"

"It's not big news. Keep going."

"You need to come meet me as soon as you can," he said. "Me and Jim Barrett."

"Nope. See? That *was* easy."

"Julia. He has the photo of your mother, you know, the one from your phone. And some other photos, too." Kel paused before he spoke again. "Ted's photos."

I closed my eyes for a moment, looking into blankness, wishing that was all the day held for me. Finally, I said, "Let me guess how he got them."

"What am I down to, three minutes now?" Kel said. "So don't guess. I pocketed them when you guys weren't looking and I gave them to Jim. I told you, I needed help to sort all this out."

"And I told you I don't."

"Never mind that I don't believe you, but look...things have gotten a little out of hand."

Now it was my turn to be silent. When my phone rang, I had pulled one of my earbuds out and left it dangling; now I removed the other and put them both in my lap, with my book. All my concentration was now centered on the voice speaking through my phone, being transmitted to me over miles and miles and miles. Through the atmosphere. Across the sky.

241

Finally, I said, "Out of hand how?"

"Do you know what an Internet blogger is?"

"I'm not an idiot, Kel. I do know what the Internet is. And I know about blogging."

"Does that mean you know who Michael Mills is?" Kel asked

"No," I admitted.

"Well, I'm afraid you're going to. This guy—Michael Mills—is a big deal in online paranormal-ville. And offline too, actually. He's got a web site, he does live chats, he posts stories video and photos...essentially, he's the new Jim Barrett. I mean, years ago he mostly focused on Big Foot sightings and haunted houses, but for the past few years, it's been aliens and UFOs all the way. He's got an international following."

"We need a new Jim Barrett?"

"Well, you pretty much helped to discredit the original, don't you think?"

"So you told me."

"Because it's true. But now Jim's hooked up with this guy, Mills ...I really didn't know about that, Julia. I'm sorry."

I closed my eyes for a moment. For a moment, I felt more deeply ex-hausted than I ever had from months of working seven days a week. I knew that what Kel was about to tell me was that the dead professor's galpal was about to be resurrected. That the mystery girl who disappeared after the brutal slaying by the alien-addled killer was going to be dragged out of hiding and made to live those horrific days and nights all over again. At least, someone was going to try to make that happen.

"So you're telling me what? That he'll post the pictures?" I said, deploying whatever reserves of denial I still had left. "Who cares?"

"You should, because he'll do more than that. He thinks he has a big story."

"Which is what?"

"It's my fault. I told Jim everything you told me—everything, Julia—and Jim passed it all on to Mills."

"Including how to find me?"

"No. Not that."

"Am I supposed to say thank you? Okay, Kel, thank you for not sending the wolves straight to my door. Which, by the way, I can close behind me without a second thought and disappear again. I'm good at that. So why don't you boys go play with the photos that Ted Devere developed in his brain pan and try to get a movie deal with your second-hand stories, or whatever it is Jim Barrett wants? I'll just wait while it all fades away again."

"That's not what's going to happen, but I'm past my five minutes."

"Way past."

"Julia," Kel said, "Mills isn't after what you think. Not exactly. There's something else."

"Oh for God's sake," I said. "Stop being so fucking dramatic or I really am going to hang up."

Kel took a breath—I could hear him on the other end of the line. "Okay," he said finally. "Listen to me: there hasn't been an abduction in almost ten years. What happened ten years ago?"

"A lot of things happened ten years ago."

"What happened to you? You specifically. Or maybe I should say, what did you do?"

*I did what I always do,* I thought. I exploded. I fought. I acted without thinking. But that's not what I said to Kel. "I disappeared. At least, I tried to."

"Julia."

"What?"

"Before that. You know what I'm talking about. You attacked the creepy crawly. Alice told Jim that you beat it to a pulp.

"So?"

"So Jim Barrett thinks that's why the abductions stopped—because of you. Because of what you did. There are still plenty of UFO sightings all over the world but no abduction reports. From the time of the Betty and Barney Hill abduction in 1961 until 1990, there were hundreds, maybe thousands of reports and then—right after John was murdered—nothing. Absolutely nothing. You do a number on one of the creepy crawlies and then they disappear, so there's got to be a connection. And that's exactly the story he handed to Michael Mills."

"Yup," I said, "that sounds totally logical. Call Gort and Klaatu. I personally stopped the invasion of earth—oh, excuse me, I think what I mean is the repopulation of earth by hybrid aliens. And how did I do that? By beating up one of the things. Wow—there's another story. Maybe somebody can make an interstellar arrest for crimes against an alien."

"I know how ridiculous it all sounds but I promise you, they *will* be selling the movie rights before they're finished. You think it was rough last time around? Just wait."

"What are you talking about?"

We had now been on the phone so long that I actually had just about reached my stop. I stood up, looped my backpack over one arm, and lurched toward the front of the bus. When it pulled to a halt, I stepped out into the street, still holding the phone to my ear. I was now standing at a windblown suburban crossroads—a strip mall behind me, a gas station across the way. Overhead, a cold, mackerel sky was laddered with gray clouds. This was the outer boundary of an otherwise high-priced neighborhood, and I had a long hike ahead of me, straight into the wind, before I got to the house I was supposed to clean. But I thought I could spare a few minutes more, so I ducked into a bus shelter set back a few feet from the road and continued my conversation with Kel.

"Face facts, Julia. It's a new world, there are new people in it." Kel said. "Ten years ago, the newspaper and tv coverage were bad enough, but now your name is going to be all over the Internet, and I don't think you really understand what that means. It'll be a free-for-all; everybody will be after you. After all of us, probably—all the experiencers. Alien abduction stories, no matter how old—and anything even connected to that—are going to be a chance for people to make money, and if not money, at least to make a career for themselves because the fact that the aliens seemed to have disappeared for now doesn't mean that they won't be back. And if they do come back, who's to say they won't be even worse than before? And maybe you know what the schedule is—I mean, if your guys are on an interstellar vacation or something, maybe they've sent you some postcards saying all is forgiven and telling you when they're planning a return trip. I'm not saying that I believe any of that—I don't, but I know who's already thinking along those lines and their names are Jim Barrett and Michael Mills and whoever else eventually latches onto the story. I'm telling you, Julia, alien hunters are going to be bigger than Batman, and don't think for a minute that any of those types are going to be like John was."

"Nobody could ever be like John."

"No," Kel said, sounding a little less frantic, "of course not. John was an idealist. He was trying to develop some real understanding of what happens to people who've had abduction experiences. I think that in the beginning, Jim Barrett was the same way. But I guess that somewhere along the line, he decided that evil wins, or something like that, and he just wouldn't let up on the idea that we're under attack. It gave him a platform and it gave him power—and a career. He made a lot of money from his books and appearances. I'm not saying he doesn't believe what he says he believes—in fact, I'm sure he does, all the more reason that he's not going to do anything to protect you from being the center of a story that is never going to come out in any shape or fashion you're going to like at all. At all. Do you hear me, Julia? Now that Jim has hooked up with Mills, I guarantee you that this is going to be as much about money and fame as it is about finding the truth. Mills' web site already pulls in big advertising dollars. And his fees for speeches and tv appearances get bigger every time he opens his mouth."

"And these are the people you went to for help?"

"I told you, I didn't know about Mills before. And Jim...what can I say? We used to just be able to talk. Not anymore, though. Once I told him that I'd seen you, that's all he wanted to hear about. He's gunning for you, Julia. He's going to find out who you really are and what you know and he's going to find a way to use it to his advantage. You have one chance here, Julia. Just one. Talk to them, to Jim Barrett and Michael Mills. Get some control of the story before it takes control of your life."

"I'll think about it," I said.

"What instinct tells me that really, you won't?" Kel said. "But think about this. Did it ever occur to you that your mother was, like consorting with the enemy?"

"What? I don't even know what you're talking about."

"Honestly? It's never occurred to you? Not even for a second? That if the creepy crawlies really do have bad intentions towards us your mother might have been helping them along? I mean, she was helping them—obviously. Even you know that. But to do what? Abduct people? Use their bodies, their

245

cells to create hybrids? Maybe she thought there was some higher purpose to it all that only she understood. Or maybe..." He paused for a moment. When he spoke again, his voice sounded forced, determined—like he had thought about stopping and had made a decision to go on talking. "Maybe she was just bored and lonely, so all this gave some importance to her life. Maybe that's why she made excuses for her involvement with the creepy crawlies. Maybe she told herself that it wasn't her fault, that she didn't have a choice."

A gust of wind rattled the walls of the bus shelter. Trash and leaf litter went scudding by my feet. I was so behind schedule now, so late, that I could already see the next bus that ran along this line approaching in the distance. I watched it for a moment, and then turned my attention back to Kel, waiting on the other end of this conversation.

"I know what you expect from me now," I said. "You're probably holding the phone away from your ear because you think I'm going to turn into a lunatic and start screaming at you. Normally, I would. I mean, you're telling me that maybe my mother was doing something really, really bad, for some really crazy reason. You covered your bases though—you started with John's reasons: maybe there was something good involved that we don't understand. That was slick, I'll say that for you. Then you could segue right into Barrett-ville: lonely, bored woman and sex-crazed aliens. That would make Laura a cooperative—no, I mean *enthusiastic*—version of Alice, which really should drive me ape shit, don't you think?" With the wind pushing at me and the leaves blowing all around, I took the phone away from my ear and put it close to my mouth. "Grrrrr," I growled. "Do you hear me, Kel? That sounds more like what you expected, right? Me getting ready to bite someone again. It would be you if you were here."

"And maybe I'd deserve it. But I'm trying to help you now. That's all I'm doing."

"I told you before, I don't need anyone's help."

"Everyone needs some kind of help. Do yourself a favor and take mine. Listen to me: at least meet with Jim and Michael Mills. Maybe you can work something out."

"Forget it," I said. "That's my message, in capital letters."

"I'm not going to tell them you said that," Kel replied. "I'm going to stall them for a while. They won't put out the story without you if they think you'll work with them."

"I'm hanging up now," I said. "For real." And that was exactly what I did; I clicked off the phone.

I was furious. Agitated and furious and in no mood to go clean someone's house. So I called the cleaning agency and left a message that I had an emergency and wasn't going to be able to do my job today. Then I crossed the street and waited for the next bus going in the opposite direction, back to the Bronx. I intended to head straight back to Besso's where I was going to get my phone number changed so Kel—along with anybody else who was looking for me—couldn't call. I had a feeling I might be able to buy something else from Nineteen, as well: some identification that would replace Laura Glazer's i.d. with another woman's. Any woman's, real or imagined. Then I was going to go home, take the cleaning products out of my backpack, stuff in whatever else I could carry and leave. Head off to parts unknown. Even Jim Barrett couldn't turn me into a sideshow attraction in his particular version of the alien abduction circus if he couldn't find me.

The bus arrived in ten minutes and it took another forty-five minutes to get home. The wind seemed to be pushing the bus all the way: the morning's gusts were turning into a steady, maddening wind. Once I got off at my stop in the Bronx, I had to fight against it every step of the way, so I decided to go back to my apartment before making the trek to Besso's. I could start packing my things first, and deal with the phone and i.d. later.

But as I moved around my place, gathering things to pile into my backpack, I began to slow down. Really, physically, to move slower and slower. It was as if as my anger wound down—because how long, really, could it sustain itself?—so did my energy until finally, I found myself sitting on my bed, holding a shirt that I couldn't decide to pack or leave behind. I listened to the wind scraping at my windows; it didn't seem to be having a problem keeping up its intensity. For a moment, I considered opening all the windows and letting the wind blow everything away.

But that's not what I did. Instead, I looked over at my open backpack and thought that if I put in the shirt I was holding and zipped it up, that was it, I would be done. I would exchange this life for some other—which it seemed to me I had been doing for as long I could remember. That backpack was like a box, and my life had been a series of boxes that I opened and closed; I was good at that, at shutting the boxes and moving on. I had done that with people and places but now, I was feeling the way I had when I'd sat by myself at the picnic table poised at the edge of a sinkhole: I didn't want to fall in. I didn't want to go anywhere. So I sat on the bed, keeping a tight grip on the shirt. I tried to picture myself in the act of getting up, shutting the door to my apartment and walking away, but I just couldn't do it. I could not move.

*Why not?* I asked myself. *You're a woman with a passport. You can go anywhere you want.*

But there was nowhere to go. No particular place, no destination. Sure, I could get on a bus and go from *here* to *there*, but the problem was that the way to *there* seemed to lead nowhere. Or everywhere. It seemed to start at a gateway through a double landscape and then lead off into just more pack-ages of time, more boxes to open and close, except that one of them refused to allow itself to be sealed. This one, this box, which I wanted to slam shut, but which would not allow it. The shirt remained in my hand. Time ticked on.

And then something occurred to me. Something Kel had said that didn't seem important to me when I was standing in the bus shelter, but was sud-denly lighting up in the back of my mind and growing brighter by the minute, like a luminous sign appearing around a bend in a dark road.

Ten years ago, a box had been closed and I had opened another. *What happened ten years ago, Julia? What changed?*

It seemed that I couldn't move from here to there, from then to now, until I answered that question for myself. And although Kel had suggested a reason, I had already told him that it didn't make sense.

Unless it did, although I couldn't imagine why my attacking one of the things—certainly not the first time I'd done that—should have had such extraordinary consequences. Well, maybe I had a limited imagination; that quality had been necessary for me to cultivate in order to survive. That's what the music and headphones and books and television were for: to limit what I did not wish to see, what I did not want to know. But now, everything seemed to be turned around: something I wanted to understand—needed to—completely eluded me. And the reason it eluded me was because I had spent a lifetime saying every version of saying *No, don't tell me*, that I could think of.

So what could have happened ten years ago, what had changed that had ended up changing everything? Though I hated the idea—totally hated it—there was someone who might be able to help me figure out the answer. One person, just one, who I could ask. One human being who was still alive.

# VIII

I HAD EXPECTED a long wait for permission to visit the women's prison ward of the Eastern State Psychiatric Hospital in Bellwood, Pennsylvania, but it took just over a week. I had to apply through a reconciliation program that was part of their treatment protocol for what they called forensic patients, meaning people whose stay in a psychiatric hospital was mandated by the courts. Another condition was that the person I wanted to visit had to agree to see me. I wasn't at all sure what the answer to that question would be, but it turned out to be yes. So, on a Friday morning at eight a.m., I was at the Port Authority Bus Terminal in Manhattan waiting for the Greyhound coach line to board. Bellwood was just outside of Philadelphia, so I had a two hour ride, which would get me to the hospital at about the right time for my appointment. I had already gone through an interview process on the phone with an administrator who didn't seem to quite believe at first that I was genuinely interested in what she called "exploring the pathways to forgiveness," but I knew what to say and how to say it in order to sound convincing. It was like a job interview, so I used the humble cleaning lady voice and played some music in one part of my mind while, in the other, whatever part of me was managing the interview pretended that nothing particularly important was at stake.

The bus let me off near enough to the hospital that I could walk the rest of the way. I could actually see the building long before I even reached the parking lot: it looked like it had been constructed out of poured concrete, one square gray block after another piled up towards a leaden sky. Not an inviting place, but not a horror show, either. It was just what it appeared to be: an institution that existed because it was necessary that it exist.

Inside, I went from an information desk to an office where I signed forms and received a day pass. Then, escorted by an aide, I walked down what felt like a mile of corridors, was directed into an elevator, then out of the elevator, and further on, through a set of double doors that led to another corridor and another office where I met a different woman than the one I had talked to on the phone. She was middle-aged, reserved but cordial enough as she explained that she was a psychiatrist who worked with the reconciliation program. She also said that she was going to be present during my visit. I could ask anything, discuss anything, and she would only intervene if she thought it was absolutely necessary.

She then led me out of her office and down another maze of corridors. There were painted lines on the floor and a map on the wall that told you how the different colors of the lines could be followed to different parts of the hospital. Outside a set of locked doors, the lines were green; when a guard buzzed us through the doors I noticed that the color changed to red.

I had expected noise and chaos, but the rooms we passed by were occupied by quiet women doing quiet things: watching television, reading magazines, sleeping. But there was a marked difference from the rest of the hospital: this was the first area where I saw uniformed guards.

Finally, we reached a room that the doctor unlocked with a key. There was nothing in the room but two chairs facing each other across a narrow table, along with a third chair that had been placed in a corner, near a window that presented a view of the dull sky hanging over an autumn landscape of small houses and bare trees.

The doctor gestured for me to sit at the table and then settled herself in the chair by the window. Five minutes went by. The doctor made some notes on a pad of yellow paper. I sat and waited, feeling uncomfortable in a kind of silence I was unaccustomed to.

Then the door opened and there she was. Alice. She looked as thin and ethereal as I remembered, but older too, and maybe a little drugged. She was wearing a hospital gown and her long blonde hair looked unwashed and dull. I wondered how much of a conversation we would be able to have with her in this seemingly diminished state.

She walked over to the table slowly, sat down slowly, as if moving through the air itself was an effort. When she was settled she looked down at the table—not at me—as she said her first words. "Thank you for coming here."

"It was probably time," I told her. "There are things we need to talk about."

Then, as if following a script, Alice said, "I have a lot to apologize to you for. What I did was...unforgivable. I've gone over and over it in my mind, and in therapy, and I think—I hope—that I really didn't mean to go through with it. How could I really have meant to kill anyone? How *could* I have really killed anyone? It still seems impossible. And of all the people in the world, John. He was so kind to me."

Finally, she looked up, though her gaze found the window, not me. Still, I searched her face. What did I see there? What did I see in her eyes? Nothing yet. Nothing I was sure of.

"I know that you didn't mean to hurt him," I said. "You were coming after me."

"It was all an accident," Alice said. "All of it. I have to believe that in order to go on living. My thinking was confused. And I was very jealous of you."

If we kept on with this, I knew that I was now supposed to reply with some sort of acknowledgement of her admission and then head down those pathways of forgiveness I had been instructed to travel along. But I decided that I had my own paths to follow and I wanted Alice to come with me, even if we had to go slowly.

"I was jealous of you, too," I said. My intention was to tell a necessary lie—the kind of thing I would say because I was untrustworthy, a person who would do anything I had to in order to slide in, out or around a problem—but in this moment, as soon as the words came out of my mouth, I knew that they were true. Because I could not trust myself, I could never trust John, or believe that he loved someone named Julia Glazer better than he loved anyone else. How could I, since most of the time, I couldn't even find that Julia under the cleaning lady's clothes where the soul of a lost and angry daughter kept itself hidden away from the world? I took a deep breath and said, "There are a lot of ways that I could have behaved differently, myself. Better." Then I went a step further. "We're probably both responsible for what happened."

Alice, who could not know what I was thinking, replied with a plain fact. "You didn't kill him."

"No," I said. "But that day...we both know I came close to killing someone else. Something."

For the first time, Alice actually looked directly at me. Some spark, some hint of life seemed to begin slowly lighting up her eyes. Then she glanced over at the woman sitting by the window, who was continuing to make notes on her yellow pad. She was trying to seem like an objective observer, attentive yet removed from what she was hearing but apparently, she wasn't fooling Alice—or me, for that matter. I had seen her head snap up for a quick moment when she'd heard what I just said.

Alice turned back to me. She said, "They don't exist, Julia. I've had a lot of time in therapy to understand why I thought what I did. Aliens, hybrids: they're just manifestations of my own anxiety, my fears, my...misunderstanding."

I let her finish this litany of damages because I was beginning to get the feeling that she was following a script she had to play out. If that was the case, then I was going to help her.

"Fine," I said. "But let's say I'm not here to discuss what happened to you, but what happened to me. Happens. Let's pretend I'm the one who believes that the aliens—the things—are real."

Again, I saw that light in Alice's eyes. "You would never admit that before."

"I'm admitting it now. To you."

"Why?" Alice asked.

I didn't answer her directly. "Have they been here?" I asked.

Knowing exactly what I meant, Alice took another cautious glance at the doctor, who still seemed occupied with her notes. She was no doubt listening to every word we said, but had not shown any sign of interrupting.

"I told you, they are..."

"I know. Manifestations of anxiety, fear, etc. So have they manifested themselves since you've been here?"

"Since I've been here? That's almost ten years." She sounded weary. She sounded like she remembered every long moment of those long, long years.

"Yes, I know. Ten years."

"I haven't seen them."

"Alice," I said, "I think that except for me, once—just once, recently—no one has."

"What do you mean," Alice said slowly. "How can that be possible?"

"I don't know," I said. "But it seems to be true. At least, that's what Kel told me and I don't have any reason to think he's not telling me the truth." I paused for a moment, since I wasn't sure Alice actually understood what I was saying "Do you remember Kel?" I asked. Alice nodded, and once I saw that she was still with me, still following my story, I continued. "That's what he told me, because that's what Jim Barrett told him. And now Jim's hooked up with some Internet guy and he's going to start all over again. What he did with you, he wants to do with me. Only in my case, I think he'd like to eviscerate me in the process. Can you imagine what he's going to say? I can: What secrets is Julia Glazer hiding? What does she know about the disappearance of the aliens? No sightings, no abductions in a decade. Where have they gone? Have they spent all this time planning something big like an invasion? Julia must know so let's rip her apart. Let's make her talk."

"So talk," Alice said.

"Really?" I snapped. "How did that work out for you?"

I shouldn't have said that and I expected an equally unfriendly response, but that would have come from the Alice I was still thinking of: the woman I had met in Jim Barrett's house, the woman walking up John's stairs one long-ago Christmas time, not the person I was sitting across from now. This quieter, more reflective woman had something different to say to me.

She leaned in closer to me, as if that would keep the doctor from hearing what we said. "You really haven't seen them in ten years? Even you?"

"Like I said, just once. But before that—and I know how weird this sounds—they showed me a movie. Me and Kel."

"That same movie Kel used to talk about? Death, reincarnation—that sort of thing?"

"Yup. Kel and I walked down to Paper Lane and then all of a sudden, it was movie night."

*Movie night.* All of a sudden, and totally unexpectedly, I heard myself laugh. In a drab and horrible room in the prison ward of a mental hospital, sitting across from a woman I should bear tremendous hatred towards, on an errand that even I wasn't sure made any sense, I found myself laughing. And I was laughing because somehow, a memory that I found comforting had managed to shoulder its way past all the bad stuff sloshing around in my brain pan and present itself as clearly as one of Ted Devere's pictures, once it pushed up through the chemicals on the photo paper and presented itself, sharp and clear.

"What's funny about any of this?" Alice asked.

"Movie night," I said. "The things. The aliens. I wonder if they got the idea from my mother."

"Your mother?" Alice said. "I don't understand."

"The things. They keep showing me pictures of my mother. And it was my mother's idea to have movie night at the Stargazer's Embassy."

"Where?"

"It's a bar in a town called Freelingburg, upstate. That's where I grew up. My mother lived with the guy who owned the bar and we had an apartment upstairs. It's also where Kel saw the movie for the first time. I never knew that until recently. I never knew he had been there."

Alice was silent for a moment as she sorted through what I had just said. "Your mother," she said finally, "she was involved with them?"

"Yes. So I've known about them all my life, just like you."

"But they act differently towards you than towards everybody else. Almost everybody. Why?"

"I don't know," I told her. And then I said, "That's a lie. I do know. At least I think I do."

"Because of your mother?" Alice guessed.

"Yes," I said. "Because of my mother."

There was more to say about that subject—a lot more—but before I got to any of it, another thought intervened, and that was, *What a strange place this is to start facing the truth.* But maybe it wasn't, really. This was the only place in the world—this world, anyway, the only one I knew—where Alice Giddings existed, where I could sit across from her and look at her and talk to her. Alice, who I could easily be sitting next to, instead, chained to her from childhood by shared circumstances. What she had seen, I had seen; what she knew, I knew. Perhaps the only difference was that fear had guided her while anger had guided me. But here we both were, now, with maybe half our lives over and the rest waiting to see what we would do. Perhaps Alice had few choices, but mine were still open. Limited, perhaps, but still waiting to be selected. I could go on as I was, doing nothing more than drifting through my own days and nights. Riding buses from here to there, cleaning other people's houses but having no real home of my own. No real future, no connections to anybody except some alien creatures in ridiculous costumes, and even they seemed capable of disappearing, though not entirely. Not altogether. They had left clues behind. They had even left a picture. And that was my other choice: to travel down that bend in the road and follow Laura past it. To follow where Laura had gone. Or at least, where she had been going. Why not? Wasn't I a kind of alien myself—hadn't I been for most of my life? A child without a mother was different than everybody else, lonelier, more disconnected. Looking for a way back into a lost life, a way to fix the unfixable, to heal what was forever broken.

"I think," I said, and hesitated only a moment before I made myself finish my own sentence, "that they are looking for my mother."

Alice looked confused. "Why?" she asked. "Where is your mother? Is she still living at that place? The Stargazer's Embassy."

"No," I told her. "She's dead. She died a long time ago."

"Then I don't understand."

"Well, that's weirdest part of this—if it's even possible for there to be a weirdest part. Laura—that was my mother's name—has been dead for a long time. They have to know that."

"I'm sorry," Alice said. "I mean, I'm sorry about your mother. You must miss her."

The words she spoke were probably automatic: that's what people say about someone who died. *I'm sorry. You must miss her.* But because we were telling each other the truth now—pretending for the eavesdropping doctor, but not for ourselves—I didn't simply say yes, of course, I do miss her, yes, it's so sad.

Instead, I tried to tell Alice what I really felt, which was not an easy thing to express. But somehow, sitting with Alice made it easier. Sitting with Alice made me channel the alien self within me, the child whose unknowable mother was lost somewhere in the past. So I faced Alice Giddings and said, "I should, right? I should miss her terribly, but I don't exactly feel that way. Miss who? I don't know who she was. If—when, once in a while—I'm lonely for her, the person I'm lonely for is like some idea of a mother, not Laura herself. Not the person, Laura, because it's like she's not real to me anymore. Maybe because I could never forgive her for bringing the things into my life. For choosing them over me, because that's what I always thought she did. And now...well, I know what I'm supposed to feel. Like I carry her memory with me or that she lives on in my heart or something like that. But I don't have those feelings. Mostly—I think, mostly—I'm just angry that she died before we got a chance to change the way things were between us. To resolve anything."

"Maybe that happens later," Alice said. "Somewhere else."

"Do you believe that?"

"I don't know," Alice replied. "It would be nice."

"Yes," I said, "I guess it would be."

"Provided, of course, that we all end up in the right place."

I laughed again. Now Alice—of all people, Alice—actually made me laugh. "Harps and angels?" I said.

She smiled at me. "Something like that.

The moment passed—the thought of angels and sweet, heavenly conversations faded away. "The things," I said to Alice, "they had someplace else in mind. They showed me a picture of my mother walking on a road, like they want to know where she went. Like they care about that, about her, more than I do. And maybe they're right. I suppose that's horrible," I said. "I suppose that makes me a horrible person."

"No," Alice said, softly. "That would be me, remember? I'm the monster."

"I don't think John would feel that way." Alice nodded. "Thank you," she said. "I try to believe that. And it helps, a little. I have this fantasy, sometimes, that if he had...survived, he would come to visit me. He'd talk to me, like he used to. He'd help me feel better, even about what happened. What I did." She paused for a moment. She had admitted a secret, had breathed it out into the dusty air of this bleak room, and needed a moment to gather it back into herself again. "It's funny, I guess, that the only person I think about visiting me is someone who can't," she said, finally. "But maybe that's because the people who could come never do, not even my parents. They say because it's too far to travel but I know it's because they're ashamed of me. Of what I did, where I am now. Of all the stories I told."

"Even if they're not stories?"

The note-taking doctor made a slight noise as she moved in her chair, crossing one leg over the other. Alice remained silent for a few moments but her eyes were becoming watery, rimmed with red. "They have to be stories," she said. "Being dragged out of my bed, over and over again. Being made unconscious and then waking up in a white room with no windows, with those gray things standing all around me. Raped with some sort of medical equipment. Used like a lab rat so they could take cells from me, eggs, whatever they were doing." Her voice went soft; she shook her head as if to banish the images she had just conjured up. "That must be a made-up memory, right? Who could live through things like that?"

"You did," I told her.

Again, she shook her head. "No. Only in my mind."

I knew that she was insisting on repeating that assertion for the doctor's benefit, so there was no point in trying to contradict her. So, I returned to what we had been talking about a moment before—the fact that she was alone in this place. "Does Jim ever come here?" I asked.

"Never," Alice told me. "Not once in all these years." She looked away from me, fixing her sight on the window. There was nothing interesting to see beyond the glass, just the same low, gray sky clamped down over the same patchy suburb that she probably saw every cold, dull day.

When she finally spoke again, she returned to the code that we both now understood we were using for the doctor's benefit. "Before I was able to accept that I was, um, deluded in a lot of ways, I used to tell myself that maybe it was a good thing that I'm here. I mean, I'm watched almost all the time so if the aliens were to come for me again..." She broke off and added, hastily, "I mean, if I thought that was what was happening to me, then finally—finally!—someone would see, someone other than the other experiencers would believe me. But if I believe *you*, what you've been telling me, then the reason they're gone has nothing to do with doctors or hospitals or prison walls. Which means they might come back. Which means I will never be safe."

"Maybe so—if you still thought that they were real," I said, trying to get us back on a conversational path that the doctor could make some approving note about. That would provide more evidence that Alice was "getting better"—and at the same time, I thought, *yes that's me speaking. Me feeling sorry for Alice.*

"Which they aren't," she added hastily, picking up on my cue. Then she sighed; longingly, deeply. "Whatever happens, I would like to get out someday. I'd like to be able to go for a walk down a street, through a field, or in a woods. Maybe in the spring, when it's sunny and fresh. And there'd be birds everywhere, and flowers."

It sounded like she was describing a greeting card—and I was hardly the right person to talk to about the pleasure of walking in fields and woods— but she didn't know that. And maybe imagining the world described by a greeting card was as close as she had gotten in a long time to any kind of life of her own.

"I could write a letter," I said spontaneously. "They told me I could do that, as part of the reconciliation program. I could endorse some kind of release program for you. I think that might help."

"You would do that?" Alice said.

"Not me," I said. "John's version of me. I think she was a better person. Had a chance to be, anyway."

"Do you still think about him a lot?" Alice asked.

"Not as much as I should," I told her. "Probably not as much as you do."

Again, Alice stole a glance at the doctor. When she turned back to me, she looked at me in a way that was different that before. It was almost like I could see her thinking, making a decision.

"I want to tell you something," she said. "About that day, ten years ago. About what I saw. *Thought* I saw," she added, cautiously. "What do you call them?"

I knew what she meant. "Things. That's all they deserve to be called."

She nodded. "Things. Well, the ones that came into the house—that I *thought* I saw—they were different. They weren't the same ones who abducted me. I don't know how to explain it but I could tell. The ones I knew, there was no way they would have tried to help anyone, not even you. They were like blank voids, empty things. *Things*," she repeated. "That really would have been the right description of them. But not of the ones who were there that day. You hurt them. They never tried to hurt you, or me. All they did was protect you. Or try to, anyway. That's what's so different about your experiences with them. That's what was so different that day in the house, ten years ago. The *things* you see are not the same ones I did. They can't be. They behaved in a totally different way."

What was she saying? It sounded like some version of what Ted Devere had said to me—something about *good ones and bad ones*. Was Alice implying something similar—that maybe there were two different groups of aliens? Maybe more?

"How is that possible?"

"I don't know. But every time I've thought about what happened, I keep coming to the same conclusion. The things who protected you looked the same as the ones I've seen—imagined I've seen—but they weren't. I'm sure of it. They weren't even the same as the thing who showed us...well, you know. You remember."

"The baby."

Alice nodded. "Yes. The dead baby. The thing who was holding it was... I don't know how else to say it. He...it...was not a part of the group who shielded you."

So was Ted right? *Good ones and bad ones.* Maybe, but I didn't see how much difference that made. Even the good ones were nightmares. Badly, stupidly costumed, but nightmares all the same.

"Julia," Alice said, and the sound of my name spoken in her voice seemed to slip through the cracks of the walls that still separated us. The cracks grew wider; air, light, time, moving images, memories, all began to leak through. "Think about this: if it's true that they're different, and maybe even if they aren't, they were willing to stand between you and a crazy woman with a knife. Why wouldn't they protect you from Jim Barrett, if that's what you want?"

"This isn't some kind of fairytale," I said, thinking of the night I had sat at the picnic table, looking into an empty distance. "I can't summon them."

"Ten years ago, you didn't have to, did you? They just came. Maybe they have their reasons for staying away but you're obviously important to them. Maybe because of your mother, maybe not—but don't you want to find out?

Either way, I'm going to guess that they'll stand between you and Jim Barrett, just like they stood between you and me. And anyone else he brings along who might threaten you."

"Taking on Barrett and that Mills guy would be a big risk," I said.

"Nothing could be worse than what's already happened." Alice Giddings said to me. "We both know that."

Suddenly, a few tones sounded over a loudspeaker. They prompted the doctor to gather her notes and stand up. She walked to the table and positioned herself next to Alice, but spoke to me. "I'm sorry," she said, "but the morning visiting hours are over."

Both a guard and a nurse appeared at the doorway. Alice rose from her seat, preparing to leave with them, but before she did, she had one last thing to say to me. "Will you come back?"

"Do you want me to?" I asked her.

She hesitated only a moment. "Yes," she said. And then she added, "Please."

Once Alice was gone, the doctor led me back to her office, where she talked to me about the visit. Had it helped me? Did I feel that Alice was genuinely remorseful? Did I think the reconciliation program was worthwhile? Yes, I said automatically; yes, I kept saying in answer to her questions, which I wasn't really listening to. My mind was elsewhere. I was going through a list of questions of my own.

When I finally left the hospital, I walked back to the bus stop on the quiet street and stood under the gray sky. I watched clouds shape themselves into ladders and roads and then break apart. I saw hawks hunting along the horizon; sparrows flying by. I felt the wind pushing at me and the cold rising up from the ground.

Finally, the bus came and I climbed aboard. I found a seat in the back and watched out the window as we headed towards the turnpike, which would lead back to New York. In a few hours, once the bus arrived at the Port Authority terminal, I could catch an uptown subway to the Bronx. Ride the number four to the end of the line and go back to my apartment.

And then what? Then, unless I did something—like go back to Besso's, as I had originally planned, change my phone number, buy another i.d. and get back on the bus to somewhere, anywhere else—I was probably in for a lot of trouble. A lot of unwanted attention and crazy times. And how would I support myself, once Jim Barrett turned the spotlight on me? If I stayed around, I didn't think the cleaning agency was going to want to employ the mystery galpal who smashed up a visitor from outer space and who might know secrets about alien abductions. I could already see the headlines hurtling like neon spikes across the electronic highways of the Internet: *Slain prof's mistress may be key to alien abduction enigma.* Jim Barrett would be back on television; he'd be writing books again, making appearances. And tons of money.

At first, my choice seemed clear: never mind what I had been thinking before because now, I had to run. Run as far and as fast as I could. It was possible that this time, I wouldn't be followed. It was possible that the things would just let me go. I hadn't exactly spelled it out to Alice, but since the night I had sat alone at the picnic table near the sinkhole, all I had felt was their absence. The picture of my mother walking on the road might have just been their last communique: maybe there simply would be no more. If I ran, I thought it was quite possible that no strangers in daisy dresses or trench coats would follow me on the bus to wherever I ended up and watch me from street corners in downtown nowhere U.S.A. Maybe they had finally boarded some cosmic bus of their own. Or an interstellar freight train, or a zip-through-the-wormhole spaceship. Or simply willed themselves from *here* to *there*. Wherever they were, they seemed, finally, to have turned away from me.

Maybe.

My bus rolled on, traveling along the Jersey Turnpike through the gray afternoon. I plugged my earbuds into my CD player and tried to lose myself in some screechy punk rock, and when that didn't work, I tried the other end of the spectrum, switching to the kind of meditation music that was supposed to zonk you into floating around in an ethereal fog, but that didn't block out my thoughts, either. And my thoughts were making some kind of uncontrolled U-turn; they were not heading off across state borders lugging a backpack and a new name. Nope. They were fixed on that *maybe* and wouldn't budge. *What's wrong with you?* I heard myself thinking. *Don't those things owe you something after all these years? Some explanation, some answers? And who says they don't know that? Maybe Alice is right: you ought to make one last try to find out.*

Well, perhaps so. But I knew it meant that gray-skinned beings with depthless black eyes weren't going to be the only creatures I would have to deal with. Not the first, anyways. As Alice and I had already agreed, there were some humans, too. Arguably human, anyway.

By the time the bus had exited the turnpike and was winding along the approach to the Lincoln Tunnel, I had made up my mind. I turned off the CD player and stuffed it into my backpack. Then I pulled out my phone. The bus was stuck in the traffic inching towards the tunnel, which left me enough time to make a call.

I dialed Kel's number and he answered pretty quickly. "It's me," I said. "I'll do it. I'll meet with Barrett and his buddy."

"That's good," Kel said. "It's the best way to handle all this."

"We'll see."

"What does that mean?"

"What do you think it means? Just that I'll talk to them and we'll see what happens.

Kel was silent for a moment. "Are you planning on bringing any friends?"

I knew what he meant. "Why does everyone think I can wave my hand or something and whammo, alien life forms appear?"

I could almost hear the wheels turning in Kel's brain. "Who's everyone?"

"I went to see Alice," I told him because I thought he might as well know. I wasn't trying to hide anything...well, at least not that.

"Jesus," he said. "And the world didn't explode?"

"She's different," I said. "So am I."

The bus was still moving very slowly, but the entrance to the tunnel couldn't be that far away. "Look, I don't have a lot of time," I said. "The phone is going to lose its signal any minute, so just tell me where Jim wants to meet."

"His house," Kel said. "You remember the place."

"Forget it," I said. "I'm not going all the way to the ass end of Brooklyn. And I want someplace public." I spent a moment or two toying with the idea of insisting that everybody meet me up in the Bronx, but I was willing to seem conciliatory, at least in offering the idea of neutral ground. The problem was that I hadn't exactly been out and about much in recent years, but then I remembered the café in the Village where John and I had sat one night long ago when he asked me to come live with him. I knew it was still open because Kel and I had walked by it on the day we had trekked over from the East Village to Paper Lane. Gargoyles with eyes like dusty gems; griffons with spiked tails painted on the walls. I described the place to Kel and gave him the address. "I'll be there tomorrow night at eight. Tell Barrett to bring the pictures of Laura. And you bring a bottle of Jack Daniels."

Now Kel sounded a little puzzled. "Of course he'll bring the pictures—that's the whole point. But why do you want me to bring a bottle of Jack?"

"Because we're going to a coffee house," I said. "They don't serve liquor."

"You think you're going to need to get drunk afterwards? Is that it?" Kel asked. "Or maybe during?"

"Me?" I said. "No."

Then I hung up the phone, but I didn't put it away just yet. Instead, I looked down at the screen. It had an almost mesmerizing glow to it—that deep blue background, the floating icons shimmering with energy. All I had to do was touch them and they would make a connection for me: tap the tiny picture of a telephone handset and I could make another call. Tap the image of an envelope and I could send an email, if I had ever bothered to set up an address. These glowing connectors, visible on my side of the screen, sat on the surface of the glowing pool of electricity, waiting to be used. But how did they work? What was behind them, on the other side of the screen? Once I touched the surface of an image and set a signal in motion, where did it go? Maybe Nineteen would have been able to answer those questions, but even if he did, I couldn't imagine that I would understand the explanation.

The telephone, the envelope; there were other icons as well, most of which had functions I had never bothered to explore. But there was one other that I knew something about—not much, but something—and now, that was where I focused my attention: on the little picture of Hello Kitty with its blank white face and round, pin-like eyes. The last time that icon had come to life, it was without my intervention and it had led to nothing. No connection had been made. Instead, I had ended up sitting at a picnic table in the middle of the night, thinking I had an appointment, which turned out to be untrue. But I had sent out a signal, anyway, using an old-fashioned method that had been around since sharpened rocks had been used to carve symbols in wood, since painted handprints had been plastered on cave walls. A double star and three smaller ones, arranged like a flat-sided triangle: that was my signal. I hoped it was enough. I hoped it was understood as I meant it: a grudging acknowledgment that for now, I would keep my hands to myself. That I wasn't going to bite. That I could control my anger. That if we could figure out how to do it, we could talk.

I looked up for a moment to take a quick glance out the window. The tunnel was right ahead of us now; the bus was about to slip into the fluorescent-lit tube under the river where my phone, everyone's phone, would likely go dead. So just before that happened, I touched the face of Hello Kitty and said, "Tomorrow night." Immediately, Hello Kitty's little black eyes began to blink.

# IX

GRIFFONS AND GARGOYLES; dim lighting and yellowed wallpaper: nothing about the café on MacDougal Street seemed to have changed since I had sat here with John a decade ago. I wasn't feeling nostalgic, though, and I hadn't expected to; the café was simply an expedient. A place I happened to remember, so it became where I chose to set events in motion and see where they would end up—if they ended up anywhere at all, achieved any kind of resolution. As far as I could tell, everything from this minute on—when I settled myself into a chair, ordered a cup of coffee from a waitress—was unpredictable. All I could do was focus my attention outward and wait. Wait, see what unfolded. Wait and then respond.

I was early, the first one to arrive. After the waitress brought my coffee, I pulled my phone out of my pocket and put it on the table. I wanted to check it, as I had been doing almost obsessively since yesterday. The little blank cat eyes had gone on blinking as the bus traveled through the tunnel under the Hudson River, but once it emerged into the light they had stopped. Since that time, no matter how many times I checked, they had not become animated again. Now, as I stared into the deep blue electronic sea of energy with its floating icons, they all remained motionless, including the wide, white cat face with its pin-sized eyes. After a minute, the screen went black. The phone had put itself silently to sleep.

I waited. Eight o'clock. Eight ten. Eight fifteen. The waitress came back to my table and I ordered more coffee. Just as she was returning, the door of the café opened and three men walked in together: Kel, scruffy and tattooed, Jim Barrett—a bloated figure looking even more overstuffed in a puffy down jacket—and another guy I hadn't met before. The Internet blogger. The paranormal investigator. The problem for me.

Kel led them over to my table and we said hello. I even managed to shake the hand Jim Barrett offered me without glaring at him. It was Jim, then, who introduced me to Michael Mills. He was younger than all of us—in his early thirties, perhaps—and he had some kind of European accent. Not English, not French, just some mélange of cultures that produced a pinched, arch-sounding voice. Immediately, he smiled at me, trying to engage, but it was Jim who started the conversation.

"I'm glad you agreed to meet with us, Julia. And I'm hoping we can just start all over again."

"Well, a lot of time has passed," I said mildly, committing to nothing.

"And a lot has changed," Jim said. "There's a lot going on."

"I thought there was nothing going on," I said. "And that's why we're here."

Jim frowned at me, but Michael Mills seemed delighted with my re-sponse. "Fantastic," he said. "Right to it then, yes? That's probably best."

When he had walked in with Jim Barrett, Mills had been carrying a messenger bag, which he had slung over the back of his chair when he sat down. Now, he reached into the bag and started pulling out all kinds of electronics that he arranged in front of him, on the table: a laptop, a digital tape recorder, and a small digital camera. He opened the laptop, touched a button on the tape recorder, and made a small show of checking the camera. I had the feeling that we were playing a kind of technology poker: my phone, with its screen blacked out in sleep mode, was already on the table, but Mills had raised the ante with his array of hi-tech devices. With his hands now poised over the laptop keys, he said, "Tools of the trade. I want to make sure I record everything, so I get your statements right. You don't mind, do you?"

*My statements.* The terminology grated on me a little; I got the message that while Mills, at least, might be planning to be pleasant enough, his intentions were to conduct an interrogation—something he would call an investiga-tion when he used his various platforms to "reveal" whatever information he got from me. I glanced over at Kel to see his reaction to what was going on, but all I could decode was a kind of quiet tension. Was he here as my friend, I wondered, or theirs?

Any further conversation was momentarily stayed by the waitress, who returned to the table to take more coffee orders. Jim also asked for a plate of biscotti. "Just something to chew on," he said when the waitress had departed. I realized that he thought he'd made a clever joke.

"So, Jim," I said. "Michael. I think I know what you want to hear from me, but I'm not sure that I have anything useful to say."

Jim Barrett's frown grew deeper. "Great," he said. "Here we go again." He turned to Kel. "I thought you said she would cooperate."

Kel shrugged and looked away. But as he did, he unbuttoned the denim jacket he was wearing and then stretched a little. That was for my benefit, because as he pushed his arms back, I could glimpse the edges of a brown paper bag tucked into an inside pocket of the jacket. *Good*, I thought. *You brought it. You are my friend.*

To Jim I said, "You want to talk, I'll talk. All I'm saying is that I don't know if I have the answers you want."

Now it was Michael Mills who took control of the conversation. "Well, let's start with the basics," he said. "The grays—the aliens. You've had contact with them? Direct contact?"

"Yes," I said. "I used to, all the time."

"Well, hallelujah," Jim said. "Finally, she admits it."

"That's right," I said. "I admit it." Then I added, for emphasis. "I've seen dozens of them, I think, though I haven't really kept count. It's been happening since I was a little kid."

"That's fantastic," Mills said. "Fantastic. Did they take you aboard a ship?"

"A what?" I asked.

"You know, some sort of space ship. Other people have described undergoing invasive exams—medical, sexual examinations—on what must be some kind of space craft."

"No one's ever taken me anywhere," I said.

Now Mills looked puzzled. "You've never been abducted?"

"No," I replied. "Nothing like that."

He turned away from me, looked over at Jim Barrett. "Then I'm at a loss," he said to Jim. "If she's not going to tell us about abduction experiences, why are we here?"

"Because she's going to tell us why the abductions have stopped. What the grays are planning next."

"I'm going to tell you that?" I said. "Well, maybe I would if I could, but I have no idea."

The waitress brought the coffee and a plate of half-moon shaped cookies. Jim barely contained himself as he waited for the woman to arrange everything in front of us, then he leaned across the table and said, "You listen to me, Julia. Don't pretend you're some kind of innocent fool, because you're not."

"Nope," I said. "Definitely not a fool."

"Then stop playing around. I know the abductions stopped after Alice killed John. She told me about that night, Julia."

"Yes," I said. "I'm sure she did. But what, exactly, did she say? That is, if you don't mind my asking."

Maybe now I was being too cordial, because he gave me a suspicious look. But for now, he just went on trading information for my responses. "She said that the grays were there. They protected you."

"That's true," I said. "That's just what they did."

"Why?" Jim asked. "Why are you so important?"

"I know that seems to be the prevailing theory, but actually, I don't think I'm really the one who's important at all. Not me."

"Dear heart," Michael Mills chimed in, perhaps thinking I would respond to charm rather than prodding, "don't be so disingenuous. You are at the center of a mystery that Jim and I want desperately to solve. Something that could have implications for the very future of humanity."

"That would be quite a responsibility," I said. "I hope I'm up to the challenge."

"Then tell us the connection, Julia. You, the abductions, the grays..."

"Things," I said. "That's what I've always called them. Kel prefers creepy crawlies." I glanced over at Kel, then, but he remained silent. He was watching me, though. Still waiting to see where all this was going.

While Michael was talking, Jim had never looked away from me. Now, his expression hardened. He reached into Mill's messenger bag, pulled out some photos, and slapped them on the table. "Tell us about these," he said.

I had expected to see these pictures so they did not disturb me. I pointed to the one showing Laura walking past the bend in the road. "That's my mother," I said. "The things put that photo on my cell phone." Then I indicated one of the Ted Devere's photos Jim had brought with him, the one showing a figure dressed in a blue sharkskin suit with skinny lapels. "And that's one of the things." I said.

*But is he a good one or a bad one?* I wondered. *And how do you tell the difference?*

"One of the grays. The *aliens*," Jim said, intending to correct me. "And your mother was involved with them from way back, right? Before you were even born. Kel told us that's what you told him."

Kel finally spoke, sounding irritated. "Leave me out of this, will you, Jim?"

"It's okay," I said to Kel. "That's probably true, as well. I'm sure she knew her visitors long before I was born. Maybe as far back as when she was a kid. I wish I'd asked her about that, but I never did."

"Really?" Jim said. His voice sounded tight, tense, almost like he was on the verge of sputtering. "Are you sure you never asked? That you don't know? Because if what you want us to believe is that you're not important to the grays, then maybe your mother was. Maybe she's the one we should be investigating."

"Probably, but good luck with that," I said. "She's been dead a long time."

"Everyone has a history. I'm very good at finding out what it is no matter how far back I have to look."

I shrugged. "Great. Let me know what you turn up."

Jim leaned forward to add emphasis to what he had to say next. "I think what I'll find out is that she was cooperating with them. So what was she doing for them, Julia? Was she luring people to them? Identifying victims for them to abduct? Maybe she was participating in their attempts to create hybrids. Has all that stopped because the aliens' plans have changed? Have they come up with some new way to replace us on this planet?"

"I told you, I have no idea."

"Julia," Jim Barrett said, "listen to me carefully. We're going to tell this story whether you like it or not." He grabbed Michael Mill's camera, pointed it at me and clicked off several quick shots. "Now I have your photo," he said. "I have these photos of your mother. And I have all the information you gave Kel, which he repeated to me and I now have on tape. Something is going on and I am damn sure going to find out what it is. And when I do, I promise you, your photo and your mother's are going to be on book covers, they're going to go viral online, and I am going to be shouting from the rooftops about how you are at the center of an alien conspiracy that poses a danger to the future of humanity."

"Yes, you said that," I replied. "But I really don't think anybody's going to listen to you. Think about the story you're going to tell: to begin with, the things are apparently so weak and helpless that they can be smacked around by a cleaning lady. Because Alice told you that, too, right? That I picked up a chair and smashed your dangerous alien in the face with it? And I'm sure Kel told you that I bit one of them when I was a kid. Bit right through its bitter skin. So what you've got is a little girl who's stronger than an evil gray alien—and she grows up to be a grieving cleaning lady who lived with a revered professor murdered by a crazy woman whose ravings you based most of your past allegations about alien abduction on. That's a romance novel, Jim, not an alien exposé. And the pictures you're going to say were delivered by aliens to the cleaning lady's cell phone were actually provided to the poor woman by a discredited con man, a janitor who most people think is a little crazy himself. And as for my mother, anyone who remembers her is likely to tell you that she was a hippie chick who liked science fiction movies and stargazing."

"I have you on tape," Jim said. He was nearly shaking with anger, so much so that even Michael Mills was looking at him with a concerned expression. Or maybe it was the dawning of doubt about the situation he had gotten himself involved in. He opened his mouth to say something, but Barrett waved his hand, meaning to silence him before he even spoke. Jim went on; he said, "You admitted to having contact with them. You admitted that they protected you."

"And I have such a great track record of being an upstanding citizen who always tells the truth. By the way, did you know I've been living the past ten years or so on a fake i.d.? My mother's, actually, but like I told you, she's dead so what kind of a nut job am I going to seem like?"

"You know what they're doing," Jim shouted—he was so loud, now, that other people in the café turned to look at him. "And I want you to tell me what it is."

His voice was still ringing in my ears—mine and everyone else's, probably—when suddenly, my phone lit up. I looked down and saw that it had awakened from sleep mode and the deep blue screen was now offering up its display of shimmering icons. And one of them, Hello Kitty, was more than wide awake: it was signaling to me. No doubt about it: the little pin eyes were blinking. Fast, repeatedly. Blink, blink, blink.

I looked up and smiled at Jim Barrett. "You want to know what they're doing? Why don't you ask them yourself?"

I raised my hand and pointed to a corner of the dim café, where there were two figures sitting at a spindly table. One was wearing a summer dress printed with daisies, the other was wrapped in an oversized trench coat and both were sporting huge sunglasses. Despite their odd dress, this was the Village, after all, so no one was paying them any attention except me. I had noticed them come into the café a few minutes ago.

Jim Barrett, Michael Mills, and Kel all turned their heads to see where I was pointing. A moment later, Jim looked back at me with a deep frown. "Those weirdos?" he said. "Friends of yours, I suppose. What have they got to do with anything?"

It was Kel who answered him. "I think we're going to find out," he said.

We were. The two figures slowly rose from their table and started walking towards us. Michael Mills—a man of manners, apparently—stood up as the figures approached.

In a moment, Daisy Dress and Trench Coat were standing above us as we remained seated—all except Mills, who was in the act of pulling two chairs away from a nearby table so "my friends" could join us. In a remarkably swift motion, Trench Coast reached out and yanked the chairs from Mills' grip. Then it put a gray hand with long, stick-like fingers on the blogger's shoulder and shoved him back down into his seat.

Mills' seemed too startled to say anything; it was Jim Barrett—seemingly ready for a fight with anybody tonight—who complained. As he began to lift himself up from his chair, he growled, "Listen you jerk, who the fuck do you think you are?"

By way of an answer, Daisy Dress removed the sunglasses from its face, unmasking its huge, expressionless black eyes. Trench Coat did the same.

271

And finally, Jim saw just who was standing before him. Slowly, his mouth agape, he lowered himself back into his chair.

Suddenly, Michael Mills seemed to remember his array of electronics. He picked up his digital camera and pointed it at the things. Trench Coat made a high, thin sound like a cat hissing, and as it did, I stole a glance at my phone, Hello Kitty's eyes, which had started blinking again. They were blinking like crazy.

Trench Coat grabbed the camera, which it tossed away. Mills' camera skidded across the floor, but again, no one else in the café paid attention—perhaps, I thought, they couldn't even see it. Or see the things—what was it Ted Devere had said? *They're not really here and we're not really there.* Maybe that meant different people saw them different ways—or not at all.

Jim Barrett turned to me with a look of terror on his face. "Do something," he whispered.

"Why?" I replied. "What's wrong? Now you've seen them yourself and you can tell the world all about it. The aliens wear dresses and trench coats and they sound like cats. That's the great menace to humanity. Oh, and one more thing—they like to drink."

"What do they want?" Barrett asked, his voice trembling.

"Probably for you to shut up. I think we'd all like that," I said.

"Please," Barrett said to me. He couldn't seem to make even one more word come out of his mouth.

"Well, I'll do something," Kel said. "He reached into his jacket and pulled out the pint bottle of Jack Daniels I had asked him to bring. He slipped it out of its paper bag and put it on the table. "That drink Julia mentioned—want to share one with us?" he asked Daisy Dress and Trench Coat. "There's only so much coffee a person can stand. Person," he repeated, "so to speak."

It was Daisy Dress who responded, reaching around Jim Barrett to pick up the bottle. As it did, Jim's gaze moved from my face to the thing's wrist where there was a dark blue tattoo. A double star and three smaller companions. A tattoo that exactly matched my own. There was no way to miss seeing it.

"You are one of them," Jim Barrett whispered to me. He still seemed almost paralyzed with fright.

"I keep telling you, no" I said, but as I did, I rolled down my sleeve and laid my arm on the table, wrist up, exposing my own tattoo. "Just think of this like a stamp from your favorite bar—you know, like when you have to leave for a while but you want to be able to get back in." Then I looked up at Daisy Dress and Trench Coat. Speaking directly to them I said, "So I guess if we're planning on doing some serious drinking, that's where we might as well go."

For a moment, the two things seemed to focus their unblinking eyes on my tattoo. Then put their sunglasses back on, turned away and walked straight out the front door, carrying the pint of Jack. I stood up to follow them. "Come on," I said to Kel. Then I smiled at Michael Mills. "Sorry about your camera. But bad things happen to people who hang around this guy," I said, tapping Jim Barrett on his shoulder. "Very bad." Then I had a few last words for Jim himself. "If you ever come near me again, or use my name in anything you say or write, watch out, because I'll come right back at you, and I just might be armed with an anal probe. Or maybe a ray gun. I think I know where I can borrow stuff like that."

I put my jacket on and walked out of the café. Kel followed right after me. He started looking around, as if he thought the things would be out on the street, but that wasn't what I expected.

He said, "Am I understanding what you meant back there? Do you seriously mean you want to go to Freelingburg tonight? How are we going to get there? We couldn't even get a bus until morning and we don't have a car. Besides, it'll take hours."

"The Stargazer's Embassy stays open late."

"Again," Kel said, "how are we going to get there?"

"I have a feeling there's something we can borrow."

I started to walk towards the end of the block, but it was slow going because MacDougal Street was very busy; even on such a chilly night, the streets were packed with tourists, locals, wanderers lingering by the jazz clubs and cafes. People were sitting on stoops, eating pizza; smoking weed, watching the passing parade. I reached the corner but didn't see what I thought I was looking for, so I started back in the other direction, all the while followed by Kel, who had finally stopped asking me questions.

I walked almost the full length of MacDougal, from West Houston to West 3rd, and still nothing. Finally, it occurred to me that maybe I was looking in the wrong place—the street was just too bright and crowded. So I retraced my steps until I reached the corner of Minetta Lane, one short, narrow street of small buildings—no stores or shops—so it was quiet, lit only by a few street lamps. Parking was not allowed here, so there were no vehicles on either side of the street, but I decided to walk down the lane anyway. Then, in an alley between two old brick townhouses, I found what I had been looking for. A motorcycle. A big one. It had no name on it, no markings of any kind.

"They seem to like bikes," I said to Kel. Then I asked, "Do you think you can still ride one of those?

He looked at the bike, then at me, then back at the bike. He was processing, he was deciding what to do. Finally, he said, "Yes. I can."

He walked over to the bike, lifted himself onto the seat, and pushed back the kickstand. I saw him flip the kill switch to the on position, then turn the key that had been left in the ignition. The bike's engine immediately revved into life, roaring with power.

"Okay," Kel said. "Get on."

I climbed onto the seat behind him. There were two mirrored helmets hanging off the back of the seat. I handed one to Kel, but before I put the other one on, I said, "Wait one sec." I pulled my cell phone out of my pocket and turned it on. Hello Kitty's little pinprick eyes were still blinking madly. I touched the face of the little icon and said, "We're on our way."

At first, the only reply I received was complete silence. But then, suddenly, a strange, tinny voice projected itself from a tiny speaker on the side of the phone.

It said, *We're already waiting for you.*

# X

FREELINGBURG'S ONE MAIN street was empty; its one stoplight blinked red, yellow, and green for no one but us, at nothing but the night and the cold stars as we drove towards the one place in town still open at this hour. Kel parked the bike outside the front door and we left our helmets on the seat. Then, together, we walked into The Stargazer's Embassy.

Inside, all the tables were empty. The movie screen was set up on the stage, but it was blank. I looked around, searching the room for any sign of movement, any presence at all, but there was nothing. In the dim light, the bar looked pretty much the same as it had the last time I had been here with John ten years ago, but it felt different. Without music playing or a movie being shown or people drinking below the star map that included the Zeta Reticuli system, the Stargazer's Embassy felt more than deserted: it felt lifeless.

Kel whispered, "Maybe you were wrong. This isn't where they are."

"It has to be," I said, "one way or another."

But could I be mistaken? I pulled my phone from my pocket—the first time I'd been able to even take a peek at it since I climbed on the back of the motorcycle—and looked at Hello Kitty. Its pinprick eyes were not moving; they were just tiny black holes in an expressionless electric face. This was not what I had expected.

275

Suddenly, a door behind the stage was pushed open and there was Nicky, looking just a little older, a little grayer—and very startled. Peering through the shadows he said, "Julia? Is that you? I can't believe it."

He walked towards me and then hesitated. I could tell that he wanted to pull me close but wasn't sure that his embrace would be welcome. Well, that was my fault and I knew it: he had tried to keep in touch with me. He had sent birthday cards and left messages on my home phone, but I had erased him from my life. I was much too good at doing that. It was time, I thought, that I stopped.

So, I walked towards him and hugged him. My old hippie cowboy sort-of-dad. A good guy who had thought the night was winding down when really, he probably had a strange hour or two ahead of him—at least, I was still holding onto that idea despite not getting any help at the moment from Hello Kitty. Now, I was going to have to explain myself to Nicky.

"I know it's really late…" I began.

"Nearly two a.m. I was just going to lock up," Nicky said.

"Don't do that yet," I suggested. "Not that I think it would matter." Again, I looked around the room. Nothing yet. No one, still. "Let's go sit down," I said.

I chose one of the tables midway between the front door and the stage, and we all took a seat. I introduced Nicky to Kel, and was trying to figure out where to start my story when my internal radar kicked in. *That* feeling, the one I always depended on to tell me that the things were somewhere around. I looked down at my phone, which I had placed face up on the table and yes, finally: Hello Kitty's eyes were beginning to blink again.

"Hey," Nicky said, looking towards the front of the bar. "Who the hell is that?"

I turned to look. So did Kel. What we saw was a tall figure standing just inside the front door near the star map. It was wearing a slim, dark blue suit with thin lapels and a pearly sheen to it, like sharkskin. The outfit was topped off with a skinny tie that looked as sharp-edged as a knife and a pair of wrap-around Ray Bans.

It was also carrying a suitcase.

"It's Sharkskin," Kel whispered to me. "The one I met here."

"Okay," I replied. And then again I breathed, "Okay." What I really meant was, *Here we go.*

Nicky hadn't heard Kel or me—he was focused on the figure at the door. "We're closed," he called out. Then he started to rise, as if to go towards this late-arriving customer.

I put my hand on Nicky's arm, signaling for him to stay in his seat. "We're not closed," I said. "Maybe never, actually. That's sort of what I wanted to tell you."

Slowly, Nicky settled back into his chair. As he did, Sharkskin removed his sunglasses, revealing his huge, almond-shaped eyes, depthless and dark. Nicky stared at the tall figure and then back at me; as he did, something in the expression on his face began to change.

"I know what you're thinking," I said to Nicky. "But you're not crazy. They're real. And that's one of them."

"My God," he breathed. "I think I've seen them before. I just never realized..." He stopped speaking and just shook his head.

"Nothing Laura ever told you was a lie," I said.

Finding his voice again, Nicky said, "Or you?"

"Or me."

For a few moments, the figure remained standing by the door. Then it took a few steps towards us. As it did, the screen behind us suddenly came to life. There was no sound, but the grainy images playing on the screen were by now, all too familiar.

"The damn death cult film," Kel said.

"What?" Nicky said, turning to look at the screen. He sounded alarmed.

"No, not a death cult," I said. "I mean, I don't think so, but I guess we're going to find out." I looked away from the figure in the dinner jacket and spoke directly to Hello Kitty. "Right?" I said.

There was no response from my phone's speaker, but Sharkskin kept walking towards us. When it finally reached our table, it stood silently for a moment, totally still. It stared down at us, seemingly waiting for something—and I thought I knew what that was.

"Get some shot glasses," I said to Nicky.

"What?" He didn't seem to be able to look away from the thing's blank, depthless gaze.

"Go," I said. "Please."

Finally, Nicky rose from his chair. Shaking his head again as if that would rid his mind of the image of a tall gray-skinned being in a sharkskin suit, he went over to the bar and returned with four shot glasses. He put them on the table and sat down again.

The thing remained standing, but it put the suitcase down on the floor. It shifted its gaze towards the glasses as it reached into an inside pocket of its jacket and brought out the pint of Jack Daniels we had given to Daisy Dress and Trench Coat and slammed it down so hard that the table shook.

Nicky and Kel looked startled, but the thing's action didn't bother me. In my mind, I was holding onto what Ted Devere had said about how the things were here, in the world we inhabited, but maybe not really, not wholly, so maybe Sharkskin didn't perceive its action as hostile to us, or aggressive. So, I just picked up the bottle, uncapped it, and poured each of us a drink.

"Anybody want to make a toast?" I said. "No? Then just drink up."

I could only sip the whiskey; it wasn't my drink. I usually stuck to beer or wine. But Kel and Nicky downed theirs quickly. Sharkskin watched them. When they were done, it reached for the one remaining glass on the table—but its movement was so fast that it was impossible to tell if it actually picked up the glass and downed the drink because the entire action passed by in a blur. I only knew it had consumed the shot by the fact that again the table shook when the empty glass was slammed down.

Sharkskin's behavior, its movements, were different than the other two we had encountered at the café in the Village, so I revised my earlier opinion: maybe it *was* trying to show some sort of aggression. Still, I wasn't going to be intimidated.

"So," I said. "I think it's time you tell me what you want." I pushed my phone to the center of the table, and touched the face of Hello Kitty with my finger. "We can use this, right?"

Again, Sharkskin raised its hand, but this time, it moved slowly enough for me to see what it was doing—and what it did was reach down to touch one gray stick-like finger to the Hello Kitty icon, just as I had done. Kitty's flat, black eyes suddenly stopped blinking, but just as suddenly, began to glow. They looked alive, electrical. Some circuit, some connection, somewhere, had been turned on.

And then Sharkskin spoke. It made a kind of hissing-cat noise that was unintelligible as any kind of speech. But as soon as the hissing concluded, a thin but fierce-sounding voice emerged from my phone. "You know what we want."

"Maybe," I said. "But why don't you tell me?"

"Laura," the voice said. "We want you to tell us where Laura is."

"She's dead," I replied. "You know that."

The thing hissed again and Hello Kitty's eyes glowed even more intensely. "Of course we know that. But where did she go?"

I was startled by the question. Completely unprepared. "Go? Nowhere. She just...died," I said.

As if what I had said made no sense the thing spoke again, through my phone. "We cannot find her," it told me.

I looked up, into the huge, black eyes of the thing. Again, there was that blur of movement; the hand with its gray, stick-like fingers, which had moments ago slammed the glass on the table was now pointing towards the movie screen. I regarded the grainy images changing from frame to frame, which seemed to depict souls, complete with white robes and wings, ascending towards the sky. Towards heaven? Well, towards somewhere: like the rest of this production, the scenes were awkward and amateurish; it was easy to see the wires pulling the white-garbed souls towards their seemingly celestial destination. These guys were as good at making films as they were at choosing outfits, but nonetheless, I knew what this scene, along with all the others I had viewed before, was supposed to suggest. Or ask, really, because the movie was like one big question—but not about death, exactly. It was about what might happen afterwards.

"Is she there?" Sharkskin asked, still pointing to images on the movie screen.

I knew that Sharkskin didn't mean heaven—at least, not some human concept of a place where you were rewarded for leading a good life, whatever *that* meant. I knew it because I remembered that Kel said my mother had told him just that, years ago, the first time he had come to the Stargazer's Embassy. Perhaps, I thought, they had even been sitting at this same table.

"I asked you a question," Sharkskin said. Though Hello Kitty's translation had its limitations, I still thought I heard some semblance of a vicious edge to this reminder. That convinced me it was probably important not to let the thing continue to tower over me, using its height to try to act intimidating. So, I stood up and looked into its face. "I don't believe things like that so...no, I guess not. I don't think my mother is in some spirit realm or anything like that."

Sharkskin regarded me in silence, perhaps contemplating my answer. Then, two quick events took place at once: the movie screen went dark and Sharkskin shoved a finger at my chest. Again, I saw only a blur, but I felt the pressure of its touch.

"Is she in you?" the thing asked.

"In me?" There were so many ways that Sharkskin could have meant that question: symbolically, metaphorically, even literally. But I had already answered that question myself, in every way, an answer I had shared with Alice. Of all people, Alice: to no one else, ever, had I confessed how completely alien I felt myself to be—with or without the things around me—because I was motherless. Because I felt that I always had been, even when Laura was alive. "No," I said. "She's not."

And then whammo: some brain cell spit out an electrical charge that sent a message to one of the dark spaces in my mind and another light went on. "Is that why you've been following me all these years? If she's not...what? Someplace else? If you can't find her anywhere—*here* or *there*, or whatever the right words are—then you think it's possible that I'm her, sort of, or she's still part of me? Do you actually believe that?"

"We don't know what to believe," Sharkskin said, sounding bitter. "Just like you." Again, it jabbed me in the chest. "So tell me what you think you are. All of you. Just things that live and die and nothing else?"

*Things?* Had I heard Sharkskin right? He was calling me—all human be-ings—*things?* That was almost funny, but not in a way that made me want to laugh. Not at all.

"Answer me," Sharkskin insisted.

By now, I was hardly even aware that the thing was communicating through my phone. I heard the fierce hissing sounds it was making but the translation was so instantaneous that the intensity with which it spoke seemed to be amplified.

"Well?" Sharkskin said.

"Why are you asking me?" I replied. "You should ask someone who thinks about questions like that. I told you, I don't."

"There is no one else to ask," Sharkskin replied.

*Really?* I was about to say. *Billions of people in the world and you think I know something they don't?* But suddenly Kel put his hand on my arm. He wanted my attention.

"Julia," he said, "I don't think it—he—means you—just you, specifically. He doesn't mean just here, in this world. I think he means anywhere. Anywhere in the universe. Maybe there isn't anyone else but us."

Another instant insight: Mr. Bad Boy, Kel, with his piercings and nail-studded boots and a coiled snake inked up his arm to his jaw, was the deep thinker when compared to me. Thanks to Hello Kitty, he was hearing Sharkskin, too, and maybe because—in another comparison I couldn't avoid—he was more unselfish than I would ever be, he was able to intuit what I could not: that "no one else" did not mean just me, personally, or even other people, other human beings. It meant exactly what Kel thought it did: *There isn't anyone else but us.* No beings of any kind, in any world. Any dimension of any universe. Anywhere, in the deep, unknowable vastness of everywhere that existed in any way or shape or form.

As if reading my thoughts, Sharkskin said, "Everywhere we have traveled, we have looked for others—and we have traveled so far and so long that not one of us can even remember when we began, or even where we started from. But in all the universe, as long as we have traveled, we have encountered no others. Only your kind. Unfortunately, though, you are all so...unpleasant."

The bottle of whiskey was empty now, as were all our glasses. I asked Nicky to get a fresh round, but he had a glazed look on his face; he seemed to have fallen into some kind of trance. In any case, he didn't appear to have heard me so Kel got up, went behind the bar and returned with a new bottle of whiskey.

Once Kel had refilled the shot glasses, I again focused my attention on the thing and what it had been telling me. "But I guess Laura—my mother—was different. She wasn't...what did you say? Unpleasant?"

Sharkskin downed its drink in another blur of motion. But then the thing paused; it put the empty glass down on the table and let one long finger linger on the rim. Finally the thing said, "Yes. She was different." And then, I experienced another impression of movement in which Sharkskin seemed to lean forward. The alien face was just inches from mine as the thing asked, "Are you sure that you are unable to find her?"

Yes, I was sure. I was about to reiterate that fact when I found myself hesitating. There were certainly no earthly boundaries I could cross to find some trace of Laura, but maybe I could turn inward again. Maybe I could try once more. And so I did. I searched inside myself for the dead.

Laura should have been there, somewhere; despite all my protestations, some element of her life, her soul—if such a thing existed—should have been encoded in some part of me, some faint electrical flare between the synapses, some chemical twined around another in my brain, around the shadow of my heart, and yet again, I found nothing. But there was also another soul, some shard of that soul, at least, that I should have been able to call out to speak to me, but I could not. John was not with me either. John and Laura. Both gone, gone, gone.

How could that be? I had watched enough tv shows, read enough books and certainly listened to enough songs to have been convinced that love should live on, no matter what happened to people who loved one another. And I knew something about that: the love between a parent and child, the intimate ache of lovers; these had been offered to me, if only for brief interludes. And yet, where those feelings should have existed inside me, all I found where whispers, traces, remnants. Just enough to understand what was missing.

Then was I the monster? The thing without feelings? Something walking all by myself along a lonely road through an impenetrable darkness—alert to threats and the need to strike out at them—but pausing for little else? Yes, that was me. It had always been me.

In the next moment it occurred to me that there was someone else in the Stargazer's Embassy who felt that way, who lived in that kind of isolation. Some *thing*. And it was standing before me in a blue sharkskin suit.

I stared at the thing, the alien, the visitor, the creepy crawly, and again, it seemed to nod. *Yes*, it was saying—and without the aid of my phone. *Yes*, it told me. *Now you know how it feels.*

Did I? And if so, then was this empathy? Was that what I felt? Empathy for Sharkskin and his fellows? For *their* aloneness?

That was certainly what John believed in—the idea that we should at least try to understand the things, or at least, understand that while we might not be able to fathom their intentions, there might be other common ground we could find with them. Other pathways to walk, other roads. Like the road Laura was walking, the one they kept showing me. The road that started *here* and went to *there*—there, beyond the bend, wherever that led. The road we were all on. All creatures, all tribes. Even if there were only two tribes: aliens and humans. Just us.

Again, as if it could intuit what I was thinking, Sharkskin said, "We are so tired of traveling. We hoped—some of us—that we might stay here. Despite the fact that you are not friendly towards us. Not at all. That was why Laura's help was so important."

"What?" I said, startled. Just as I was beginning to mellow in my feelings towards these things—and towards my mother—was Sharkskin really telling me now that everything Jim Barrett had suggested was true? That there was some alien plot to seed humanity with their own kind, and Laura was some sort of collaborator, helping them along?

But before I lost myself in that horrifying idea, I heard Sharkskin sigh. It was still a fierce and angry sound, but sad as well. Deeply, fearfully sad. It said, "We tried so many different ways to stay. But you are all so unwelcoming that the only way was to blend in as best we could. We tried to put ourselves into children we made, but they were empty things. They had no mind, no being. We could not enter them and they never existed very long."

Sharkskin reached out with a long, gray arm; its movements, now, looked to me as jerky as the stop-motion action of an animated movie, as if it was making an effort to slow itself down, to have its intentions visible to us. To me and Kel, anyway: Nicky still seemed to be in some frozen state. His eyes were wide open and his breathing, though slow, seemed regular—but I was still sure that he was not exactly with us. Not hearing or seeing what was going on around him.

Sharkskin lifted the bottle of Jack Daniels and poured himself another drink. His movements had completely changed now: from blindingly fast, he suddenly seemed to be moving in some sort of exaggerated slow motion, as if he had adjusted his actions for my benefit. He lifted the shot glass to the thin slit of his mouth, which seemed to me barely able to open, and then slowly drank the amber colored whiskey. When he was done, he said, "We don't understand you. How do you live? What happens when you die? As far as we can tell, you are the same as all the animals around you. Perhaps that was why we could not enter the half-human children we created. The strength of your being is so faint that mixed with ours, it was like nothing. You fear everything. You understand nothing. You know nothing."

"Really?" I said. "Just what is it you think we're supposed to know?"

*Slam.* Sharkskin was moving like a blur again, and this time, when he banged his glass down on the table, the whole building seemed to shake. "Where the road goes!" he cried out. "When we found you we always hoped you would know. But you are useless to us. Useless in every way." Then, seeming to quiet down, to collect itself once more, Sharkskin said, "Most of you, anyway."

I thought that was an outrageous declaration. "And that's why you think it's alright to terrify people? Because we're useless animals?" I felt like I was asking this not only for myself, but also for Alice. And for John; for the idealist he was who would have wanted to know the truth for all the patients he treated, all the experiencers. "Is that what you were doing? Using human beings to breed your hybrids?"

Sharkskin waved his hand dismissively, again, in that slowed-down, stop-motion way that ensured I could see what he was doing. "That was not us," he said. "We never forced anyone to help us. It was the others."

"What others? You said you never found any others."

"There are divisions among us," Sharkskin said. "Just as with you." And then, if it was possible for Sharkskin to smile with that nearly im-mobile slit of a mouth, it did smile. A kind of bizarre smirk. "Good ones and bad ones," it said, pulling my own thoughts from my mind. "We are the good ones. Imagine what the others are like."

I could imagine—they were the reality of Alice's nightmare encounters. But what did my mother have to do with all this? I still didn't understand. "Was Laura one of your...volunteers?"

Sharkskin didn't exactly answer me. What he said was, "She was the only one who could comfort the empty creatures we created. If they needed comforting. Who knows? She held them, cradled them. And then she showed us where to dispose of them. She showed us how—insisted that it be done... ah, correctly."

"Dispose?" Kel said, breaking in. "*Correctly?* You mean she made you bury them, right? Because that's what people do when human beings die—even if they aren't really human, I guess. So you put them in the cemetery near

Freelingburg, where I met the creepy crawly that night. Lucky me," Kel said.

Sharkskin turned towards Kel, again controlling its movements so we could see what it was doing. "Useless," it spat.

"Hey," Kel protested, but then immediately shut up, probably because he wasn't exactly sure what failure he was being accused of and thought better of trying to find out.

Once more, Sharkskin focused on me. "Your mother believed in all possibilities," it said. "Whatever road she took, we thought we could follow. We are so tired of the one we are on. I told you, we can't even remember anymore where it began. And not one of us has any idea where it is leading. But we thought with Laura's help we might find out. But then, suddenly, she was just gone, and in all this time, she has given us no sign of where she is. So if you don't know—if she is not reborn in you—then there really is no hope. We have to go on. There is no choice. The children were a failed attempt to stay here, to put ourselves into them so we could follow Laura's road. We believed she would look back, she would guide us, but as you see, nothing seems to work. Nothing."

Suddenly, Kel stood up. It seemed like he had acted on an impulse and when he found himself on his feet he stopped and looked at Sharkskin as if expecting to be told to sit down again. But the thing said nothing, so I watched as Kel strode quickly over to the star map painted on the wall of the Stargazer's Embassy. "Is this where you're from?" Kel said, pointing at the star system of Zeta Reticuli. "Is this your home?"

In response, Hello Kitty laughed. It was such a harsh sound that it made me remember how I was hearing Sharkskin—through an icon on my telephone. The perfectly round, blank cat face laughed, while Sharkskin himself kept those huge, dark eyes on me. But it was Kel's question he responded to.

"Didn't I say that we don't remember where home is? Where we began? Those stars are just a marker we follow. A configuration that repeats and repeats throughout the universe. I showed them myself to Betty and Barney Hill, but they misunderstood. When people are with us—and those who have visited with us have agreed to come—we can talk to them without the phone toy," Sharkskin said, "but there is still so much that gets confused. We don't know who, or what, has caused that star pattern to be placed across the cosmos, and we don't even really remember anymore why we have to follow them. But we do. That's how our story begins—the story of our origin. What went before—who knows? But the road through the cosmos must lead somewhere, and until we find out, what else can we do but follow the signposts?" Then Hello Kitty made some sounds again—a sigh full of static, as if it was translating something Sharkskin had not meant me to hear. But I heard it anyway because I had become attuned to the icon's speech pattern, its tones and rhythms. And what I heard it say was, "We should have moved on long ago."

Kel must have heard that, too. He came back to the table and perhaps emboldened by what he perceived as a momentary crack in Sharkskin's aura of aggressiveness, he said, "So you live and die on what? Spaceships?"

"There are no spaceships." Sharkskin said. "That's a ridiculous idea."

So, in my mind, I said goodbye to Gort and Klaatu and their great, round flying saucer ship; goodbye to UFOs gliding out from behind the clouds; goodbye to whatever people thought they saw hovering above them in the night sky. Maybe they were only as real as the myths John had told me about long ago: ghostly wheels spinning in the sky, flying ships trailing their anchors. But how then, did the things travel? How did they traverse their cosmic road? Perhaps they walked, I thought. Perhaps they dreamed their way across the universe. Or perhaps there was some other form of transitioning from *here* to *there* that they experienced—one that would finally explain why they were so sure that Laura could not possibly, simply, be gone.

The idea that came to me seemed impossible and yet, I knew it was true. "You never really die, do you?" I said to Sharkskin.

"Of course we do," the thing said. "At each signpost. Each marker. But we are reborn at the next, into these same bodies." Again, I heard that long, crackling sigh from Hello Kitty. "It just goes on and on." Sharkskin said, ignoring the sound that came from the icon on my phone. "And it will just continue until it ends. If it ends. That, it seems, is impossible to know."

All this time, Sharkskin had remained standing. Now, suddenly, I saw a blur of motion and when I was able to focus again, what I saw was Sharkskin halfway towards the front door of the Stargazer's Embassy, walking away from us. And it was holding the suitcase it had been carrying when it first walked in.

"Hey," I called after the thing. "You can't just leave like that."

Sharkskin stopped and turned to face me. "Why not? Isn't that what you want?"

"I want to know, once you leave, if I'm really free of you. What about the others?"

Sharkskin knew who I meant. *The bad ones.* Alice's tormentors. "They left years ago," Sharkskin said. "Right after you attacked one of us that last time."

"You mean when John died?"

"Yes. You did serious harm to the body of that traveler. There was doubt as to whether it would ever recover."

*The traveler.* Now I knew, finally, what they called themselves. "And what would have happened if it didn't recover?"

"That also cannot be known, since it has never happened before. We told the others and they were frightened." Once more, I saw, or thought I saw, a smile on the thing's long, blank face. "Nothing has ever frightened them before and so they fled. At least the ones we are in contact with. That we know about."

And there, finally, was the explanation for why the abductions had stopped. The bad ones were gone. *At least the ones they knew about.* That bit of information took a moment longer for me to process.

"Are you telling me there are more of you?" I asked.

"Some must be ahead of us on the road. Some must be behind us—or so we assume. The divisions among us happened so long ago that those travelers are just part of our story now, what we tell each other. But," the thing said, its dead eyes seeming, now, to glitter, "you should be prepared."

"*I* should be prepared? Why? I've had enough of you. All of you."

"You're marked," the thing said. "And the mark is above the front door of this place. That's what they will look for."

"If there are more of you. If they even exist. You said that you aren't even sure."

Sharkskin acted as if it hadn't heard me. It said, "Offer them a drink. Or smash them in the face with a bottle. Do what you like. That's what you always do, anyway, isn't it?"

As it said those last words, Sharkskin started advancing towards the front door again. But then, suddenly, it stopped. It seemed to hesitate for a moment, almost as if it couldn't help itself, and turned to regard the star map on the wall. Slowly, it reached out a long, spindly arm to touch the painted stars. The gesture seemed almost reverent.

And then it sighed. A long, deep, painful sigh.

Immediately, Hello Kitty began to crackle with sighs—one sigh, then another, then another, until the sound became wave of sighs: mournful, wistful, weary. But underneath the sound there was something else, some echo of anger that could only come from a living being rattling the chains that confined it in the dark. I knew that anger: it was what I had felt every day of my life that I tried to find some peace for myself but knew it was impossible.

Sharkskin seemed to hear the wild sighs as well, which now seemed fill the Stargazer's Embassy. It put down the suitcase again and turned around to look straight at me. "Apparently," it said, "we are not done yet."

The sighing became even louder. "Now what?" Kel said, though I could hardly hear him above the noise. "What's going on?"

I had no idea. All I could think to do was look down at the phone, where Hello Kitty's eyes seemed to have changed shape. No longer blank round dots or even glowing orbs, they had morphed into alien eyes—long and almond shaped, black and depthless as a night without a single star.

And when I looked up again, Sharkskin was not alone.

"Kel," I whispered. "Look who's here."

They all were: every creepy crawly, every thing, phone phreak—*traveler*—I could remember. Some were as tall as Sharkskin, some much shorter, as if different variants of whatever race of beings they were had become intertwined. But still, I remembered many of them because I remembered the bizarre outfits that Ted Devere had explained were the result of their not being able to actually assess or understand the human reality they were trying to interact with. I saw Daisy Dress and Trench Coat, but others, too—dozens and dozens of travelers, wearing ill-fitting raincoats, farmers' overalls, odd feathered hats, pajamas, rainboots, and baseball caps. Some wore sunglasses. Only a small group appeared to be unclothed, and I remembered them, as well: the two or three I had met with Laura, when I was a child—these were the ones that were my height, so I had thought of them as children, as well, though clearly, they were not. All of them had arranged themselves behind Sharkskin and each one was carrying a suitcase.

Where had they come from? Their presence seemed like the result of a curtain being lifted, or a new scene being inserted into a familiar movie. Now, all the players were present. All the travelers who had surrounded me all my life.

Well, almost.

Suddenly, one of the travelers stepped forward. It was dressed in boots and a cape, and draped around its neck was a loop of what appeared to be steel teeth. I recognized this traveler immediately, but not only because of its outfit. What I recognized was my own handiwork: the body of the traveler was broken and bent so that it appeared to be stooped over. One arm hung limply from its side and the top of its head looked crushed in. Yes, my handiwork—this was the traveler I had attacked on the night Alice had killed John.

It walked towards me with difficulty. Then it stopped, just a few feet away, as if it was important to display its injuries. For me to see what I had done.

When it seemed sure that I'd had a good look, it started to repair itself. Everything happened quickly, in what was becoming a familiar blur of motion, but I saw the traveler's bent body straighten up, its broken arm become supple, and its crushed head smooth out and take on the long, ovoid shape of the others. In a moment—half a moment—the traveler was whole again, completely uninjured.

"That's a nice trick," I said. "If you were going to stick around, I might ask you to teach it to me."

From Hello Kitty, I heard a derisive snort. Then the newly rejuvenated traveler pointed to the tattoo on my wrist. "One life," it said. "Useless."

"Maybe so," I said to the traveler. "But yours doesn't seem so much better."

"One life," the traveler said again, and Hello Kitty managed to convey these words with even more accentuated derision. Then, apparently, the traveler attempted a laugh. "Ha," it said. "Ha, ha."

As it walked back towards the others massed near the front door, the traveler stopped right next to Sharkskin and paused for a moment to speak to him. "Now we can leave," he said.

But it was impossible for me to let this snarky thing turn its back on me without some kind of retort. "Listen," I called after it, "if this mark means

289

that all I have is this one life, so what? One tattoo—that's all I've ever seen on any of you," I said, though really, it was only tonight, back at the café, that I, personally, had ever seen the star mark on any of them at all. Could that mean everything I'd heard from Sharkskin was a lie? The idea was disturbing in many, many ways, not least of all the fact that maybe, it made them more like me than I wanted to even contemplate.

It was Sharkskin who replied. "We have nothing to prove to you."

Now it was my turn for scorn. "Why? What makes you so important? So much better than us? Is that what you think? Or do you feel that this supposed quest you're on to find—well, what? Who created the universe? Why you were sent wandering through time and space?—is so much harder, so much more an impressive feat of endurance than just living the one life of a human being? Even if I believed any of that, if I felt sorry for you for one second and thought it somehow justified that when you get tired of it, when you want to stop, you feel free to set up some experiment that means you get to rip people from their beds, shove instruments into their bodies..."

"I told you, that was not us!" Sharkskin bellowed.

"Excuse me, I forgot. You're the good ones."

It glared at me—again, this was more of an impression than any visible expression on its face, but I felt that glare, that sense of bile rising in an alien throat.

"You have no idea," Sharkskin said. "How we suffer to exist. Born and reborn and reborn—and for what? If there is no reason, that would be unbearable. But each time we are reborn, we mark ourselves to remember that we have to keep going, keep traveling from signpost to signpost. Why should we share that with you?"

"Because I'm asking you to," I said. "Because I want to see."

I did. Suddenly, I did, very much. I wanted to see *something*. I was owed something after a lifetime of being stalked—or accompanied as I traveled through my days and nights, which is probably the way these things would have put it; accompanied in a way that had assured me they were always with me somewhere, somehow, but that no one else would be. Could be. Forced me to walk their road, and no one else's—and along the way, I had lost my mother, I had lost John, and even Nicky. Now, I wanted something back. These things—these aliens—had marked me and if that was something we shared, I wanted to see. Alice had said that was how they marked their children, and even if I wasn't one, not really, I wanted to know that at least, at the end of where this road led for me, I had been told the truth.

Sharkskin's answer was to pick up his suitcase once more. He continued to glare at me for a moment longer and then turned to walk away. As he did, he began to disappear into a blur, but suddenly, something stopped him.

There had been one being—one traveler—missing from the group that include Daisy Dress, Trench Coat, and all the others. One being who I had expected to see, but did not.

Until now.

The front door of the bar swung open and another tall figure appeared. This one was wearing a mirrored helmet, black leather motorcycle jacket, boots, and a pair of jeans. Now, he was standing in front of Sharkskin, blocking his way.

The two travelers said nothing to each other—at least, nothing that Hello Kitty translated for me. The Biker—which I now recognized as the costume the second tall thing was wearing, and I had to accord some sort of grudging credit here, since the clothes looked almost authentic, almost *right*—removed his helmet and for the first time, I saw his face, his gray, almond-shaped face and unblinking eyes. He and Sharkskin simply stared at each other for a few moments, and then Sharkskin backed away, as if acknowledging The Biker's authority.

Then, in the next moment, The Biker was standing right in front of me. I hadn't seen him move at all—first he was *there*, and now he was *here*, standing in front of me.

"We've met before," he said.

Without waiting for a reply from me, The Biker crossed his arms in front of him so that my attention was drawn to them. I noticed that one sleeve of his jacket had a rip in it, on his forearm. Under most circumstances, you wouldn't think a child could bite through leather but then, this wasn't most circumstances. Not now, and not all those years ago.

"Sharp teeth," The Biker said, and somehow, Hello Kitty managed to convey what sounded like amusement in his voice.

Finally, I spoke, because I had something to say. Something important to me. "I'm not sorry about that," I told him.

"I didn't think so. But then neither am I," he countered. "About anything."

I shrugged. I didn't feel like giving him the satisfaction of allowing him to think that affected me. It didn't matter, though: he knew. He knew anyway.

"Yet you still think we owe you something."

"Yes," I answered.

"I don't."

"Then why are you here?"

"That depends on what you mean," The Biker said. "If you mean here—the Stargazer's Embassy, well, we can just say that it's on the way. A place to stop. Someone we knew used to live here, but apparently, she's gone. There's no denying that now, no reason to go on hoping she will come back. Or send word. So, it's time to go."

"But others might show up, right? Or was telling me that just a threat?"

"It wasn't a threat—just the truth, as far as we know it. There may indeed be others. But who's to say? As you've been warned, the others might be difficult to deal with."

"So am I," I replied. "Isn't that why we're having this conversation?"

For the first time, I thought I saw something in The Biker's eyes, some spark, some light that belied their appearance of being soulless black voids. Then he cocked his head, slightly. It was an almost human gesture, like he was considering whether or not to reply to me. Or perhaps, what to say.

His decision surprised me. Instead of speaking, he reached over to me and touched the tattoo on my wrist. Then, finally, he said, "You could have had this removed."

"But I didn't," I told him.

"Why not, if you hate it so much?"

"I never said that I hate it."

At the corner of The Biker's mouth, I thought I saw a slight movement, as if it meant to smile—another human-like gesture that once again caught me off guard. "At last," he said. "Some sign of appreciation."

If Hello Kitty had been capable of conveying sarcasm, I knew that was what I would have just heard. But that realization was swiftly consumed by another: the memory I had recovered ten years ago, the thin gray hand inking stars on my wrist, now belonged to a particular creator—the one standing before me, wearing a motorcycle jacket. For years, I had suspected as much, but now I knew it was true.

"It was you," I said, touching the stars on my wrist. "You're the one who did this."

The Biker nodded. Then he turned to Kel. "A superior job, wouldn't you say? I'm asking as one expert to another."

"I don't usually force people to get tattooed," Kel said.

The Biker waved his hand, as if swatting away Kel's gibe. "It's an interesting custom, don't you think? A representation of individual expression. Imbuing art with meaning, symbols with power. Scarring the body so it can bear the evidence of what the mind dreams. Or is driven to dream, yes?" Again, The Biker seemed to smile. "It makes one wonder where the practice originated."

"What are you suggesting?" Kel asked. I could tell that wheels inside of wheels were turning in his mind. "That we learned tattooing from you?" He sounded incredulous.

"From me?" The Biker said. "Us?" Now he gestured towards the others who were still standing around him. They were silent. Motionless. "Hardly. We are just passing through. Though we have considered the possibility that you are, too."

"What does that mean?" I broke in.

"It's just a thought," The Biker said.

Though his mouth remained immobile—barely a slit that never seemed to open or close—I really could have sworn that he was smiling at me. Joking with me, sort of. Teasing. If nothing else, the feeling I got from him, which grew stronger as the minutes passed, was that he was capable of expressing something I had never even intuited from any of the others—a sense of humor. Or maybe irony? Whatever it was, he was beginning to seem almost relatable to me, like it might have been possible to forget that I was dealing with a *thing*, a creepy crawly. A traveler. With Sharkskin, and other others, I had been ready to do battle, but despite myself, my own default setting, which was almost always set to dial up antagonism, I was beginning to feel differently about this one. Perhaps it was Sharkskin that Kel had seen sitting with Laura in the bar but if any of the things had been some sort of friend to her, it must have been this tall traveler, who I now had yet another name for: the Tattoo Artist. *My* Tattoo Artist. The thought made me glance down at the stars etched on my wrist, and I realized that no matter how much I denied my ability to feel a connection to my mother, here was a link that would be unbreakable, always visible for all the days that I was alive: these stars, this tattoo. And not only that we both bore the same mark but also the fact that we seemed to have chosen friends—one human, one not—with the same propensity for creating skin art with ink.

Maybe my Tattoo Artist had some idea of what I was thinking because he suddenly said, "You look like her. Like your mother. Very much, actually. The photographer told you that, too, didn't he?"

I knew he meant Ted, but that wasn't what engaged my attention even more deeply. Instead, it was what I heard: there was something in my Tattoo Artist's voice—something I didn't think Hello Kitty was adding for him—that I thought I recognized. Something a child without a mother might know about. Something that would make her feel like an alien in her own life, hardening herself so that the feeling would never penetrate to her hidden core.

Still, the idea was astonishing to me. "You miss her," I said. "You, personally. Is *that* what this has always been about? Just that? *Why?*" I said.

But apparently, I wasn't the only one who could turn cold at a moment's notice. I received no answer—none that was spoken, anyway. My Tattoo Artist just reached out once more and wrapped his thin fingers around my wrist. With his other hand, he traced the outline of the stars he had drawn on my skin. "Your one life," he said. "I wish you good luck with it."

And then he let go of me. That was it—that was as far as we were going to get. If he thought of saying anything else about me or Laura, he had decided not to. I thought, then, that the moment had come when he and all the others would finally vanish from The Stargazer's Embassy. Finally turn their backs and leave, forever. But still, he lingered, with the others standing silently behind him.

"Maybe," I said, "you should let me wish you good luck as well." And then I added, "Or would safe travels be better?"

Once again, I had the feeling that my Tattoo Artist meant to smile. "You really do have to see, don't you?"

"I want to," I told him. "Yes." And then I added, "I need to."

He said nothing, but for a moment or two, he just stood there, looking at me with those strange eyes. Then, almost imperceptibly, I thought I saw him nod.

In the next moment, a blinding disturbance split the air, causing it to move in a way that resembled visible layers—layers of atoms, particles— scraping sideways against each other. And when these elements rearranged themselves and finally disappeared, I saw that my Tattoo Artist had removed his clothes. The leather jacket and jeans lay in a pile on the floor.

Another moment passed. And then my Tattoo Artist began to remove his skin.

Or that was what I thought was happening until I realized that it wasn't. In fact, what he was doing was peeling off some sort of covering—something like a body suit or second skin that he removed and tossed away. Then he raised his long, stick-like hand and made a gesture to the others who were now standing behind him—a whipping motion with his fingers that must have meant that they should all undress, as well, because they quickly obeyed. Even Sharkskin, though Hello Kitty growled a protest for him, a deep, angry sound.

Still, he too did as he had been commanded. And then, there they were. All of them, with their clothes—trench coats, dresses, hats, jackets, sun-glasses, boots—piled at their feet. And what I saw was that every inch of their bodies, on every single one of them, was covered with tattooed stars.

The tattoos were the same as mine: a double star and three smaller companions, repeated over and over and over again. From what Sharkskin had explained, I understood what they meant: each tattoo signified a life, a repeated birth and death—but another transition as well. The star con-figuration marked each passage from signpost to signpost in the cosmos, so each tattoo was like a stamp in a passport. And there were so many stamps—countless, endless, it seemed—that on some of the travelers, they had blurred, blended together. How many years—eons? Millennia?—did the tattoos signify? How many more did they have to go?

I had already asked these questions, and had my answer: no one knew. Not us, not them. The road through the cosmos just went on and on. If they ever found anything—what was beyond the bend, where the road might finally end—how would we ever know? Or if we were the ones who some-how discovered what lay beyond our own human horizon, how would we ever tell them? If indeed, any of us ever spoke again.

That was my thought as a sudden, deep silence overcame the Stargazer's Embassy. My reaction was to glance down at my phone where I saw that my Hello Kitty icon had lost its electronic glow: its eyes were back to the shape of tiny black pinpoints, and their blinking had ceased.

And when I looked up again, all the travelers, along with their suitcases and their clothes, were finally gone.

# XI

AROUND SEVEN O'CLOCK the next morning, I was sitting on the bench outside the Stargazer's Embassy, feeling a little weary but otherwise okay. I had only slept a few hours, conked out on the bed in my old room upstairs, and when I woke up, wanting coffee, I had decided to walk a few blocks to the diner at the other end of Main Street instead of making it myself. The diner was the only place in town open at this hour, so as I sat and sipped my coffee from a cardboard container printed with the words, "Welcome to the Gorgeous Gorges! We ♥ our customers!" there wasn't much to look at except the empty street with its one stoplight stretched out beneath a watery gray sky, with the hills in the distance letting the wind unwrap them from the morning mist. Still, I wouldn't have wanted to see any other landscape this morning. I wanted to be here right now. I wanted to be home.

I had my jacket zipped up, but I wasn't all that cold: it was getting on to winter here, in this far north region of the state, a season that would linger for a long time. But spring would come. It was already waiting its turn, somewhere, and it wasn't hard for me to imagine that the tail end of the chilly breezes that whipped by left behind the faintest scent of flowers and new grass. I closed my eyes for a few moments and thought about days to come when maybe, I could sit out here under sunny skies.

"Jules?"

*Jules.* It sounded good to hear John's old nickname for me, even though I knew it was Kel who had just spoken. Even though I couldn't remember Kel ever having used it before.

I opened my eyes. "How did you sleep?" I asked. He had spent the last few hours on the couch in the living room upstairs. I remembered throwing a blanket over him before heading off down the hall to my room.

"I'm okay," he said, sounding almost surprised. He sat down beside me on the bench and pointed to my cup of coffee. "I could use some of that, though," he added. I handed over the coffee and he took a couple of deep gulps. "How's Nicky?" he asked.

"Still sleeping. I don't think he's going to remember much about what happened."

"No," Kel agreed, "probably not."

Kel had helped me lead Nicky up to his room last night. Even after the travelers had disappeared, he seemed to remain in a dazed state, glassy eyed and confused. I had checked on him after I got up a little while ago and he looked comfortable enough, lying on his bed, snoring away.

"The bike's gone," Kel said suddenly, as he looked out at the empty street.

"I guess it went with them. If it was ever really here."

He smiled. "Don't start all that yet. It's too early in the morning." He yawned, then stretched his arms out over his head. When he settled back down again he said, "How are we going to get home?"

"There's a bus," I told him. "It stops down by the diner. That'll take you to Ithaca, and then you can get another bus back to the city."

"It doesn't escape me that you didn't just say 'we' can get a bus."

"I'm going to stay here," I said.

"And do what?"

I shrugged. "Well, you know. Serve drinks. Cook up some burgers. Wait."

"Don't you think that's a little crazy? You heard what they said last night. There could be more of them on the way."

Now it was my turn to smile. "You said not to start."

"Well, we already did. So?" Kel said.

"So let them come."

"Let them come?" Kel looked at me with total disbelief. "Why would you ever want to see one of those creepy things again?"

"I've met actual people who were a lot worse."

Kel was silent for a few moments. A gust of wind blew some pages of a newspaper down the street. Kel shivered, but I still thought that I could catch a hint of spring.

"You liked them," he said, with a kind of grim astonishment, as if he had just solved a puzzle but wasn't happy about the solution.

I had to think about that, but I finally came up with an answer. "No," I said. "I didn't like them. Well, not all of them, anyway." I smiled at him. "Maybe I just have an affinity for tattoo artists."

*Or maybe more than just that*, I thought—though not for the first time this morning. I had awakened with an idea that had probably been brewing somewhere in my mind throughout my brief hours of sleep and had finally revealed itself as soon as I opened my eyes. Last night, I had gotten no real answer about Laura, no explanation about why the travelers were so sure that she wasn't just dead and gone, whatever that really meant. In the movie they had shown me, they suggested human answers for what might lie beyond the endpoint of this one life, but maybe they were hoping, instead, that the alien horizon was where she had crossed and therefore, perhaps she could still be found. But even so, why would she be so valuable to them, so important?

Because, I had decided somewhere in my dreaming, that maybe my Tattoo Artist and his friends were exactly what I had accused them of being—liars. Not good ones, not bad ones, but liars all the same—which meant that maybe, not all their hybrid babies had really been the empty creatures they described to me. Maybe one of them had survived. Maybe that was why Laura had been so comfortable with them. And why—though he didn't admit it—my Tattoo Artist had seemed to be genuinely missing her, why he had sent so many others to search for her, because now I knew it must have been him. He was the one in charge. Clearly that was so because all the others had deferred to him, even snarling, angry Sharkskin. They had backed off when faced with his authority—or maybe what empowered him was something even stronger than that. Maybe it was his love that overrode every other directive they were following, and not just the love of a friend. Maybe what drove him was the one thing I knew nothing about, or at least, way too little: the love of a parent.

*There was a blood test*, Nicky once told me. *You are a perfectly ordinary girl.*

Well, maybe. But Laura could have lied about the results of the test, if there really ever was one. And who knew, anyway, if traces of alien blood, removed by a generation—if they even *had* blood—would even show up in some lab technician's test tube?

"Was that a compliment?" Kel said, pulling me out of my own thoughts and back into our conversation. "Nice try to throw me off track, but it's not working. If you really had an affinity for tattoo artists—at least this one— you'd listen to me. You'd take my advice, which I have lots of, and it starts with this: come back to the city with me. Right now. Because if you don't, I'm getting the feeling that what you're going to do instead is send up the bat signal and stand out here every night, waiting for more. More of them." He turned around then, and pointed at the entrance to the bar. "Oh wait," he said, "you don't need the bat signal because you've got that." He meant the five stars—the twin and its companions—painted on the escutcheon fixed above the door. The Great Seal of the Stargazer's Embassy to the World. To the universe. "Well, here's more advice," he said. "You should take down that sign. Paint over the damn star map on the wall. And then go into Ithaca and have someone remove that tattoo from your wrist. If I recall, that was one of the suggestions made last night."

"No it wasn't," I said. "Not exactly."

"Who cares? Again, let me suggest that you come back to the city with me and *I'll* remove the damn tattoo for you. Keeping all that stuff—the sign, the star map, the tattoo—it's like an open invitation." He gave me an unhappy look. "Which, because you're crazy, is what you're counting on, right?

"I don't feel crazy," I told him. "In fact, I don't even feel particularly angry today, which is a good thing for me. So why don't we both just hope that lasts a while? Julia, in a better mood, might tell you that the invitation even extends to you. In fact, if another bunch of travelers does, show up, I'll give you a call, first thing. You can find another bike and pay me—us—a visit."

"Didn't you hear me?" Kel said. "I've had enough. Enough for like, forever."

"Well, we'll see about that." I said. "Maybe someday you'll change your mind."

"You can keep thinking whatever you want," he said, "but you're wrong. From now on, all this crap has nothing to do with me. No more creepy crawlies, no more mystery motorcycles or weirdo movies. And I may never drink a drop of whiskey again."

I didn't argue with him, but I didn't think I had to. He was a smart guy and eventually, he was going to figure all this out for himself, then decide how he wanted to deal with it. After, all, I wasn't the only person—well, maybe mostly a person, anyway—who had been shown the death movie. Who had been asked where they thought some lost soul had gone. Which meant that maybe more than one hybrid baby had survived in some long ago generation. Some parent, grandparent or ancestor. Some other traveler whose hybrid offspring had produced a wild child with an affinity for etching tattoos.

Kel and I finished our shared cup of coffee, and then we went inside where I brewed another pot in the kitchen behind the bar. I filled a thermos for Kel to take with him and then walked him to the bus stop. I knew the schedule by heart, and I heard the bus before I saw it rattling its way around the bend in the road that led into town.

Before we said good-bye, I asked Kel to do me a favor. I gave him two envelopes; one contained a letter I'd written a few days ago and the other I'd addressed when I had waited for the coffee to percolate. I asked him to mail them for me when he was back in Manhattan, since I thought they would get where they was going faster than if I left it at the local post office. Mail meant to leave the town of Freelingburg could wait for a while until someone actually got around to processing it.

Kel looked at the envelopes, one of which was addressed to the director of the reconciliation program at the hospital where Alice was incarcerated. "I know what this is," he said. "You're suggesting they let her go."

I shrugged. "Well, it might not make a difference but I said I would do it, and so there it is."

"And what's in this other one?" He shook the envelope, which I had addressed directly to Alice and covered with stamps, since it weighed more than a regular letter and I wanted to make sure it had a swift, safe passage. Kel must have figured out what was inside because he said, "Well, this really is your day for invitations, isn't it? But do you think Alice will know what this means?"

"I hope so," I said. "I did tell her about this place, but if not, she'll write to me and I'll explain."

"You'd actually let her come here."

"Maybe," I said. And then I smiled, which felt good. Really good. "Stranger things have happened, right?"

Then the bus pulled up to the curb, the door opened and Kel climbed aboard. I called after him, saying I'd be in touch. He waved to me, and then the bus pulled away.

So then there I was, standing alone at the end of Main Street, with many miles of road between me and the next town, the next city. This town, Freelingburg, was finally beginning to wake up, just a little bit. Someone rolled by in an old pickup truck. A light went on in one of the stores across the street from the diner.

I turned to head back to the Stargazer's Embassy. It was a quick walk, but I had enough time to make a few small plans, which included placing a call to the superintendent of the apartment building in the Bronx where I had been living and do some bartering: I was going to tell him he could keep all the electronics in the place—the radio, the CD player and all the discs, even the tv—if he'd just box up my clothes and send them to me. I didn't think I was going to be needing anything else. I didn't want to block out the world around me anymore. I wanted to hear what was going on. I wanted to see.

When I got back to the Embassy, I didn't bother, yet, to turn on the lights. I sat on a stool at the bar, sipping more coffee and enjoying the quiet, the watery gloom. I felt like I was suspended between a kind of before and after; like I was resting up—or maybe a better way of putting it was that I was gathering strength—for when it was time to face whatever came next.

But *next* was not going to come today. Maybe it wouldn't come for a long time—maybe even never, though I didn't really believe that. Still, I couldn't stop myself from pulling my phone from my pocket and taking a look at Hello Kitty. The little icon looked dull, drained of energy. Its tiny pinpoint eyes looked dead. Blank.

Oh well. Maybe, I didn't have to wait for any new visitors to show up in order to give Kel a call—maybe I'd do it sooner than that. At lot sooner. Not just to see how he was doing but also to suggest that perhaps he could go pay Ted Devere another visit. See if he had any updated phone apps he might want to share with me. I could even trade him something for it: what I had in mind was a new Stargazer's passport—if I could find where Nicky kept them. That is, if he even gave them out anymore. This morning, when I had looked around for them, I couldn't find any. What I had put in the envelope I had given Kel to mail to Alice was my own passport, the one I had been carrying around for years. If Nicky didn't have any new ones, I was going to get him to have more of them made. A whole new supply.

Which was only the beginning of the conversation we were going to have to have. I was sure he would be happy enough to hear me say that I wanted to stay here, in Freelingburg, but of course, there was a lot more we had to talk about. First up, I was going to have to try to explain what had happened last night. It was all going to be pretty confounding for him even though he probably already understood that he was going to have to change just about everything he'd ever thought about Laura, and about me. That was just for starters.

The big question was, what were we going to do here at the Stargazer's Embassy? Before I tried to work that out with Nicky, I had to figure out the answer for myself, but I had an idea that I already knew what it was, and that was pretty much exactly what I had told Kel. We would just go on. We would live our lives. We would hire the occasional band to play music, keep showing movies, hang with the locals, welcome the tourists and students who wandered in from the city down the road, and keep serving drinks. Beer on tap, wine by the glass, Jack straight up in a shot glass, if that's how you liked it. We'd just make extra sure to watch out for whoever ordered it that way.

And we'd keep the front door open way late into the night—not that that was unusual for the Stargazer's Embassy. We were always open late. Open and welcoming to whoever walked in. Of course, you never knew who that would be. You just had to be prepared to deal with the bad types, if they were the ones who showed up. But you hoped for the good ones. Hoped they'd bring good days, good endings, a little enlightenment. Hoped something like that was what you'd find around the next bend in the road.

# ABOUT THE AUTHOR

Eleanor Lerman, who lives in New York, is the author of numerous award-winning collections of poetry, short stories, and novels. She is a National Book Award finalist, the recipient of the Lenore Marshall Poetry Prize from the Academy of American Poets, and was awarded a Guggenheim Fellowship as well as a fellowship from the National Endowment for the Arts. In 2016, her novel, *Radiomen*, was awarded the John W. Campbell Prize for the Best Book of Science Fiction. This is her fourth book with Mayapple Press.

# OTHER RECENT TITLES FROM MAYAPPLE PRESS:

Eric Torgersen, *In Which We See Our Selves: American Ghazals*, 2017
    Paper, 44pp, $14.95 plus s&h
    ISBN 978-936419-72-2
Toni Ortner, *A White Page Demands Its Letters*, 2016
    Paper, 40pp, $14.95 plus s&h
    ISBN 978-936419-70-8
Rivka Basman Ben-Haim, tr. Zelda Newman, *The Thirteenth Hour*, 2016
    Paper, 94pp, $15.95 plus s&h
    ISBN 978-936419-71-5
Nola Garrett, *Ledge*, 2016
    Paper, 94pp, $15.95 plus s&h
    ISBN 978-936419-68-5
Amanda Reverón, tr. Don Cellini, *El Silencio de las Horas / The Silence of the Hours*, 2016
    Paper, 70pp, $15.95 plus s&h
    ISBN 978-936419-67-8
Toni Mergentime Levi, *White Food*, 2016
    Paper, 82pp, $15.95 plus s&h
    ISBN 978-936419-65-4
Allison Joseph, *Mercurial*, 2016
    Paper, 42pp, $13.95 plus s&h
    ISBN 978-936419-64-7
Jean Nordhaus, *Memos from the Broken World*, 2016
    Paper, 80pp, $15.95 lus s&h
    ISBN 978-936419-56-2
Doris Ferleger, *Leavened*, 2015
    Paper, 64pp, $15.95 plus s&h
    ISBN 978-936419-47-0
Helen Ruggieri, *The Kingdom Where No One Keeps Time*, 2015
    Paper, 80pp, $15.95 plus s&h
    ISBN 978-936419-55-5
Jan Bottiglieri, *Alloy*, 2015
    Paper, 82pp, $15.95 plus s&h
    ISBN 978-936419-52-4

For a complete catalog of Mayapple Press publications, please visit our website at *www.mayapplepress.com*. Books can be ordered direct from our website with secure on-line payment using PayPal, or by mail (check or money order). Or order through your local bookseller.